AMNESIA

An avid reader since childhood, Beverly Barton wrote her first book at the age of nine. Since then, she has gone on to write well over sixty novels and is a *New York Times* best-selling author. Beverly lives in Alabama in the U.S. For further information on Beverly Barton, visit her website at www.beverlybarton.com

Visit www.AuthorTracker.co.uk for exclusive updates on Beverly Barton.

By the same author

Close Enough to Kill

Beverly Barton

AMNESIA

AVON

AVON

A division of HarperCollins*Publishers*
77–85 Fulham Palace Road,
London W6 8JB

www.harpercollins.co.uk

This paperback edition 2007

2

First published in the U.S.A by
Kensington Publishing Corp.
New York, NY, 2006

Copyright © Beverly Barton 2006

Beverly Barton asserts the moral right to
be identified as the author of this work

A catalogue record for this book is
available from the British Library

ISBN-13: 978-1-84756-001-8
ISBN-10: 1-84756-001-6

Set in Times New Roman

Printed and bound in Great Britain by
Clays Ltd, St Ives plc

For John Scognamiglio, editor extraordinaire,
and
Richard Curtis, agent par excellence.
Thank you both for excellent professional guidance.

Also, with great appreciation to Michael Speltz,
my research "partner in crime."

Acknowledgments

Thanks to Michael Speltz, Reserve Inspector with the Shelby County Sheriff's Department, with thirty-plus years of service and a lifelong resident of Memphis and Germantown, Tennessee. Mike's assistance in doing research for this book proved invaluable.

A special Thank You to Mike's wife, Pat, owner of Pat Speltz Media Consultant in Germantown, Tennessee, who drives writers in the Memphis and Jackson, Tennessee, Oxford, Mississippi, and Blytheville, Arkansas, area. Pat also helped with research on this book.

And to Mike's brother-in-law, Ben Payne, retired captain of the Memphis Police Department, whose assistance is greatly appreciated.

Prologue

Lulu Vanderley was rich, blond and beautiful. Women envied her. Men wanted her. She had it all. Everything. Except . . . There was one thing she wanted that could never truly be hers. Quinn Cortez. And knowing she couldn't have him made her want him all the more.

They'd been lovers for several months, ever since they'd met through mutual acquaintances in Vail. In the beginning, a hot affair had been enough for both of them. He'd made it clear from their very first date that he was a no-strings-attached kind of guy. And she'd been well aware of his love-'em-and-leave-'em reputation. But that was before she fell in love with the gorgeous hunk, before she decided that she wanted to become Mrs. Quinn Cortez. And as a general rule, Lulu got what Lulu wanted.

She stared at her reflection in the mirror and smiled devilishly. No man had ever been able to resist her. And that was one reason she and Quinn were perfect for each other. They were two peas in a pod—a couple of gorgeous, irresistible philanderers.

Tonight she would spring the trap, the age-old trap that had caught many a poor fool. Quinn wasn't invulnerable. He was as susceptible as any man to feminine wiles and little white lies. She'd weep and swear she didn't know how it could have happened. She'd told him the first time they had sex that she'd been on the pill for years and since he'd also used a condom every time, convincing him she was pregnant might not be easy. But all he had to do was talk to her doctor. Lulu was definitely six weeks along.

Running her hands over her tall, slender body, from waist to narrow hips, she studied her image. Her beauty had always gotten her whatever her family's wealth wouldn't buy. But neither could give her what she wanted most.

Quinn might be a womanizer, but he wasn't a heartless cad. If he believed she was carrying his child, then there was a good chance he'd do the honorable thing and marry her.

And if he doesn't, what will you do?

She'd get an abortion, of course. No way in hell did she want to get tied down with a squalling baby unless the little brat served some purpose.

The mantel clock struck the hour, reminding her that Quinn would be arriving soon. Her stomach tightened. Lulu laughed. It wasn't like her to be nervous.

Everything was ready. A bottle of champagne was chilling. A second bottle. She'd already drunk three glasses from the first bottle in an effort to steel her nerves and lull herself into a tranquil haze. Not good for the baby, she supposed, but what the hell. The silk bed linens were turned down, soft music was playing and she was wearing her most alluring sheer black teddy.

Quinn had just won another high profile case, this time involving country singer Terry McBryar. The Nashville jury had come back with a not guilty verdict in the case against McBryar, who had been accused of murdering his manager. Of course, this victory was only one in a long line for Quinn Cortez, who was one of the nation's most highly acclaimed trial lawyers.

The fact that Quinn had a reputation for being ruthless excited Lulu. She'd always been fascinated by bad boys.

When she had telephoned him earlier today to congratulate him on his big win, she'd heard reluctance in his voice the minute she invited him to drive over to Memphis this evening so they could celebrate together. But in the end, she had persuaded him. Telling him that she'd be waiting in her bedroom, wearing only a teddy, and eager to suck his dick had given him all the incentive he needed.

"I can get there by eight," he'd told her. "Is your extra key in the usual place?"

"Right where it always is," she'd said. "Just let yourself in. I'll be waiting."

Thinking about the night ahead, Lulu shivered with excitement. She'd had dozens of lovers, but none compared to Quinn. The guy was a real stud, in every sense of the word. She'd give him a blow job, then they'd drink champagne and cuddle by the fireplace here in her bedroom. After he was relaxed and mellow, she'd spring her big surprise.

Guess what, Quinn, you're going to be a daddy.

Laughing, pleased with her almost foolproof plan to trap her man, Lulu twirled around the room.

She heard a noise. The front door opening? Her heartbeat accelerated. Quinn was here. He'd arrived early. He must have broken every speed limit between Nashville and Memphis. That had to mean he was eager to see her.

Hurriedly, she turned off all the lights and lit the candles she had arranged on top of the sleek, modern cherry dresser. Only the candlelight and the glow from the flickering blaze in the fireplace illuminated the room. The right ambience was so important.

"Quinn? Darling, I'm back here waiting for you."

His footsteps tapped quietly over the hardwood floors in the foyer and down the hall.

"You got here early, didn't you?" She licked her lips.

Why wasn't he answering her?

She scratched her long fingernails over her nipples, hardening them instantly. "Come on back here, big boy. I've got what you need."

She stood by the fireplace, primed and ready, eager for

what lay ahead. When she saw him standing in the doorway, her heart caught in her throat. She did love this man, loved him to distraction. He stood there in the shadows, a tall, dark silhouette. Broad shouldered, lean hipped. Six one. And every inch a man.

She held open her arms. "Come to mama. Let me take good care of you."

He took several steps toward her. His blue-black hair glistened in the firelight. God, he was handsome. Ruggedly handsome in that exotic way only men of mixed heritages were. Quinn was a delicious mixture of Mexican and Irish.

As he neared her, she thought how incredibly young and sexy he looked tonight. Even men looked better by candlelight. At forty, he possessed a body any twenty-year-old would envy. And she knew from personal experience that he had the stamina of a man half his age.

"Hello, Lulu," he said, and she thought there was an odd tone to his voice. He didn't sound quite like himself.

She took a tentative step toward him, closing the gap between them. When she looked up into his piercing black eyes, she gasped. "Quinn?"

"Were you expecting someone else?" he asked. "Another lover?"

"No, I wasn't expecting anyone else." She felt a sudden sense of unease. What was wrong with him? He was acting so strangely. And he looked odd.

Maybe it wasn't him; maybe it was her. After all, she had drunk three glasses of champagne. Perhaps she was picking up on strange vibes where there were none.

He reached out and grasped her shoulders. She quivered.

"What's wrong? You're shivering," he said.

She stared directly at him, studying his tense features, as his big hands bit painfully into her shoulders. *Oh, God, how could this be?* She didn't understand what was going on.

"You're acting as if you're afraid of me."

"I—I am." She tried to pull away, but he held her in his strong grip. "Let go of me." When she struggled against him, he pushed her backward, his dark eyes boring into her with unadulterated hatred. "I don't understand—"

She felt addled, her thoughts fuzzy, her mind playing tricks on her.

As he shoved her backward, she somehow managed to escape his tenacious grasp. She had to get away from him. She turned and ran, intending to lock herself in the bathroom and use the telephone in there to call for help. But before she reached the bathroom door, he caught her by the wrist, whirled her around and flipped her over and onto the bed.

The satin sheets felt cold and clammy against her bare arms and legs. The dark shadow of the man hovering over her appeared menacing and dangerous. Why hadn't she realized sooner that something wasn't quite right?

Because you drank too much champagne.

He came down over her, bracing his knees on either side of her hips, trapping her beneath him. She opened her mouth in a silent scream, her voice paralyzed by fear.

Don't panic. Maybe he just wants to play rough. Maybe he isn't going to hurt you.

"You're a fool, Lulu," he said in that strange tone of voice. "And I feel sorry for foolish women."

"What—what are you talking about? Please—"

"Do you know what I do to foolish women?"

He reached over and picked up one of the king-size pillows from the head of the bed. She tried to shove him off her, but without success. He was too big, too strong. He lifted his knee and pressed it against her belly, effectively holding her in place and enabling him to use both hands to maneuver the pillow.

"I kill foolish women," he told her. "I kill them softly . . . tenderly . . . and put them out of their misery."

"No!" She managed to scream once before he covered her face with the huge pillow. Oh, God, he really was going to kill her. Smother her.

Help me, please, dear God, help me.

She wriggled and squirmed, thrashing her head about,

seeking air, but he kept the pillow securely in place. With
what little strength she had left, she grasped his wrists, but
the effort proved useless. Within seconds her hands loosened. Her arms dropped languidly to either side of her still
body. Her chest ached. Swirling gray circles appeared in the
blackness behind her pillow-covered eyes.

Lulu had one final coherent thought.

I can't breathe. I can't breathe!

Chapter 1

Jim Norton figured it was going to rain. His arthritic knees were giving him fits and had all afternoon. But what could an ex-jock, who'd had bones broken, muscles strained and ligaments torn, expect when he hit forty? His ex-wife had once dubbed him her six-million-dollar man because he had so many artificial body parts.

Jim groaned. The last thing he wanted on his mind tonight was Mary Lee. Their marriage had ended six years ago. It was past time he got over her.

"What are you grunting about?" Chad George asked. "Pissed because Inspector Purser assigned us this case right before you were scheduled to go on vacation?"

"Nah, nothing like that. I didn't have any special plans. Mary Lee nixed my idea of taking Kevin camping for a week. I can always reschedule my time off. Besides, Purser knows when to send in the best the homicide division has to offer."

"Gee, thanks, Jim. I had no idea you thought so highly of me."

"Go fuck yourself, Boy George."

Chad's face turned beet red, a close match to his wavy auburn hair that he kept cut military short.

"I'm getting damn sick and tired of the jokes about my being pretty enough to be a girl," Chad said. "What do I have to do to get you and the other guys to ease up on the ribbing— run my face through a windshield or let some knife-happy perp slice-and-dice my rosy cheeks?"

Jim chuckled. "The only reason we dish it out is because you can't take it. Act like you don't give a shit and it'll stop soon enough."

Chad harrumphed as he turned their black Ford Taurus onto Galloway Drive. "I'd like to believe that."

"Believe it."

Jim had been partnered with the darling of the department on a string of cases these past three months since Chad's former partner, Bill Delmar, retired. Jim couldn't fault the kid on his professionalism. But on a personal basis, newly promoted Sergeant Chad George could be a pain in the ass. He was often a bit too cocky and always a bit too sensitive. Hell, at twenty-eight, the guy should have wised-up. A police officer, especially one in the homicide department, wouldn't last long if he didn't learn to distance himself from the job just enough so that the intensity of murder and mayhem didn't bleed over into every aspect of his life. It was no secret to anyone who knew him that Chad lived and breathed his job. Odds were he'd make lieutenant in a few years and just keep moving right on up. Of course, it didn't hurt that he had his own personal angel—none other than Congressman Harte, who was Chad's uncle-by-marriage.

Jim had been a lot like Chad at his age—minus the angel—but he figured there was no point in telling the boy to do as he said and not as he'd done. Ten years ago, Jim hadn't listened to older and wiser men on the force who'd tried to warn him. If he had listened, maybe his former partner would still be alive. Maybe he and Mary Lee would still be married. And maybe he'd get to see his son whenever he was off duty and not just on alternate weekends and a couple of holidays a year.

"It's not every day there's a homicide in Chickasaw Gardens," Chad said.

Jim glanced out the window, visually skimming over mansion after mansion in this old, well-established Memphis neighborhood, where homes often sold for somewhere between one and two million dollars. And in Tennessee, million-dollar houses were far from the norm for the average citizen.

"Who'd they send out from the Central Precinct?" Jim asked.

"A couple of one-man cars. Don't know the officers' names."

Jim nodded.

Within minutes, they reached the address they'd been given when they were dispatched from downtown. Two white police cars, trimmed in red and blue, a black Chevy Trailblazer, an ambulance and a small group of curious neighbors blocked their path. Chad parked behind one of the two police vehicles. The minute they emerged from the sedan, they made their way up the sidewalk to the two-story brick traditional shaded by large oak trees. Curious stares and a hum of murmurs followed them. Jim scanned the area, left and right, forward and backward. He noted a sleek, silver Porsche convertible parked in the driveway.

A young uniformed officer stood outside the front door, nervous sweat dampening his face on this cool spring night. Chad approached, identified himself and Jim, and then turned to the crowd.

"Folks, I'm going to have to ask that y'all leave the yard. Your presence here could very well compromise our crime scene."

A loud grumble rose from several in the group, but to-a-person they moved hurriedly out into the street.

Jim noted the embarrassed look on the young policeman's face. His name tag read Jarnigan. "The medical examiner already here?" Jim thought he recognized Udell White's SUV parked behind the police cars.

"Yes, sir. He arrived just a few minutes ago," Officer Jarnigan replied, then swallowed hard.

Chad zeroed in on Jarnigan, who Jim figured was fresh out of John D. Holt police academy. If he was a rookie that would explain his nervousness. Sometimes it seemed like only yesterday that he had graduated from the Academy. He'd been young and stupid enough to think he could conquer the world. He should have known better. After all, his dream of turning pro had been dashed when an injury his senior year at the University of Tennessee had ended his football career. After his body had been refurbished through a series of operations, he had been able to function normally, at least enough to meet the force's physical requirements. After losing out on a pro career and making a ton of personal and professional mistakes, Jim didn't have big plans anymore. He just took each day one at a time.

"What other officer responded to the call?" Chad asked.

"Del Treacy. He's inside with the ME." Jarnigan's voice trembled.

Jim gave Chad a back-off glance, then stepped up on the porch where Jarnigan stood, guarding the open front door, and put his hand on the man's shoulder. "Take it easy, son. We're all on the same team here."

"Yes, sir."

"This your first murder case?"

"Yes, sir." Jarnigan sighed deeply.

Jim turned to Chad. "Why don't you go out there and get the names of the curious and find out if they know anything about what happened. I'll take over here."

Chad bristled. Too bad. Jim still outranked him. He probably should have sent Jarnigan to interview the bystanders instead of ordering his partner to do the job. But it was liable to be a long night and a little bit of Chad went a long way. He figured he'd better separate himself from the cocky kid as much as possible so he didn't lose his cool with the department's darling boy.

"Yeah, sure." Chad grunted, then headed down the sidewalk.

Jim pulled out a notepad and pen from his inside coat pocket, then asked Jarnigan, "What time did y'all arrive on the scene?"

"Ten forty-seven."

Jim made a note of the time, then jotted down the address, the approximate temperature and weather conditions. Sixty-three degrees. Cool, clear, stars in the sky. "Tell me what y'all found when you arrived."

"Uh . . . er . . . the guy who'd called 911 met us at the door." Jarnigan glanced over his shoulder. "Del's got him inside. In the living room."

"Go on."

"He said he found the victim when he arrived. They . . . er . . . they had a late date. He said she was already dead when he got here."

Jim nodded as he glanced around, taking note of the specifics of the old brick house. One door—a double door at the front. Four long, narrow windows. All four shut tight.

"I'm going inside," Jim said. "You stay out here and help Sergeant George. And don't let him intimidate you."

"No sir. I mean, yes sir, I won't."

Jim entered the large marble-floored foyer and eyed the sweeping staircase leading to the second floor. A crystal chandelier glistened brightly overhead. A set of double pocket doors to the left were closed, but the matching set to the right were open, revealing the twenty-by-twenty living room. Hardwood floors. Fireplace. No fire. Intricately carved wooden mantel. Traditional decorating, probably created by an outrageously expensive interior designer.

A stocky, black-uniformed officer stood talking to a man wearing an expensive dark suit, a white shirt and a red tie.

When Jim approached the entrance to the living room, both men glanced at him.

"Officer Treacy, I'm Lieutenant Norton. Homicide."

"Yes, sir."

"Who's this you've got with you?"

The tall, broad-shouldered man turned all the way around and faced Jim. Wavy black hair and dark eyes, bronze skin and handsome Hispanic features. *Good-looking devil,* Jim thought. Not a pretty boy like Chad. Just damn impressive.

"I'm Quinn Cortez." The man's black eyes narrowed as his gaze met Jim's. "I'm the one who found Ms. Vanderley's body."

The muscles in Quinn's belly tightened as he studied the homicide detective. The guy looked vaguely familiar. Rugged features. Short brown hair. Somewhere between thirty-five and forty. Quinn never forgot a face. He'd said his name was Norton. His identity didn't come to Quinn immediately, but it would. Lieutenant Norton was a couple inches taller than Quinn, well-muscled and lean, with a world-weary look in his pensive blue eyes that hinted of pain, both physical and emotional.

"*The* Quinn Cortez?" Norton asked, his hard face emotionless.

Quinn grunted. "Yeah, I'm *the* Quinn Cortez."

"You just won that McBryar case over in Nashville," Norton said. "What brought you to Memphis tonight?"

"Lulu—Ms. Vanderley called earlier and invited me. Our get-together was supposed to be a celebration."

"Want to take me, step-by-step, through what happened from the minute you drove up in the driveway until the officers showed up?"

"Sure." Quinn knew the routine. Being a criminal lawyer, he had cultivated friendships with as well as made enemies of numerous lawmen in a number of states, where pro hac vice rules allowed him to practice outside his home state of Texas.

"That your Porsche parked in the drive?" Norton asked.

Quinn nodded. Was Norton one of those men who would automatically dislike Quinn because he was rich and famous? He'd run into his share of green-with-envy yo-yos who had tried to give him a hard time, but they'd all learned they couldn't intimidate Quinn Cortez, nor could they scare him. But he'd never been in a situation such as this, had never been a suspect in a murder case. And he knew as well as he knew his own name that since he had found Lulu's body and the two of them had been lovers, he would immediately top the police's persons-of-interest list.

"I got here around ten-thirty," Quinn said. "I parked, got out, walked to the door and let myself in with the key Lulu kept hidden beneath the doormat." When Norton squinted and frowned, Quinn nodded. "Yeah, I know it wasn't very smart of her to keep a key in such an obvious place, but Lulu was like that. She enjoyed flirting with danger."

"Did she now?"

"Hell, yes. Why else would she have lived the way she did? In case you don't know anything about Lulu, let me tell you that the lady liked her thrills. She was into skydiving, mountain climbing, deep-sea diving and she had run through as many bad boys as possible since she turned fifteen."

"You've known the lady that long—since she was fifteen?" Norton asked.

Quinn shook his head. "No, but she liked to brag, and her friends who've known her for years verified what otherwise I would have thought were tall tales."

"So, Cortez, were you just one more bad boy to Ms. Vanderley or were you somebody special?"

Quinn shrugged. "I've never given it much thought, but I suppose I was just one more in a long line. Lulu and I are—were—a lot alike. Neither of us was into serious relationships."

"You were lovers?" Norton asked.

"Yeah," Quinn replied. "On and off. It wasn't an exclusive relationship by any means."

"Before tonight, when was the last time you saw Ms. Vanderley?"

"About six weeks ago. She drove up to Nashville and stayed a couple of days."

"Hmm . . . Okay, pick up with when you arrived tonight and let yourself into the house."

"I walked inside and called Lulu's name, but she didn't respond, so I went down the hall and straight to her bedroom. I assumed she was in there waiting for me."

"The master bedroom is downstairs?"

"That's right."

"And was she in the bedroom?"

"Yes. She was lying on the bed, flat on her back, wearing a black teddy and . . . well, at first I thought she was asleep." Quinn clenched his teeth. Lulu had looked lovely lying there, her eyes closed, her body resting in a languid pose. He'd bent down over her, intending to kiss her. But the minute he touched her shoulder and she didn't even flinch, he'd known she wasn't simply sleeping, even though she'd still felt warm to the touch. At that same time, he'd smelled the stench of death and had noticed, there in the dim candlelight, the waxy, translucent look of her skin. "She was dead. Probably an hour or less at the time I found her. Rigor mortis hadn't set in and her body was still warm."

"Hmm . . ."

Quinn could tell by the quiet, contemplative way the lieutenant was studying him that the guy would probably wind up hauling his ass down to headquarters for further questioning. There was only one way out of this mess and that was complete cooperation. Tell the police the truth and prove he hadn't harmed a hair on Lulu's pretty little head.

But could he prove he didn't kill Lulu? He had no alibi

for the time of her death—he'd been en route from Nashville and had stopped for a quick nap when he'd gotten so groggy he couldn't keep his eyes open. He'd pulled off Interstate 40 somewhere between Nashville and Jackson and had slept for well over an hour and a half.

Norton glared at Quinn. "Considering you and Ms. Vanderley were lovers, you don't seem too torn up about her death."

"I'm not the emotional type. I don't fall apart in a crisis. If I did, I wouldn't be *the* Quinn Cortez. But I'm not a completely heartless bastard." Quinn looked Norton right in the eyes. "I cared about Lulu, as a friend. And as a lover. If I could change what happened to her, I would. But all I can do—all any of us can do now—is determine how she died. And if she was murdered, find the person responsible."

Norton eyed Quinn skeptically.

"And no, lieutenant, I didn't kill her. I had absolutely no motive."

Before Norton had a chance to respond, a man of probably fifty, with a receding hairline and a potbelly hanging over his belt, came into the room.

"That you, Jim?" the man asked.

Norton turned and nodded. "Yeah, it's me. What have you got for us, Udell? Suicide? Accident? Murder?"

Jim Norton. Jim Norton. Quinn repeated the name several times and suddenly a light clicked on inside his brain. Jim Norton, a running back for UT twenty years ago. That's where Quinn had seen Norton. Norton had been star-athlete Griffin Powell's teammate and best friend. The entire South— and that included Texas—had kept track of the two men who'd been destined to turn pro. Oddly enough, considering both had had NFL star quality written all over them, neither man had played professional football.

"Murder," the ME said. "Asphyxiation."

Quinn had suspected as much. When he had found Lulu lying there so peacefully, he'd desperately wanted to believe she wasn't dead, that he could somehow save her. His first impulse had been to perform CPR, but when he'd lifted her right arm to check for a pulse and seen her bloody hand, he'd known that he had arrived too late. If only he hadn't stopped for that damn nap, he might have gotten here in time to prevent her death.

"There's one other thing," the ME said.

"What's that?" Jim Norton asked.

"The index finger on her right hand was amputated Postmortem."

Annabelle Austin Vanderley was at her best playing hostess. It was a role she'd been born and bred to perform, as had generations of women in her family. Tonight's gala event—a buffet supper to raise funds for the Christopher Knox Threadgill Foundation—hosted society's elite from Mississippi, Alabama and several other surrounding states. Tickets had been a thousand dollars each and all proceeds went directly into the foundation that Annabelle had established ten years ago, shortly after her fiancé, Chris Threadgill, had become the victim of a nearly fatal car crash that left him a paraplegic. The foundation was dedicated not only to research, but also to assisting paralysis victims and their families. Not everyone was as fortunate as Chris had been—to have been born into a wealthy family who could afford to provide him with the best possible care.

Almost two years had passed since Chris's death and even now Annabelle found it difficult to accept that he was gone. She had made him the center of her life for many years, even though they had never married. His choice, not hers.

Annabelle strolled from room to room in her uncle Louis's antebellum mansion, where the charity supper was being held, checking on everything from the string quartet playing in the front parlor to the caterers working feverishly in the kitchen. She was the consummate hostess, with the ability to multitask with the aplomb of a juggler balancing half a dozen balls in the air at once. But this event was only one of three she had overseen this month—the other two being a circus for underprivileged kids and a Winner Takes All charity event at one of Biloxi's many gambling casinos.

At twenty-three, when she'd been planning her wedding to Chris, she had thought by the time she was thirty-four, she would be the mother of several children and the wife of either the governor or a senator. Chris had been destined to follow in his father's and grandfather's political footsteps. But instead of living her dream, she was still single, childless and filled her days—and as many nights as possible—with overseeing the various Austin and Vanderley philanthropic organizations.

"You look lovely tonight, Annabelle," her cousin, Wythe Vanderley, said as he came up behind her and slipped his arm around her waist.

Annabelle froze to the spot. Then forcing a smile, she eased away from Wythe and turned to face him. "And you look handsome, as always." Wythe was an attractive man, in an aristocratic way that drew women to him like moths to a flame. And most of those women—the ones who'd gotten too close to that flame—had been badly burned. Wythe was a scoundrel and despite their being first cousins, Annabelle disliked him intensely. He'd been a disappointment to Uncle Louis, who supported Wythe in grand style, as he did Wythe's younger half sister, Lulu. To quote her aunt, Perdita Austin, "Neither of Louis's children are worth a damn."

"Lovely but cold Annabelle," Wythe said softly so that no one passing them in the hallway could overhear. "The right man could thaw you out and melt that frigid heart of yours."

"If you'll excuse me, I have—"

Before Annabelle could escape her annoying cousin, he grasped her wrist to halt her. She glared at him, her look demanding he release her immediately.

"I'm volunteering for the job, you know," he told her. "I'm just the man who could heat you—"

"Unless you want to make a spectacle of yourself, I suggest you release me," Annabelle said with absolute conviction. "Otherwise, I'll have no choice but to slap that smug look off your silly face."

He released her instantly, but leaned close and whispered, "One of these days, bitch, you'll get yours."

She offered him a deadly smile. "Maybe so, but I won't get it from you."

Annabelle rushed away as fast as she could walk without bringing undue attention to herself. If she didn't adore Uncle Louis and feel tremendously sorry for him, she'd never come to this house again, never subject herself to her cousin's harassment. As she made her way down the hall toward the dining room, intending to make sure everything was in order, she smiled and spoke to half a dozen acquaintances. Annabelle knew everybody who was anybody and cultivated superficial friendships as easily as she performed her hostess duties.

When she entered the dining room, her uncle Louis's butler, Hiram, spoke her name quietly as he came to her side. "Miss Annabelle . . ."

"Yes, Hiram, what is it?"

"Sheriff Brody's at the front door, ma'am, and he's asked to speak to you."

"Sheriff Brody? Did he say what it's about?" Had Wythe gotten in trouble again? Except for Uncle Louis's wealth and political connections, Wythe would already be in prison for statutory rape. Everyone in the county knew Wythe Vanderley had a penchant for teenage girls. And a sick hunger for rough sex.

"No, ma'am, but it can't be good. He said it's about Miss Lulu and he wanted to speak only to you."

How could something Lulu had done be of any concern to Sheriff Brody? Lulu had moved off to Memphis five years ago and was living in her mother's old house there in Chickasaw Gardens, the house Uncle Louis had bought his ex-wife as part of their divorce settlement when Lulu was twelve.

"Show Sheriff Brody into Uncle Louis's study, please, Hiram, and take him around the back way. Tell him I'll join him as soon as possible."

"Yes, ma'am."

Whatever had brought the sheriff to their door, Annabelle didn't want their guests to be aware of the lawman's presence. After making her rounds through the dining room to check that the champagne was ready for the midnight toasts due to begin shortly, Annabelle discreetly slipped away and hurried to her uncle's study. The minute she entered the room, Sheriff Brody, a stocky, middle-aged man, removed his hat and walked toward her.

"Ms. Vanderley, I'm afraid I've come with some awfully bad news," he said.

Annabelle's heart caught in her throat. "Bad news about Lulu?"

"Yes, ma'am."

"Has she been in an accident? Is she badly hurt?"

"I hate to be the one to tell you, but . . . your cousin Lulu is dead."

Annabelle's stomach knotted painfully. "Lulu's dead? How? When?"

"Tonight," Sheriff Brody said. "She was found dead in her bedroom. The Memphis police are treating her death as a homicide."

"Are you saying someone murdered Lulu?"

"It appears so. I'm terribly sorry, Ms. Vanderley. You can contact the Memphis PD, if you'd like, either tonight or in the morning. The lead detective on the case is Lieutenant Norton."

Annabelle shook hands with the sheriff and thanked him

for coming personally to give her the terrible news about her cousin. As she turned and asked Hiram, who'd been waiting in the hallway, to escort the sheriff out, all Annabelle could think about was how on earth she was going to break the news to her uncle. Lulu was—had been—the apple of Uncle Louis's eye. He doted on his younger child, who'd been born when he was fifty. With his health already so precarious, learning that the little girl he'd spoiled rotten and loved to distraction was now dead might easily kill him.

Chapter 2

Sitting alone in a quiet tenth-floor office of the Criminal Justice Center on Poplar Avenue, drinking a cup of coffee and waiting for his lawyer, Quinn Cortez kept telling himself that things weren't as bad as they seemed. After all, the police hadn't arrested him. He hadn't been charged with Lulu's murder. Not yet.

Not yet? Not ever. You didn't kill her. There is absolutely no evidence that you did. If the detectives suspect you—and they probably do—there is no way in hell they can prove you murdered Lulu.

Yeah, but there's no way you can prove you didn't.

Quinn's head pounded as if a couple of giant hammers were being repeatedly thumped against each temple. He leaned his head back against the wall and using his forefingers, massaged the pressure points.

When he had awakened from the nap he'd taken when he'd pulled off the road on his trip from Nashville to Memphis, his head had been throbbing; and downing a couple of aspirins hadn't helped. Finding Lulu dead and then dealing with the police had only increased the tension, which had reached migraine proportions. He'd been healthy as a horse all his life, but during the past eight or nine months he'd had several really bad headaches. First came the extreme grogginess that led to an odd blackout spell. The headaches came after he awakened, lasted for a while and then went away. He probably should have seen a doctor, but he'd kept putting it off, thinking each headache would be the last. After all, there hadn't been all that many spells—only three, counting the one tonight.

Although he'd defended countless clients accused of murder, he'd never been on this end of a murder case. Never been a suspect. And he'd never discovered a dead body.

Poor Lulu. God in heaven, who could have killed her? And why? She might have been practically worthless as a human being, having never worked a day in her life or gone out of her way to help another living soul, but she certainly had never intentionally harmed anyone. She'd been a free spirit, living life for the sheer pleasure of it. She was a good-time girl, fun to be around, and a damn good lay.

Quinn winced. *That's no way to think of the dead,* he reminded himself, then huffed out a pained chuckle. Who was he kidding? Lulu would love being described as a damn good lay. She prided herself on her sexual prowess. The woman had been a tiger in the bedroom.

I don't know who killed you, honey, or why, but if the police can't find your murderer, I will.

The door opened and Sergeant George poked his head in and said, "Your lawyer's here."

George had been a real pain in the ass, but Lieutenant Norton had conducted himself like the old pro he was. And it wasn't a matter of good cop/bad cop. It was a basic difference in men.

Quinn eased his fingers down over his cheekbones, then let his hands drop to the tops of his thighs as he glanced up at the cocky, young policeman. His gut instincts told him that no matter what the circumstances were under which he might have met Chad George, he wouldn't have liked the guy.

"We haven't charged you with anything. And we weren't interrogating you, just asking you a few questions," the sergeant said. "You really didn't need to call in a lawyer."

"Oh yeah, I think I did." Quinn rose to his full six-one height and looked the policeman in the eyes. George wasn't a large man. Five ten, one sixty-five. And too damn pretty to be a man. Bet he got plenty of ribbing from the other officers about being so movie-star handsome. Like a young, red-headed Brat Pitt.

George's lips lifted in a hint of a smile, then he stepped backward and out of the way as Kendall Wells charged past him. She ignored the sergeant as if he were invisible. And when she closed the door behind her, Quinn grinned, imagining the guy's indignant reaction to not only being ignored, but also having the door practically slammed in his face. Bet Chad George wasn't accustomed to women treating him that way. But then, Kendall was no ordinary woman.

"I hope you've kept your mouth shut," Kendall said as she approached Quinn, her three-inch black heels tapping against the floor.

Quinn inspected his lawyer from head to toe. Ms. Wells was a looker. Tall, slender, leggy and though not classically pretty, attractive nonetheless. She dressed in the best her money could buy. Tailored suits. Simple gold jewelry. Her bright red, sculptured nails made a statement that said although she was feminine, she could also be dangerous, possibly lethal.

He'd known Kendall for a number of years. They'd worked together on one of her first cases after she joined Hamilton, Jeffreys and Lloyd, which was now Hamilton, Jeffreys, Lloyd and Wells. At forty-four, she didn't look a day over thirty-five. By keeping her body toned and the gray in her hair covered with a dark rinse, she managed to fool those who didn't know her true age. But Quinn knew. He knew a lot about Kendall. They'd been lovers briefly and she liked to talk—mostly about herself—in the afterglow of lovemaking. Even though he hadn't seen her in nearly five years, she'd been the first person he'd thought of when he decided he needed a top-notch Memphis lawyer right away.

"You're looking good," Quinn said.

Kendall smiled. "You look like hell."

He rubbed his head. "I've got a killer headache."

"Discovering a lover's dead body would give anybody a headache."

Quinn narrowed his gaze and looked directly at Kendall. "I didn't kill Lulu."

"That's good to know."

Inclining his head toward the closed door, Quinn asked, "Do they think I did it?"

"Probably. The boyfriend or the husband is always a suspect. You know that."

"I told them the basic facts of my having a late date with Lulu, driving in from Nashville, showing up at her house and finding her dead in her bedroom. But when Sergeant George starting implying I might have had a reason to want to kill Lulu, I called a halt to the questioning."

"And telephoned me. Smart boy."

"Mrs. Cortez didn't raise no fools."

"*Did* you have a reason to want to see Lulu Vanderley dead?"

Quinn lifted his brows and glowered at his lawyer. "Playing devil's advocate a little early in the game, aren't you, counselor?"

Kendall shrugged. "They'll pin this on you if there's any way they can. You're a big fish. A headline maker. Just think what it could do for not only George's and Norton's careers but the DA's. I know Steven Campbell. He's as ambitious as they come. He'd love nothing better than to convict *the* Quinn Cortez of murder."

"I had absolutely no reason to kill Lulu. We were friends . . . lovers."

"Nothing serious between you two?"

"Now when have I ever had a serious relationship with a woman?"

"Hmm . . ." Kendall looked him over from head to toe. "What about Lulu, did she want more than you were willing to give?"

Quinn shook his head. "Not that I know of. She drove up to Nashville and spent a couple of days with me about six weeks ago. I hadn't seen her since. She called this afternoon to congratulate me on winning the McBryar case and invited me to Memphis for a personal celebration."

"What about other boyfriends? Do you know if she was seeing someone else—someone who might have been the jealous type?"

"We didn't discuss other lovers when we were together."

"I sure hope she had a jealous boyfriend. That would at least take some of the focus off you."

"Look, honey, we can talk particulars later. I'd like to get out of here. Tonight."

"That can be arranged. If they want to ask you more questions, we can come back in the morning. This early in the investigation, they apparently don't have any reason to hold you." Kendall slipped her arm through his. "Do you have a place to stay tonight?"

"I'll check into the Peabody or—"

"You'll stay with me."

Quinn gave her an inquisitive look. The last he'd heard, Kendall had gotten married about four years ago.

"We're separated," she said as if reading his mind. "The divorce will be final next month."

"Sorry it didn't work out."

"Yeah, me, too." She shrugged. "He was a nice man. Widower. A couple of teenage kids. I thought it was what I wanted, but it wasn't. I should have stuck to my own kind."

"And that would be?"

"No-good heartbreakers like you, Quinn."

* * *

"Annabelle?" Wythe Vanderley's voice vibrated with anticipation. "Hiram said you wanted to see me immediately. Dare I hope you've changed your mind about—"

Annabelle whirled around and glared at her loathsome cousin. "For God's sake, don't say anything else."

He stared at her, speculation in his gaze. "You've been crying. What's wrong?"

When he approached her, she held up a restraining hand. He stopped immediately.

"Sheriff Brody just left. He came personally to deliver some bad news . . . about"—she swallowed fresh tears—"about Lulu."

Wythe's face turned pale. "What's happened? Has she been in a car wreck? Damn, how many times have I warned her not to drive so fast."

"It wasn't a car wreck."

"What is it? What? Is she in the hospital? Do we need to—"

"Lulu was murdered," Annabelle forced the words, hating the very sound of them. Saying them aloud made the unbearable truth more real.

"Murdered?" Wythe shook his head. "No, that's not possible. Who'd want to hurt Lulu? Everybody loved her. You know that." Pale and trembling like a leaf in the wind, Wythe stared at Annabelle, a dazed look in his eyes.

"Pull yourself together. Right now. I can't have you falling apart. I need you to help me tell Uncle Louis."

"Daddy? Oh, Lord, this will kill him."

"What I want you to do is telephone Dr. Martin and tell him what's happened. Ask him to come over to the house immediately," Annabelle said. "I have duties to attend to, but as soon as Dr. Martin arrives, the three of us will take Uncle Louis aside and tell him."

"You know I was never jealous of her." Wythe smiled, the

expression on his face pathetic. "I was fifteen when she came along and I should have hated her, but I didn't. I adored the little puss from the first moment I saw her. Even knowing Daddy loved her far more than he ever did me didn't change the way I felt about her."

Annabelle did not want to hear this. Not now. Not ever. She had no time—and no stomach—for any of Wythe's confessions. And she felt he was on the verge of one.

"Use the phone in here to call Dr. Martin." As Annabelle walked past her cousin on her way to the door, she paused momentarily and offered him a sympathetic glance. The caring, nurturing part of her wanted to reach out and hug him, offer him comfort. But she could not bring herself to touch Wythe, not knowing what she did about him.

Once outside in the hallway, she hurried down the corridor, her head held high, her eyes dry. And all the while her heart was aching. Poor Lulu. No matter how wild and crazy she'd been, no matter how useless her life or how many times she'd disappointed her father, she didn't deserve to die. The murder of a Memphis socialite, the daughter of a Mississippi multimillionaire and the reigning emperor of the Vanderley empire, would be front-page news by morning. Once she told Uncle Louis about Lulu, she'd make plans to drive to Memphis first thing in the morning. She would take charge, do her duty and represent the family. She intended to make it her mission to see that Lulu's murderer was found and punished.

Quinn parked his Porsche in the two-car garage alongside Kendall's BMW. She waited for him to retrieve his overnight bag from the trunk, then held the door open for him to enter through the kitchen of her South Bluff home, a downtown terraced house. As he followed her into the great room, he noted that the decorating style reflected the lady herself. Sleek, smart and modern. Nothing homey about the place.

Lots of glass and mostly basic black-and-white, with a few tans and creams thrown in for good measure.

He was a man who noticed details, had built his career on his shrewd intuition as much as his intelligence. The house told him clearly that Kendall slept here, occasionally ate here and probably had sex here, but this place wasn't her home. The woman didn't have a home anymore than Quinn did. They were, by nature and nurture, vagabond loners.

He owned a penthouse in Houston, a vacation home in Jamaica and a time-share in Vail. But he didn't have a home. Not even the ranch he'd bought in the hill country adjoining his old friend Johnny Mack Cahill's property was really home.

He'd never needed a home. He'd been too busy building a career and getting filthy rich to be bothered with matters as mundane and unimportant as a home. But that had been in the past. He now had everything he'd ever wanted. And more. So why did he feel so empty? And so alone?

Kendall paused by the counter separating the state-of-the-art, stainless-steel kitchen from the great room. "I could fix us some hot tea or if you prefer, I can make you a stiff drink."

"How about some hot tea and a couple more aspirins." He rubbed his left temple with his forefinger.

"Hot tea and aspirins coming right up." She nodded toward the hallway opening to the right of the great room. "I have two guest bedrooms. Take your pick. They both have their own private bath."

Quinn nodded. "I'm not picky. Not tonight. I'm just grateful you offered me a place to stay. At a time like this, a little tea and sympathy is appreciated."

She looked at him suspiciously, as if doubtful about his sincerity. "I'll give you all the tea you want, but no sympathy."

Quinn heaved a deep sigh, then chuckled mirthlessly. "I meant that literally, honey, not metaphorically. I didn't think you'd brought me home with you so you could have your way with me."

She raised an eyebrow. "You've changed."

He shrugged. "Not really. Not much. But all I want from you is a cup of tea, a couple of aspirins . . . and maybe a little genuine sympathy. I haven't been on the wrong side of the law since I was a teenager. I don't like the feel of it—being a suspect in a murder case. And even though Lulu and I weren't in a serious relationship, I did care about her."

"As much as you can care about a woman. That's what you mean, isn't it?"

"Did I hurt you . . . back when we—"

Kendall laughed. "God, what an ego. No, you didn't hurt me. And before you jump to any other erroneous conclusions—I have not been pining away for you all these years. It's just that I know you. Correction, I knew you."

"I never realized how much you disliked me," Quinn said.

"I didn't dislike you back then and I don't dislike you now," she told him. "Hell, Quinn, if I disliked you so damn much, do you think I'd have come when you called, that I'd have invited you to stay here with me if—"

She stopped midsentence as she watched him drop his overnight bag on the floor and walk toward her. When he was within a foot of her, he reached out and caressed her face with his fingertips. "It's not me, is it? It's your ex. The guy must have done a real number on you."

Kendall sighed, then turned and moved away from Quinn. With her back to him, as she reached up in a cabinet for the box of tea bags, she said, "His name was Dr. Jonathan Miles. I was madly in love with him. The sex was great. His kids were holy terrors and both of them hated me. We thought that would change. It didn't. In the end, he chose his kids. Can't blame him. After all, he was still in love with his wife—his dead wife—and they were her kids."

"You're well rid of him, honey. The man didn't deserve you."

"No, he didn't." Kendall blew out a deep breath, then filled a kettle with water and placed it on the eye of her ceramic-top range. She glanced at Quinn and offered him a weak smile. "Why don't you pick out a bedroom, freshen up and by then I'll have the tea ready. I don't figure you'll get much sleep tonight."

He nodded, then headed down the hall. No, he probably wouldn't get any sleep tonight. He didn't want to close his eyes because he knew what he'd see. Lulu's lifeless body lying there on her bed. Beautiful and sexy, even in death. And her bloody hand, one digit missing. Why would anyone cut off her index finger?

Annabelle waited for Dr. Martin on the far side of her uncle's bedroom, Wythe at her side. He'd been remarkably well-behaved, keeping his own emotions in check and actually putting his father's needs first. She supposed in his own selfish way, Wythe did love Uncle Louis.

"No, please, please, tell me it isn't true," Louis Vanderley moaned as the sedative his personal physician had given him began to take effect. "My little Lulu. My precious baby girl. She can't be dead."

"Just lie back and relax, Louis," Dr. Martin said.

"Annabelle?" her uncle called for her.

She went to his bedside. Dr. Martin looked at her sympathetically, then moved aside. Annabelle leaned over and took her uncle's hand.

"I'm right here," she told him.

"Go to Memphis. Find out what happened. Our Lulu can't be dead."

She squeezed his age-spotted hand. "I'll leave first thing in the morning. And I'll call you as soon as I know anything."

"Someone has lied to us," Louis said, his voice a mere whisper. "Lulu isn't dead."

Annabelle leaned over and kissed her uncle's forehead. He closed his eyes and sighed heavily. She eased the satin coverlet up and over his chest. Uncle Louis was her father's elder brother. Her father had been the youngest of four, fifteen years his elder brother's junior. There had been two sisters born between them. Meta Anne, who'd passed away only a few years ago, an unmarried, childless career woman who'd devoted herself to helping Louis oversee the vast Vanderley empire. And Annabelle, the sister who'd died in the forties with infantile paralysis at the age of three. That Annabelle, as well as the present Annabelle Vanderley, had been named in honor of a great-great-grandmother who'd come from France as the bride of Edward Vanderley in 1855.

"Rest, dearest." Annabelle adored her uncle Louis, who'd been a second father to her since her own father had died of a heart attack seven years ago. "I'll find out what happened to Lulu. I promise."

Dr. Martin stopped her on her way out of the room. "Annabelle?"

"Yes?"

"He's seventy-eight, in poor health and has received a terrible shock," Dr. Martin said.

"Are you trying to tell us that he might die?" Wythe asked.

"Hush." Annabelle glanced at her uncle, who seemed to be asleep, then glowered at Wythe. "He might hear you."

"He's out cold," Wythe told her.

"All I'm saying is to prepare yourselves," Dr. Martin said. "Louis could well survive this, but . . . Well, it will depend on his will to live, at least in part. I've seen it happen before, patients who give up the will to live and die in a few weeks or a few months."

"I'll give him something to live for," Annabelle said. "Once he accepts that Lulu is dead, he'll want to see her killer punished. That alone will keep him going."

Dr. Martin shook his head. "Revenge can be a strong motivator. Just be careful that it doesn't turn on him. And on you."

"I wasn't referring to revenge. What I want—what Uncle Louis will want—is justice."

Quinn lay in the bed, the back of his head resting in his cupped hands, his fingers entwined. A cup of tea, a couple more aspirins and a sympathetic ear had partially eased his headache but hadn't helped him fall asleep. In a few short hours, he would have to return to police headquarters and answer more questions. Be grilled about Lulu's death.

God, how he wanted to turn back the clock and—and do what? Decline Lulu's offer to come to Memphis? Arrive at Lulu's house in time to stop her killer?

He flopped over and glanced at the digital bedside clock. Four forty-three.

Lulu had loved life about as much as anybody he'd ever known. There wasn't anything she wouldn't try, at least once. At twenty-seven, she'd had her whole life ahead of her. Marriage, kids, divorces and more marriages and divorces. Quinn laughed quietly to himself, remembering Lulu and the fun times they'd had. She'd been his female equivalent. Unkind people called her a whore. Those who knew her well thought of her as a free spirit. She enjoyed men in the same way he enjoyed women. Their rules of encounter were pretty much the same. No holds barred. Everyone was fair game. No commitments. No promises. Sex for the sake of sex. And love was never involved. Love was for fools. And Lulu had no more been a fool than Quinn. She knew the score.

Had she gotten herself involved with someone who had refused to play the game by her rules? Had someone decided that if they couldn't have Lulu exclusively, then no one could have her?

If the police concentrated all their efforts on proving he

killed Lulu, then the real killer might escape. He couldn't let that happen. He would not only find a way to prove his innocence, but he'd also move heaven and earth to bring Lulu's murderer to justice.

Chapter 3

Mary Lee Norton cried out with release when her climax exploded inside her. She was a screamer. Something he liked in a woman. He never wondered with Mary Lee whether or not he'd satisfied her. He'd heard that women in their mid to late-thirties were in their sexual prime and from his experience with older women, he'd found that to be true. It was certainly true of his partner's ex-wife. The woman had an insatiable hunger for sex.

Chad grasped her hips and tossed her off him and over onto her back, then delved deep and hard, seeking his own release. Within a couple of minutes, he came. Groaning with the headiness of satisfaction, he slid off her damp body and onto the bed. She cuddled against him and kissed his shoulder.

"You're good, sugar pie," she whispered in a husky, Southern drawl that hinted she was a heavy smoker.

Turning to her, he smiled as he noted the faint lines that edged her hazel eyes. At thirty-seven, she was still a looker, but give her a few more years and a couple of decades of smoking and sun worship would catch up with her. By the time she was forty-five, she'd need a face-lift. Of course, what she looked liked a few years down the road was no concern of his. Mary Lee was a temporary fixture in his life, a brief liaison that had to end before Jim Norton found out his partner was bonking his ex-wife.

"Am I as good as your ex?" he asked and could have kicked his own ass for letting his insecurity show.

Usually Chad was confident. Some said overconfident. And about most things he was. After all, why shouldn't he be? He was highly intelligent, good-looking, the ladies loved him and he was moving up fast in the department. But ever since he'd been paired with Jim Norton, he'd had a few moments of self-doubt. Without consciously doing anything to cause the effect, Jim intimidated the hell out of other guys. Even Chad. And why that was, he didn't know for sure. After all, Norton was nothing more than an ex-jock who'd nearly ruined his life and his career before Chad had graduated from college.

Mary Lee curled herself around Chad like a purring kitten and laughed as she ran her fingernails up and down his chest. "Comparing you to Jim is like comparing apples to oranges, sugar."

He grabbed her by the nape of her neck, trapping a few strands of her short black hair between his fingers. "Are you screwing him, too? Everybody knows that he's still got a thing for you."

"So I've been told, but you can't prove it by me." She stared right at Chad. "I've made the offer more than once since our divorce, but he hasn't accepted."

"He must be nuts to turn you down."

"Jim's unforgiving," she said. "I'm warning you, if you ever do anything to get on his shit list, you'll be on it for life. He doesn't forgive and he doesn't suffer fools gladly."

"So, what'd you do that was so unforgivable?"

Mary Lee pulled away from him, reached over on the nightstand and picked up a pack of cigarettes. He watched her as she lit the cigarette and took a couple of draws off it.

After blowing out a puff of smoke, she grinned at him. "I got tired of being ignored, of him working all the time. I looked elsewhere."

"And Jim found out."

"Jim caught us in the act. He came home unexpectedly and found our son's T-ball coach scoring a home run with me."

"What'd he do? Beat the hell out of the T-ball coach?"

"You'd think that's what a rough and rugged guy like Jim would do, wouldn't you?" She shook her head, then puffed on the cigarette. "He just stood there in the doorway for a couple of minutes. Didn't say a word. Then he turned around and walked away, right out of the house, and got back into his car and drove off."

"I'd never peg Jim for—"

She put her index finger over his lips to silence him. "You don't know the man at all, do you? He left so he wouldn't kill us. He wanted me dead just as much as the guy I'd been fucking. And I figure there was about a minute there when our lives hung by a thread. But Jim has incredible self-control. That's why he could walk away."

"Hmm . . ."

"Surely you've heard the rumors, haven't you? Jim Norton believes in the old adage about revenge being a dish best served cold."

A shiver zinged up Chad's spine. Yeah, he'd heard the rumors. And if he believed them, like others in the department did, then he knew what Norton was capable of doing. He sensed that Mary Lee admired her ex-husband, maybe still even cared about him. And he also sensed that if she were totally honest about which man was the best—at sex or anything else—she'd choose Lieutenant James Norton over him or any other guy.

Needing to erase such thoughts from his mind and bring back the casual mood, Chad jumped out of bed and headed for the bathroom, keeping his hand over the sagging condom clinging to his penis. He paused in the doorway and glanced back at his partner's ex-wife. "I've got to shower and shave, then get downtown and meet Jim. We're questioning a murder suspect this morning and I don't want to be late."

"Go ahead." She waved him off as she got out of bed. "Want me to put on a pot of coffee?"

Standing there in his bedroom, naked, tousled and sated, Mary Lee Norton got a rise out of him. A partial rise anyway. If he had time, he'd toss her back into bed and— Another time, he told himself. It wasn't as if he couldn't have Mary Lee anytime he wanted her. The lady was definitely hot-to-trot.

"I'll grab a cup at headquarters," he told her as he removed the used condom and dumped it in the wastebasket. "But feel free to fix yourself a pot and hang around as long as you'd like."

She didn't respond, so he had no idea what she'd do. By the time he had showered, shaved and dressed, he found the house empty. Mary Lee had left a note attached to the refrigerator with a magnet.

You're as good as he is, just different.

She'd scrawled her initials beneath the succinct note.

Chad grinned. He'd be seeing the lady again. Soon. And he'd make damn sure and certain her ex-husband didn't find out.

Quinn nibbled on the high protein bar Kendall had provided along with a cup of coffee. The coffee was good— black and strong, the way he liked it. The protein bar tasted like cardboard coated with cheap chocolate. He preferred his breakfast protein in the form of steak and eggs. At home and when out of town on a case, his routine seldom varied. He was accustomed to having his needs met by a small contingent of well-paid employees, who traveled with him. After the McBryar acquittal yesterday, he'd sent his entourage back to Houston, expecting full well to be on a plane back home no later than Monday morning. Those plans had been made when he'd thought he would be spending the weekend with Lulu.

"I've got some low-fat wheat bread," Kendall said. "I could fix you some toast."

He glanced at Kendall, who sat on the bar stool next to him at the kitchen counter. How was it possible that she looked so awake and refreshed at seven-twenty in the morning, when it had been nearly three when they'd finally gone to bed. Her tan suit fit her to perfection and matched her heels and the clutch purse lying at the end of the counter alongside her burgundy leather briefcase. Everything about her was perfect, from her stylish short hair to her subtle makeup.

"Don't bother. I'm not hungry." He laid the bland protein bar atop his napkin and lifted the coffee cup to his lips.

"Did you get any sleep?" Kendall asked.

"Some," he lied. He hadn't slept at all. Only dozed a couple of times.

"Do I need to remind you to think like a lawyer this morning when you're questioned and not like a suspect in a murder case?"

"Be calm, in control and logical," he replied. "Don't get emotional. And remember when to let my lawyer talk for me."

"Good boy."

"Honey, I've never been a good boy in my entire life." Quinn Cortez had been a lot of things, to a lot of people, but being a good boy wasn't one of them. As far as he was concerned, goodness was overrated. He preferred being rich, being powerful and being a winner. Maybe he'd sacrificed some important things along the way on his road to success, but he had to admit that if he had it to do all over again, he wouldn't change a thing.

Not unless he could go all the way back to the beginning

when Rico Cortez had married Sheila Quinn because he'd gotten her pregnant, then conveniently disappeared a few month's after his son's birth.

Kendall laughed. "I happen to like your cockiness, but how about downplaying it just a little this morning. And for God's sake, act a little broken-up about Lulu Vanderley's death, will you?"

"It won't be an act," Quinn said. "Not entirely. I'm not all broken-up, but . . . I want to make sure whoever killed Lulu is caught and punished."

"Finding the real murderer will get you off the hook."

"I want to see to it that her murderer pays for what he did. And not just for selfish reasons, but because Lulu didn't deserve to die." Quinn slammed his half-full cup down on the counter, splashing the black liquid onto his hand. He reacted to the heat instantly, raised his hand and rubbed it across his mouth.

"You really liked her, didn't you?" Kendall reached over and patted Quinn's arm.

He cut his eyes toward her. "Do you find that amazing— that I'd actually like a woman who's my lover?"

"No." Kendall gazed at him contemplatively. "What I find amazing is that you'd actually like a woman, any woman."

"What the hell do you mean by that? I love women. All women. You should know that, honey. Ask anybody who knows me and they'll tell you that Quinn Cortez is a ladies' man."

"You may love women—all women—but you don't like them as a general rule. If you liked women, you wouldn't treat them the way you do."

"I've never had any complaints." The flip response shot out of his mouth instantly.

"I'm sure no woman has ever complained about your prowess as a lover," Kendall told him. "But what about all the hearts you've broken? Don't you think there are dozens

of women out there who would love to see the great Quinn
Cortez brought to his knees and begging for mercy."

"I thought you said that I didn't hurt you, back when
we—"

"This isn't about me. It's about your reputation. Don't
you realize that if Lulu told just one person that she wanted
more from you than a passionate fling, the police could build
a case around that fact—that she was clinging to you and
you couldn't shake her without killing her?"

"Lulu never once said she wanted more from our relationship."

"She didn't say that to you, but can you be one hundred
percent sure she never implied to anyone else that she was in
love with you or wanted a committed relationship?"

Quinn slid off the bar stool and stood. "I can't be certain
of what she might or might not have told someone else. But
I'm telling you that Lulu wasn't looking for a permanent relationship with me or anybody."

"I hope her family and friends will verify that fact."
Kendall bit off a chunk of protein bar, chewed and washed it
down with coffee.

"Lulu's family . . ." Quinn groaned. "I'd forgotten all about
them. She has an elderly father and a half brother over in
Mississippi somewhere. The old man still runs the Vanderley
empire, with the help of a cousin. I can't recall the cousin's
name. Abigail or Adelaide or something like that. I can hear
Lulu saying, 'Abi . . . Adel—Annabelle . . .' That's it, Annabelle.
She'd say, 'Annabelle is a real saint, a true martyr. I love her
like a sister, but God, she's such a bore.' I suppose the
Memphis police notified—"

Kendall stood, put her arms around Quinn and hugged
him. "Don't consider it a weakness to allow Lieutenant Norton
and Sergeant George to see this I-actually-do-give-a-damn
side of your personality."

Quinn stepped back and looked directly at Kendall. "You

think they're going to charge me with Lulu's murder, don't you?"

"I think that if they don't find another suspect and they can come up with the least bit of evidence against you, no matter how circumstantial, they just might try to pin this on you."

On the way to the Criminal Justice Center, Jim Norton sipped on a container of black coffee as he maneuvered his seen-better-days Chevy truck along Poplar Avenue. He'd downed a cup of the high octane brew before he left his apartment in the Exchange Building, right after wolfing down a bowl of corn flakes. The alarm clock had gone off at six-thirty, but he'd hit the snooze button twice. He'd gotten all of maybe four hours sleep. He'd tried to get in touch with his ex-wife last night without any luck. He didn't really give a damn where Mary Lee was or who she was with, but he sure as hell wanted to know where his son was. Spending the night with a friend again? Whenever Mary Lee needed to scratch an itch, she'd send Kevin to a friend's for the night.

He could complain. He had in the past. But Mary Lee had pointed out to him that he was lucky she didn't have sole custody. "What if you didn't even have visitation rights?" she had asked him when he'd suggested she let him keep Kevin whenever she had a date. "All things considered, you're lucky I let you see Kevin as much as I do. After all, if I hadn't agreed to your getting some visitation rights—"

He'd just call her again later this morning—or at least try to—to make sure she hadn't forgotten that he was supposed to pick up Kevin this evening and keep him until Monday morning. He'd made plans for them to spend tomorrow with his sister Susan's family. Kevin enjoyed spending time with his three cousins, twin boys only a year older than he and a girl two years younger. Jim liked the idea of his son seeing

what a real family was like. That's what he'd wanted for
Kevin—that all-American, mom-and-apple-pie life he and
Susan had had as kids. But both he and Mary Lee had
fucked up big time. And now, thanks to them, Kevin would
never have what Jim had wanted most for his son.

He could blame it all on Mary Lee. And sometimes, especially when he'd had too much to drink, he did blame it all
on her. But when completely sober and in the cold light of
day, he knew he had to accept his share of the blame. Way
back when he'd been a young hotshot with great ambition,
he had neglected his wife and son. His arrogance and cockiness had gotten his partner killed, had put him in the hospital
and had landed him in a heap of trouble with the department.
By the time he'd healed physically and emotionally, he'd already lost his wife, even if they didn't divorce until nearly
three years later.

After pulling into his parking place and releasing his
safety belt, Jim removed his cell phone from its holder and
hit the button that instantly dialed his ex's home phone number. Much to his surprise, she answered on the fifth ring.

"Mary Lee?"

"Yeah. Who were you expecting, the Queen of Sheba?"

"I tried calling last night."

"I had a date."

"Stayed out kind of late didn't you?"

She laughed. "I stayed out all night. Just got in."

If she thought telling him she'd spent the night with some
guy would bother him, she was wrong. He had actually given
a damn that she screwed another guy only one time. The
time he'd caught her in the act. After that, she could have
done it with every guy in Memphis for all he cared. He just
hated that Kevin's mother had gained a reputation as a . . . as
a what? A slut who'd spread her legs for just about any guy?

Mary Lee had always been a little wild and God knew she
hadn't been a virgin when they got married, but he hadn't

cared. He'd been crazy about her. Hog-wild crazy. And she'd loved him, too. He knew she had.

"I just wanted to remind you that I'll be picking Kevin up at six-thirty this evening," Jim said. Now wasn't the time to get into it with Mary Lee about Kevin spending too many nights at other people's houses.

"He'll be ready. He's been looking forward to seeing you."

"Yeah, me, too."

"Jim?"

"Huh?"

"I saw in this morning's *Commercial Appeal* where you and your partner are working the Lulu Vanderley murder."

"Yeah."

"Lulu Vanderley was somebody real important, wasn't she? If you solve this one and bring her killer in, it sure won't hurt your career, will it?"

"I don't worry as much about my career as I used to," he told her.

"You don't worry as much or care as much about a lot of things."

"That's the way life is." He took a deep breath. "Tell Kevin I'll see him at six-thirty."

Before giving Mary Lee a chance to say anything else, Jim hung up. One of these days he'd be able to have a conversation with his ex and not think about what might have been. "If only" was a game for idiots.

Annabelle emerged from her white Cadillac, hoisted her leather bag over her shoulder and took a deep, calming breath. On the drive over from Austinville, she'd made a dozen phone calls, using her On-Star system, which made phoning while driving an easy, risk-free task. She'd spoken to the president and two vice presidents at Vanderley, Inc., and helped their top PR person word a press release about Lulu's murder. She'd also spoken to her uncle twice and it had broken her heart to hear the sound of his weak, trembling voice. Knowing that Dr. Martin had arranged for nurses to be at Uncle Louis's side twenty-four/seven gave her some comfort.

Before leaving early this morning, she'd fielded numerous calls from local, state and even national newspapers and televisions stations. Her cousin's murder was front-page news throughout the state of Mississippi and most of the South. Even now, a good twelve hours after hearing the news from Sheriff Brody, Annabelle was having difficulty believing it was true. Accepting the death of a family member was always difficult—she'd gone through the agony with her aunt Meta Anne's and both her parents' deaths and again when she lost Chris. When someone young died, someone only twenty-seven as Lulu had been, the loss seemed all the greater because you felt that the person hadn't gotten a chance to live a full life. She'd felt that way when Chris died two years ago. He had been the center of her world for so long that shortly after the funeral, she'd fallen apart completely. But in typical Annabelle style, she hadn't allowed herself to wallow in self-pity for very long. She'd pulled herself up by the proverbial bootstraps, dusted off her bruised and bloody emotions and thrown herself back into work. Thank God for work. It had been her salvation more than once over the years.

As she approached the Poplar Avenue entrance to the Criminal Justice Center, she recited the directions she'd been given over the telephone by the helpful police officer she'd spoken to an hour ago while she'd been en route. With her mind on other matters—finding the homicide division of the police department within this huge complex, as well as thinking about what she'd be told concerning Lulu's murder—Annabelle failed to notice the small crowd gathering around her. Suddenly, someone shouted her name. She jerked her head up and searched for the speaker.

"Ms. Vanderley? Annabelle Vanderley?" A short, wiry man with a camera in hand moved toward her.

"Who are you?" she asked. "What do you want?"

"You are Lulu Vanderley's cousin, Annabelle, aren't you?" a small, slender blonde holding a microphone in her hand asked as she zeroed in on Annabelle.

"We'd like to ask you a few questions," another reporter joined in the fray.

"I have no comment," Annabelle told them. "The spokesperson for Vanderley, Inc. will make a statement at noon today at our headquarters in Jackson, Mississippi."

"Is it true that Lulu was killed by her latest lover?"

"Was she raped and then killed?"

"How was she killed? Was she shot? Strangled? Stabbed?"

The questions bombarded her as the reporters drew closer and closer, shoving microphones and cameras in her face.

"Please, leave me alone." She tried to move past the throng that seemed to be multiplying by the minute, but she was surrounded. Try as she might, she couldn't find an escape route.

As if from out of nowhere a tall, broad-shouldered man cut a path through Annabelle's tormentors, slid his arm around her waist and all but shoved the reporters aside. When they complained, he paused, faced them and snarled. With her breath caught in her throat, Annabelle took a good look at her rescuer. The fierce expression on his face would have backed down the devil himself. The reporters continued to grumble, but didn't make the slightest move in her direction.

Whoever this man was—her protector—he took her breath away.

"You heard the lady. Leave her alone," he said, his voice baritone deep and rich.

Annabelle sighed with relief as she offered her white knight an appreciative smile. *Who is he?* she wondered. Could he possibly be a plainclothes police officer?

She studied him hurriedly, taking in his appearance. He

was a devastatingly attractive man with wavy jet black hair and large dark brown eyes. Handsome, but not pretty. Suave yet rugged. He was dressed in an expensive navy blue suit. Tailor-made, unless she missed her guess, which meant he was rich. So he probably wasn't a policeman. She doubted the base pay, even for a detective, was more than forty or fifty thousand a year. This man's suit had probably cost several thousand.

He kept his arm around her waist, her body pressed against his side. Annabelle's heart beat faster and her stomach fluttered. Sheer nerves, she told herself.

"Thank you so much, Mr.—"

"Cortez. Quinn Cortez."

"I appreciate your coming to my rescue, Mr. Cortez." Her gaze locked with his as they stared into each other's eyes. He was looking at her as if he wanted to say something.

"These people can be real jerks," he told her. "You've just lost your cousin—"

"How did you . . . Oh, you probably read about Lulu in the newspaper."

A tall, dark-haired woman came through the crowd and walked straight up to Quinn. "I'm sure Ms. Vanderley will be fine now," the woman said. "We have an appointment"— she tapped her gold wristwatch—"in five minutes. You don't want to be late."

He didn't budge and made no move to release his protective hold on Annabelle.

"Please, don't let me keep you from an important appointment," Annabelle said. "I'll be fine now. Surely they won't follow me."

His gaze caressed her, creating a fluttering sensation along her nerve endings. "Let me see you safely inside."

Suddenly one of the newspaper reporters shouted out, "Ms. Vanderley, how well do you know Mr. Cortez? Obviously you don't think he had anything to do with your cousin's murder, right?"

What had the reporter said? Why would he think Mr. Cortez had any connection to Lulu's murder?

Annabelle broke eye contact with Quinn and looked right at the reporter. "What are you talking about?"

"Did you and your cousin both have a romantic relationship with Mr. Cortez?" the same reporter asked.

When Annabelle glared at him, puzzled by his question, he added, "Seeing how chummy you are with Mr. Cortez and how he came rushing to your rescue, are we to assume that you two are close . . . friends?"

"I never—" Annabelle realized she wasn't handling this media attack very well. Speechlessness and shock wouldn't work in her favor.

"Ignore them," Quinn whispered in her ear as he urged her into movement.

Escape was the best plan of action, so she allowed him to guide her toward the entrance.

"You didn't kill Lulu, did you, Ms. Vanderley, when you found out she was sleeping with Quinn Cortez?" The blond reporter held out her microphone as she trailed behind Annabelle, Quinn and the dark-haired woman.

Annabelle turned and faced the reporter. "Go away. Leave me alone. I don't know what you're talking about and I don't care."

"You don't care that your cousin was murdered or that Mr. Cortez might have been involved?" Someone in the crowd shouted the question.

"Let's go inside and get away from them," Quinn said. "Then I'll explain what's going on."

"Explain now." She jerked away from him.

"Don't give them a chance to exploit you and me and Lulu," Quinn warned.

She stood still as a statue and glared at him. "Were you and Lulu . . . were you—"

He spoke softly, saying the words for her ears only. "Lulu and I were lovers. We had a date last night. I'm the person who found her body."

Chapter 4

Although stunned by Quinn Cortez's confession, Annabelle managed to maintain her composure. Just barely. Odd how discovering her rescuer was one of Lulu's numerous lovers actually bothered her. And the fact that he'd been the one who had discovered Lulu's body concerned her. Hadn't the reporters implied that Mr. Cortez might have been somehow involved in the crime?

Was she murdered by a lover?

When one of the reporters asked that specific question, she hadn't paid much attention. But staring Quinn Cortez in the eyes, that question suddenly became of paramount importance.

"You—you discovered Lulu's body?"

"Please, Ms. Vanderley, you don't want to do this here, in front of the reporters," Quinn said.

She nodded. "Yes, I suppose you're right."

When he gripped her elbow, she instinctively jerked away from him, but when he and his female companion flanked her in a protective manner, she followed them straight into the building. The last thing she wanted was to give the reporters a show.

"They'll follow us," the woman said. "You two go on ahead and I'll deal with them."

"Thanks, honey." Quinn bestowed a devastating smile on his companion. "I'll meet you upstairs."

The woman eyed him speculatively. "Don't get side-tracked." She looked pointedly at Annabelle.

"I won't." Quinn grabbed Annabelle's elbow and ushered her forward. "Let's go now, while we can, and let Kendall handle things here."

"Kendall?"

"Kendall Wells, my friend and lawyer."

Lawyer? Did this man need a lawyer? Was he guilty of a crime? Was he a suspect in Lulu's murder?

Despite her uncertainty, Annabelle didn't protest his assistance in their escape from the media and willingly allowed him to lead her into the building and through the metal detectors. Neither spoke a word until they were securely inside the building and safe from prying eyes. When they reached the two banks of elevators across from each other, she pulled away from him, tilted her chin and narrowed her gaze. He faced her with the same devastating smile he'd used on his friend and lawyer. She punched one of the elevator UP buttons.

"You and Lulu were lovers?" she asked as they waited.

"Yes, we were."

"You had a date with her last night and you found . . . you discovered her body."

"That's right."

When the elevator doors to their right swung open, Annabelle entered, punched the tenth-floor button and turned to Quinn, who was still at her side.

"Do the police suspect you were involved?"

"Probably. In any murder investigation, the victim's closest relatives and friends are usually suspects, at least in the beginning."

"You say that as if you—"

"I'm a lawyer," he told her. "I'm surprised you haven't heard of me. I'm famous. Or perhaps I'm infamous." He grunted sarcastically.

When she stared at him, a tight knot of apprehension clutched her stomach muscles. "Lulu often chose influential, powerful men as her friends. And usually those men were quite a bit older than she was."

"I'm thirty-nine. I suppose twelve years makes me somewhat older. But I know for a fact that she enjoyed her share of guys her age and younger."

"You seem to know more about my cousin than I do."

"You two weren't close," Quinn said. "At least not since you were kids."

"She told you about me?"

He nodded. "Your name came up once or twice. Apparently she never mentioned me to you."

"As you said, we haven't been close in a very long time. Lulu and I chose very different paths in life."

"You say that in a very superior manner, Ms. Vanderley. I take it that you didn't approve of your cousin's hedonistic lifestyle."

The elevator doors opened on the tenth floor. Annabelle hadn't even thought about the fact that they were both headed for the same floor, that they probably had the same destination.

Instead of responding to his comment, she asked, "Are you being interrogated concerning Lulu's murder this morning, Mr. Cortez?"

After stepping out of the elevator, he placed his hand so that he could keep the doors from closing on her. "I'm being interviewed."

"What's the difference?" She stepped out of the elevator, taking every precaution to make certain her body didn't so much as graze his.

Ignoring her question, he said, "I want you to know something, Ms. Vanderley."

"What's that, Mr. Cortez?"

Staring at each other, eye to eye, tension vibrated between them. Subconsciously, Annabelle held her breath in anticipation.

"I didn't kill Lulu," he said.

Annabelle swallowed. Why was it that she so desperately wanted to believe him? What possible difference could it make to her whether this man was innocent or guilty?

"I don't think there's any reason for us to continue this conversation or for us to see or speak to each other again," Annabelle told him. "So I'll take this opportunity to thank you again for coming to my rescue with those reporters, but—"

"I want to find out who killed Lulu just as much as you do. Lulu and I weren't family, but we were friends. Close friends."

"The way you and Ms. Wells are friends?"

Annabelle groaned mentally. Why had she asked him such a personal question?

His lips twitched. "Yes, the way Kendall and I were once close friends."

There, I guess that answers your question, doesn't it? He and his lawyer are more than friends. And he didn't mind telling you.

"Finding another suspect would certainly be to your advantage, wouldn't it?" She wanted to get away from this man as quickly as possible. He had the strangest effect on her and she didn't like it. *I believe it's called charm,* she told herself. No doubt this man has been charming women all his life. She shouldn't flatter herself by believing she was different from countless others he had charmed or that she was in any way important to him. Except . . . ? Except as Lulu's cousin and the official representative for the Vanderley family, it would work to his advantage if she liked him, if he could persuade her to trust him.

This man could be Lulu's killer. Never forget that fact.

"Whatever my motives are, you and I want the same thing," he told her, his dark eyes roaming over her with disturbing familiarity. "If we were to work together—"

"Ms. Vanderley, is this man bothering you?" The masculine voice came from behind her.

Whipping around, she faced a beautiful young man with short auburn hair and a deadly serious expression on his flawless face. She wasn't sure she'd ever seen a prettier man in her entire life.

"No, Mr. Cortez wasn't bothering me," she said. "We were just . . . talking."

"I wasn't aware that you two were acquainted." The young man looked right at Quinn.

"We aren't," she said. "I mean we weren't until a few minutes ago when Mr. Cortez rescued me from a marauding band of reporters."

Giving Quinn a harsh look, the other man held out his hand to Annabelle as he focused all his attention on her. "I'm Sergeant Chad George, ma'am. My partner and I are the detectives in charge of the investigation into your cousin's death."

"Her death? I was told she was murdered."

"Yes, ma'am, she was," Chad said. "Allow me to offer you my condolences."

"On behalf of the Memphis police department?" Quinn asked. "Or are you offering Ms. Vanderley your personal condolences, sergeant?"

Annabelle sensed a hostile tension between the two men as they glowered at each other. And she had the oddest sensation that, for the moment, she was the prize in this particular battle of wills.

"Both," Chad said sharply, then softened his voice when he spoke again. "Ms. Vanderley, if there's anything I can do for you . . ."

"I would like to speak to you and your partner and anyone else involved in this case. I will be representing my family in this matter and expect to be kept informed about anything and everything involving my cousin's murder."

"Certainly. Lieutenant Norton and I have an appointment with Mr. Cortez"—Chad glanced at his wristwatch—"right now, so allow me to escort you to the director's office. He's expecting you and can answer some of your questions. Then when Norton and I are free, we'll be glad to do whatever we can for you."

Annabelle gave Quinn Cortez a sidelong glance. "Is Mr. Cortez a suspect?"

Silence.

Annabelle glanced back and forth from one man to the other. "Knowing if Mr. Cortez is a suspect falls under keeping me informed about anything and everything to do with Lulu's murder."

Chad cleared his throat, then said hurriedly, "Mr. Cortez discovered the body. We will be questioning him again this morning, with his attorney present."

As if on cue, Kendall Wells stepped off the elevator directly behind them. "What have we here, a little informal powwow?" she said as she approached her client. "You've been behaving yourself, haven't you, Quinn?"

"Don't I always?" he replied.

His lawyer gave him a censoring glance, then zeroed in on the sergeant. "We're here on time and ready for the interview. Let's get this over with so Mr. Cortez can—"

"We'll be ready for y'all shortly," Chad snapped his response, then turned to Annabelle, all smiles and concern. "Ms. Vanderley, if you'll follow me, I'll show you to Director Danley's office." He took her arm and tugged gently.

Annabelle went with him, all the while fighting the urge to look back at Quinn Cortez.

"Don't make us cool our heels too long," Ms. Wells called after them.

Sergeant George mumbled under his breath. "I apologize for someone not meeting you outside and escorting you in.

It's unfortunate that you had to be subjected to meeting Quinn Cortez, especially this morning, so soon after . . . Well, I am sorry."

"Exactly who is Quinn Cortez and why did he think I should have heard of him?"

Chad harrumphed. "The man's an egomaniac. He thinks the whole world knows who he is because he's a criminal defense lawyer who has gotten quite a few murderers off scot-free. He just won a big case over in Nashville. The Terry McBryar case."

"Oh, yes, I seem to recall hearing something about that trial on the news. Wasn't McBryar's lawyer some hotshot from Texas?" Annabelle gasped as she remembered what one newscaster had said about McBryar's lawyer, whose name she'd forgotten.

He not only has a reputation as a dangerously formidable opponent in the courtroom, but also as a real lady-killer in his personal life.

She wasn't sure why that comment had stuck with her when she had forgotten the man's name and had no memory of seeing him on the newscast. The words *dangerously formidable* and *lady-killer* repeated themselves again and again in Annabelle's mind.

"A far as I'm concerned, Cortez is scum," Chad told her. "He's an immoral moneygrubber. A real shyster."

"Are you saying you believe the man has no conscience? If that's the case, then he's capable of murder, isn't he? Is that what you think—you think he killed Lulu?"

Chad coughed, then cleared his throat. She glanced at him and noted a slight pink flush to his cheeks.

"Here we are." He paused in front of the closed door to the Director of Police's office.

She realized that Chad George had no intention of answering her question about Quinn Cortez. Why was that? Couldn't he give her a simple yes or no response?

"Director Danley, Ms. Annabelle Vanderley has arrived," he announced through the closed door.

A deep, gruff voice responded. "Don't keep the lady waiting. Go get her and show her in. We've got enough trouble with the press as it is. The last thing we want—" When he opened the door and saw Annabelle standing at the sergeant's side, the director quieted immediately. "Ms. Vanderley?"

She nodded.

"Please, come into my office." Danley cast Chad a scurrilous glare. "Don't you have somewhere to be right now, sergeant?"

"Yes, sir." The younger man all but clicked his heels before he turned and walked away, leaving Annabelle with Director Danley.

Jim Norton rubbed the palm of his hand across his face as he studied Quinn Cortez. *The* Quinn Cortez. There had been a time when he'd been *The* Jimmy Norton, renowned UT running back and teammate of the even more renowned quarterback, Griffin Powell. Jim understood what it was like to have your reputation precede you and to often follow you around like a ghost from the past, a ghost from which you couldn't escape.

He'd listened carefully to everything Cortez had said and he'd interpreted the way in which the man had responded to questions. He'd also studied his body language as he'd sat there, cool as a cucumber, for the past hour. Jim's gut instincts told him that Cortez didn't kill Lulu. First and foremost, the man had no motive. At least none they knew of. And secondly, Jim had been impressed with the way Cortez had dealt with Chad George's hostility and rudeness. His partner seemed damned and determined to make Cortez confess to the crime. Jim had come close to asking Chad to step outside a couple times before he crossed the line with his unprofessional interrogation. His reaction to Cortez wasn't the norm for Chad, who often acted on emotion rather than logic, but always conducted himself in a professional manner.

Jim followed the rules, never broke them—not in a long

time—and bent them only when absolutely necessary. Dealing with a lawyer as smart as Cortez put an extra burden on the Memphis police department and the bottom line with Jim was making sure neither he nor Chad did anything that even hinted of illegality.

Been there. Done that. Wouldn't repeat that mistake.

"Are we about through here?" Kendall Wells asked as she rose from her chair and snapped shut her briefcase.

"Maybe," Chad said.

"Yes, we're though," Jim corrected his partner. "And we want to thank Mr. Cortez for being so cooperative."

"Then my client is free to go?"

"Certainly."

"Free to return to Houston?" she asked.

Jim grunted. "At this point, I'd rather not make what I'm going to say official . . ."

Ms. Wells sighed loudly. "He's free to walk out of the Criminal Justice Center, but not free to leave Memphis. Is that it?"

"We don't have all the facts in this case. Not yet," Jim said. "Once we have the autopsy report and we've interviewed—"

"I won't leave Memphis." Cortez stood. "I'll be available if you need anything else from me. But don't mistake my co-operation for acquiescence. If y'all don't find Lulu's killer in a big hurry, the public and the Vanderley family are going to bring a great deal of pressure down on Director Danley. I don't intend to stand idly by and do nothing until y'all arrest me for a murder I didn't commit."

"What's the matter, Cortez? If you're so damn innocent, why are you afraid we'll pin the murder on you?" Chad came out of the corner where he'd been standing quietly for the past ten minutes. "We'd have to have some really good evidence before we did that. You must be scared shitless that we'll find that evidence."

Cortez glared at Chad, a killer stare that Jim figured had

made many a man quake in his boots. Chad took a step back, but didn't break eye contact with Cortez.

"Lieutenant Norton, I advise you to rein in your partner." Cortez eased his gaze from Chad to Jim.

"We're out of here." Kendall Wells patted Cortez on the back.

"We'll be in touch," Jim said.

Just as Cortez passed by Chad, Jim heard Cortez warn his partner in a soft whisper, "Annabelle Vanderley is off-limits to you."

Before Chad could respond, Cortez and his lawyer were out the door. Jim clamped his hand down on Chad's shoulder. "What was that all about?"

Chad shrugged. "God damn son of a bitch. He's the one who'd better steer clear of Ms. Vanderley."

Jim rubbed the back of his neck, then shook his head. "What did I miss? What's going on with you, Cortez and Annabelle Vanderley?"

"Nothing. It's just that Cortez played white knight to her outside earlier when some reporters were harassing her. We should have sent someone to meet her and escort her inside to protect her from—"

"Someone meaning you?"

"Yeah, why not?"

"I take it that this Ms. Vanderley is quite attractive and that fact didn't escape either you or Cortez." Jim tightened his hold on Chad's shoulder. "So help me God, if you instigate a personal pissing contest between you and Cortez, I'll—"

"I didn't start anything. He—"

"I don't give a damn who started what. Just make sure you don't get involved. Steer clear of Cortez except on official business. Do I make myself clear?"

"I swear I'll steer clear of Cortez until we have some evidence against him. And I'm telling you, there's bound to be evidence. He may be smart, but he's not nearly as smart as he thinks he is. If he killed her—and I say he did—then he slipped up somehow and all we've got to do is figure out how."

Quinn had wanted to stick around and speak to Annabelle Vanderley again. But he'd thought better of the idea— actually Kendall had warned him in no uncertain terms to stay away from Lulu's cousin. And she was right. What good would it do either him or Annabelle if he sought her out again simply because she intrigued him. Lulu had talked about her cousin several times and he always sensed that she both loved and hated Annabelle. From what Lulu had told him— that her cousin was plain, placid and prudish—he hadn't expected the woman to practically take his breath away the moment he saw her.

Lulu had been gorgeous. All Barbie doll leggy, bosomy and blond. And as spoiled rotten as her daddy's millions could make her. She'd been Quinn's type—an easy lay who wouldn't complicate his life.

Annabelle possessed a cool, reserved elegance. A Grace Kelly beauty that hinted of hidden fires burning deep inside and saved for one lucky man.

Was that it, the reason she fascinated him so much? Did he see Annabelle as a challenge? God knew he hadn't found a woman challenging in . . . Hell, he couldn't remember when.

After the police interview, Quinn had driven back to Kendall's, fixed a fresh pot of coffee and considered his options. Kendall had given him a key and told him to make himself at home, for the time being. He appreciated her hospitality, but if he was going to be stuck in Memphis for a while, he'd need his own place.

Setting his coffee mug aside, Quinn punched the preset number on his cell phone and waited for Marcy to answer, which she did on the third ring.

"Hello."

"Marcy, I need you to round up Aaron and Jace and y'all get the first flight out of Houston to Memphis."

"What's going on? I thought you planned to get some R&R before even thinking about taking another case."

Marcy had been Quinn's personal assistant for nearly ten years. Their association had lasted longer than a lot of marriages. He relied on her, trusted her and paid her an ungodly salary to be at his beck and call twenty-four/seven. In all their years together, she'd never let him down, which was more than he could say for most of the women in his life, past and present. And that was the reason he'd never allowed their association to change from the friendship level to something more intimate. It wasn't that he hadn't been tempted. Marcy was a doll. Cute as a button. All of five one and a hundred pounds soaking wet. But he wouldn't do anything to risk losing her. Lovers were a dime a dozen; a great personal assistant was irreplaceable.

"Lulu Vanderley was murdered last night before I arrived at her house," Quinn said. "I discovered her body."

"Holy shit."

"Yeah, my sentiments exactly."

"So, unless you're phoning from the police station, I take it they haven't arrested you."

"Not yet, but I'm suspect numero uno."

"You were told not to leave town, huh?"

"It was more of a request than a demand."

"I'll have to find Aaron and Jace. Might be tomorrow before they can fly in, but I can be there by this evening if you want—"

"Just wait and the three of you fly in together tomorrow. But you could do something for me from there. Two things actually."

"Name them."

"Check out renting us a place here in Memphis. Something I can lease by the month. I could be stuck here a week or two or if they try to pin this thing on me—"

"I'll take care of it. What else?"

"Get me Griffin Powell's home phone number."

"Ask me to move the Smoky Mountains to Hawaii."

Quinn chuckled. "I know it'll take a minor miracle, but you're good at pulling off the impossible."

"Flattery will get you what you want," she told him. "And maybe performing another minor miracle will get me a raise."

"You're overpaid already."

"I wish." She paused for a couple of seconds, then said, "Quinn?"

"Yeah, honey?"

"I know you didn't kill Lulu Vanderley."

"You're one in a million, kiddo."

"And don't you forget it."

"I won't," he said. "Besides, if I do, you'll remind me."

"Got that damn straight."

"Get me Powell's number as soon as possible," Quinn said. "He's the best money can buy and—"

"You always buy the best."

"You know me too well." Quinn grunted. "I want my own private investigator to assist the Memphis police in their job of finding Lulu's killer. Unless they come up with something damn quick, they may not look any further than me."

Chapter 5

He could hear her footsteps coming closer and closer. Any minute now she would open the door to his room and come inside, just as she always did whenever he had displeased her. He tried so hard to be good, to make her happy, but it seemed that he couldn't do anything right. Everything he said and did was wrong. Even the way he looked angered her.

"You're much too handsome," she had told him repeatedly, from as far back as he could remember. "You're going to break a lot of hearts if I don't stop you."

"I won't. I promise I won't."

"You've always been a liar. If I don't punish you for your sins, God will. You'll burn in hell if I can't beat the evil out of you."

Sitting in the middle of his bedroom floor, he trembled as he watched the doorknob turn. He had locked the door once, but when she'd removed the hinges and taken the door off the frame, she had been wild with anger. His punishment had been severe. She'd broken his arm that time. And when he'd hidden in the closet, she'd whipped him so severely that he still bore the scars on his buttocks.

The door opened. His heart beat like crazy, thumping so

loudly that it deafened him to the sound of her voice. He couldn't understand what she was saying as she stood there hovering over him, a stern look on her face. He knew she was screaming, outraged by what he'd done.

He dared a quick glance up at her, his gaze focused not on her face, but on the erect index finger she pointed directly at him. Whenever she scolded him, she used her index finger to emphasize her point. God, how he hated that judgmental finger.

Suddenly, she stopped ranting. He held his breath, knowing what would come next. She lifted her hand and brought it down across his face, slapping him so hard that he reeled backward. He lay there, feeling completely helpless as she pointed her finger at him again and continued berating him. Cuddling into a small protective ball, he lay there waiting for the next blow. He didn't have long to wait. She removed the thick leather belt from around her waist, folded it in two and then snapped it. He cried out with fear.

He hated that belt, the instrument of his torment. She wore it with every pair of jeans she owned. A brown leather belt with a wide brass buckle.

She kept talking, but still he couldn't hear her, only the drone of her agitated voice. But he knew what she was telling him to do. With trembling hands, he slid his pajama bottoms down his hips and trembling legs, then kicked them off. He dared another glance up at her. She smiled at him.

Oh, God, help me. Don't let her beat me again.

She motioned for him to roll over, which he did. The first blow to his backside stung something awful. Those first few blows were always the worst. After about a dozen strikes over his flesh, the pain was so bad that it began to become a part of him.

Tears welled up in his eyes.

Begging and pleading wouldn't do any good. He'd tried that over and over again.

I love you, Mommy. I want to obey you. I'll try harder. I promise I'll be good.

*She hit him repeatedly, so many times that he finally lost
count. The pain surged through him as blood oozed from the
stripes covering his bare buttocks.*

*"It's my duty to punish you, to save you from yourself and
your evil ways."*

Tears trickled down his cheeks.

*"You know I'm doing this for your own good, don't you?"
When he couldn't manage a reply, she reached down, grabbed
him and shook him. "You've been a very bad boy, Quinn."*

The scream inside him ripped him apart.

His eyelids flew open as he shot straight up in bed. It wasn't
real. Not anymore. It was a nightmare. That's all. He'd been
asleep, taking a nap, and as so often happened, his subconscious forced him to relive those horrific days from his
childhood. With his heart thundering and sweat glistening
on his skin, he took several deep breaths.

That same nightmare or one very similar plagued him relentlessly. No matter what he did, he couldn't escape. No
matter how many miles or years he'd put between the two of
them, she would never release him completely. She'd be a
part of him until the day he died.

But she can't hurt you, he told himself. *She can never
hurt you again.*

Griffin Powell didn't go into the office on the weekends,
and unless he was personally working on a case, he didn't do
anything work-related on Saturday and Sunday. After all, a
man had to make time for a social life. He'd spent most of
the afternoon working out in the gym he had designed to fit
into the basement of his Knoxville home. Keeping physically fit was one of his top priorities. After wiping the perspiration from his face, he hung the small white towel
around his neck and headed for the shower, but before he
reached the bathroom adjacent to the exercise room, Sanders
appeared at the foot of the stairs.

Sanders had been Griffin's assistant for a number of

years, ever since he'd been at Griffin's side on his personal
journey to hell and back. They shared a comradery only
those who've depended upon each other to stay alive truly
understood.

"Sorry to bother you, sir, but I've taken two phone calls
that were made to your private number."

Griffin cocked an inquisitive eyebrow.

"One was from Quinn Cortez. He wants you to investigate a murder case. It seems he discovered his lover's dead
body last night and as of right now, he is a person of interest
to the Memphis police department."

"Quinn Cortez, huh? *The* Quinn Cortez." Griffin's lips lifted
with amused interest. "I'll call him after I take a shower."

"There was a second telephone call."

"Someone more interesting than Quinn Cortez?"

"This person's call makes Mr. Cortez's call even more interesting."

"And this person is?

"Annabelle Vanderley."

"Annabelle? Why didn't you put her through to me immediately?"

Griffin recalled the one and only time he'd met the lady.
And she was a lady, down to the very marrow in her bones.
Born and bred to Mississippi royalty, the descendant of two
wealthy, prestigious families—the Vanderleys and the Austins.
They'd been introduced by a mutual friend at a charity function in Chattanooga three years ago and he'd found Ms. Vanderley vastly intriguing. He'd made subtle overtures, which
she'd ignored. He was unaccustomed to being rejected, so
out of curiosity, he had asked their mutual friend for details
of Annabelle's personal life. Once he'd been told she had a
crippled fiancé to whom she was devoted, he hadn't ask anything else. Encroaching on another man's territory wasn't
Griffin's style.

"I wasn't aware you knew the lady," Sanders said, his face
expressionless.

"We met briefly several years ago."

"And she made a favorable impression."

Griffin nodded. "What did Annabelle want?"

"She also wants to hire you to investigate a murder case. It seems her cousin was murdered in Memphis last night and—"

"Damn! Annabelle's cousin and Quinn Cortez's lover are one in the same, right?"

Sanders nodded his slick bald head. His keen brown eyes studied Griffin. "What do you intend to do? You'll have to turn one of them down. Mr. Cortez's call did come in first, if that helps you decide what to do."

"It doesn't."

"You have met Ms. Vanderley, so perhaps—"

"Telephone each of them, on my behalf. Naturally, don't mention anything about one of them to the other. And arrange for a suite for me at the Peabody. If we can get the suite set up today, I'll fly to Memphis this evening and meet with Ms. Vanderley and Mr. Cortez tonight. Let's say around eight o'clock."

"You plan to speak with both of them at the same meeting?"

"It'll save time."

"Yes, sir."

When Sanders turned and headed up the stairs, Griffin called to him, "See what kind of background check we can come up with on both of them by tonight."

Sanders didn't reply verbally, but Griffin knew he'd heard him. They had worked side by side for so many years that they were practically psychically linked. When a man saved another man's life, it bonded them in a way nothing else could.

Vanderley Inc. kept an executive apartment in Memphis since a great deal of their business was conducted in this city. Heading up the Vanderley family's numerous philanthropic organizations, Annabelle came to Memphis several

times a year, the last time less than three months ago. At that
time, it had been over a year since she'd seen Lulu and nearly
six months since they'd spoken over the phone. Only at her
insistence had Lulu agreed to meet her for dinner that
evening. As usual, they wound up in an argument. And as
usual, it was about the same things—money, Uncle Louis
and Wythe.

Annabelle snapped open her overnight bag that she had
placed on the suitcase rack at the foot of her bed. She had no
idea how long she'd be in Memphis, how many days or perhaps even weeks it would take the police to find Lulu's killer
and formally charge him with her murder. If she needed
more clothes, she'd send home for them. Or she'd just buy
something off the rack at a department store. Whenever she
stayed in any of the apartments Vanderley Inc. maintained in
various cities, one of the first things she did was unpack and
put everything in its place. Being neat was simply a part of
who she was. She despised clutter.

After taking her toiletries into the bathroom, she arranged
them carefully on the vanity and inadvertently caught a
glimpse of herself in the mirror. She stared at her reflection
for a moment. When they were children, she and Lulu had
been close, despite Lulu being nearly seven years younger.
Family and friends had thought it sweet that Annabelle had
been like a big sister to her young cousin. More than one
person had mentioned how much the girls resembled each
other, both blue-eyed blondes with strong Vanderley features. But that had been before Lulu reached puberty and
blossomed into a model-thin, bosomy, leggy version of her
mother, who'd been Uncle Louis's third wife and twenty-five
years his junior.

Annabelle glanced away from the mirror and returned to
the bedroom. No one would have noticed anything more
than a vague resemblance between the cousins in the past fifteen years. Lulu had been considered the family beauty;
Annabelle had been thought of as the brains. It wasn't that

she envied her cousin—quite the contrary—but there had been times when she'd wondered what it would be like not to feel the heavy weight of family responsibilities she bore on her shoulders. Lulu had been irresponsible and frivolous, but Annabelle knew only too well that her cousin's life had been far from perfect.

Just as she zipped her overnight bag closed, the telephone rang. Rounding the bed, she lifted the receiver from the base on the bedside table. "Hello."

"Ms. Vanderley."

"Yes." She didn't recognize the man's voice.

"This is Sanders, Mr. Powell's assistant. I'm calling on his behalf."

"Yes, Mr. Sanders—"

"Just Sanders, ma'am."

"What's your message from Mr. Powell?"

"He'll be in Memphis tonight and would like to meet with you at the Peabody at eight. Shall I let him know to expect you?"

"Yes, of course. And please, tell Mr. Powell thank you."

"For what, ma'am?"

Slightly flustered by the man's comment, Annabelle said, "Uh . . . hmm . . . well, I assumed that if he's coming to Memphis, he plans to work for me."

"Possibly, but I couldn't say for certain."

"Oh, I see."

"Good day, Ms. Vanderley."

The dial tone droned in her ear. She replaced the receiver. *Odd man,* she thought. Such strange comments. But surely if Griffin Powell was coming to Memphis this evening, he intended to take her case. Why else would he make the trip?

She remembered meeting Mr. Powell several years ago at a charity function in Chattanooga. More than likely anyone who ever met the man, never forgot him. Like Quinn Cortez, Griffin Powell possessed enormous animal magnetism, albeit a more subtle charisma. If she hadn't been engaged and totally devoted to her fiancé when she met Mr. Powell, she might have accepted his overtures, but at that time Chris had still been the center of her universe.

Suddenly, her mind was filled with images of three different men. Chris, her first love, who would always be a part of her. She liked to remember the way they had been before the accident, the two of them young and in love and looking forward to a lifetime together. But more and more lately, thoughts of Chris during the last few years of his life haunted her. Helpless. Melancholy. Begging her to make a new life for herself and yet clinging to her at the same time. And now memories of Chris became overlaid by images of two men she barely knew—men who, each in his own way—had made a strong impression on her. Big, blond Griffin Powell. A reserved, secretive man who reminded her of the old saying about still waters running deep. And then there was Quinn Cortez—dark and dangerous.

Annabelle shivered. Had Quinn Cortez killed Lulu? Had the man who had come to her rescue this morning murdered her cousin last night?

If the police had any proof whatsoever that he had killed Lulu, they would have arrested him. Right? Of course they would have. He'd been Lulu's lover, the person who discovered her body, so naturally he headed their list of possible suspects.

Stop thinking about Quinn Cortez. If he's an innocent man, then he is of no interest to you. Your only concern must be making sure Lulu's murderer is caught and punished.

Uncle Louis was counting on her. He trusted her to do what he was physically and emotionally unable to do. Staying the course until the family could achieve closure on this matter could well be the only thing that would keep her uncle alive. After all, he'd said more than once that Lulu was his only reason for living. Not Wythe. Never Wythe. No father could be proud of a son like Wythe. Spineless, bloodsucking leech. That's what Uncle Louis had once called him.

The telephone rang again. Annabelle sighed. Now who?

Please God, don't let it be a phone call from home about Uncle Louis.

Her hand trembled slightly as she picked up the receiver. "Hello."

"Annabelle, darling girl, it's Aunt Perdita. I just spoke to Hiram and he told me what happened and where I could get in touch with you."

"Oh, Aunt Perdita, I'm sorry I didn't try to contact you, but—"

"No apologies necessary. I understand. What I want to know is if you need me to come to Memphis tonight. If you do, I can skip this damn wedding and try to catch a flight out right away."

"Wedding?"

"Joyce and Whit Morris's daughter, Cynthia. You'd forgotten, hadn't you, dear? No mind. It's a tediously dull affair. But since I was once engaged to Whit's brother, that makes me practically Cynthia's aunt and—"

"No, please, don't miss the wedding."

"I'll be there no later than tomorrow night. I'll book reservations right away for the first flight from Louisville to Memphis, hopefully in the morning."

"There's really no need for you to come. I'm perfectly fine."

"Really, dear? Are you sure?"

Her aunt Perdita knew her better than anyone, perhaps because she had shared confidences with her mother's younger sister, had told her things she'd never told another living soul. Aunt Perdita was the only other person who knew that she'd been unfaithful to Chris, that she'd had two brief affairs during their eight-and-a-half-year engagement.

"I'm numb right now, Aunt Perdita," Annabelle admitted. "I'm just going through the motions. Hopefully, the police will find Lulu's killer very soon and I can return home, at least until the trial starts."

"Do they have any idea who killed her or why?"

"Not really."

"No suspects."

"No." Not unless she counted Quinn Cortez and for some unfathomable reason, Annabelle didn't want to think of him as a suspect.

"If you're sure you're all right—"

"I am."

"Then I'll phone you in the morning. And if you need me, I'll come running. I know how alone you are."

Annabelle said good-bye, then headed for the kitchen, which was kept fully stocked. She hadn't eaten a bite since the cup of coffee and cheese Danish she'd had before leaving home early this morning. As if on cue, her stomach growled when she opened the refrigerator.

She removed an apple and a bottle of Perrier. For dinner tonight, she'd either order in or make reservations at a nearby restaurant for six o'clock. She had an eight o'clock appointment at the Peabody with Griffin Powell and didn't want to be late. She suspected the man appreciated punctuality. Something they had in common.

After settling onto the living room sofa, she turned on the television to the history channel, then opened the bottled water and took a sip.

I know how alone you are. Her aunt's words reverberated in her mind.

As Annabelle munched on the Granny Smith apple, she told herself that Aunt Perdita was wrong. She wasn't alone or lonely. She had servants who lived in at the home she'd inherited from her parents. She had a secretary, a personal assistant and dozens of friends. Her social calendar was full. And if she wanted to date, she could have her pick of eligible men.

Her solitary life was by choice. She enjoyed her freedom. And she wasn't interested in getting married just for the sake of marrying. If she couldn't love someone as much as she'd loved Chris, she had no intention of settling for anything less.

* * *

The moment Kendall Wells entered her house, she smelled the delicious aroma of food. Smiling to herself, she tossed aside her jacket and briefcase, then undid the top two buttons on her silk blouse. Quinn Cortez was in her kitchen. That meant he was cooking. Remembering their brief affair, she sighed when she recalled that not only was the man extremely talented in the bedroom, but he was also a master in the kitchen. If he hadn't decided there was more money in being a lawyer, Quinn could have been a chef.

Kendall paused and sucked in a deep breath as she watched Quinn. Wearing a large white apron—one of hers—around his waist, he stood over the stove, stirring some kind of sauce in an stainless-steel pan with one hand and sipping on a glass of red wine that he held in the other hand. What a man! Exotically alluring with his rich bronze skin, his wavy black hair and eyes so dark and fathomless that looking into them was like being sucked into a sensual black hole. Once a woman dived in, she would be forever lost.

"Welcome home." He offered her one of his cream-your-panties smiles. God, the man was lethal, even in small doses.

Scratch that thought, she told herself. Considering the fact that Quinn was a suspect in a murder case, she didn't want to associate the word lethal with him, not even in her thoughts.

Think about something other than how much you'd like to drag the man off into your bedroom and keep him there all weekend. And for goodness sake, don't even consider the possibility that he might be a murderer. You know Quinn better than that.

Or at least she thought she did.

"Something sure smells good," she said.

"Nothing fancy. I found some things in the freezer and in the pantry. So how does stuffed pork chops, asparagus with hollandaise sauce, twice baked potatoes and a pear salad sound to you?"

"You found the makings for all that in my kitchen?"

He nodded. "Take off your shoes, sit down and let me pour you a glass of wine. You look tired. What's kept you so busy on a Saturday?"

Kendall stepped out of her shoes, then sat on the sofa in the great room and waited for Quinn to bring her the wine before she said anything. "Sit down here with me." She patted the sofa cushions.

With his own wineglass refilled and in hand, he sat beside her. "Your working on a Saturday has something to do with me, doesn't it?"

"I have a bad feeling about this case," she told him. "Sergeant George is an ambitious young man. If he could pin this murder wrap on you, arrest you and the DA could win a conviction, it could make both his career and the DA's. The media would have a field day if one of the most famous criminal lawyers in the country was arrested for Lulu Vanderley's murder."

After taking a couple of sips of wine, Quinn set his glass on a coaster atop the coffee table, then reached over and circled the back of Kendall's neck with his big hand. As he caressed tenderly, she sighed. His touch was like magic—erotic magic.

"If the worst happens and I'm arrested, you'll make a name for yourself by getting me acquitted."

"Do you have that much faith in me?"

He took her glass from her hand and put the crystal flute to her lips. She took a sip, all the while keeping her gaze riveted to his. His black eyes were mesmerizing. God damn it, she thought she was over him, that she'd dealt with any leftover romantic feelings she had for him. Undoubtedly, she'd been wrong. Right this minute, she wanted Quinn as much as ever. Maybe more.

"I have all the faith in the world in you, honey." He set her glass down on a second coaster, alongside his. "Besides, I'm innocent. I did not kill Lulu."

"I believe you," she told him, her heart beating erratically as he inched his fingers up her neck and into her hair. When he cupped the back of her head and pulled her toward him, she gasped, knowing full well that when he kissed her, she'd give in completely.

"Kendall, I don't want you to think I'm trying to take advantage of you . . ." He waited, not kissing her, only staring deeply into her eyes. "I'd be lying if I said I didn't want you, but"—he heaved a deep sigh—"we both know that mixing business with pleasure is a stupid move."

Kendall shoved him away and jumped to her feet. Standing over him, breathless with sexual frustration, she cursed under her breath. "Damn you, Quinn."

"Honey, I'm sorry if—"

"I thought I could handle this—being your lawyer, having you staying here with me. But it appears that I'm not as immune to you as I thought I was. It seems that once Quinn Cortez is in your system, it's not so easy to get rid of him."

Quinn stood, but made no attempt to touch her. "I'm getting a place of my own, just in case I'm stuck in Memphis for more than a few days. The gang's coming in tomorrow. I'll be out of your hair then. Once this thing is over . . ."

He grinned and that killer smile was her undoing. *Killer smile? Lethal? Stop using that type of terminology when you think about Quinn.* What was wrong with her? She'd always known Quinn's sex appeal was lethal, that he possessed a killer smile. Those words had never bothered her before now. But that was before Quinn became a murder suspect. Before the thought had crossed her mind that he might have actually killed Lulu Vanderley.

"Kendall, honey, are you all right?"

"Huh?" Had her doubts translated into a facial expression that concerned him? God, she hoped not.

"I didn't mean to—"

"No!" She shook her head to dislodge such idiotic thoughts. "No, this isn't your fault. I've probably been sending out mixed signals. So let's forget all this nonsense and go back to safe ground. We're friends and nothing more for the duration. We're not saying no to each other, just not now. Not yet."

"Agreed," Quinn said, then nodded toward the kitchen. "Dinner is ready and it would be a shame to let it go to waste. What say we eat, then you can go with me to the Peabody to meet with Griffin Powell. I have an eight o'clock appointment with him tonight."

"Griffin Powell? You're hiring Griffin Powell?"

Quinn headed for the kitchen. "Refill the wineglasses, while I put dinner on the table. Eating in here in the breakfast room is okay with me if it is with you."

"You contacted Griffin Powell and plan to hire him to do what—investigate Lulu Vanderley's murder?" Kendall followed him into the kitchen area.

"I don't intend to take any chances, in case the police don't cover all the bases. We both know that they could concentrate all their efforts on finding evidence against me. I want a private investigator who's on my payroll, somebody who'll be working to find the real killer, to prove me innocent."

"Damn it, Quinn, I'm your lawyer. You shouldn't be doing anything without running it by me first."

"I'm taking you with me to meet with Powell tonight. That's running it by you, isn't it?"

"And if I disagree with you?"

"About Powell?"

"About anything?"

"Honey, you're a very good lawyer. I trust you. But we both know that I'm the best damn criminal lawyer there is. As much as I trust your judgment, I trust my own more."

"Then maybe you'd better defend yourself if you wind up going to trial."

Quinn zeroed in on her, his gaze freezing her to the spot. She held her breath as he came toward her, grasped her by the shoulders and held her tightly in place.

"Don't do this. You're pissed at me because . . . well, because you're all hot and bothered, because you want me, because we want each other, but we agreed jumping into bed together might not be a good idea."

She glared at him.

"I need you, Kendall. Together, we'll make an unbeatable team."

Clenching her teeth, she grunted, admitting to herself that he was right. "Okay, this situation with Lulu's murder could wind up meaning your life is on the line, so I'm not going to argue with you. Besides, I should have known we'd have to play this game by your rules."

He smiled. "It's the only way I play."

Chapter 6

Griffin Powell opened the door to his suite and met Annabelle with a cordial semismile. His lips curved upward ever so slightly, but not enough to be a true smile. He was just as she remembered him from their one and only meeting and she found him just as overpoweringly mesmeric now as then. A large, broad-shouldered man, with platinum-blond hair and a pair of dark blue eyes that seemed blank and lifeless one moment, then pensive and calculating the next.

"Please, come in, Ms. Vanderley."

"Thank you." She walked into the suite as he stepped aside to allow her entrance. When he followed her into the lounge area, she turned and faced him. "I can't thank you enough for agreeing to meet with me. I hope I can persuade you to take this case."

"Won't you have a seat?" He indicated the sofa with a hand gesture. "Would you care for something to drink?"

Annabelle sat on the sofa, folded her hands and placed them in her lap as she slid one ankle demurely behind the other. She had learned at an early age, at her grandmother Austin's knee, the proper way for a young lady to sit. "I wouldn't care for anything to drink, but thank you."

Griffin sat across from her, on the gold brocade wing chair, and dropped his clasped hands between his knees as he leaned forward and looked directly at her.

"I'm very sorry about your cousin. It's tragic when someone dies so young, but even more so when murder is involved."

She offered him a weak, agreeable nod. "Yes, you're right. Lulu would have turned twenty-eight in a couple of months. I'm still finding it difficult to believe that she's really gone. And my uncle Louis—Lulu's father—is taking her death very hard. He's an old man, with numerous health problems. I believe the only thing that will keep him alive now is finding out who killed his daughter."

"And that's where I come in?"

"Yes. I want to hire you to investigate Lulu's murder."

"Isn't that a job for the Memphis police department?"

"Yes. Certainly. But I don't want any stone unturned, no avenue not taken. The police don't have any real suspects and it's been nearly twenty-four hours. Don't they say that the first twenty-four hours is crucial to solving a crime?"

"Do they?" Griffin cocked an inquisitive eyebrow.

Not quite sure how to interpret his comment, she chose to ignore it. "I can't imagine why anyone would want to harm Lulu. She didn't have a mean bone in her body. Everyone who knew her liked her on some level. She had an electric type of personality and—"

"Did you like her?"

"I beg you pardon?"

"Did you like your cousin Lulu?"

Annabelle caught herself before she automatically said yes and gave her reply some thought. "I loved Lulu because we were cousins and very close when we were young. And I did like her, at least part of the time. She could be selfish and irresponsible and I certainly didn't approve of the kind of life she lived. Does that answer your question?"

He nodded. "You're aware that the media seems to be

putting out their own scenarios concerning Lulu's death," Griffin said. "Their favorite appears to be that it's possible her latest lover killed her. How do you feel about that?"

"I've been ignoring the media as much as possible, but I'm well aware that not only is that scenario a favorite with the press, but also with the police."

"You know the identity of your cousin's latest lover, the man who discovered her body, don't you?"

"Yes . . . I . . . uh . . . I met Mr. Cortez this morning, at the police station."

"Did you? So what do you think? Could he have killed your cousin?"

Annabelle didn't know how to answer these unexpected questions. How could she tell Griffin Powell that she did not want to believe Quinn Cortez was capable of murder because he had struck a personal chord deep inside her, that her reaction to Lulu's lover had been that of a woman relating to a highly desirable man? The very thought of her response to Mr. Cortez's protective gestures made her feel cheap and sleazy. It was so out of character for her.

"I don't know Mr. Cortez well enough to have an opinion," she said.

"Hmm . . ."

"If you agree to take this case, naturally I'll want you to investigate Mr. Cortez, even though I'm certain the police will put him under a microscope."

"Yes, I'm sure they will, since he was her lover and he discovered the body. They will want to rule out any possibility that he killed her before they look further and that's the reason he has—" A repetitive knock on the door interrupted Griffin midsentence. "If you'll excuse me." He stood and walked to the door.

Annabelle turned halfway around and focused her gaze on Griffin as he opened the door. Her heart caught in her throat when she instantly recognized the couple who entered the suite. Kendall Wells, followed by Quinn Cortez.

What are they doing here?

"Please, come inside and meet my other guest," Griffin said.

Kendall Wells stopped instantly the moment she saw Annabelle. Quinn Cortez paused, did a double-take, then glared at Griffin.

"I see you already have a guest," Quinn said. "Did I get the time wrong? Was our appointment for later?"

"No, you're here right on time," Griffin replied. "Ms. Vanderley was a few minutes early."

"What's she doing here?" Kendall asked.

Annabelle's gaze connected with Quinn's. An odd sensation hit her in the pit of her stomach. His gaze was not friendly; it even bordered on hostile, but she couldn't look away.

"It seems that Ms. Vanderley is in need of a private investigator, just as Mr. Cortez is," Griffin explained. "Imagine my surprise when I realized that both of my prospective clients want the same murder investigated."

"I see," Kendall said. "So you decided to meet with both Ms. Vanderley and Mr. Cortez and see who's willing to bid the highest for your services."

"Humph." The sound that came from Griffin was a combination of amused chuckle and disgusted irritation.

"I think you insulted Mr. Griffin," Quinn told Kendall. "Perhaps you should apologize."

"If I'm wrong, I'll say I'm sorry." Kendall shot Quinn a withering glare, then focused on Griffin with glowering intensity. "Am I wrong?"

"You're wrong," Griffin told her, a cold, indifferent expression on his face. "I set up this meeting to see if Ms. Vanderley and Mr. Cortez would be willing to work together to find Lulu Vanderley's murderer."

"You what?" Kendall glanced back and forth from Quinn to Annabelle, then said to Griffin, "You're suggesting that they both hire you and the two of them join forces to track down Lulu's murderer. Is that correct?"

"No, I—I don't think that would work," Annabelle said. The last thing she wanted was to spend anymore time with Quinn Cortez than she already had.

"Why wouldn't it work?" Kendall asked. "I think it's a brilliant idea."

"But only if Ms. Vanderley believes I'm innocent," Quinn said as he walked toward the sofa. Stopping when he was less than two feet away from Annabelle, he looked right at her. "And you're not sure, are you? You believe there's a possibility that I killed your cousin."

Aaron shoved the naked girl over and positioned her so that she had to catch herself from falling by bracing her open palms flat against the bed. While she gasped and shivered, he ran his hand over her sleek butt, then lifted his penis and rammed it into her. Damn, what a feeling. Grasping her hips, he maneuvered her back and forth, quickly increasing the speed and the pressure. Their naked flesh slapped together and that friction combined with her feminine moisture created a smacking sound. Despite the fact that this was their third time tonight, he was on the verge of coming. But hell, he was twenty-six and hadn't been with a woman in weeks. He'd built up a lot of steam and it was going to take awhile to blow it off.

The louder her grunts and groans, the more excited he became, the closer to losing it. He slid his arm around her, eased his hand between her legs and fingered her clitoris. Within a couple of minutes, she keened deep in her throat, then cried out when her climax hit. That was all it took to send him over the edge.

In the aftermath, sweaty and panting, they fell across the bed. As he lay there looking up at the dark ceiling, he sighed. He'd met Gala in a downtown bar this evening and they'd hit it off from the first hello. It had taken him all of thirty minutes to talk her into coming back to his apartment with him. They'd practically ripped off each other's clothes the minute they got here and he'd humped her on the sofa the first time. The second time had been an hour later and he'd taken the missionary position, with her lying under him in bed.

"I'm hungry," she said.

"I don't think I have anything," he told her as he worked the condom off his deflated penis and dropped it on a magazine lying on the floor beside the bed. "I've been out of town and haven't had a chance to restock."

Gala cuddled up against him. "Do you really work for Quinn Cortez?"

"Yeah, I really do." He reached down and pulled the sheet and blanket up and over them, covering him to just above his waist and her to the top of her tits.

"And you were with him in Nashville during the Terry McBryar case?"

"Every day he was there, I was there. I told you, I'm part of his personal staff."

"What's it like being that close to a man like Quinn Cortez?" She curled several strands of his chest hair around her index finger. "I mean the guy's like famous and all."

Gala wasn't the first woman he'd impressed by telling her that he worked for Quinn and she sure wouldn't be the last. He'd told Quinn about using his name to get chicks and his boss had just laughed and said, "If it gets you laid, go for it." Quinn was that kind of guy. When it came to scoring with a woman, nothing was off-limits. All was fair in love and war. And Quinn always won at both. Aaron figured there wasn't a woman alive Quinn couldn't conquer. And the man never lost when it came to courtroom warfare.

Gala propped herself up with her elbow and gazed down at Aaron. "You know, you look like him a little. Same black hair and brown eyes. You're Hispanic, too, aren't you?"

"You guessed it, sweetie. Me and Quinn are like two peas in a pod."

He wasn't Hispanic—not even half—and any resemblance to Quinn was purely superficial. They were about the same height at six one and they had similar coloring, although without a tan, Aaron was several shades lighter than Quinn. He owed his ethnic heritage to his maternal grandmother, a Navajo who still lived on the reservation. But since he'd probably never see Gala again, why spoil the image of him she had in her mind?

A loud, aggressive pounding at the door brought Aaron up out of bed and sent Gala scooting toward the bathroom, picking up some of their discarded clothing as she went.

"You expecting somebody?" she called to him from the bathroom.

"Nope." He'd deliberately unplugged his phone after they'd done it the first time and turned off his cell, too. He didn't want anything interrupting what he'd hoped would be an all-night love-a-thon.

"Whoever it is, get rid of them." She winked at him before she shut the door.

Aaron grabbed his jeans off the floor, shimmied hurriedly into them and headed out of the bedroom. The knocking grew more intense.

"Hey, man, if you're in there, open the damn door," Jace Morgan shouted.

What the hell was Jace doing here? After returning to Houston, Jace, Marcy and he had gone their separate ways, as they always did after the end of a business trip. Quinn's personal staff worked like a well-oiled machine when together, despite the difference in their personalities; but the minute a case ended, they didn't make contact again until Quinn called them together. He usually gave them at least a week's downtime after a big case. And the Terry McBryar case had been one of the biggest. He expected to get a really nice bonus, something else Quinn did after winning a case. He was the kind of guy who took care of his people.

"Hold your horses," Aaron said as he raced through the living room. When he opened the door, he was surprised to see Marcy Sims with Jace. He knew instantly that something was up. "What's wrong?"

Not waiting for an invitation, Marcy swept past him and into his apartment. "Quinn's in trouble. He wants us in Nashville by tomorrow."

"What kind of trouble?" Aaron asked.

"That Lulu Vanderley he was going to Nashville to see got herself murdered last night." Jace closed the door and came inside behind Marcy.

"You're shitting me?"

"Quinn found her body," Marcy said. "So you know what that means."

"He's a suspect," Aaron replied.

"He didn't do it. He didn't kill her," Jace said emphatically. "The boss would never murder anybody."

"Yeah, you're right, he wouldn't," Aaron agreed. "But I'll bet there are a lot of people who're getting a big laugh out of this. The most famous criminal lawyer in the country, who's gotten dozens of accused murderers acquitted, might get charged with murder himself."

"They can't arrest Quinn for murder." Jace's cheeks flushed with emotion. "We gotta do whatever we can to help him."

Sometimes Aaron found it amusing the way Jace hero-worshiped Quinn. But then the kid owed Quinn a lot, didn't he, even more than he and Marcy did? They were all three misfits, kids who'd been in trouble, heading for a life of crime. Marcy had been abused by her father and wound up on the streets, ready to turn tricks at sixteen. A cheerleader-type blonde with big brown eyes, she could have made a fortune as a prostitute. Her salvation had been that the first guy she'd approached on her first night on the job turned out to be Quinn Cortez, a real crusader for kids in trouble. He'd gotten her placed in a good foster home, helped her attend junior college and then hired her as his personal assistant.

Aaron's story wasn't much different, except he'd wound

up at the Judge Harwood Brown Boys' Ranch, a place built and run by Quinn and several other guys who'd been boys in trouble themselves way back when and had been saved by old Judge Brown. When Aaron turned eighteen, Quinn had encouraged him to go to college, but he'd known college wasn't for him. He wasn't stupid, but he was no Einstein either. He made Quinn understand that he didn't have the smarts for college. He'd been working for Quinn as his chauffeur and all-around gofer ever since. The pay was good, the benefits great.

Jace, another Judge Harwood Brown Boys' Ranch alumnus, had been working for Quinn for the past year. He was a pretty kid, with hazel eyes and curly sandy brown hair that he kept short to control the curls, but Jace's story wasn't a pretty one. He'd admitted that he had been molested by a priest when he was twelve, which had screwed him up pretty bad. And it didn't help that he'd grown up without a dad and had lost his mother, too, only a couple of years ago.

"I've booked us flights for tomorrow morning," Marcy said. "And I've lined up a four-bedroom house and a rental car. I'm hoping the police will clear this up pretty quickly and we can all head home in a few days, but—"

"Aaron, who was at the door?" Wearing only his rumpled shirt, Gala stopped dead still in the doorway between the bedroom and living room. "Oops. Sorry."

"We . . . er . . . we were just leaving." Marcy started backing toward the door.

"Don't leave on my account," Gala said. "Stick around. I was just going to order pizza."

Marcy looked directly at Aaron. "Jace will pick you up at eight-thirty in the morning. Be ready."

"No problem," Aaron told her.

"Quinn's counting on us, man," Jace said, eyeing Gala disapprovingly. "We can't let him down."

"I get it, okay," Aaron said. "I'll be ready to go at eight-thirty in the morning."

As much as Aaron admired and respected Quinn, he wasn't in love with the guy like Marcy was nor did he worship the man the way Jace did. But he'd cut off his right arm before he'd let Quinn down.

"Let's look at this rationally," Griffin Powell said. "I can't take on each of you individually as clients for obvious reasons, even if I assigned one of my employees to handle the case for one of you. However, if you two could work together, you could hire me jointly. After all, I assume you both want the same thing—to discover the identity of Lulu Vanderley's murderer and see him brought to justice."

Annabelle nodded.

"Yes, that's what I want." Quinn thought Powell had brass balls for even recommending such an odd proposition. Selling Annabelle on this unholy alliance wouldn't be easy.

"I believe one of us should simply hire another agency," Annabelle said.

"Griffin Powell is the best." Quinn looked her square in the eyes. "I hire only the best."

"Are you suggesting that I look elsewhere?"

"Yes, I am. Unless you're willing to work with me."

She stared at him quizzically and he caught a glint of something peculiar in those cool blue eyes. Did the lady want to be persuaded? Was that it? Did the thought of their working together intrigue her as much as it did him?

You're a fool, Cortez. The very last thing you need in your life right now is a personal relationship with Lulu's cousin, a woman who thinks it's possible you might have killed Lulu.

"I believe we have a stalemate," Kendall said. "Apparently neither Quinn nor Ms. Vanderley is willing to accept second best."

"I'm flattered," Griffin said. "But I think you should know that unless I can take you both on as clients who have consented to work together, I won't take this case."

"What!" Annabelle whipped around and glared at Griffin. "You can't mean that."

"If you knew me better, you'd know that I always mean what I say."

"And say what you mean." Quinn made an instant decision, one that surprised him as much as it did everyone else in the room. He motioned to Kendall. "Let's go. I withdraw my bid to hire you, Mr. Powell. Feel free to take on Ms. Vanderley as your client."

"What the hell—" Kendall gasped when Quinn grabbed her arm and led her toward the door.

"Wait!" Annabelle rose from the sofa. "Please, Mr. Cortez, don't go."

Quinn stopped, but kept his back to Annabelle and Griffin.

"What are you pulling?" Kendall spoke to Quinn so softly that only he could hear her.

"Why should I stay?" Quinn asked Annabelle.

"Mr. Powell is right—we do want the same thing. If you can accept the fact that I don't trust you completely, then I believe we might be able to work together."

"Hmm . . ." Kendall grinned at Quinn before he turned around to face Annabelle.

"You don't know me well enough to trust me. Not yet," Quinn said. "I'm willing to wait and earn your trust. I didn't kill Lulu and I want to find her murderer as much as you do."

Annabelle looked at Griffin. "Let's set up some ground rules."

"All right," Griffin said, then glanced at Quinn. He nodded.

"First and foremost, Mr. Cortez and I share all the information," Annabelle said. "You will be working for both of us, so what you tell one of us, you tell both of us. No secrets. No hidden agenda." She glanced at Quinn. "And we share all the expenses, fifty-fifty. Are you in agreement, Mr. Cortez?"

"Yes, I'm in agreement. And since we'll be working closely together, don't you think you should call me Quinn?"

"If that's what you want."

"It's what I want."

"Fine. And you may call me Ms. Vanderley . . . because that's what I want."

Chapter 7

Jim had taken Sunday off, despite his boss's recommendation that he not take any downtime right in the middle of a high profile case.

"Look, Ted, I've made plans with my son that are important to both of us. It's not as if I get a chance to be with Kevin very often. Besides, Chad's on top of everything. If he's going to get all the glory for breaking this case wide open, then let him do the work."

Inspector Ted Purser, who was the head of homicide, had grumbled a little, but in the end he'd allowed Jim to take the day off. Ted knew as well as Jim did—as well as everyone in the department—that Chad George was on his way up. By hook or crook. And it was also a well-known fact that Jimmy Norton was on a one-way street to nowhere. He'd be lucky if he could hang on to his job long enough to draw his pension.

On his own, Chad was bound to screw up. Not because he was stupid. Quite the contrary. The guy was highly intelligent. Nah, he'd screw up because he was an inexperienced homicide detective who was too damn cocky to realize he had a lot to learn. It was Jim's opinion that Chad was a know-it-all who needed taking down a peg or two. Not that he'd intentionally do anything to bring that about himself. Nah, he figured all he had to do was wait around and sooner or later Chad would shoot himself in the foot. Figuratively, of course.

Jim chuckled softly.

"What's so funny, Dad?" Kevin asked.

Jim glanced over at his eleven-year-old son sitting in the passenger seat of his battered, old truck and grinned. Kevin was the one good thing that had come out of his marriage to Mary Lee. He might regret all the wasted years he'd spent hung up on a woman who hadn't loved him enough to stick with him through the bad times and had repeatedly betrayed their marriage vows, but he'd never regret fathering Kevin. On the really rough days, when nothing in his world seemed right, all Jim had to do was think of Kevin and he remembered he had a very good reason for living.

"Just thinking about my partner," Jim told his son.

"Chad George?"

"Yeah, you've met Chad. I introduced you to him a couple of months ago."

"I know Sergeant George."

Jim picked up on something in his son's voice before he glanced at him and noticed Kevin had his head hung low and was staring at the floorboard.

"What's the matter?"

"Nothing."

"Is it something about Chad? Did he say or do anything that—"

"I'm not supposed to tell you."

"Who told you not to tell me?"

"Mom did."

Don't lose your cool. The last thing Kevin needs is to feel he's caught between you and Mary Lee, even if he is. Whatever she told him not to tell you, don't press him about it.

Jim kept the truck on Highway 78, heading straight toward Holly Springs where his sister and her family lived. He'd planned this trip so they would arrive at Susan's just about the time church let out and right before Sunday dinner.

He needed to concentrate on the positive—on sharing a family day with his son. Grilling Kevin about Mary Lee's secrets would ruin not only their day together, but also injure their already fragile relationship. Even though he couldn't prove it, he knew his ex-wife worked at undermining his relationship with Kevin. And she did it just because she could, wanting to hurt Jim and not caring that their son was the one who'd be harmed the most.

"Dad?"

"Huh?"

"You don't care who Mom dates, do you?"

"No, I don't care," Jim said. And he didn't. Not now, although for years after their divorce he'd been jealous of every man she'd dated. But that was when he'd still been in love with her.

"Then I don't understand why Mom doesn't want you to know that she's dating Sergeant George."

Jim grasped the steering wheel with white-knuckled tension. Mary Lee and Chad? Goddamn son of a bitch. He couldn't help wondering which one of them had instigated their affair. Six of one and half dozen of the other. Them's the odds. Mary Lee would love for him to find out she'd been screwing his young partner. She actually thought he still cared. And Chad—God how he must love fucking Jim's ex-wife. At least four other officers had told Jim to watch his back where Chad was concerned.

"Your mom's dating Chad, huh?"

"Yeah, for about a couple of weeks now. But it's no big deal, right? I mean, you don't care, do you?"

"Your mother and I are divorced," Jim said. "We both have the right to date anybody we want to. It's fine with me if Mary Lee is dating Chad."

Dating? Maybe they were dating—dinner, movies, dancing, that sort of thing. But Jim figured their dates were spent in bed, doing the horizontal. That was the only kind of relationship Mary Lee was any good at. And he hated like hell that he could remember so vividly just how good she'd been.

* * *

Annabelle had expected to spend a quiet day at the apartment, catching up on work-related e-mails and making plans for Lulu's funeral. Although the plans couldn't proceed until the autopsy had been completed and Lulu's body released, Annabelle didn't want to leave things until the last minute. The family expected her to handle all the details and see to it that Louisa Margaret Vanderley's funeral would impress everyone in attendance. The Vanderleys always arrived and departed this life in grand style. It was a family tradition.

Annabelle had slept later this morning than she intended. She was, by nature, a creature of habit and hated to alter her sleep schedule. But she'd tossed and turned half the night, not able to rest until sometime after four. If only she could have turned off her thoughts and disconnected her mind. Thoughts of Lulu tormented her. She wondered if she had tried harder to maintain a close relationship with Lulu, would her cousin still be alive? If she had looked after Lulu a little more closely, would it have made any difference? *Don't be silly. You couldn't have done anything to prevent what happened.*

For most of her life, Annabelle had been a caretaker. Perhaps she'd been born an old soul with the need to nurture everyone around her. She'd always had a deep-rooted need to please others, to keep everyone happy. Being a spoiled only child could have turned her into a self-centered, demanding bitch, but instead being the center of her parents' universe had placed a heavy burden on her young shoulders. She'd actually believed that it was her duty to make her parents happy, and by the time she reached adulthood that feeling had transmitted itself to everyone around her.

"You care so deeply about everyone and everything," Aunt Perdita had once told her. "Your devotion to Christopher is quite admirable, my dear child, but you must occasionally think of yourself. You're a healthy young woman, with a woman's needs. And what you need is a man."

Her aunt had been half right about her needing a man. She had needed the man she loved to be whole again, for Chris to be as he'd once been—her friend and lover. But that had been an impossible dream. Her darling Chris had been a paraplegic for nine years before his death, completely paralyzed from the waist down and unable to function sexually. And two very brief and completely secret affairs had shown her that sex for the sake of sex was not what she wanted or needed.

There had been times when she'd wished she could be more like Lulu, who could so easily go from man to man with no regrets. She doubted that Lulu's conscience had ever bothered her. *What must that be like?* Annabelle wondered.

After setting her cup of chocolate caramel coffee beside her laptop on the desk, Annabelle pulled out the chair. When the telephone rang, she jumped. Her nerves were shot. Not only had memories of Lulu as well as concerns about her cousin's death and all that entailed kept her awake, but so had thoughts about Quinn Cortez. Ever since agreeing to become partners with the man in hiring Griffin Powell, she'd had a million and one second thoughts.

On the third ring, Annabelle lifted the receiver from the base on the desk. "Hello."

"Ms. Vanderley?" a man's voice asked.

"Yes, this is she."

"This is Sergeant George, ma'am. I was wondering if I could come by and talk to you?"

"I—er—when?"

"Right now, if that's convenient. I can be there in no time."

"Do you have information about—"

"No, not really. Sorry. There's nothing new," he said. "But if you could spare the time, I'd like to go over a few things with you."

"Yes, of course. I take it that you're nearby."

"Yes, ma'am."

"Then come right over. I want to do whatever I can to help the police."

"Thank you."

The minute she hung up the receiver, Annabelle dashed into the bedroom and stripped out of her comfy fleece sweat-shirt and pants. Her wardrobe was limited since she'd brought only a couple changes of clothes, but thank goodness she'd brought along a pair of jeans. After dressing hurriedly in jeans, white shirt and slip-on loafers, she had just applied pink blush and lipstick when her guest arrived. Taking a deep breath, she rushed through the apartment.

Flinging open the door, she gasped when she saw the man standing there. Not Sergeant George. Definitely not the handsome young police officer.

"Mr. Cortez, what are you doing here?"

Wearing faded blue jeans, a beige turtleneck sweater and a brown leather jacket, he didn't look like a wealthy lawyer. But even in casual attire, he possessed an aura of power and strength. And danger.

"I thought we needed to talk," he said. "After we settled things with Griffin Powell last night, you rushed off in quite a hurry before we had a chance to discuss the situation."

Go away. Leave me alone. I don't want to see you or talk to you or think about you.

"There isn't anything to discuss," she said. "Not until Mr. Powell has some information for us."

"May I come in?" he asked.

"I don't see the need. Besides, I'm expecting company any minute now."

"This shouldn't take long. What if I come in and stay until your company shows up? Then I'll leave."

He wasn't going to take no for an answer. It was that plain and simple. Short of slamming the door in his face—which is probably what she should do—her only alternative was to give him what he wanted.

"Very well, Mr. Cortez, you may come in for a few min-utes."

As he entered the apartment, he paused and their gazes locked. "I thought we agreed last night that you'd call me Quinn."

Heat suffused her, warming her from head to toe. "Please, come in, Quinn."

"Thank you, Ms. Vanderley."

When he smiled at her, the bottom dropped out of her stomach. Dear God, had she gone so long without a man that she had become little more than a bitch in heat? What was wrong with her? She never—not ever!—reacted this way to a man.

Annabelle cleared her throat. "Would you care for something to drink? I just made a fresh pot of chocolate caramel coffee."

"Yes, thanks. That sounds good."

"Please, have a seat." Annabelle all but ran from the room, glad for any excuse to get away from Quinn.

While safe in the kitchen, she grasped the edge of the tile countertop and closed her eyes. *Get control of yourself. And do it now.*

She took her time preparing his coffee, calling out once to inquire about sugar and cream. He took his coffee black.

When she reentered the living room, she found him sitting on the sofa, looking like he belonged there. He exuded an air of confidence as if he controlled the world and everyone in it.

Instead of handing him the cup of coffee, she placed it on a coaster atop the cocktail table. No need to risk their hands accidentally touching. She sat across from him in one of two straight back wooden chairs that doubled as dining chairs and matched the small dining table in front of the windows.

"I don't bite," he told her, glancing pointedly at the sofa cushions where he had apparently thought she would sit. "At least not without an invitation."

"Do you find that comment amusing?"

"You really are uptight, aren't you, honey?"

"I am not your honey."

"Do you dislike me because you think I killed Lulu? Or do you object to the fact she and I were lovers? Or is there another reason . . . a more personal reason?"

Annabelle jumped up, balled her hands into tight fists and kept her arms straight down on either side of her body. "Why are you really here, Mr. Cortez? You know as well as I do that we have nothing to say to each other. I agreed to become partners with you in hiring Mr. Powell because I believed doing so would be the lesser of two evils. But let's get something straight—I do not want to become better acquainted with you. I do not want to be your friend or your lover."

He rose from the sofa in one quick, fluid move. Annabelle gasped when he rounded the coffee table and came over to her before she realized his intent. Nervous and taken by surprise, she tried to retreat, only to encounter the chair behind her. The backs of her thighs hit the wooden edge.

She shook her head and held up a restraining hand. He was close. Too close. She couldn't breathe.

"What makes you think I want to be your friend . . . or your lover?" His black eyes bored into her. "My God, you're afraid of me, aren't you?"

Annabelle's pulse pounded. "Why shouldn't I be afraid? After all, you might have killed Lulu."

A mocking smile played at the corners of Quinn's mouth. "No, that's not it. You're not afraid of me because you think I might be a murderer. You're afraid of something else."

"Don't be absurd."

He reached out toward her. Shivering, she stood her ground, despite wishing she could bolt and run. When his fingertips touched her cheek, she gasped.

"You shouldn't believe everything you hear about me." He caressed her cheek. "I know I have a reputation where the ladies are concerned, but I can assure you that I've never forced myself on an unwilling woman."

"I—I haven't heard anything about you. I don't know your reputation."

"Believe me, Ms. Vanderley, I don't want anything from

you except your cooperation. And maybe your trust." He eased his hand down her throat, allowing his thumb to skim her bottom lip before resting on her chin. "Work with me to find Lulu's killer. I need for you to believe I'm innocent."

She felt as if she were suffocating. "We are working together. We hired Mr. Powell jointly."

When Quinn removed his hand and stepped backward, Annabelle drew in a deep, cleansing breath, then let it out on a long, rushed sigh.

"I think we can help Powell and the police if we put our heads together and try to figure out who might have had a motive for wanting Lulu dead. You're a member of her family and I'm a member of her social set. The two of us probably know most of the people in Lulu's life."

"What you say makes sense," she told him. "But I have no reason to trust you. You could be using me, knowing that as the Vanderley family representative if I believe you didn't kill Lulu, then the media and even the police might—"

"Tell the damn police that you think I might be guilty. Call a press conference and tell the media you think I killed Lulu." He grabbed her by the shoulders and shook her. None too gently. Fear raced through her at breakneck speed. "If that's what you want to do, then do it."

He released her so quickly she almost lost her balance and just barely managed to keep herself from falling backward onto the chair.

"I came here hoping—hell, I don't know what I was hoping. I must have been out of my mind to think you'd give me a chance." Quinn strode toward the door.

Annabelle cried out his name silently, inside her mind. *Quinn, don't go. Stay. I want to believe you didn't kill Lulu. I want to trust you.*

After opening the door, he paused and glanced over his shoulder. "You said you didn't want to be my friend or my lover. That's your loss, honey. I make a good friend. Ask any of my friends and they'll tell you that I'm loyal to a fault. I stand by my friends and would do anything for them." He narrowed his gaze, raking her with a contemptuous glance. "And if I ever became your lover, I'd satisfy you the way no man ever has."

Annabelle stood there, her eyes wide and her mouth agape as Quinn walked out of her apartment and disappeared down the hall.

Chapter 8

Quinn zipped his Porsche along the street, forcing himself to go no more than five miles over the speed limit. The last thing he needed was to be stopped by the police. He'd had his fill of the Memphis PD, especially Sergeant George. As he'd exited Annabelle's apartment building, he caught a glimpse of the pretty boy cop heading for the elevator. They'd barely missed running into each other.

So that was the company she'd been expecting. Even if Annabelle thought the sergeant's visit pertained to nothing more than official police business, Quinn knew better. Nobody with eyes in his head could have missed the way Sergeant George had looked at Annabelle yesterday. As if she were a Christmas present he couldn't wait to unwrap. But who could blame him? The lady projected a hands-off attitude that a man couldn't help but take as a challenge.

Was that why he'd gone to see her today? Maybe. Probably. What's that old saying about a leopard not changing his spots? He'd been a ladies' man since reaching puberty. Was it his fault that the opposite sex found him irresistible? It was that combination of Mexican and Irish genes that gave him his rugged good looks, just about the only good thing he'd inherited from his parents. Having been jerked up by the hair of his head instead of being raised properly had made him a bad boy. And women loved bad boys. Every damn one of them thought they'd be the woman to tame him.

Quinn had some regrets, things he'd done that he wished he hadn't. And a few things he hadn't done that he wished he had. But for the most part, he didn't look back. For years he'd looked to the future as he scratched and clawed his way out of the gutter. Money and power were his gods. Romancing the ladies was his hobby.

If he was arrested for Lulu's murder, everything he'd spent a lifetime building would be destroyed. He couldn't let that happen. He'd do whatever it took to save himself. Hell, he was a survivor, wasn't he? If he hadn't been, he'd have never made it through childhood. Not with Sheila Quinn Cortez as his mother.

Forget about trying to convince Annabelle Vanderley of your innocence. You don't need her. Let her doubt you. Let her suspect you. As long as she doesn't work against you, you can get out of this mess without her help.

But not without Griffin Powell.

No, not without the investigator coming up with at least one other viable suspect. Considering how many men Lulu had known—in the biblical sense—there had to be at least one angry, jealous ex-lover. It was just a matter of finding him.

Quinn whipped his Porsche off the street and into Kendall's driveway. At least here he was assured of a warm welcome. He'd be heading across town later this afternoon to the house Marcy had leased for their indefinite stay in Memphis. She and the guys had flown in earlier today and would have everything set up by tonight. But in the meantime, he was in need of a little ego soothing. Who better than Kendall? She was a willing woman, wasn't she?

She's your lawyer. You're a fool if you mix business with pleasure. It's one of your cardinal rules. If you break it, you'll regret it. Besides, they had come to an agreement, of sorts, this morning, hadn't they?

Kendall met him at the door. Smiling. And looking damn

good, even if she wasn't the blue-eyed blonde who'd given him a hard-on.

"How did it go?" she asked.

"Let's just say I didn't earn any brownie points with Ms. Vanderley."

Kendall looked into his eyes and he realized she knew what was going on with him. He reached for her then, right there in the open doorway. She didn't hesitate. Not for a second. When he grasped the back of her neck and drew her to him, she threw her arms around him and pressed herself intimately against his erection.

Kendall's mouth was warm and wet and sweet. Her tongue darted out and into his mouth. He groaned deep in his throat. Images of another woman flashed through his mind. Her mouth would be sweeter, hungrier.

Quinn shoved Kendall backward, into the foyer, then reached behind him and closed the door. While they kissed, he ran his hands inside her spandex slacks and panties, cupping her buttocks. Inserting her hands between their bodies, she worked his belt loose and unzipped his jeans.

Lifting his head, he paused long enough to ask, "Are you sure about this?"

She answered him by removing a condom from her pants pocket and handing it to him. Then she yanked off her slacks and panties.

Quinn freed his sex, sheathed himself and lifted Kendall so that she straddled him. He braced her back against the foyer wall and rammed into her. With his eyes shut, he pretended he was fucking Annabelle Vanderley, taking her with brutal force and giving her what she so desperately needed. Kendall came first, crying out and raking her fingernails deep into the material of his brown leather jacket. His climax hit him hard, releasing the pent-up anger and sexual hunger his encounter with Annabelle had created.

As he eased Kendall down and onto her feet, he opened his eyes and found her staring at him. "Thanks, honey. I needed that." Realizing how impersonal his comment had sounded, he added, "I needed you."

Smiling sadly, she shook her head. "Don't you think I know what that was all about? I knew you'd come back here frustrated. Why do you think I had a condom in my pocket?"

"What are you—?"

She placed her index finger over his lips. "Hush. Don't lie to me."

"Kendall, I . . ."

"You weren't fucking me. You were fucking Annabelle Vanderley. I had a pretty good idea when you left here that you'd come back to me with your tail tucked between your legs." Laughing, she shrugged. "That's how much I wanted you—enough to let you use me."

"Honey, I'm sorry. I never meant to—"

"I know. And I'm okay. Really. It's not your fault that we women are such fools when it comes to you. You don't make any promises. You're honest up front. And yet we still give you whatever you want, knowing you'll break our hearts."

"Kendall?"

"This was a one-time-only thing." Her gaze didn't quite connect with his; it settled somewhere in the middle of his chest. "From here on out, I'm just your lawyer. It's better for both of us that way. So, the next time you need a warm body—and you will—find somebody else." She bent over and picked up her discarded clothing.

When she walked away from him, he wanted to say something to soothe her hurt feelings, but what could he tell her that wouldn't be a lie? Damn, he felt like the biggest heel of all time. What was it about him that made him hurt people? He never meant to hurt anybody, least of all a great gal like Kendall.

Not for the first time, he thought there must be some horrible defect in him because not once in his life had he ever truly loved a woman.

* * *

Quinn's in there right now screwing his lawyer. She's as big a fool as all the others. How many have there been? Hundreds? Why were they all such stupid cunts? He doesn't love her anymore than he loved any of the others. They mean nothing to him; they're just willing sex partners.

I can't blame him, can I? What man wouldn't take what was so freely offered? But how many lives has he destroyed? How many women have gone mad after they lost him? And who should know better than I do what it's like for those poor foolish women? How they suffer. How they make others suffer.

I can't believe that he's finally been caught in a trap of his own making. But it was inevitable. And with the police investigating Quinn and that private detective searching for another suspect, it's only a matter of time before the truth comes out about those other women.

I shouldn't stay here any longer. Someone might see me, might remember this car. No one must ever suspect that I keep close tabs on Quinn, that I know every move he makes.

Chad George patted his chest, directly over the inside pocket of his sports coat. Finding Lulu Vanderley's date book might turn out to be of no help to the investigation at all. On the other hand, if they could rule out the other men in Lulu's life as suspects, then they could concentrate only on Quinn Cortez.

His gut instincts told him Cortez was as guilty as sin.

But they had one major problem—they had no real evidence against the guy. Not yet.

Chad had made copies of the twenty pages in the date book and brought them with him to show Lulu's cousin. He and Jim had read over the entries a couple of times yesterday and found little of interest. Except one guy's name kept popping up. And it wasn't Quinn Cortez. Randy. Randy who?

Lulu had seen this Randy guy half a dozen times in the past couple of weeks or at least she'd written times and places in her date book that implied they had made plans. The people they'd questioned—friends, acquaintances and neighbors— had no idea who he was or if they did, weren't telling. Other than Quinn's name and Randy's name, there were a few odd entries about somebody Lulu referred to only by a nickname— Broo. "Broo called and we talked for an hour," had been written in the margins of the date book. "Called Broo and told him the big news," was written down on the date for three days ago.

Who was Randy? Who was Broo? Could either of them have killed Lulu and if so, why? He sure as hell didn't want either of these people to be the person who'd killed Lulu. He wanted it to be Quinn Cortez. Yeah, he'd admit the truth to himself. Nailing a guy with Quinn Cortez's prestigious reputation could make his career.

Besides, he didn't like Cortez.

The elevator stopped on the fourth floor. Chad stepped out and headed down the corridor. As he passed a large decorative mirror, he paused to check his appearance. He knew he was handsome and women usually responded to his good looks by fawning over him. He'd never had a problem dating. He'd kept a steady girlfriend through high school and college, although not the same girl. He'd changed every six months or so, usually when his latest girlfriend found out he'd been cheating on her. He'd broken up with his most recent girlfriend about a month ago, after she'd stopped by his place unexpectedly and found him bonking Mary Lee Norton.

Chad knew he'd have to get married in the next year or so. A man with his aspirations needed the right kind of woman at his side, a lady who would impress people. There were a couple of suitable candidates right here in Memphis, but he'd been biding his time before deciding which one to pursue. That of course had been before Annabelle Vanderley walked into his life yesterday morning. She had everything he wanted in a wife—and more. The fact that she was stinking rich was simply icing on the cake. Annabelle was attractive, intelligent and a real lady. Right now, he was nothing to her. Barely a bleep on her radar. But if he could draw her into the police investigation, that would give him a reason to see her often. The upcoming days were bound to be difficult for her. She'd need a shoulder to cry on, wouldn't she? By the time he nailed her cousin's killer and ingratiated himself to her and her family, she'd already think of him as a dear and trusted friend.

Humming to himself silently, Chad smiled at his reflection in the mirror, then sauntered down the hall and straight to Annabelle's door.

Wythe Vanderley poured himself another drink. Scotch and soda. His third in the past hour. How many would it take for him to get stinking drunk? How many before the pain eased, before he could think about Lulu and not cry? His mind knew she was dead; his heart didn't. He had loved Lulu more than anyone on earth and he'd hated her with equal passion. She had been many things to him over the years, giving him the greatest joy and the most agonizing pain. She'd toyed with people's feelings as if she were a puppet master who enjoyed pulling the strings and controlling lives. At least he could take comfort in the fact that he wasn't the only one who had danced to Lulu's chosen tune. Their father had been as much her slave as he had been; and now the old goat was hanging on to life by a thin thread.

Their father? When had Louis Vanderley ever been a real father to him? He had only vague memories of his dad during his childhood and even fewer after he'd been shipped off to military school at twelve, only months after his mother died. The old man had been running Vanderley, Inc. back then and was far too busy to waste his time on a child—even his own child. But by the time Lulu came along, things were different. From the moment she was born, their father had doted on her. As much as Wythe had loved his little half sister, he'd hated her because dear old dad had given her all the love, adoration and time he'd never given Wythe.

What did it matter now? Lulu was dead.

Wythe lifted his glass tumbler in a salute. "Here's to you, Lulu, my love. You finally got what you deserved."

Emotion tightened in Wythe's chest, making it difficult for him to breathe. Tears swam in his eyes and trickled down his cheeks. As he took a hefty swig of the Scotch and soda, salty tears dripped into his mouth.

A mournful keening sound rose from inside him and erupted in an agonized cry. He threw the tumbler across the room. When the glass hit the wall, it shattered into several large chunks and numerous tiny shards. Wythe dropped to his knees and wept.

"I tried to warn you, didn't I? I told you to be careful. But you liked playing with fire. None of them loved you the way I did. Didn't I tell you that I was the only one you could count on, that I was the one who'd never leave you?"

Wythe sucked in deep gulps of air and forced his emotions under control. Now wasn't the time to fall apart. He had to show the old man that he could count on him just as much as he counted on Annabelle. Dear cousin Annabelle. Blessed Saint Annabelle.

He should be the one in Memphis representing the Vanderley family. After all, Lulu was his sister. If he was there instead of Annabelle, he'd be the one who could tell his father when Lulu's killer was caught and brought to justice.

It's not too late, he thought. *I can still go to Memphis. I have every right to be there.*

Wythe came up off his knees, stood shakily on his feet and went straight to the telephone on the nightstand beside his bed. Earlier today, he had memorized the number for the Vanderley apartment in Memphis, intending to call Annabelle to check on the investigation into Lulu's murder. He sat on the edge of the bed, lifted the receiver and dialed the number.

Annabelle answered on the second ring. "Hello."

"I assume you don't have any news I can relay to Father," Wythe said.

"No, Wythe, I don't. If I had news, I would have called Uncle Louis."

"Don't the police know anything more than they did yesterday?"

"Wythe, have you been drinking? You sound odd. If you're drunk, whatever you do, don't go in to see Uncle Louis until you've sobered up. The last thing he needs is—"

"You always know what everyone needs, don't you, Annabelle? Well, you sure as hell didn't know that Lulu needed protection, did you? You didn't see that one coming, did you?"

"Please, don't drink anything else. Have Hiram prepare you some coffee and—"

"I'm coming to Memphis."

"What?"

"She was my sister. I loved her. I'm the one who should be there overseeing things, not you."

"Wythe, do not come to Memphis."

"I'm coming. And you can't stop me."

Annabelle sighed. Wythe hated her little exasperated sighs, those disgruntled utterances that let him know how displeased she was with him.

"If you're determined to come to Memphis, at least wait until you've sobered up."

"I'll leave first thing in the morning," he said. "I'll stay there with you, of course."

"No, you won't. Get a suite at the Peabody."

Wythe laughed. Damn the high-and-mighty bitch. "You get a suite at the Peabody if you don't want to share the family digs there in Memphis. I have as much right to stay there as you do." Before she could say anything else, utter one more word of protest, he hung up on her.

Somebody needed to take dear cousin Annabelle down a peg or two. She was much too sure of herself and he was sick and tired of her thinking she was superior to him. They were both Vanderleys, weren't they? What gave her the right to treat him as if he were dirt under her feet?

"You'd better start treating me good, Annabelle, 'cause if you don't, you'll be sorry. I'll bet Lulu's sorry that she was so mean to me the last time I saw her."

As the dial tone hummed in Annabelle's ears, she suddenly realized that someone was at the door. Taking a minute to compose herself after her less than pleasant conversation with Wythe, she replaced the receiver, squared her shoulders and tilted her chin. *That's probably Sergeant George,* she thought, then sighed. At least with the young policeman, she'd be safe from confrontation. She'd had enough of that for one day, first with Quinn Cortez and then with Wythe.

When she opened the door, she greeted her guest with a cordial smile, one she hoped told him that he was welcome. "Please, come in."

He entered, then waited for her to close the door and move ahead of him into the room. "I appreciate your seeing me, Ms. Vanderley."

"May I offer you something to drink?" she asked.

"No, thank you. Not right now." He studied her closely. "Are you all right?"

"Yes, I'm fine. Why do you ask?"

"Your cheeks are flushed."

"Oh, it's nothing. I just had a disagreement with my cousin Wythe over the phone. My face tends to turn pink when I get upset. It's the curse of having a very fair complexion."

Chad smiled warmly, then asked, "Wythe is Lulu's brother, right?"

"Half brother. Same father, different mothers."

Chad nodded.

"Where are my manners? Please, sit down, Sergeant George." She hoped he wouldn't ask her any questions about the disagreement with Wythe. Her personal animosity toward her cousin and the reasons for it were no one else's concern. Like the rest of the Vanderleys, she believed that family business should stay in the family.

"I'd like it if you called me Chad."

"All right . . . Chad. And you must call me Annabelle."

After sitting on the sofa, Sergeant George—Chad—reached inside his jacket pocket and pulled out a neatly folded packet of papers. "These are copies of Lulu's date book entries for the past couple of months. My partner and I have gone over them and on the surface, there doesn't seem to be anything there that might help us . . . except . . ."

"Except?"

Annabelle sat beside Chad and when he held out the papers to her, she took them from him. Even though her nerves were still a bit ragged after dealing with both Quinn Cortez and Wythe in the space of fifteen minutes, her hands were steady. She prided herself on keeping herself in check, in holding everything deep within her. Her emotions were private, not for public display. She'd learned how to pretend to be happy when inside she was dying during the years she struggled to be Chris's faithful and devoted companion.

"Except there are two men, other than Quinn Cortez, mentioned in her date book during the past two months and I—we—were wondering if you know either man."

Reading through Lulu's date book seemed like an invasion into her cousin's privacy. Seeing the little notes she'd scribbled in the margins, the funny doodles she'd made here and there, reminded Annabelle what a great sense of humor Lulu had. As a teenager, wherever she wrote anything, she'd always dotted the letter *i* with cute heart shapes and used hot pink and bright purple inks.

"Do you have any idea who Randy is?" Chad asked.

"Randy? I'm not sure, but it could be Randall Miller. Or it might be Randolph Chamness. I know Lulu was involved with Randolph in the past, but I don't recall her mentioning him in a couple of years. I'd start with Randall Miller. I seem to recall that Lulu called both men Randy. Actually, she referred to them as 'my Randy boy one' and 'my Randy boy two.'"

"Does Randall Miller live in the Memphis area?"

"As a matter of fact, he does. He's in real estate, I believe."

"That Randall Miller?"

Annabelle smiled. "Yes, the one who's on TV and all the billboards. Mr. Memphis Real Estate."

"Isn't he like fifty and married?"

"Yes, he is."

"Would he have a reason to kill Lulu?"

Annabelle sensed that Chad wanted her to assure him that her cousin's married lover had no reason to want her dead. The sergeant thought he already had his man. He wanted Quinn Cortez to be guilty. But why?

"As far as I know, no one had a motive to kill Lulu."

"Miller is a married man. If Lulu had threatened to tell his wife—"

"That wasn't Lulu's style," Annabelle said. "She wasn't into long-term relationships. It wouldn't have served any purpose for her to have told Randall Miller's wife about the affair."

"Okay. We'll check Miller out, ask him a few questions. If he has an alibi for Friday night, then that'll be that."

"And if he doesn't?"

"We'll dig a little deeper."

Annabelle flipped through the copied pages of Lulu's date book and her heart stopped when she read the first entry that mentioned Broo. Scanning hurriedly she noticed the name at least half a dozen more times. "What's the other name you wanted to ask me about?" she inquired, knowing full well what he would say.

"Do you know someone Lulu referred to as Broo?"

Gripping the date book pages, Annabelle considered her options. She had two—tell the truth or lie. She chose the former. "Broo was a nickname Lulu used for her brother Wythe. When she was a toddler, she couldn't say the word *brother*,

which is how Uncle Louis referred to Wythe. When she tried
to say brother, it came out Broo. The name stuck. I don't
think Lulu ever called Wythe anything else."

"Then these notations—phone calls and dates—were with
her brother?"

Annabelle nodded. "Yes. They were very close and kept
in touch on a regular basis."

"I hate to ask this, but is there any reason—"

"Wythe was at home Friday night, attending a charity
function there that the Vanderleys were hosting."

Chad smiled. "No way a man can be in two places at
once, is there?"

"No, I suppose not."

"I realize we've already asked you this, but I thought now
that you've had time to think about it—do you recall anything Lulu might have said to you recently about someone
threatening her or an argument she might have had with
someone?"

"I hadn't spoken to Lulu in several weeks. I phoned her to
give her an update concerning Uncle Louis's latest doctor's
visit."

*Lulu had said, "I'm glad Daddy's doing as well as he is.
Give him my love and tell him that I'll be home for Easter
and I'm bringing a guest. I have a big surprise for him, for
all of you."*

"What did you two talk about during that last conversation?"

"Nothing much. The entire conversation didn't last five
minutes." Annabelle considered whether to share anything
else with Chad—with the police. *You might think it means
nothing, but what if by telling them what Lulu said, it might
help in some way?* "Lulu told me that she had a surprise for
the family, but she didn't even give me a hint as to what it
might be."

"And you don't have any idea what—"

"None whatsoever."

"Did she say anything else?"

"Just that she was bringing someone home with her for Easter. And before you ask, no, she didn't say who and I don't know."

"Was she in the habit of bringing guests home for holidays?"

"Lulu wasn't in the habit of coming home for holidays. She hadn't been home even for Christmas in two years and it's been four since she came home for Easter."

"What did you make of what she said?" Chad asked. "A guest for Easter and a big surprise might have meant a special man in her life and maybe an engagement."

"Yes, that thought did cross my mind."

"Apparently she wasn't contemplating marriage to Randy, since he's married. Or to Broo, since he's her brother. By process of elimination, that leaves only one other man mentioned in Lulu's date book these past six or seven weeks."

"Quinn Cortez."

"If Lulu was expecting a proposal and didn't get one, she might have gotten angry, turned on Cortez, perhaps even threatened him and when that happened, he lost it and killed her."

Annabelle clenched her teeth tightly as she strained not to cry. Since learning of Lulu's death, she had managed to rein in her emotions so that she could handle things for the family, but every once in a while, her grief rose to the surface, despite her best efforts to control it.

After swallowing that tight knot in her throat, Annabelle said, "With what could she have threatened him?"

With disappointment etched on his features, Chad grunted. "Yeah, you're right. That scenario will work only if Lulu had something she could hold over Cortez."

"And as far as we know, she didn't."

"As far as we know. But my instincts tell me that if we dig a little deeper, we'll find something."

"You want Quinn Cortez to be guilty, don't you?"

Chad narrowed his gaze, reached out and took her hand in his. "I believe he is guilty, Annabelle. And I intend to prove it. Once Cortez is tried and convicted, you and your family can at least have closure. I want to do that for you."

"Thank you, Chad . . . thank you."

But what if Quinn Cortez isn't guilty?

Chapter 9

Jim hated Monday mornings, especially after he'd had a Sunday off to spend with Kevin. And this Monday was no exception, only worse than usual. With the Lulu Vanderley murder hanging over their heads, the Director of Police, the DA and the mayor were demanding an arrest ASAP. If they didn't find another suspect soon, Jim figured they might have to arrest Quinn Cortez on the barest circumstantial evidence Jim had ever seen in all his years on the force. Chad was chomping at the bit to pin this rap on Cortez; Jim was just as eager to prove the guy innocent. *Why was that?* he asked himself. Did he really believe that Cortez didn't do it or was he just automatically lining up against Chad? He'd like to think that his personal doubts about Chad and having recently discovered that his partner was sleeping with his ex-wife wouldn't affect his judgment. But he had to face facts—he was as human as the next guy, as easily influenced by his own gut reactions as anybody else.

The homicide department was buzzing with activity. Inspector Purser was playing host to a prestigious visitor right now, someone who might or might not play a crucial role in the Vanderley murder case. If Randall Miller didn't have an alibi for Friday night, then as far as Jim was concerned, the guy should head their list of suspects, far above Cortez. After all, at this point, Cortez didn't appear to have a motive.

After downing the last drops of his third cup of coffee since waking this morning, Jim crushed the Styrofoam cup and tossed it into the nearest wastebasket.

"We're questioning Randall Miller first," Chad said as he approached Jim. "I want to get that over with and eliminate him as a suspect so we can concentrate on Cortez."

Jim gave Chad a sidelong glance. "What makes you so sure that Randall Miller didn't kill Lulu? He's a well-known, highly respected married man who had an affair with the deceased. In my book that makes him a prime candidate as a suspect."

"My money's on Cortez."

Jim grunted. His gaze followed Chad's as he watched Inspector Purser's office door open. Jim instantly recognized the distinguished silver-haired man who emerged from the office as local real estate czar, Randall Miller. Miller shook hands with the inspector, his broad smile exposing a set of perfect, snowy white teeth. Ted Purser looked downright uncomfortable, probably well aware that his detectives were watching the exchange. Ted was a good guy who played by the rules. However, in his position he couldn't forget that it wasn't in his best interest to do anything that would deliberately upset the director or the mayor. Ted was a team player, just as Chad was. There had been a time, years ago, when Jimmy Norton had been, too. But not now. All he cared about professionally was keeping his job. And sometimes he wondered if this damn job was worth occasionally having to kiss ass, albeit, his version of kissing ass amounted to little more than begrudgingly going along with the status quo.

Ted made eye contact with Jim, then held up his hand and motioned to him.

"That's our cue," Jim said.

Chad placed his hand on Jim's shoulder. "Let me do all the questioning with Mr. Miller, okay?"

Jim shrugged off Chad's limp clasp and, without replying, headed toward the inspector and Randall Miller. Chad caught up with Jim quickly and had his hand held out in greeting to Miller before Jim had a chance to say howdy.

"Good morning, Mr. Miller. I'm Sergeant Chad George"— he nodded toward Jim—"and this is my partner, Lieutenant Norton." Chad exchanged a cordial handshake with Miller. "If you'll come with us, we'll make this as quick and pain- less as possible."

Ted Purser smiled, relief showing plainly in his facial ex- pression, a look that all but cried aloud, "Thank goodness Chad's handling this thing with kid gloves." After all, it was no secret that Randall Miller had been one of the mayor's biggest supporters in the last election and that he and the DA, Steven Campbell, were not only fraternity brothers, but were both deacons in the same local Baptist church.

"I'm at your disposal," Miller said, his ear-to-ear smile a bit irritating, at least to Jim. "I certainly want to do all I can to help the police find out who murdered poor little Lulu. Such a darling girl. My wife and daughters were quite fond of her."

"What about you, Mr. Miller?" Jim asked as he motioned toward the interview room.

Miller looked at Jim, his thousand-watt smile dimming to five-hundred watts.

"Were you quite fond of Ms. Vanderley?" Jim asked pointedly.

"Yes, of course. We all were."

So, this was how the guy intended to play it—Lulu had been a family friend and nothing more. But that's not what Annabelle Vanderley had told Chad and that's not what Lulu's date book entries implied.

A couple of minutes later, when the three of them were behind closed doors and Miller was seated, Chad said, "Would you care for some coffee, Mr. Miller?"

"No, thank you."

"How long had you known Lulu?" Jim asked, interrupting Chad playing cordial host.

"A little over a year," Miller replied. "My wife and I met her at a dinner party held at a friend's home."

"I apologize for our having to question you," Chad said. "But your name was in Lulu Vanderley's date book with entries mentioning she'd met with you several times during the past two months."

Without missing a beat, Miller explained. "Lulu was interested in selling her house and buying something a little more modern."

Miller kept smiling that phony, insincere grin that made Jim want to slap the guy.

"So all those meetings with Lulu were strictly business?" Chad asked.

"Mostly, yes. We'd have a drink, talk business and discuss a few personal things, too."

"What kind of personal things?" Jim asked.

"Oh, she'd always inquire about Valerie and the girls and I'd ask about her father. Just chitchat."

The guy was slick. Jim would give him that. Smiling, not a drop of perspiration on him, hands steady and his body relaxed, Miller projected total self-assurance that implied he knew the police had nothing on him.

"Just a couple of more questions if you don't mind," Chad said.

"Sure thing."

"First of all, do you know anyone who might have wanted to harm Lulu? And as much as I hate to ask, where were you this past Friday night between seven and ten?"

Miller's smile wavered ever so slightly and he clamped his teeth together for half a second before recovering fully and responding. "I can't imagine anyone wanting to harm Lulu. She was a charming young woman. As for where I was Friday night—I was at the office late. I left around nine or so and arrived home well before ten. Feel free to check with my wife to verify the time."

"We'll do that," Jim said.

Momentarily dropping his friendly facade, Miller glowered at Jim, then bestowed his locally famous TV smile on Chad. "If that's all, Sergeant George, I'd—"

"Before you leave, I have one more question," Jim said.

Not even glancing his way, Miller asked, "And what would that be?"

"Does your wife know that you were having an affair with Lulu Vanderley?"

Miller looked at him again, his gaze scowling. "Be very careful about making unfounded accusations."

"I take that as a no."

"Take it however you'd like," Miller said. "If we're through here, I'd like to leave."

"Certainly, that's all. And thank you for your cooperation." Chad escorted Miller to the door, opened it for him and followed him.

Jim stood in the doorway and called, "If we have any more questions, we'll be in touch."

Miller didn't respond, just shook hands with Chad and walked away hurriedly. Chad turned around and gave Jim a damning look.

Bring it on, pretty boy. Tell me that I should have left the questioning to you. Tell me there was no reason to antagonize Miller. Ask me why I always like to stir things up. Just one Goddamn word out of you and I'm liable to punch your lights out.

Don't do it, Jim told himself in no uncertain terms. So he's screwing Mary Lee. What difference does it make? She'd screwed dozens of guys before, during and after their marriage. Yeah, but none of those guys had been his partner, and none of those guys had fucked Mary Lee solely because she was Jim's ex-wife.

Chad opened his mouth to speak, but before one word

came out, Annabelle Vanderley and some slender, lanky guy dressed to the nines entered their line of vision on the way to the inspector's office. Chad moved toward Ms. Vanderley like a lion stalking a gazelle.

"Good morning, Annabelle," Chad said. "I didn't realize you were coming in this morning. Is there anything I can do to help you?"

"Thank you, Chad, but no. Inspector Purser telephoned to tell me that the results of Lulu's preliminary autopsy should be available this morning."

Chad glanced at the debonaire blond man accompanying Annabelle. "I don't think I caught your name."

"Wythe Vanderley. I'm Lulu's brother."

"Mr. Vanderley, please accept my deepest condolences."

Jim thought he'd be sick. Chad was such a suck-up. And just when had Chad become so chummy with Annabelle Vanderley, enough so that they were using each other's given names? Probably yesterday when he'd questioned her about Lulu's date book. He'd hand it to Chad—he worked fast.

"Thank you. Dear cousin Annabelle tells me that you've been very kind, Sergeant George." Wythe Vanderley smiled weakly, his manner rather condescending as if he thought Chad—and probably any other civil servant—was his social inferior.

Jim figured Wythe did everything weakly because he was weak. He had that look about him that all but shouted to the world that he was soft and refined and much too good for this dog-eat-dog world into which he'd been born. Jim's gut instincts warned him that there was something not quite right about the guy, something more than him being a snobbish prick.

"Would y'all care for coffee?" Chad asked. "I'd be glad—"

"No, thank you," both Vanderleys said in unison.

"I hope the press didn't give y'all too much trouble this morning." Chad gazed adoringly at Annabelle.

Give me a break, Jim thought. How obvious could a guy be?

"As of this morning, I have a bodyguard who is doubling as my chauffeur, at least for now," Annabelle said. "He took care of the press for us and saw us into the building and up to the tenth floor."

"I'm sorry you felt it necessary to hire a bodyguard," Chad said.

"That was a smart move, hiring a bodyguard to keep the press off your back." Jim approached them, thinking it was high time he stepped in and made his presence known.

Annabelle snapped her head around and faced Jim. "I suppose y'all should know that I have hired Griffin Powell's agency to investigate Lulu's murder and it's his agency that is providing me with a bodyguard whenever I'm concerned about being harassed by the press."

"I'm afraid Annabelle has done something quite foolish." Wythe Vanderley gave his cousin an I'm-telling-on-you smirk. "She's gone into partnership with Quinn Cortez in hiring Mr. Powell."

"What!" Chad's face darkened with shock and anger.

"It was the only way Mr. Powell would take the case," Annabelle explained. "It was either take the case for the two of us together or not take it at all."

"But Quinn Cortez is still a suspect—" Chad paused, cleared his throat and said, "He's a person of interest in your cousin's murder. I don't see how you could have agreed to—"

"An unholy alliance," Wythe finished Chad's sentence as he looked squarely at Annabelle. "That is what you called your partnership with that notorious Latin lover, isn't it?"

Annabelle gave Wythe a withering eat-dirt-and-die glare.

Inspector Purser's door opened. Ted called from where he stood in the doorway. "Sergeant George, please contact Quinn Cortez and ask him to come in as soon as possible."

All eyes turned to the inspector.

"Yes, sir," Chad replied and headed off to do as he'd been told.

Jim gave Ted a questioning glance.

"Ms. Vanderley . . . Mr. Vanderley . . . if y'all will come into my office, please."

"What is it?" Annabelle asked. "Has something happened?"

Ted shook his head. "Nothing unexpected. The ME just telephoned me with the preliminary results of Lulu's autopsy and I think it's best if we speak in private."

When Wythe grasped Annabelle's hand, she jerked it away, then hurriedly walked past Ted and went into his office. After glancing around to see if anyone had noticed how decidedly his cousin had rejected his touch, Wythe followed her.

Ted motioned to Jim. "Come on in. Chad can join us after he contacts Cortez."

Quinn got out of his Porsche, retrieved his carryall from the trunk and flung it over his shoulder. He'd phoned Marcy last night to let her know he wouldn't be moving into the place she'd rented for them until this morning. He hadn't intended to spend the night with Kendall, but they'd both wound up forgoing their good intentions. He'd used Kendall and she knew it and had let him do it anyway. This morning he had some regrets. Mostly he regretted that she didn't mean as much to him as he did to her. He did care about Kendall, just not the way she wanted him to care. She had admitted that she was in love with him. In a way he wished he felt the same, but he didn't. He wasn't in love with her. He'd never been in love, didn't even believe in that kind of emotion. Not for him.

When he reached the front entrance of the condo, the door flew open and Marcy stood there frowning at him. He knew she didn't approve of his philandering ways. Jace had told him that Marcy hated all the other women in Quinn's life because she was probably in love with Quinn herself. He'd dismissed Jace's suspicions as nonsense, but in the back of his mind, he wondered. If there was any chance whatsoever Jace was right, that was yet another reason to keep his relationship with his pretty, young assistant on a strictly friendship basis. Marcy was the last woman on earth he'd want to hurt. Without meaning to, he'd broken quite a few hearts over the years. Although he'd never lied to a woman, never made any promises he didn't intend to keep, he wasn't entirely blameless.

"Did Jace and Aaron come in with you yesterday?" Quinn asked, knowing full well that they had. Marcy always followed his instructions to the letter.

"Aaron's eating breakfast. Jace is still asleep." Marcy reached out and took Quinn's carryall. "I'll put this in your bedroom. This place has four, one for each of us, although two are quite small. And if you're hungry, there's coffee and an assortment of cereal and fruit in the kitchen."

"Coffee will be fine." Quinn closed the front door behind him and followed Marcy through the foyer and into the living room of the fully furnished condo. Sleek and modern. Light wood. Dark leather. Chrome and glass. Not one personal touch in the house. But that was what Quinn had become accustomed to, what he expected. The only place Quinn kept personal mementoes of any kind was at the old frame farmhouse on his ranch in the hill country. Most of those were photos of him and his fellow juvenile delinquent buddy from their teen years, Johnny Mack Cahill and Johnny Mack's wife and kids. Even his penthouse in Houston possessed a sterile, unlived-in feel. He was a man without sentiment, with few personal ties, only a handful of friends and no family whatsoever. Money and power ruled him. Carnal pleasure was simply an enjoyable pastime.

"You might want to shower and shave," Marcy told him as she headed up the stairs. "The master suite is on the second floor, up this way."

"Any special reason I need to shower and shave?"

"Other than that you look like hell this morning?"

Quinn grinned. "Yeah, other than that?"

"A Sergeant George from the Memphis PD telephoned

about ten minutes ago and requested the pleasure of your company this morning downtown at the Criminal Justice Center."

Chad George. The bastard! Quinn's latest nemesis. "Did he say why?"

"He wasn't specific. More questioning about Lulu Vanderley's murder, I suppose. I called Ms. Wells. She'll meet you there in half an hour."

"Kendall's due in court this morning," Quinn said as he followed Marcy into his bedroom.

"Another member of her law firm will be taking her place in court today."

Marcy opened the folding wooden doors to the closet and placed his carryall on the floor. He noted that half a dozen of his suits hung in a neat row in the closet, six silk ties adorned a metal tie rack and four pairs of shoes sat side-by-side on a shoe rack at the bottom of the closet. No doubt his laundered shirts were lined up in the chest, along with his underwear and socks.

"Kendall should have sent the associate to meet me instead of coming herself," Quinn said.

Marcy gave him a condemning stare.

"Don't look at me that way. Kendall should have known that I don't expect her to jump through hoops for me."

Marcy groaned. "God, Quinn, get real, will you? You spent the past twelve hours with her, making love to her. Of course she's going to put your welfare first . . . above everything else."

"The way you do," a deep male voice said from the doorway.

Both Quinn and Marcy shot quick glances in that direction. A barefoot Jace Morgan, wearing a T-shirt and worn jeans, grinned at them. "Sorry, I just came up to say hi to Quinn. Didn't mean to eavesdrop."

Ignoring Jace's comment, Marcy looked at Quinn. "You'd better hurry up. You've got thirty minutes to get ready and make your appointment on time."

"Where are you going?" Jace asked.

As she walked past him and out into the hallway, Marcy told Jace, "Quinn has to meet his lawyer at police headquarters this morning for further questioning."

"Want me to drive you?" Jace asked.

"Thanks, but not today." As Quinn headed into the bathroom, he paused and glanced over his shoulder. "Look, how about not saying things like that to Marcy again."

Jace shrugged, an I-could-care-less expression on his face. "Sorry, it just slipped out. But you know as well as I do that she's nuts about you. If you gave her the slightest encouragement, she'd jump you in a minute."

"I doubt that's true, but even if it is, Marcy's my assistant and my friend. And that's the way I intend for it to stay. But it wouldn't hurt if she found herself a boyfriend. Maybe you should ask her out sometime."

All color drained from Jace's tanned face. "She's not my type. Besides, I don't want your leftovers. I'd be a fool to get involved with a woman who's in love with you. Nobody can compete against you. You're The Man."

Quinn wasn't sure how to respond, wasn't sure if Jace's comments had been a compliment, a slur or if he'd simply been stating the facts as he saw them. "Just go easy on her from now on. Okay?"

"Sure thing. Whatever you want, boss."

Quinn nodded.

Quinn had spent the night with Kendall Wells. She was his lover, just as Lulu had been. Another foolish, foolish woman. Didn't she know that he would break her heart again? Didn't she know that he had used her, the way he'd used so many other women over the years? She didn't mean anything to him. None of them did.

She deserved to die, just as the others had deserved to die, so killing her would be easy. The first time had been difficult, despite having good reason to kill the bitch, but with each woman, each death, it had become a little easier.

Just like with Lulu and the others, when I cover her face with the pillow, I know that I'll be putting her out of her misery. I'll be saving her from the agony of loving Quinn Cortez.

A voice from yesterday growled inside his head. "You've been a bad boy, Quinn. I'll have to punish you for your own good."

No, God, no, make her voice go away. Make her leave me alone. Doesn't she realize that everything I've done has been good, not bad. I don't hurt them. I help them. I give them peace. I kill them softly, tenderly.

Annabelle sat in one low-back, metal and vinyl chair across from Inspector Purser's desk and Wythe sat in the other. Before sitting, she had deliberately scooted her chair as far from his as possible. She hated that her animosity to her cousin was so apparent, but at least no one here had been ungentlemanly enough to inquire why she appeared to loathe Lulu's brother.

Wythe had shown up at the Vanderley apartment yesterday evening, just as he'd warned her that he would. She had hoped he wouldn't come, that as he so often did, he'd threatened her with some action or other simply to get a reaction from her. When he arrived, she had tried to keep him from entering. She had stood her ground and told him to go to the Peabody. He'd laughed in her face.

"Either we share this place or you go to the Peabody," he'd told her.

And that's what she'd done—packed her things and gone straight to the hotel. She'd shown up on Griffin Powell's doorstep at seven-thirty and had drinks with him until a suite could be prepared for her. During her hour with Griffin, he'd suggested that he provide her with a bodyguard whenever she was in public and would have to deal with the press. She had accepted his offer of providing one of his employees for the task.

"I just spoke to Udell White, our medical examiner, concerning the preliminary autopsy report," Inspector Purser said.

Annabelle snapped out of the mental fog she'd been in, thankful to put last night's unpleasant episode with Wythe out of her mind.

"Cause of death on the death certificate will read asphyxiation," the inspector said.

The office door opened and closed. Inspector Purser glanced at the person who had entered. "Come on in, sergeant."

"Yes, sir."

"Did you take care of that matter?" Purser asked.

"Yes, sir."

Purser glanced from Annabelle to Wythe. "Lulu was suffocated, which we pretty much already knew. She was smothered with one of the feather pillows on her bed."

Annabelle hadn't realized she'd gasped aloud until she felt a man's hands touch her shoulders with gentle comfort. She glanced up to see Chad George standing behind her.

Inspector Purser gave Chad a censoring glare, which prompted him to immediately remove his hands from Annabelle's shoulders. She sighed, feeling the loss of that tender touch. Chad had been so kind to her, so caring.

"Was she . . . was she raped?" Wythe asked in a low, weak voice.

Annabelle glowered at him.

"There is no evidence of rape," Purser said. "Actually, there is no evidence of sexual activity shortly prior to her death."

"Thank God," Wythe said. "I couldn't bear it if I thought she had been violated that way."

Annabelle gritted her teeth. *Count to ten,* she told herself. *Just don't say or do anything you'll regret later.*

Once again the inspector glanced from Annabelle to Wythe. "Were either of you aware that Lulu was pregnant?"

"What?" Wythe and Annabelle cried simultaneously.

"She was approximately six weeks pregnant," the inspector said. "I take it that neither of you knew."

"No, I didn't," Annabelle said, then cast a suspicious glance at Wythe. "Did you know? Did she tell you?"

"No. I swear to God, she never said a word to me."

She didn't believe him. The bastard lied so easily and so frequently that she doubted he knew the difference between the truth and a lie. If Lulu had been pregnant, she would have told Wythe.

"I was hoping she had confided in one of you," Purser said. "It would help us in the investigation if we knew who the father is."

Annabelle couldn't speak, could barely breathe. Please, dear Lord. Please don't let it be him.

"Perhaps we should ask Mr. Cortez for a DNA sample," Chad said. "If he is the father and Lulu expected him to marry her and he refused, this could have given Cortez a motive for murdering her."

Chapter 10

"The baby wasn't mine." Quinn vehemently denied the accusation that Sergeant George had hurled at him.

"How can you be so sure?" George leaned down and got right in Quinn's face. "You had sex with Lulu Vanderley, didn't you? Weren't you two together approximately six weeks ago?"

Quinn narrowed his gaze as rage built inside him. He gripped his knees with white-knuckled strength to stop himself from attacking the cocky young sergeant. When Kendall reached out and grasped his wrist, Quinn lifted his hands and balled them into tight fists, then glanced at her. He swallowed a portion of the rage he felt, taking his lawyer's warning glare to heart. The last thing he needed to do right now was lose his temper.

"I don't have unprotected sex," Quinn said, his voice deadly calm.

"Never?" Chad George smirked. "Not in your entire life?"

Quinn didn't reply. The question didn't warrant a response. Yes, of course, when he'd been very young and very stupid, he'd screwed around a few times without using a condom. But God, that had been twenty or more years ago, when he'd been a horny teenager. But even then, he'd used a condom at least seventy-five percent of the time.

"Condoms fail," Sergeant George said.

No shit, Quinn thought, but kept his mouth shut. Could he be one hundred percent sure the child Lulu had been carrying hadn't been his? No, of course not. But the odds were in his favor. Besides, could a person ever be a hundred percent sure of anything?

"I think Lulu told you she was carrying your baby and she put pressure on you to marry her," George said. "When you told her there wouldn't be a marriage, she got upset, maybe threatened you in some way and you lost your temper and in a fit of anger, you killed her. Isn't that what happened?"

Quinn growled, deep in his throat. He wanted nothing more than to rip out Chad George's heart.

"And after I smothered her in a fit of anger, I chopped off her finger," Quinn said. "Since you seem to have all the answers, sergeant, want to tell me why I did that?"

Suddenly George backed away, putting some distance between Quinn and him. *Smart move on his part,* Quinn thought. Sooner or later, things would come to a head between the two of them. But not now. Not until Quinn was no longer a suspect. The one thing those who knew Quinn understood about him—he always paid back in kind.

"We'd like you to give us a DNA sample," Lieutenant Norton said. "Do you have any objections to—?"

"I'll give you a sample," Quinn replied. "I did not get Lulu pregnant. The child she was carrying wasn't mine. And I did not kill her."

Saying he hadn't been the father didn't make it so, but on a gut instinct level, Quinn believed it was true. He'd been careful. Was always careful. Fathering an unwanted child was the last thing he'd ever want to do, considering he'd been one of those unwanted, unloved kids with a mother who'd reminded him every day of his childhood that he'd ruined her life.

Kendall squeezed Quinn's arm, then turned to the lieutenant. "Mr. Cortez has agreed to give y'all a sample of his DNA to compare with the fetus's DNA. If that's all you need my client for today, then we'd like to get this done right away. And I would appreciate it if you would personally handle things and not the sergeant."

Bristling, Chad George opened his mouth for what Quinn figured would be an outraged cry, but before he uttered one word, Lieutenant Norton cut him off.

"Chad, why don't you get in touch with Mr. Miller about that matter we discussed while I finish up here with Mr. Cortez?"

"All right, if that's what you want," the sergeant agreed reluctantly.

"If y'all will wait right here, I'll arrange things for Mr. Cortez to go straight over to the Med to give his DNA sample as soon as possible."

The minute the detectives left them alone, Kendall zeroed in on Quinn, her nostrils flared, her eyes bright. "Are you very sure you couldn't have been the father of Lulu's baby?"

"What's the matter, counselor, don't you believe me? If my own lawyer doubts my word, what are my chances with the police?"

"Don't get cute with me. Just answer my damn question."

"Am I one hundred percent sure? No. But I never had unprotected sex with Lulu."

"But you did have sex with her six weeks ago, right?"

"Yes, give or take a few days," Quinn said. "She came up to Nashville for a couple of days during the McBryar trial."

"So the timing is right for you to have gotten her pregnant."

Yeah, the timing had been right. But surely he wasn't the only guy Lulu had been with six weeks or so ago. And what were the odds that even one of the condoms he'd used had been defective?

"You realize that if your DNA matches the fetus's DNA that fact alone will give you a possible motive for killing Lulu," Kendall told him.

"That's only if people buy Sergeant George's theory that Lulu told me the baby was mine and expected me to marry her and I killed her so I wouldn't have to marry her." Quinn rose from the chair and looked directly at Kendall. "If—and that's a big if—Lulu's baby was mine and she'd told me about it, which she didn't, then I doubt she'd have wanted marriage any more than I would have. Hell, I'm surprised she didn't get an abortion as soon as she found out she was pregnant."

"If that baby was yours . . ." Kendall rolled her eyes toward the ceiling. "Damn it, Quinn, Sergeant George wants to pin this on you. You know that. The DA could call dozens of witnesses to testify to the fact that you're a heartless womanizer and just as many who'll testify that when shoved up against a wall, you have a deadly temper."

"Neither fact proves I killed Lulu." Quinn sucked in a deep breath. "And don't forget the fact that somebody cut off Lulu's right index finger. In my experience, that bit of evidence shouts serial killer."

"Maybe. Possibly." Kendall shrugged, then laid her hand on Quinn's arm. "I believe you're innocent, but . . . Look, there had to have been other men in Lulu's life and the police probably already know who they are. They'll want to get DNA samples from any guy Lulu's been with in the past couple of months."

"Are you thinking maybe the scenario Sergeant George came up with might be correct, but he's got the wrong daddy in mind?"

"Just in case the police haven't been quite as thorough as they should have been, I think you should ask Griffin Powell to find out who else might be a candidate for father of the year."

"I'll give him a call the minute we get out of here."

Randall Miller poured himself a drink. Bourbon. Straight. He wasn't in the habit of drinking this early in the day—before lunch—but by God it wasn't every day he was asked to give the police a DNA sample. What the hell would he do if it turned out the child Lulu had been carrying was his? If that happened, he couldn't continue denying their affair. And if Valerie found out, which she would if he was arrested for murder, would she ever forgive him? It was one thing for her to suspect that he cheated on her. But it would be another thing if news of his infidelity became public knowledge. Valerie had chosen to look the other way, to pretend she was unaware her husband had a wandering eye, because she enjoyed being Mrs. Randall Miller. She loved their historic home on Belvedere in the Central Gardens area of midtown almost as much she loved playing the social grande dame. She had been willing to pay whatever price necessary to keep up the facade that they were happily married. Valerie would rather die than become a laughing stock in the community.

"Is something wrong?"

Hearing his wife's voice startled Randall so badly that he almost dropped his glass. He hadn't expected her to be at home today. It was Monday and she always had lunch with several of her friends every Monday at the Memphis Country Club.

Turning to her, he plastered a smile on his face. "Darling, what are you doing home?"

"I could ask you the same question."

What explanation could he give her that she would believe? Some version of the truth might be his best bet. "I'm afraid I got dragged into the Lulu Vanderley murder investigation. I had to answer a few questions about our relationship with the girl."

Valerie entered the living room, removed her cashmere jacket and laid it and her leather clutch purse on the sofa. "I wasn't aware that *we* had a relationship with Ms. Vanderley."

Randall downed a large gulp of bourbon, wheezed slightly and released a long sigh. "We knew her socially and I met with her on several occasions to discuss her selling her house in Chickasaw Gardens."

"Really?" Valerie stared at him questioningly. "You never mentioned it to me."

"Didn't I?"

She shook her head. "Why did answering a few questions for the police rattle you so badly?"

He could tell her everything, fall to his knees and beg for mercy. After all, if the police questioned her, they would discover that he hadn't come home straight from the office on Friday night, that he hadn't been home with his wife as he said he'd been.

"It seems someone put the ridiculous idea in their heads that I was having an affair with Lulu." He forced a laugh, which sounded ridiculous, even to his own ears.

Valerie walked over to him and looked him right in the eyes. "Are you a suspect in her murder?"

"No. Not yet."

"Did you kill her?"

"Valerie!"

"Did you?"

"No, of course I didn't."

"Do you have an alibi for the time she was murdered?"

"Not exactly."

"What did you tell them when they asked you where you were?"

"I told them I was working late at the office and came straight home."

"Will Geneva lie for you?"

Randall shook his head, knowing full well that his secretary would not lie to protect him. "I don't think so. But she can truthfully say I was at the office until seven."

"Did you tell the police you came straight home?"

"I messed up. I couldn't think straight. I told them I left the office around nine and came right home."

"That was very stupid of you, wasn't it?" Valerie took the half-full glass of bourbon from his shaky hand and set it on the portable liquor cart. "If you're asked again, you'll tell them that you were confused about the time. You left the office at seven and came directly home. You and I spent a quiet evening alone together since Friday night is the staff's night off."

"Valerie, my dear, how can I ever thank you for—"

She placed her index finger over his lips. "Randall, you're a philandering swine. You've cheated on me with so many women that I've lost count. But you've been a good father to our daughters and an excellent provider. I ceased to love you years ago and haven't given a damn for ages what you did or with whom you did it. I don't care that you had an affair with Lulu Vanderley and I really don't care if you killed the little bitch. But I will not allow anything you did to affect me and our daughters. Do I make myself clear? Whatever I do, it won't be for you. It will be for me and the girls."

"For whatever reason, I'm grateful. And I swear to you that I didn't kill Lulu."

Annabelle took the elevator from her suite at the Peabody to Griffin Powell's suite that afternoon only moments after he phoned her. She had parted company with Wythe at the police station, warning him when he followed her outside to steer clear of her during his stay in Memphis. He knew her well enough to take her seriously, especially with Griffin's employee, Bruce Askew, working as her part-time body-guard. She'd never come right out and told Wythe she knew the sordid details of his perversion, but she suspected he was aware she possessed some knowledge of his numerous sins. After all, he'd have to be a total idiot not to realize how thoroughly she detested him and to what lengths she'd gone to for several years now to avoid his company.

And neither of them would ever forget that day, shortly after Chris's funeral, when Wythe had tried to rape her. Naturally, he told her that he'd simply misunderstood the situation, that he had thought she wanted him because she'd come on to him and led him on.

Lies. All lies. Fabricated in his sick mind.

When Annabelle reached Griffin's suite and knocked, he opened the door himself and escorted her into the lounge. She stopped dead still when she saw Quinn Cortez standing near one of the windows, the afternoon sunlight turning his hair a shiny blue-black. Her stomach did an evil flip-flop.

"When you phoned me, you didn't mention that Mr. Cortez was here."

"I assumed you'd know he was either here or on his way here," Griffin said. "I work for both of you, jointly. Whatever I have to say, I say to both of you at the same time."

"Yes, of course. I understand."

"Why don't we all sit down and I'll bring you both up to date on what we've found out so far." Griffin indicated the seating area with a hand sweep.

Both men waited for Annabelle. After she sat in one of the chairs across from the sofa, Quinn and Griffin sat on opposite ends of the striped silk couch. They were both large, broad-shouldered men, Griffin several inches taller and a good twenty-five or more pounds heavier. They were like two sides of a coin. One a blue-eyed, blond Viking. The other a dark-eyed, black-haired savage.

Good heavens, where did such vividly descriptive thoughts come from? she wondered.

"I'll tell you both up front that when I take a case, I always do a check on the client," Griffin admitted. "In this case, I ran a check on both of you."

"Was that necessary?" Annabelle asked.

"Find out anything interesting?" Quinn crossed his arms over his chest and surveyed Annabelle from head to toe. "I'd love to hear all about Ms. Vanderley."

Griffin looked at Annabelle. "It's standard procedure as far as I'm concerned. That's all." He turned to Quinn. "I learned all I need to know about both of you. And anything you want to know about Ms. Vanderley, I suggest you ask her."

Grinning, Quinn nodded. "I just might do that."

"Hmm . . ." Griffin nodded toward a file folder on the coffee table. "That's a preliminary report on Louisa Margaret Vanderley. I concentrated on the past two months since one of the scenarios the police are considering is that the father of Lulu's baby killed her and they're betting that you, Quinn, turn out to be the father."

"I'm not," Quinn said.

"Let's hope you're not." Griffin readjusted his large frame so that he could relax more into the sofa back. He crossed one leg over the other at the knee. "That report only scratches the surface, of course, since we've just begun the investigation. But we already know that Quinn wasn't the only man in Lulu's life these past two months."

"Yes, I'm aware of that fact," Annabelle said. "The police showed me the entries in her date book. She was seeing quite a bit of Randall Miller, but he swore to the police that it was strictly business. But the man lied to Sergeant George when he said Lulu had consulted him about selling her house."

"How do you know he lied?" Quinn asked.

"Because Lulu never would have sold her home. It meant too much to her. It was her mother's house and Lulu loved the memories of the time she shared with her mother there after her parents divorced."

Griffin nodded. "Randall Miller is married and a highly respected Memphis businessman. If Lulu's baby was his . . ."

"Then they were having an affair?" Quinn asked.

"More than likely," Griffin replied. "But Lulu also saw quite a bit of another man, but of course, we can rule him out."

"Why's that?" Quinn asked.

Annabelle knew the answer. "Because that man was Wythe."

"Yes," Griffin said. "One of the men she spent time with was her brother."

"One of the men?" Quinn asked.

"She didn't see much of the other man, but we have reason to believe that they had a sexual relationship and that they had sex at least once, about six weeks ago."

"Then he could be the father of Lulu's baby," Quinn said. "Who is he?"

"Aaron Tully." Griffin watched Quinn for a reaction.

"Who is Aaron Tully?" Annabelle sensed that the name meant something to Quinn.

"Lulu was sleeping with Aaron?" Quinn shot up off the sofa. "Where the hell did you get your information?"

"Aaron Tully is Quinn's employee, a sort of valet/butler cum gofer," Griffin explained. "As for where we got that information—Quinn's personal assistant, Marcy Sims, claims that she caught them in the act one afternoon when Lulu was in Nashville visiting." Griffin glanced at Quinn. "When you were in court one day, Lulu and Aaron had sex . . . in your bed."

Quinn stomped around the room for a couple of minutes, then stopped and laughed. "It's a wonder he survived Lulu, a kid like him. She had a way of chewing a man up and spitting him out in little pieces if he didn't know how to protect himself."

Griffin cleared his throat. "Are you forgetting that Lulu was Annabelle's cousin?"

Quinn's eyes closed to mere slits as he focused on Annabelle. "You have no illusions where Lulu's concerned, do you? You know what she was, how she treated people, especially men. Lulu had no respect for a man unless he could give as good as he got. She was a man-eater. If I'd known she was sniffing around Aaron, I'd have tried to protect him from her."

"I'm well aware of the fact that Lulu was no saint, but . . ." There are reasons she was the way she was, Annabelle wanted to shout. But she didn't. Some things should remain secret. For the sake of the family, this one secret would go to the grave with Lulu. "If she slept with Tully, then he could be the father of her baby. We'll have to tell the police. They'll want a DNA sample from him, too."

"Griffin can inform Lieutenant Norton," Quinn said. "I

trust Norton. But even if it turns out Aaron was the father, the police can't pin Lulu's murder on him."

"Why not?" Annabelle asked.

"Because he wasn't in Memphis when Lulu was killed. He was on a plane with Marcy Sims and Jace Morgan heading back to Houston that Friday night."

"As a matter of fact, he wasn't," Griffin told them. "The three didn't actually travel together to Houston that night." Griffin stood, bent over and picked up the file folder. After leafing through it, he pulled out several sheets of paper. "Ms. Sims took a late night flight out of Nashville, leaving at ten-fifty. Tully and Morgan took a morning flight."

"I don't understand," Quinn said. "I thought all three of them went back to Houston together Friday night. They didn't mention anything about Marcy taking a separate flight and Jace and Aaron not leaving Nashville until Saturday morning."

"Any reason why they should have told you?" Griffin inserted the pages back into the file folder and laid it on the table. "They were off duty, weren't they? Don't you usually give them a vacation of sorts after you've won a big case like the McBryar trial?"

"Yeah, sure. And what they do in their free time isn't any of my business, as long as they keep their noses clean. You probably already know that all three of them were kids in trouble with the law before they came to work for me. But I'm telling you right now that Aaron might have fooled around with Lulu, but there's no way in hell that boy is capable of murder."

"Would you stake your life on it?" Griffin asked.

Chapter 11

Griffin excused himself and went into the bedroom to take a telephone call, leaving Annabelle and Quinn alone. Quinn could tell by the way she wouldn't look directly at him and by the stiffness of her spine that the lovely Ms. Vanderley felt decidedly uncomfortable. The very fact that she was not only unavailable, but also completely unresponsive to his charm made her all the more intriguing. She posed a challenge to him, on every conceivable level.

"Do you suppose that call will take long?" she asked, but glanced anywhere but at him.

"Depends," Quinn replied. "If it's personal, it could take a while. If it's business, it'll depend on who called and what they have to say."

"Aren't lawyers capable of one-word answers?"

Quinn chuckled.

She hazarded a glance his way. He took full advantage of the moment by smiling at her and gazing into her big blue eyes. He figured she'd look away and do her best to avoid making a direct connection to him; but she surprised him. She kept her gaze linked to his. A strange undercurrent swept through him, drawing him deeper and deeper into unknown waters. What was it about Annabelle that not only fascinated him, but also unnerved him?

She wasn't centerfold material, the way Lulu had been. Annabelle was several inches shorter, a few pounds heavier, not as bosomy, but elegantly lovely. Her hair was a darker blond, probably natural, whereas Lulu had lightened hers to almost white. And where Lulu's skin had been tan from hours spent in tanning beds and on beaches at private resorts around the world, Annabelle possessed a peaches-and-cream complexion.

"Do you suppose that phone call has anything to do with our case?" she asked.

"Our case?" Smiling, Quinn maintained eye contact as he rose from the sofa and walked toward Annabelle. She broke eye contact immediately and leaned back in her chair, her shoulders tensing, her spine stiffening. "You really hate having to share Griffin Powell with me, don't you?"

"Yes."

That one word said a great deal. For one thing it told him that Annabelle wouldn't lie to him for the sake of courtesy or to spare his feelings. She might be a lady to whom good manners was of tantamount importance, but she could be direct and absolutely honest if the circumstances called for it.

"I'm sorry you've been put in this situation," he said. "And you may not believe me when I say that we both want the same thing."

"I want to find Lulu's murderer and see him brought to justice."

"That's exactly what I want."

"I'd like to believe you."

Quinn knelt down in front of her and reached out to take her hands. She slid her hands on either side of her hips and drew them into tight little fists. "You really would like to believe me, wouldn't you? You'd like to believe I didn't kill Lulu," he said. "I appreciate the fact that you aren't convinced I'm guilty. It means a lot to me that you're willing to keep an open mind."

"Why does my opinion matter one way or another?"

He clasped her chin, cradling it in the hollow between his thumb and forefinger. Gasping softly, she met his gaze head-on.

"Do you want the honest truth?" he asked.

"Yes." Her voice quivered ever so slightly.

"I don't know," he admitted, then released his hold on her chin. Of their own accord, as if he had no control over them, his fingers glided gently down the side of her neck, pausing when he felt the beat of her pulse. "I usually don't care what anybody thinks of me. I've always lived my life by my own rules and thumbed my nose at society. When you're as rich and powerful as I am, people tend to cater to you, not the other way around. Being a Vanderley, you understand what I'm saying, don't you? You've had people kowtowing to you all your life."

Her pulse quickened as her heartbeat accelerated. He could feel her life's blood pumping beneath his fingertips. She was either excited or agitated. Perhaps both.

"The difference between us, Mr. Cortez, is that having been born to wealth and privilege, I was taught at an early age not to abuse my wealth and power. My parents told me that with great privilege comes great obligations. I don't live my life by my own rules and I do care what other people think of me."

He eased his hand from her neck and moved across her shoulder. She trembled. He lifted his hand away, but remained kneeling in front of her. "Haven't you ever wanted to break free? Don't you sometimes dream of what it would be like to walk on the wild side, just once?"

She stared at him as if he were an alien creature speaking in an unknown tongue. Was she so totally buried in Vanderley tradition that she had lost the ability to think for herself? How was it possible that she and Lulu were first cousins? He'd never known two women as vastly different.

"What are you suggesting?" she finally managed to say.

"Take a chance. Throw caution to the winds. Trust me completely, Annabelle."

"I can't."

"Yes, you can. You want to." He stood up and held out his hand to her. "Tell me that you know I didn't kill Lulu, then work with me to prove who did."

She glared at his offered hand, then looked up at him. "We're already working together to find Lulu's murderer. Isn't the fact that I agreed to be your partner in hiring Griffin enough for you? If I truly believed you'd killed Lulu, do you think I'd have done that?"

"Tell me. I need to hear you say it." He hated the urgency in his voice, a pleading tone he hadn't used since he was a kid. Was she aware of the fact that he was practically begging her to believe him? Until that very moment, he hadn't realized how desperately he wanted Annabelle to believe in his innocence. And heaven help him, he honest-to-God didn't know why.

She stood slowly, as if fighting a battle within herself. When she faced him, only inches separating them, she tilted forward as if her body was drawn to his by some invisible magnet.

"I don't think you killed Lulu."

He let out the breath he didn't even know he'd been holding. Exhilaration welled up inside him. He couldn't explain how he felt except to say it was as if he'd been given a rare and precious gift. Annabelle's trust.

Quinn wanted to kiss her. *Don't do it,* he told himself. *Don't even attempt it. If you touch her, you'll want more than a kiss.*

"Sorry about that," Griffin Powell said as he came out of the bedroom.

Annabelle jumped as if she'd been shot and moved hurriedly away from Quinn. The tightly wound tension inside him momentarily coiled tighter and he had to fight the arousal that had been building since the moment he touched Annabelle.

Griffin glanced from Quinn to Annabelle. "Is everything all right in here?"

"Yes," Annabelle replied.

"Was that phone call anything we need to know about?" Quinn asked, eager to change the subject and take his mind off how much he wanted Annabelle.

"Why don't we all sit down," Griffin suggested.

"What is it?" Annabelle asked. "Whatever it is, just tell us."

"The *Commercial Appeal* is going to run an exposé on Lulu's life in tomorrow's paper," Griffin said. "They're going to show what they believe was the real Lulu, warts and all."

"Oh, God!" Sudden tears glistened in Annabelle's eyes. "How much do they know? And will they really print things about her personal life knowing the family will sue the paper?"

"They're going to paint Lulu as a fun-loving party girl who handed out her sexual favors as if they were candy," Griffin told them. "And my bet is they won't print anything that can't be substantiated. They will maintain that every word is the truth and not slander."

"But why would they—?" Annabelle asked.

"To sell papers," Griffin said, then looked right at Quinn. "And exposing the fact that Lulu had a legion of lovers will make it appear that Quinn, despite the fact he found her body, was only one man of many who *might* have had a motive to kill her."

"Are you accusing me of something?" Quinn asked. "Like leaking this story to the newspaper?"

"The investigative reporter who's doing the exposé on Lulu somehow found out that she was pregnant." Griffin stayed focused on Quinn. "The police department or the ME's office could have a loose-lipped employee, but according to my sources, someone in the law offices of Hamilton, Jeffreys, Lloyd and Wells made a phone call to the *Commercial Appeal* today."

"Kendall?" Quinn didn't want to believe that his friend

and lawyer—and his lover—would have done something that unethical, although it was something that under different circumstances, he might have done himself. In order to win, he'd always been willing to do whatever it took, no matter how underhanded or borderline illegal. "You think my lawyer leaked the news about Lulu's pregnancy?"

"There's no way to prove it, of course," Griffin said. "But, yes, I think Kendall Wells is planning ahead, just in case you are charged with Lulu's murder. She's smearing Lulu's reputation now and keeping her own hands clean, thereby keeping yours clean, too."

"If Kendall did this—and I'm saying if—I didn't know anything about it." Quinn turned to Annabelle. "I swear to you that I had nothing—"

"I can't do this right now." Annabelle held up a protective hand, warning him to stay away from her. "I'm going back to my suite. I need to contact some of our people and see if we can stop this exposé from coming out. It's possible we have enough pull to influence the publisher. If not, we'll have to come up with some damage control."

"Your cousin's going to be exploited in the *Commercial Appeal* and your main concern is damage control for Vanderley, Inc.?" Quinn shook his head. "If that's the case, then I think I've misjudged you. You're not the woman I thought you were."

She pinned him with a stern, rueful look. "I don't give a damn what people think of Lulu because she apparently didn't care. If she had, she would have lived her life differently. But I do care that if Uncle Louis finds out the truth about his precious little girl, it will break his heart. The damage control I mentioned isn't to apply a Band-Aid to Lulu's public image, but to somehow keep the news from reaching my uncle, and if that fails, to convince him that everything being said about Lulu is a pack of lies."

Annabelle turned and practically ran to the door.

Calling out her name, Quinn headed after her; but Griffin grabbed his arm, halting him.

"Let her go," Griffin said. "You can apologize to her later."

Quinn took the time during his drive to his newly leased Memphis house to collect his thoughts and allow his temper to cool. He could blame everyone else, but when it came right down to it, he had no one to blame but himself. He'd been the one who had insulted Annabelle, the one who'd mouthed off without giving her the benefit of the doubt. In his own defense, he could say that he had simply judged her by the other women he'd known, but he knew that defense wouldn't hold water with her. She had taken a giant leap of faith and admitted to him that she believed he hadn't murdered Lulu. And how had he repaid her? The very first time his faith in her was tested, he'd failed. Failed miserably. He had all but accused her of being a cold, heartless, business-first bitch. God, how could he have been so stupid?

Was there any way he could repair the damage? Maybe if he crawled on his hands and knees over hot coals or broken glass, she might give him a second chance.

Ask yourself why the hell you care? Annabelle Vanderley is just a woman. Attractive. Rich. Cultured. With a pedigree reaching back to Adam and Eve. He'd known her type before and had had his pick. So what if he'd seen her as a challenge. He'd conquered other women who'd been just as great a challenge, hadn't he?

Stop thinking about her. Concentrate on more important issues. He had to regain control of his life, even while being forced to remain in Memphis. Kendall had made an important decision—to leak information to the local newspaper about Lulu's personal life—without discussing it with him first. They needed to talk. He'd make her understand that although she was his lawyer, he would have the final word in everything that affected him. But first, he needed to have a powwow with a couple of his loyal employees—one who'd ratted on another and one who'd bedded Quinn's lover in

Quinn's own bed. After he confronted Marcy and Aaron, he would telephone Kendall at her office and leave a message with her secretary for her to call him.

By the time he reached his home away from home, he had cooled off considerably and was thinking clearly. There was no need to rip into either Marcy or Aaron, but they both needed to be aware that in the future, he wouldn't tolerate such behavior.

When he unlocked the front door, he halfway expected Marcy to meet him as she often did. Instead the living room was empty and no one was there to greet him. Wondering if all three of them had gone out, he walked across the tile-floored foyer and toward the hallway. That's when he heard voices coming from the kitchen, so he veered left and swung open the kitchen door.

Jace was emptying the dishwasher and putting away dishes. Perched on a bar stool, Aaron hunched over the counter working on a crossword puzzle. Marcy was busy stirring what smelled like spaghetti sauce in a pan on the stove.

Jace was the first one who noticed Quinn, who stood in the doorway studying the threesome. "Hey, Quinn, I thought you wouldn't be back this soon. Did you finish up with that private detective?"

"Yeah, we're through for now," Quinn said.

Marcy turned the temperature down on the stove eye, laid the wooden spoon on a folded paper towel and studied Quinn for a moment. "What's wrong? You're glaring at me."

"Was I?" Quinn pulled out the second bar stool and sat down beside Aaron. "Maybe it's your imagination. Or perhaps your guilty conscience."

Marcy flushed. Aaron looked up from the crossword puzzle. "What's going on? Why should Marcy have a guilty conscience?"

"I had a very interesting conversation with Griffin Powell. Would you believe that he knows more about my employees than I do?"

"I know I should have told you myself," Marcy said, a

plea for understanding in her voice and in her eyes. "But I didn't want to cause trouble between you and Aaron. We're like a family and I was afraid that if you knew what he'd done, you would be hurt and angry and . . ."

Aaron slid off the bar stool and inched away from Quinn, then grabbed Marcy's arm and shook her. "What are you talking about? Who did you tell what about me?"

Marcy jerked free of Aaron's hold and looked back and forth from Quinn to Aaron. "I never would have said anything, but when Mr. Powell told me that it was important for the police to be aware of all the men Lulu Vanderley had been with for the past two months—"

"Hellfire, Marcy, you didn't!" Aaron stomped across the floor, shaking his head as he clenched and unclenched his hands. "You swore to me you'd never tell." He paused, looked at Quinn and said, "Hey, she came after me. I swear. You know I'd never betray you. I tried to get away from her, but she just wouldn't take no for an answer. God, man, I'm sorry. I—"

"Aaron, what did you do?" Jace asked, a worried frown marring his handsome young features.

Quinn slid off the bar stool, reached out and clamped his hand down on Aaron's shoulder. "I don't care that you fucked Lulu. Or knowing Lulu the way I did, I should probably say I don't care that she fucked you. But the police are going to care that you had sex with her because Lulu was pregnant. Six weeks pregnant."

"Oh, God!" Jace's face went white as a sheet. He nervously fiddled with his glasses, readjusting them farther up his nose.

"You're shitting me," Aaron said. "Lulu was pregnant?"

"The baby she was carrying could have been fathered by any man she had sex with five or six weeks ago," Quinn told him. "Me, Randall Miller and you and God knows who else. The police think that maybe whoever fathered her child killed her. And right now they're laying odds I'm the daddy."

"Don't you see, that's why I told Mr. Powell about Aaron being with her six weeks ago," Marcy said. "So the police would know somebody else might have fathered her child. When Mr. Powell said she'd been pregnant—"

A barfing sound came from the sink area. Quinn, Marcy and Aaron turned to see Jace throwing up.

"Are you okay?" Marcy asked as she rushed to Jace and rubbed his back.

Jace lifted his head, tore off a paper towel from the spindle rack and wiped his mouth. "Yeah, I'm okay. It must have been that burger I ate for lunch." He turned on the faucets and washed out the sink, then tossed the paper towel into the garbage.

"Why don't you go lie down for a while," Quinn said. "Everything is okay here. Nobody's mad at anybody."

"I—I think I'll go out, maybe ride around and get some fresh air." He looked at Marcy. "Mind if I take the rental car?"

"Go ahead," she told him. "I've been thinking about renting a second vehicle, maybe even one for each of us. Is that all right with you, Quinn?"

"Sure, whatever you think y'all will need while we're here," Quinn said.

"I'll probably call the rental place and make arrangements for an SUV of some kind. It'll be good for picking up supplies and all."

After removing his glasses and wiping them off with the edge of his sweater, Jace grabbed the car keys from the counter, then glanced at Aaron and said, "You shouldn't have done it. Lulu Vanderley might have been a whore, but you had no right to— She belonged to Quinn." Jace ran out of the room, his glasses clutched in one hand.

"Poor Jace, he's so high-strung and emotional," Marcy said.

"He'll be okay." Aaron didn't make eye contact with anyone else in the room. "And he was right about my screwing around with Lulu. Quinn, I'm sorry. I tried to steer clear of her, but a part of me wondered what it would be like to get it on with one of your women."

"You men are all alike," Marcy shouted. "All you ever think about—no, scratch that. Y'all don't think. At least not with your brain."

"Okay, now that everybody has had their say, let's put this whole thing into the proper perspective and move on." Quinn patted Aaron on the back and held out his hand to Marcy. When she came to him, he put his arm around both her and Aaron. "No more fighting among ourselves. We're a team. Let's act like one. Okay?"

They both replied in unison, "Okay."

"Marcy, go rent yourself an SUV and, Aaron, if you need a vehicle—"

"I don't." He shook his head. "Jace and I can share the car."

"If you change your mind, rent whatever you want."

"Yeah, sure."

"I've got a phone call to make and then I'm going out again," Quinn told them. "Don't wait on me for supper tonight."

Thinking it might be safe now to leave Marcy and Aaron alone, Quinn walked out of the kitchen and into the living room. After removing his cell phone from his pocket, he sat down and dialed Kendall's office number again.

Marcy came out of the kitchen, a frosty mug in her hand. She set it on a granite coaster atop the coffee table, offered Quinn a halfhearted smile and disappeared down the hall toward the bedrooms. Quinn eyed the iced tea. Wherever they were, Marcy always made certain she kept a pitcher of unsweetened tea made for him. Neither she nor the guys would touch the stuff, preferring traditional sweet tea. And Marcy knew he liked his tea, milk and most beverages served in a frosted glass, so she always kept glasses in the freezer.

Despite their occasional squabbles, Quinn's personal entourage worked well together as a general rule and made day-to-day living much easier for him.

"Yes, this is Quinn Cortez," he said to the receptionist at Hamilton, Jeffreys, Lloyd and Wells. "May I speak to Kendall Wells, please."

"Just a moment."

Quinn lifted the tea and took several sips. He frowned. The tea tasted a little bitter. Maybe Marcy had changed brands.

"I'm sorry, Mr. Cortez, Ms. Wells isn't here," her secretary told him. "She left early to have drinks with a client and then she was going home. You can probably reach her there in about half an hour or so."

"Okay, thanks." Quinn returned his cell phone to his pocket, downed two-thirds of the glass of tea, then got up and called to Marcy and Aaron. "I'm leaving now. You two behave yourselves, especially around Jace."

After getting into his Porsche, Quinn didn't immediately start the engine. He sat there for a few minutes trying to decide whether or not he should try to talk to Annabelle before he drove over to Kendall's. Probably not. But he could stop by a florist shop and order her some flowers. A dozen red roses. No, not red roses for Annabelle. He wanted to send her something else, not the standard red roses he'd sent to so many other women.

Yellow roses as golden as her hair? Or perhaps pink roses as soft and feminine as she was? Or even cream roses as alabaster as her complexion?

Why not a dozen of all three colors? Yeah, why not? Three dozen might be a little extravagant, but if his goal was to impress her with how sorry he was, maybe he should send six dozen.

Kendall entered the great room through the garage entrance, tossed her briefcase, purse and car keys on the counter and headed straight for her bedroom. She wanted to strip out of her suit, heels and pantyhose, take a quick shower and then prepare an easy microwave dinner. She should probably call Quinn later tonight and tell him what she'd done—having her secretary telephone Bob Reagan at the *Commercial Appeal* to reveal the true story about Lulu Vanderley. Quinn might be pissed, but on the other hand, he might agree that she'd made a wise decision. Either way, he had to know that she'd done what she thought was best for him.

After stripping, putting her suit in a bag to take to the cleaners and her underwear and pantyhose in the handwash laundry bag, Kendall turned on the faucets in the shower to allow the water to heat up. Just as she turned to the vanity and removed the lid from her jar of face cream, she thought she heard a noise. Had the sound come from inside or outside? She stood perfectly still, barely breathing, and listened. Quiet. Absolute quiet. Then she heard the clink of ice dropping from the machine in her refrigerator freezer into the plastic holding container. Breathing a sigh of relief because she'd figured out what the noise was so quickly, Kendall smeared her face with cold cream. Using a washcloth, she removed her makeup and rinsed out the cloth. Staring at herself in the mirror, she groaned. Although she was still a fairly good-looking woman, age was beginning to catch up with her. Tiny lines around her eyes and nose and mouth. Laugh lines. And there were several small age spots on her cheeks that could easily be mistaken for freckles, only Kendall's dark skin never freckled.

After taking a fresh washcloth from the stack on the vanity, she opened the shower door and stepped inside, sighing as the warm water peppered her naked body.

There was that noise again. Louder. And it wasn't the ice machine.

Stop being paranoid, she told herself. *It's barely dark. Whatever you're hearing is probably outside, one of your neighbors doing something noisy.*

She should have turned on her alarm system again, but

she never rearmed it until bedtime. She'd always felt perfectly save here in her own home.

Kendall lathered her hair and massaged her scalp.

There it was again. That noise. Her fingers, forked through her wet, soapy hair, then paused as she listened.

Were those footsteps she heard?

It's your imagination, she told herself.

But she hurriedly rinsed her hair and bathed herself, then opened the shower door and listened, but heard nothing. She had a gun in her nightstand drawer. But she didn't keep it loaded. If someone was inside the house, could she get to the gun and load it before the intruder caught her?

There was no intruder. Houses creaked and groaned. Ice machines made noise. The sound of a neighbor walking on his deck next door might easily be mistaken for footsteps inside her house.

Kendall wrapped a towel around her head, dried off and grabbed her silk robe from the hanger on the back of the bathroom door. She stood there behind the closed door and listened. Quiet. No noise at all. She breathed a sigh of relief, then opened the bathroom door and hurried into her bedroom. There in the doorway leading into the hall, she caught a glimpse of a shadow. A man's shadow.

Adrenaline flooded her body. Fear clutched her throat.

Who was inside her house? How had he gotten in?

Oh, God. Oh, God!

The nightstand was on the other side of the bed. If she tried to get to it, whoever was hovering in her doorway would see her. Not only was her gun in the nightstand, but also the telephone was sitting on top of it. And her cell phone was in her purse, out there in the kitchen.

What was she going to do?

The shadow moved.

He was coming into her bedroom.

Light from the bathroom cast a soft glow over the man, partially revealing his features. Kendall sucked in a deep breath. Then she thought she recognized her uninvited visitor.

Releasing a relieved sigh, she called, "Quinn, is that you? My God, you scared me half to death."

She had recognized him, had called him by name and had felt relief that she knew and trusted the intruder. Poor darling.

As he drew closer, the fading light from outside peeking through the closed blinds in Kendall's bedroom, her welcoming smile wavered. Was she wondering what it was about him that had changed? Did she realize she was dealing with someone she really didn't know? He wasn't the Quinn who had been her friend and lover.

When he stood directly in front of her, she reached out as if to touch his face. Her hand froze in midair. He saw realization dawn in her dark eyes. Now she knew the truth, and just as the others had done, she looked at him in horror.

"There is no reason to be afraid," he told her.

"What . . . who . . . My God!"

He clasped her hand, brought it to his chest and laid it over his heart. "I promise I will make it quick and painless."

She snatched her hand away. "No. No . . . don't . . ."

She opened her mouth to scream. He couldn't allow that to happen. If she screamed, someone might hear her. And if anyone came to help her, it would ruin his plans.

He grabbed her and clamped his hand over her mouth. She struggled. Why did they always struggle so hard against him when all he intended to do was put them out of their misery? Didn't they understand how much better off they would be once he gave them release from all their pain?

Kendall fought like a wildcat, kicking and thrashing, doing her best to get away from him. But he was far stronger than she, making her effort to escape totally useless. Keeping one hand over her mouth, he turned her so that her back was to his chest, then he dragged her toward the bed. When he flung her around and down onto the bed, her loose-fitting robe came apart several inches, revealing the inner curves of her breasts.

For half a second she stared up at him, agonized fear in her eyes. She probably thought he was going to rape her.

"Did you kill Lulu Vanderley?" she asked in a breathless, quivering voice.

So like a lawyer, he thought.

"Yes, we killed her."

"We?"

He laughed. "That's right, you've never met bad Quinn, have you? Not until tonight."

"Bad . . . ? You're bad Quinn."

He nodded.

"You're going to kill me, too, aren't you?"

He nodded again.

Trembling, her features etched with sheer panic, she moaned deeply, then tried to scream, but only a screeching whimper emerged from her throat.

Hovering over her, straddling her hips, he grasped her wrists, flung her arms over her head and pinned her to the bed. He stared deeply into her terror-stricken eyes and felt pity for this unhappy, lovesick woman.

"Poor foolish darling," he told her. "Don't you know you shouldn't waste your love on someone who can never love you in return?"

"What—what are you talking about?" Her voice quivered.

Smiling, he loosened his hold on her hands. "We can never love you."

The moment he released her wrists, she reached out for him, but before she could claw at his face, as he was sure she had intended to do, he lifted the pillow from the other side of the bed and brought it down over her face. She fought him, cursing and crying all the while.

"It's useless to struggle," he told her. "I'm doing what is best for you . . . for us."

He pressed the pillow down harder and harder. Her struggles grew weaker and weaker until she finally stopped moving.

When he was certain that she was dead, he rose up and off her. Standing beside the bed, he gazed down at her lifeless body and sighed.

"Now, that's better, isn't it? You aren't suffering anymore?"

Reaching inside the pocket of his jacket, he removed a small glass vial filled with formaldehyde and set it on the nightstand. Then he took the switchblade from his other pocket and snapped it open. For several seconds he stared at the sharp edge of the knife, mesmerized by the shiny metal surface.

"This won't hurt a bit," he told her as he spread out her right hand and eased her index finger apart from her other fingers.

Gripping her index finger tightly, he took the knife and hacked off the long, slender digit, just above the knuckle.

Humming softly to himself, he closed the dirty knife, dropped it back into his coat pocket and then studied the prize he held in his other hand. Such a pretty finger, the nail painted a bright red. He unscrewed the lid to the vial, dropped the finger into the formaldehyde and recapped the vial before slipping it into his pocket.

He would add this one to his collection. A reminder of his good deed—he had put one more foolish woman out of her misery.

Chapter 12

Annabelle stared at the single cream white rose nestled in the long, narrow florist box that had just been delivered. Knowing before she read the enclosed card exactly who had sent the rose and why, she hesitated. *Dump the box, flower, and card all in the trash,* she told herself. *And do it now before you talk yourself out of making the wise choice.* Halfway to the wastebasket in the bathroom, she paused to take another look at the rose. Long-stemmed, fragrant and perfect. Most men would have sent a dozen red roses as a way of apologizing. Someone like Quinn Cortez had probably sent dozens of women dozens of red roses. She had figured him for the type who would have gone the extravagant route and sent her half a florist shop. But no, not even half a dozen flowers. Only one. Cream white. Why only one and why white? Odd that she'd misjudged him. Ordinarily she had a knack for sizing up people correctly.

Don't pick up that card, her inner self warned. But she didn't listen. Acting purely on instinct, she laid the box on the vanity, removed the card and read the message.

Forgive me. Quinn

Straight to the point and succinct. Was the sentiment heartfelt and sincere? She had no idea, but she wanted it to be. And that fact bothered her greatly. She shouldn't care how Quinn felt or what he thought or even what he did. The man meant nothing to her—unless he turned out to be Lulu's murderer. And that was a definite possibility. She couldn't allow herself to forget that fact.

Annabelle dropped the card back into the florist box, closed the lid and dumped the box into the trash.

Apology not accepted.

Apology not really necessary.

Quinn didn't know her—the real Annabelle Vanderley—anymore than she knew him. They were practically strangers who had been brought together only because of a terrible tragedy. And they were temporarily bound to each other because of their business arrangement with Griffin Powell. If there was another family member she could trust to work with Griffin, there would be no need for her to ever see Quinn Cortez again. But there was no one else. If Wythe were the man he should be, the son his father wanted him to be, the brother Lulu had deserved, he would be here in Memphis alone, representing the family. But Wythe was weak, mentally sick, his mind warped.

Several fast, firm knocks at the outer door of her suite vanquished unpleasant thoughts of her cousin. She hadn't been expecting anyone, but as she squared her shoulders and walked out of the bathroom, a flash of insight hit her.

That's probably Quinn.

He had no doubt timed his arrival perfectly, so that his apology in the form of one perfect white rose would be delivered shortly before he showed up at her door. She had several choices, but was uncertain which to choose. If she didn't answer the door, he might simply go away. But if she did that, he would probably come back later. If she opened the door and told him to go away, how would he react? Or she could invite him in and try to make him understand that whatever he wanted from her—understanding, friendship, a new conquest—he would never get.

Licking her lips nervously, Annabelle peeped through the

viewfinder. An odd sense of disappointment fluttered inside her. The man standing outside in the hallway was not Quinn.

Opening the door, Annabelle smiled warmly. "Good evening, Sergeant George. Is there news about—"

"I'm not actually here in any official capacity," he told her. "I just wanted to drop by and see how you're doing and find out if there's anything you need."

"That's very kind of you." Chad George was incredibly good-looking in a male model sort of way, as if Mother Nature had airbrushed out all the physical imperfections. "Won't you come in?"

"Thanks." He entered the suite and followed Annabelle into the lounge area. "I hope you won't think I'm stepping over the line here, but I was wondering if you'd like to go out for dinner? Nothing fancy. And if you need someone to talk to about things—about Lulu, her murder, the suspects. Anything. I'm a good listener."

Why not? Why not go out to dinner with this handsome detective?

"You aren't married or engaged or anything are you?" she asked.

Chad laughed. "No, ma'am. If I were, I wouldn't be asking you out, even if this won't actually be a date. I wouldn't want to put that kind of pressure on you. It'll just be two people sharing a meal and getting better acquainted."

"That sounds an awful lot like a date to me," she told him, her tone light, the comment made jokingly.

He grinned. "Is that a yes?"

She nodded. "Give me a few minutes to freshen up."

"Take your time. I didn't make reservations or anything."

Annabelle rushed off to the bedroom, then called out before closing the door, "I'll be right back."

There was no point in changing clothes since she looked perfectly presentable and her available wardrobe was limited. *Brush your hair, use some mouthwash, add a fresh coat of blush to your cheeks and put on some lipstick.*

While flying about from one thing to the next, she considered the fact that she hadn't been out on a date of any kind in ages and she was looking forward to spending the evening with Chad. What woman wouldn't? After all, he was young, handsome, charming and trustworthy.

Quinn awoke gradually. Groggy and slightly disoriented, he opened his eyes and looked around, wondering where he was. Then it all came back to him—he'd been on his way over to see Kendall and had stopped by the florist to order flowers for Annabelle. He had decided on a single white rose instead of the six dozen he'd considered sending in way of an apology. A cream white rose as smooth and beautiful as Annabelle's flawless skin.

Lifting himself upright from where he'd been halfway slumped on the car seat, Quinn glanced outside and noticed it was dark. Where was he and what had happened?

Think, man, think.

He'd left the florist and thought about going straight to the Peabody to see Annabelle, then decided it wasn't such a good idea. Better to let the rose and the note speak for him. At least for the time being. She needed time to forgive him.

After nixing the idea of seeing Annabelle, he returned to his original plan and headed toward downtown. But he hadn't made it to Kendall's, had he? He vaguely remembered feeling odd, of becoming terribly drowsy.

Taking another look outside, he realized he was in a parking lot that serviced a restaurant and several shops. Had he pulled off the main thoroughfare and parked here? Yeah, that's what he'd done. He remembered now, remembered thinking he should stop for coffee because he was so damn sleepy. Stress, restless nights, constant worry. It all added up. He'd probably just been totally exhausted and— No, that wasn't it and he knew it. He'd had an odd spell like this before—several in the past year. How many episodes had there been? Two or three? No, this one made four. He had dismissed it the first time, could barely remember when it had happened or the details. The other episodes of feeling woozy, then passing out and coming to an hour or more later had occurred months apart, but this spell had happened only days after the last one, which had occurred the night of Lulu's murder.

Maybe he shouldn't keep putting off seeing a doctor.

But now wasn't the right time, considering he was embroiled in a murder case where he was one of the suspects. Later, when all this hullabaloo about Lulu's death had been cleared up, when her real killer had been caught and put behind bars, he'd have a complete physical. But there was no rush, was there? It wasn't as if these spells had any real effect on his life. Having four blackout spells in the span of a year hardly warranted any real panic. After all, once he came to after an hour or two, he was able to function normally despite a headache that lingered for several hours.

Rubbing his palm across his face, he grunted, then leaned over and looked at himself in the interior rearview mirror. Other than his hair being slightly disheveled, he didn't look any worse for wear. But he had a damn crick in his neck. As he massaged the back of his neck, he twisted his head from one side to the other.

Quinn checked his watch. Seven fifty-two. Damn, he'd been out over an hour and a half. After spearing his fingers through his hair, he turned the ignition key, started the Porsche and exited the parking lot. Realizing he was only a few miles from his destination, he wondered why he'd stopped here instead of trying to make it to Kendall's house. He must have been really out of it when he left the flow of traffic.

With the late afternoon rush hour over and the streets not as congested as they had been earlier, it shouldn't take him long to get to Kendall's. He backed up his car and headed toward the main thoroughfare. His head hurt like hell. When he arrived at Kendall's, he'd get a couple of aspirin.

Less than ten minutes later, when he turned onto the street where Kendall lived, he saw the whirling lights of an ambulance and patrol cars. A tight knot formed in the pit of his belly. *Whatever's going on, it's not at Kendall's house,* he told himself. *Don't expect the worst, don't think something's wrong with Kendall just because you were the one who discovered Lulu's body.*

He slowed the Porsche to a crawl as he drew nearer the emergency vehicles, which were parked in a row along the street in front of Kendall's house. A small group of neighbors were huddled together in the street on both sides of Kendall's place, curiosity and concern fostering their vigil.

God, not again! This can't be happening. Please, let Kendall be all right. She can't be hurt. She can't be dead.

Quinn drove by slowly, going several houses down from Kendall's before he pulled his Porsche over to the curb and parked. After killing the engine, he sat there for a couple of minutes, willing himself under control. Although his gut was telling him he could now expect the worst, he couldn't quite wrap his mind around the possibility that something bad had happened to Kendall. Filled with dread, Quinn got out of his car and walked up the street. When he drew closer, he saw a patrolman manning the perimeter, keeping curiosity seekers and nosy neighbors at bay. He made it halfway to the front door when the young, freckle-faced officer stopped him.

"Sir, I'm going to have to ask you to stop."

"What's wrong?" Quinn asked. "I know the lady who lives here. Kendall Wells. She's my lawyer and a good friend."

"I'm sorry." The officer's cheeks flushed. "I can't give you any information at this time."

Just as the paramedics came out of the house via the front door, a black Chevy Trailblazer pulled up behind one of the patrol cars parked on the street. Quinn immediately recognized the man who emerged. Memphis's medical examiner, Udell White.

Quinn's heart sank. Somebody inside Kendall's house was dead. If not Kendall, then who? As the ME came closer, he glanced at Quinn and apparently recognized him immediately.

"Did this guy find the body?" the ME asked the young officer.

"No, sir. He just showed up. The victim's ex-husband actually discovered the body. He's inside with—"

"Kendall's dead." Quinn felt sick. "How . . . who . . . ?"

"Cortez, you'd probably better wait around," Udell White said. "I'm sure Norton and George are on their way. They're bound to have a few questions to ask you."

"How did she die?" Quinn asked. "Did her ex-husband kill her? Was it an accident? Did an intruder—?"

"Keep him out here," the ME told the young policeman, indicating Quinn with a hitch of his thumb in Quinn's direction as he headed straight for the front door.

"Sir, if you'll just stay out of the way and wait here, I'd appreciate it," the policeman said to Quinn.

With his head pounding and his stomach churning, Quinn nodded, then turned and walked to the curb. Disregarding his surroundings and the murmurs of the small crowd nearby, Quinn sat down on the curb, hung his head and dropped his clasped hands between his knees. How was it possible that in the span of seventy-two hours, two of his lovers had died?

Annabelle found herself enjoying Chad George's company a great deal. Since being seated and ordering dinner at Pat O'Brien's, located two blocks south of the Peabody on Beale Street, they hadn't mentioned Lulu or anything connected to her murder. Chad had relayed basic personal facts and she'd done the same. He was nearly thirty, never married, his mother was a widow who taught English at Memphis State, his uncle was a congressman and his older sister was a pediatric nurse who lived with her husband and one daughter in Horn Lake, Mississippi, which was pretty much considered a suburb of Memphis.

The waiter had just brought their after-dinner coffee when Chad's beeper went off.

He glanced at the number displayed, frowned and said, "Sorry, but I need to call in about this."

"Certainly. Go right ahead." Annabelle lifted the cup to her lips, tasted the hot coffee and sighed. Delicious.

Using his cell phone, Chad made the call. When he groaned, Annabelle glanced at him and noted his furrowed brow.

"Say again." Chad's features hardened. "Yeah, I heard you. Have you contacted Norton? Okay. I'm on my way. I'll meet him there."

"What's wrong?" Annabelle asked.

"I'm afraid I have to leave now. There's been a murder in the South Bluff area. I have to go, but I'll drop you back by your hotel."

"Yes, of course, but I assumed you were off duty."

Chad stood. "I am, but this murder—this possible murder—well, it might be connected to another case my partner and I are working on."

Annabelle's stomach muscles tightened. "Lulu's case?"

When she stood, Chad placed his hand on the small of her back. "The victim—the deceased—is Kendall Wells," he whispered, for her ears only.

Annabelle gasped. "Quinn Cortez's lawyer has been murdered?"

Chad grasped her elbow and led her through the restaurant and out to the street. "I don't know any details, except that Ms. Wells is dead and the ME has been called. But, yeah, it looks like foul play, according to the first officers on the scene."

"Don't waste time taking me back to the hotel," Annabelle told him. "I'll go with you."

"That's not a good idea."

"I'll stay in the car and out of the way. I promise. But if Kendall Wells was murdered and her death is in any way connected to Lulu's, then I want to know. I need to know."

"I shouldn't take you along," Chad said as he led her to his parked car, but when she gazed at him pleadingly, he gave in without putting up much of a fight. "You stay in the car, out of sight and keep quiet."

"I will. I promise." She reached out and grasped Chad's hand, then smiled appreciatively at him as she twined her fingers with his and squeezed. "Thank you."

When Jim Norton arrived on the scene and saw Quinn Cortez sitting on the curb outside Kendall Well's house, a jolt of déjà vu hit him.

Jim nodded toward Quinn. "What's he doing here?" Jim asked freckle-faced Officer Vickers. "Don't tell me he found the body." Just the fact that Cortez's lawyer was dead, probably murdered, was peculiar enough, but if Cortez had discovered the body, what were the odds anyone would believe he hadn't murdered her? After all, he was already a prime suspect in Lulu Vanderley's murder.

"No sir, he's just a friend and client who showed up a few minutes ago," Officer Vickers said. "Ms. Wells's ex-husband, Dr. Jonathan Miles, is the one who discovered the body. He told us that he stopped by to see her occasionally, that their divorce, which isn't official yet, was an amicable one and they were still friends. When he arrived, he noticed the side door was wide open, so he went in and called out to Ms. Wells. When she didn't answer, he went through the house searching for her and found her in her bedroom."

"How did she die?" Jim asked. "Was she shot, stabbed—"

"No visible wounds of any kind, except . . ." Vickers swallowed. "Her right index finger had been cut off. And there was a pillow lying over her face, so we figured she'd been smothered."

"Goddamn," Jim grumbled. "Is Udell White in there now?"

"Yes, sir."

"The guy over there sitting by the curb . . ." Jim indicated Quinn. "How much did you tell him about what happened here?"

"Nothing. I swear. I didn't tell him anything."

"He wasn't told that you suspect Ms. Wells was suffocated? Or that her index finger had been cut off?"

Vickers shook his head. "No, sir. I'd never . . . I mean I know what to do and what not to do. I'm not exactly a rookie. I've been on the force for over a year now."

Jim patted the guy on the back. "I'm sure you handled things just fine. It's just that the man over there on the curb is Quinn Cortez. He's a possible suspect in a recent murder and—"

"That's Quinn Cortez, huh? I thought he looked familiar. Strange isn't it that his lawyer's dead now, only a few days after his girlfriend was murdered. You think there's a connection?"

"It's possible. But since we don't have any of the facts in Kendall Wells's death yet, it's a little too soon for suppositions," Jim said, although he figured that with this killer's MO appearing to be identical to Lulu's killer's MO, it was more than coincidence. "I'm going inside to speak to the ME. When my partner shows up, let me know." Jim walked away, then paused and glanced back over his shoulder. "Keep an eye on Cortez, will you? I might want to question him later."

Jim showed the officer inside Kendall Wells's house his ID, then glanced at the middle-aged man sitting at the kitchen table, tears streaming down his pale face. The ex-husband, Jim surmised, then headed up the hall. When he reached the bedroom, the door stood wide open. He surveyed the area and noted that nothing appeared to be out of place. The bed was still made, but the spread was wrinkled beneath the body as if Kendall Wells had wriggled around on it. Or had struggled against an attacker. She lay there perfectly still, a towel still partially wrapped around her head, a few tendrils of dark hair poking out against her forehead. The silk robe she wore was belted, but spread slightly apart so that one long, slender thigh showed plainly and the inner curve of each breast was visible.

And her right hand rested at her side, the index finger missing. A small spot of dark blood stained the spread beneath her hand.

"What can you tell me?" Jim asked when Udell White turned and looked right at him.

"I'd say there's a good chance that either we've got a serial killer on our hands or this is a copycat murder. She was probably smothered with the pillow." Udell indicated the large pillow lying at the foot of the bed. "It was over her face. There are signs of a minor struggle, as if she tried to fight her attacker, but he overpowered her. No outward signs of sexual assault. And as you can see, her killer removed her right index finger." Udell shook his head, making a silent comment.

"This seems very similar to the Lulu Vanderley murder," Jim said.

Udell nodded. "Just like with the Vanderley woman, it's as if she knew her killer. There's no indication that she ran from him or fought him at all until he had her down on the bed."

"Time of death?"

"A couple of hours, at the very most."

Something didn't sit quite right with Jim about this whole thing. If Quinn Cortez killed Lulu Vanderley in a fit of rage because she was pregnant and demanding marriage, then who killed Kendall Wells and why? Even with a strong motive, Cortez would have to be an idiot to kill a second time and in exactly the same manner. Either an idiot or a psychopath. He didn't think the man was either.

Chad parked behind a line of other cars, cautioned Annabelle to stay put and then got out and spoke to the policeman standing outside the house. Annabelle had met Kendall Wells several times, always with her client, Quinn Cortez. It seemed odd to think that the woman was dead. Had she been murdered, as Lulu had been? It would be unbelievable if she'd been murdered, wouldn't it, considering her close connection to Quinn.

Slightly uneasy, her mind filled with questions, Annabelle glanced out the windows, scanning the area in every direction. This was a lovely neighborhood, upscale and modern. People were gathered in the streets. Neighbors, no doubt. Police vehicles, cars and SUVs lined the street and driveway. Was this what it had looked like at Lulu's house the night she was killed? A shiver tingled through Annabelle's body.

Suddenly, her gaze paused on a lone man sitting by the curb, his head bowed, his hands resting on either side of his head. Illumination from a nearby streetlight shined directly on the man. Annabelle's heart skipped a beat. No, it couldn't be. What would he be doing here? But when the man dropped his hands down between his knees and turned his head to one side, Annabelle gasped.

Quinn Cortez!

What was he doing here? Had he discovered Kendall's body as he had Lulu's? Did the police believe he had killed his own lawyer? Surely, if the police suspected him of murdering Kendall Wells, they would have arrested him, not left him sitting alone on the curb. When Annabelle caught a glimpse of his face, she fought the tender sympathy that overwhelmed her. He looked like a lost soul, a man in mourning.

Quinn was not a murderer. She felt it deep inside her, at a gut level. Of its own volition, her hand reached for the door handle and before she realized what she was doing, she stood outside Chad George's car. As if drawn to him by some unknown and overwhelming force, Annabelle moved past the car and walked up the street toward Quinn. Then without warning Chad came marching toward Quinn from the other direction. Annabelle stopped and held her breath.

"Cortez!" Chad bellowed the name.

Quinn glanced behind him, saw Chad and shot up off the

ground. When Chad was within two feet of Quinn, he paused and the two men glared at each other.

"Did you kill her?" Chad asked, his voice loud but calm.

"Sergeant George, what the hell do you think you're doing?" Jim Norton called from the open front door.

Annabelle's gaze darted from Quinn and Chad to Lieutenant Norton, who came out of the house and headed toward the other two men.

"Then she really is . . . dead," Quinn said, a catch in his voice.

"Yeah, she's dead," Chad replied. "Quite a coincidence, don't you think—first your latest lover and then your lawyer. Both women murdered. And Kendall Wells was one of your lovers, too, wasn't she?"

"Damn," Jim Norton cursed under his breath as he approached the two men. "Mr. Cortez, we'll probably have a few questions for you tomorrow, but for now, why don't you go on home. I'll contact you in the morning."

Quinn nodded. "Was she—was Kendall murdered?"

"You know damn well she was," Chad said. "What is it with you, Cortez? Do you get off on killing your lovers?"

"That's enough!" Lieutenant Norton told Chad as he walked between the two men.

Quinn snarled. Annabelle noted the rage in his black eyes, the way his nostrils flared and his jaw tightened. Acting on instinct, she ran toward them and when she reached Quinn's side, she put her arm through his. His muscles were so tight they felt like stone. "I need a ride back to the hotel," she said. "Would you mind driving me to the Peabody, Mr. Cortez?"

"Annabelle, no—" Chad held out a restraining hand toward her.

Jim Norton grabbed Chad's arm and said, "We've got work to do. I don't know how Ms. Vanderley got here or why she's here, but I think it's a good idea for Mr. Cortez to take her home."

"It's all right, Chad," she told him. "We'll talk later. To-morrow or whenever you're free." She turned to Quinn. "I'm ready to leave now, if you are."

Quinn didn't respond verbally; instead he nodded, and then led her down the street. When they reached his silver Porsche, he opened the passenger door. After she slid into the seat, he rounded the hood and got in on the driver's side. Once inside, he sat there for several minutes, staring at Kendall Wells's house.

"Aren't you afraid to be alone with me?" he asked, bitter-ness in his voice.

"Should I be?"

He faced her then and something purely feminine and nurturing inside her reacted. She reached out and touched his cheek. "You cared about Ms. Wells. You're in pain right now, mourning her death."

He stared deeply into her eyes and for a split second she thought he was going to open up to her, to share his sorrow. But he jerked away abruptly, as if her touch had burned him.

"Why did you do that?" He inserted the key into the igni-tion and started the car.

"Why did I do what?"

"Come to Sergeant George's rescue. You knew I was on the verge of hitting him, didn't you?"

"Yes, I sensed that you might do something foolish—like hit Chad."

"Chad, huh? You two have become very chummy. Did you come here with him tonight?"

"Yes, I did. We were having dinner when he got the call about Ms. Wells."

Quinn laughed, the sound harsh. Anguished.

"Why do you automatically assume that it was Chad I was trying to protect?" she asked.

He cut his eyes in her direction, his gaze puzzled.

"Maybe I came to your rescue. Did you ever think of that?" she asked. "If you'd hit a police officer, you'd have been in a great deal of trouble. Don't you think you have enough problems as it is?"

"Are you saying you whisked me away from there to save me, not to protect Chad George?"

"Would you believe me if I told you that I felt I needed to save you from yourself?"

Chapter 13

Jace Morgan met her at the door. "Where the hell have you been?"

"What's it to you?" Marcy knocked into him as she shoved him aside to enter the house.

"I came home a few minutes ago and nobody was here," Jace said. "Aaron's home now and he said he'd gone to the store because you forgot to pick him up some Cokes. I wish y'all had at least left a note so I wouldn't have been—"

"What's the problem, Jace—afraid of the dark?"

"What's wrong with you all of a sudden? You're acting like you're mad at me. As a matter of fact, lately you've been acting like you're mad at the whole world."

"Just leave me alone, will you? I've got a headache, I've had a rotten day and all of you are pissed at me because I ratted on Aaron." She stopped in the middle of the hallway and turned around to face Jace. "You'd have thought Quinn would be at least a little upset with Aaron, wouldn't you? The guy slept with Quinn's girlfriend and Quinn acted like it was no big deal."

"It wasn't a big deal to Quinn. You know how he is with women. None of them mean anything to him."

Marcy heaved a deep sigh. Yeah, Jace was right. In the ten

years she'd worked for Quinn, women had come in and out of his life and he'd never been serious about any of them. She had fantasized that she'd be the woman who'd finally capture his heart, that one day he'd look at her and realize she was the only woman for him. But that hadn't happened and it never would. She'd been fooling herself to think she'd ever be more to Quinn than a friend and an employee. He'd told her numerous times how much he valued her as his assistant and as his friend. There had been a couple of times when, if she'd taken advantage of the moment, they might have become lovers, but she wanted to be more than Quinn's lover. She wanted to be the love of his life.

But why should he want her, even as a temporary lover, when practically every woman he met fell at his feet? She hated all those other women, especially the ones who kept coming back into Quinn's life—ones like Lulu Vanderley and Kendall Wells. She had despised Lulu. The woman had treated her as if she were nothing more than a servant, someone she could order around and then dismiss with a wave of her hand.

"Earth to Marcy." Jace wiggled his fingers in front of her face.

"Huh?"

"Where'd you go?"

"What? Where I've been is none of your business."

"Jeez, you're really out of it. I wasn't asking where you'd been tonight. Why should I care? I just meant where'd your mind go. You were off in la-la land somewhere."

Before she could thoroughly process Jace's question, Aaron came out of the kitchen, a Coke in one hand. "Don't you know that any time Marcy's daydreaming, she's thinking about the boss?"

Whirling around, she shot Aaron with a deadly look. "Shut up. You don't know anything."

"I know you've had the hots for Quinn as long as I've been working for him." Aaron put the canned cola to his mouth and downed a hefty swig.

"I said shut up!" *Get hold of yourself. Stop overreacting. Aaron knows how to push all your buttons. He likes getting a reaction out of you.*

"Ah, leave her alone, will you? The boss wants us to lay off her." Jace frowned at Aaron. "Besides, it's not like she can help herself. What woman could resist Quinn?"

"You know, Jace, old buddy, this hero-worship act of yours is wearing a little thin," Aaron said. "We all like Quinn. We're all grateful to him for helping us, for being a great boss and a real friend. But he doesn't expect you to bow and scrape and he's the last one who'd want you putting him up on a pedestal."

Behind his wire-framed lenses, Jace's eyes widened with concern. "Has Quinn said something to you about—"

"Nah, man, that's just me talking." Aaron swigged on his cola as he headed toward the living room. After sitting on the sofa and picking up the TV remote, he said, "Where have you two been? I was going to order pizza, but I waited for y'all to get back."

"I just rode around," Jace said. "Kind of took in Memphis. I drove downtown, checked out Beale Street."

Think fast, Marcy, she told herself. *It's none of their business where you've been or what you've done. It's not as if Aaron actually cares. He's just making conversation. You can tell him a half-truth. That should satisfy him.*

"I called the car rental place and had them pick me up so I could rent an SUV for myself," she said. "That way we don't have to share a vehicle and Quinn did give me the okay to do it."

"Want me to order that pizza?" Jace asked, apparently hoping his question would diffuse the tension in the air.

"Sure, kid, go ahead," Aaron said. "Order enough for Quinn, too, just in case he comes home tonight. Remember, he likes extra pepperoni."

"I can finish up the sauce and boil some pasta if y'all would rather have spaghetti instead." Marcy glanced from Jace to Aaron.

"Don't bother," Aaron said. "Save it for tomorrow. We'd rather have pizza."

Grinning, Jace nodded and headed for the kitchen. The minute they were alone in the living room, Marcy walked over and blocked Aaron's view of the TV. He had the sound muted, but his gaze was focused on the screen.

Aaron glanced up at her. "Want something?"

"I want you to stop ribbing Jace. He's just a kid, not even twenty. He looks up to Quinn, sees him as a role model."

"Jace knows I don't mean anything by what I say, but if you really think my kidding is getting to him, I can cool it."

"I'd appreciate that."

When she kept standing in front of him, Aaron hardened his gaze. "Is there something else?"

"You do realize that Jace isn't the only one who sees Quinn as a role model, don't you? In your own way, you admire him as much as Jace does. You'd like to be just like Quinn and that's the reason you slept with Lulu Vanderley."

Aaron shrugged. "Are you psychoanalyzing me? You think you've got me all figured out. Is that it?"

Aaron surprised her by shooting up off the sofa and getting right in her face, which meant him looking down at her since he was so much taller. Marcy's heartbeat accelerated as Aaron reached out and grabbed her shoulders. Gasping at his unexpected move, her gaze clashed with his.

"Have you ever thought maybe there's only one of Quinn's women I really want? The one he's never had?"

Marcy couldn't breathe. Aaron was too close. And he was confusing her by the way he acted and by what he said. Surely he didn't mean he wanted her. They'd been buddies, of a sort, ever since Aaron came to work for Quinn nearly six years ago, but there had never been any sexual chemistry between them. At least not on her part. But then again, she'd been so nuts about Quinn for such a long time she barely noticed other men.

Marcy gulped. "I—I don't know what to say."

Loosening his tight grip on her shoulders, Aaron eased

one hand down to clasp her waist and the other up to cup the back of her neck. "Say that you suddenly realized you'd rather have me than Quinn."

Marcy's heart fluttered maddeningly. "I'm confused. You've never acted like . . . sometimes you treat me as if I irritate the hell out of you."

"You do irritate the hell out of me, especially when you're mooning over Quinn."

Aaron looked at her as if she was the most important thing in the world to him. All she had to do was stand on tip-toe and lift her face to him and he'd kiss her. But did she want that? Did she want Aaron to—?

"Pizza's ordered. Be here in twenty-five minutes," Jace called just before he came out of the kitchen.

Marcy and Aaron jumped apart as if they'd been caught on the verge of committing a crime. Heat rose up from inside Marcy, flushing her face, creating moisture on her upper lip and between her breasts. When Jace walked into the living room, she forced a casual smile.

"Why don't you see if you can find us something to watch on TV," Marcy said. "I'm going to change into my sweats. Be right back."

She practically ran out of the room, but not before she caught a quick glimpse of Aaron, who had the oddest expression on his face. Whatever he was thinking, however he was feeling had to be a jumble of thoughts and emotions as crazy as hers. He had to know that things would never be the same between them. Not after he'd all but come out and said he wanted her. Wanted her the way a man wants a woman. At twenty-eight, she should be sexually experienced; but she wasn't. Of course, she wasn't a virgin either. Her own father had sexually abused her from the time she was eleven until she ran away from home at sixteen. She hadn't seen either of her parents since and a part of her hoped they were both dead. She blamed her mother as much as her father for those years of abuse because her mother had known and done nothing to stop it. And although she'd been halfway in love with Quinn since he'd rescued her and helped her turn her life around, there had never been anything of a sexual nature between them.

Once inside her bedroom, she went straight into the connecting three-quarter bath, turned on the faucets and filled her cupped hands with cold water. After splashing her face several times, she yanked a hand towel from the rack and patted her skin dry. Lifting her gaze, she stared at herself in the mirror.

"How do you feel about Aaron?" she asked herself aloud.

You quivered inside when he touched you. Got butterflies in your tummy and your heart beat ninety to nothing. And when you thought he was going to kiss you, you didn't try to turn away from him. Did you want him to kiss you?

"Yes," she told the image staring at her from the mirror. "Yes, I wanted him to kiss me."

Quinn hadn't spoken a word to her since they drove away from Kendall Wells's house and headed away from South Bluff. His big hands gripped the Porsche's steering wheel forcefully. With his jaw taut and his eyes glued to the road ahead, Annabelle more than sensed his anxiety—she actually felt the edgy unease radiating from him. Alone with him in the semidark confinement of his car, she wondered what had possessed her to come to his rescue, to whisk him away from what she perceived as harm's way. Yes, it was in her nature to be a protector, a caretaker, to soothe and nurture. But why Quinn Cortez of all people?

Have you forgotten that he's a suspect in Lulu's murder?

No, she hadn't forgotten. And for all she knew, he might wind up being a suspect in Kendall Wells's death, also. But every instinct within her told her that this man was no murderer.

Was she a fool to trust her own instincts when everything feminine within her was drawn to all that was masculine in Quinn? She had never been so physically captivated by a man, so sexually enticed, so emotionally connected. These odd yet powerful feelings confused her. How could she be so strongly attracted to a man who was not only a stranger, but possibly a dangerous stranger? A wise woman would steer clear of him or at the very least learn everything she could about him before she disregarded common sense. If she asked Griffin Powell for a condensed report on Quinn, enough to give her some insight into who the man really was, would he share that information with her?

When Annabelle realized how close they were to her hotel, she felt a strange urgency to keep Quinn with her. *Do something*, she told herself. *Don't let him drop you off and drive away.*

She said the first thing that popped into her mind. "You don't suppose Griffin might have a report for us by now, do you?"

Quinn let out a long, deep breath as if her breaking the silence eased some kind of ache trapped inside him. "I doubt it. Nothing that would actually help us."

"We could call him," Annabelle said. "Or just drop by his suite."

Quinn pulled the Porsche up to the front entrance of the Peabody. "If you don't want me to leave, just say so." Turning to face her, he draped his arm over the passenger seat and leaned toward her.

Annabelle's breath caught in her throat. "I don't want you to leave."

Squinting his dark eyes into mere slits, he studied her, his gaze raking over her face with pensive intensity. "I'm trouble, honey. Bad trouble. Trouble with a capital *T*. Are you sure you can handle me?"

With her nerves quivering and her femininity clenching, she shook her head. "When it comes to you, Mr. Cortez, I'm not sure of anything."

* * *

Wythe rushed out of the elevator and ran down the corridor to the apartment that Vanderley, Inc. maintained in Memphis. His pulse raced. His heart was practically jumping out of his chest. When he tried to unlock the door, his hand shook so badly that he nearly dropped the key.

God, what if someone had recognized him? If anyone found out where he'd been and what he'd done—no, he couldn't let that happen. He'd been discreet, taken every precaution. But what if the police were already involved?

Finally managing to insert the key, he unlocked the door, opened it and hurried into the apartment. Thank God Annabelle hadn't stayed here with him; otherwise she'd be here now and might suspect what he'd done.

Wythe locked the door behind him and went straight to the bathroom. He needed to shower and get rid of his clothes. He'd send them to the cleaners first thing in the morning. Just in case. No point taking any chances.

Once he had stripped and stood under the delicious warm water, he sighed. She wouldn't identify him. He'd made sure of that. He hadn't meant to hurt her. He never meant to hurt any of them. But sometimes he simply couldn't stop himself.

Griffin Powell stared at the faxes in his hand. A gnawing sense of unease spread through him as he considered the implications of the information in both faxes. It was too soon to jump to conclusions, not without more facts. Initially, he'd put three of his best people on this job, investigating Lulu Vanderley's murder at the same time the Memphis PD was scrambling to find and arrest her killer. His people understood how important it was to stay just under law enforcement's radar whenever possible. It was counterproductive to step on John Law's toes. The Powell agency didn't actually work with the law, but rather alongside it and never in opposition.

He scanned the first fax sent from his Knoxville office. If

this was true, then Wythe Vanderley was a real sicko. Griffin grunted. He had no sympathy for sexual predators, no matter how mentally ill they might be or how badly they might have once been abused themselves. He was a man who believed in basic, ancient principles. Some people didn't deserve to live. If he had his way, sexual perverts would be wiped off the face of the earth. And if half of what his investigators had discovered about Wythe Vanderley was true . . .

There was no point in confronting Annabelle with these findings. Not yet. It was possible she had no idea what kind of man her cousin Wythe actually was. But she had vacated Vanderley Inc.'s executive apartment as soon as Wythe had moved in, so that had to mean something.

Griffin put the second fax atop the first. This was the one that filled his mind with questions. Questions he wanted answered. Questions it would take more than three investigators to track down and unearth the answers to.

If the MO wasn't identical and if Quinn Cortez wasn't involved, he could chalk it up to coincidence. One of the things he'd told his crew at Knoxville headquarters to do was start searching for any other murders similar to Lulu Vanderley's, starting with Tennessee and working out to surrounding states.

New Orleans lounge singer Joy Ellis had been murdered in her apartment. Smothered to death. No report of rape or any physical violence, other than what it took to subdue her. And no evidence leading to a suspect. Another investigative team might not have dug any deeper, but that's why his agency was the best. They always went one step further. Far enough in this case to learn that the lady's right index finger had been severed. Postmortem. A fact never released to the press.

Griffin huffed. *Damn, Quinn, if you knew about this, why didn't you tell me? By hiring me, you had to know I'd find out.* That fact led Griffin to believe there was a good chance Quinn had no idea that Joy Ellis, the woman with whom he'd shared a very brief affair when he'd vacationed in New Orleans almost a year ago, had been murdered the day he left town.

Was it possible Quinn killed both Lulu and Joy?

Griffin survived by his instincts. They had kept him alive in numerous dangerous circumstances. He never ignored what he felt in his gut. And his gut told him Quinn Cortez was capable of killing, just as he was, just as most people were, given the right set of circumstances. But unless he'd badly misjudged the guy, Griffin didn't believe Cortez was a murderer.

"Excuse me, sir." Sanders stood in the doorway to his bedroom.

"Yes, what is it?" Griffin kept his back to his old friend.

"You should turn on the television. They've interrupted local broadcasting to go live to the scene of a murder in the South Bluff area."

Griffin glanced over his shoulder at Sanders. The man never made idle requests. Griffin nodded, then walked over, picked up the remote control and turned on the power to the television.

"Channel three. WREG's late night news."

He clicked in the number, then focused on the screen.

"The police have not commented on any details of the murder," the reporter said. "We've been told that Director of Police Jay Danley will issue a statement in approximately an hour. This is the second murder of a well-known and highly respected Memphis resident in seventy-two hours and speculation is running high as to whether or not there is a connection, considering renowned trial lawyer Quinn Cortez was involved with both women."

A tight knot formed in Griffin's gut. He cast Sanders a Goddamn-it glance before returning his attention to the television screen.

"Kendall Wells was Mr. Cortez's lawyer and it's rumored the two have been close personal friends for a number of years," the reporter continued.

Griffin clicked the OFF button, dropped the remote onto the coffee table and stomped across the room to the telephone. As he dialed the number, he looked at Sanders. "See if you can get in touch with Cortez. I want to see him. Tonight."

"Yes, sir."

Griffin nodded, then when the office manager for Powell Investigations answered her home phone, Griffin said, "This is Griffin Powell. Hunt down Ben Sullivan and tell him to contact me ASAP. I need half a dozen more investigators on the Cortez/Vanderley case and I need them on it yesterday."

"Yes, sir. I'll find Mr. Sullivan and give him your message. Is there anything else I can do for you, Mr. Powell?"

"Not unless you're psychic, Charisse, and can tell me if one of my clients is a murderer."

Chapter 14

As they started to enter the elevator at the Peabody to go up to Annabelle's suite, Quinn's cell phone rang. She tensed. Flush with the anxiety of admitting to Quinn and to herself that there was something sexual between them, Annabelle tried not to think about what lay ahead for them tonight. The rational part of her mind warned her that she shouldn't become just one more of Quinn Cortez's women, that their becoming lovers was an unwise course of action. But the purely emotional part of her that acted and reacted on gut instinct rather than pure logic wanted this man as she'd never wanted another.

Quinn whipped his cell phone from his pocket. "I have to take this call."

Pausing at his side, Annabelle nodded, then glanced around to see if anyone else was nearby, either hotel employees or guests. Oddly enough, they seemed to be all alone, as if they were the only two people on earth. Crazy notion.

Quinn answered the phone call. "Cortez here."

Noticing Quinn's frown, Annabelle assumed the call wasn't good news. But then how could there be any good news, considering two women—both important in Quinn's life—had been murdered in the past seventy-two hours?

"Yeah, Marcy. Thanks for passing along the message. I'm at the Peabody now, with Annabelle Vanderley. We'll go straight to Mr. Powell's suite." Quinn flipped his cell phone closed and shoved it back into his coat pocket.

"We're going to see Griffin?" Annabelle asked.

Quinn grasped her arm and herded her into the elevator, then punched the number for Griffin's floor. "That was my assistant, Marcy, on the phone." Quinn slipped his arm around Annabelle and maneuvered her so that she faced him. When she looked up at him, he said, "I suppose Griffin has heard about Kendall. No doubt it's on the local newscasts."

"Tell him you didn't kill Kendall and he'll believe you." *Just as I believe you. Or at least, I desperately want to believe you. I will not allow myself to think that a man I'm so strongly attracted to could be a murderer.*

"Do you believe me? Can you honestly tell me that you know"—he gently tapped her in the center of her chest— "deep down inside, that I didn't kill either Lulu or Kendall?"

Annabelle's mouth gaped open, the words caught in her throat. In that moment of hesitation, Quinn released his hold on her and his facial expression hardened. She wouldn't lie to him.

Before she could think of an acceptable response, the elevator stopped and a middle-aged couple holding hands smiled at them. "Going down?" the man asked.

"Going up," Quinn replied, then hit the CLOSE button and within seconds, the elevator continued its ascent.

"I don't think you killed Lulu or Kendall," Annabelle said softly. "Is there even the slightest bit of doubt in my mind? Yes, of course there is. I don't know you. Not really. We're little more than strangers. You could be hiding all kinds of deep, dark secrets and I'd have no way of knowing."

"I told you before we got out of the car a few minutes ago that I'm trouble. My track record with women is abysmal and I'll be the first to admit it. There has never been one special woman in my life. That's not my thing. Commitment. Fidelity."

"I already figured that out about you."

"Yeah, sure." Quinn's grimace conveyed his barely controlled anger. "As for deep dark secrets . . . I've never killed anybody. Although when I was thirteen, I came damn near close to beating the hell out a guy. You see, I had a shit childhood. No father and a worthless bitch mother. When mama dearest's latest boyfriend tried to beat the crap out of her, I stepped in and did to him what he'd been trying to do to her."

"I'd say you were justified in what you did. After all, you were defending your mother."

The elevator stopped on Griffin Powell's floor. Quinn's gaze locked with Annabelle's. "I'll bet your mother was as beautiful and elegant as you are," he said. "And I'll bet she loved you more than anything and was very proud of you."

Tears born of tender sympathy filled Annabelle's eyes.

"Don't cry for me, honey," Quinn said. "It would be a waste."

Blinking several times to dissipate the tears, Annabelle wanted to put her arms around Quinn, hold him and tell him whatever it was that he needed to hear. All those things his mother apparently never told him. That he was special. Handsome. Smart. And loved.

But she didn't love him. She couldn't love him. She didn't even know him.

When Quinn stepped out of the elevator, Annabelle joined him in the corridor. He grasped her arm and said, "Why don't you go to your suite and let me see Griffin Powell alone? I'll call you in the morning."

She shook her head. "I'm involved in your life now, whether I want to be or not. We're partners in hiring Griffin and we're . . . well, we're something. Not friends."

"And not lovers. Not yet. And if you're smart, you'll get the hell away from me and stay away."

"If you try this hard to run off every woman you meet, then I'm amazed that you consider yourself such a Don Juan."

"Don't say I didn't warn you." Quinn slid his hand beneath her elbow and guided her down the corridor to Griffin's suite.

He knocked; they waited.

"You should ask Griffin to let you see the report he has on me," Quinn said. "I'll give him permission to let you read it. If that doesn't make you run from me as far and as fast as you can, then nothing will."

A tall, muscular man with a shaved head and pensive dark eyes opened the door to Griffin Powell's suite. On first sight, the man was intimidating, but the minute his wide mouth curved slightly into a semismile, he seemed a little more welcoming.

"I'm Quinn Cortez and this is Annabelle Vanderley. I believe Mr. Powell is expecting me."

"Yes, sir, he is. Please come in."

Once they entered the suite, the man announced them. *Was he Griffin's servant?* she wondered. Odd that she hadn't met him before now, but perhaps he had just arrived in Memphis.

As they walked toward the lounge area, Quinn ran his fingers beneath the high collar of his lightweight turtleneck sweater. Was he nervous? Was he concerned about why Griffin had requested his presence?

Griffin stood with his back to the windows. When they approached him, he turned, came forward and instructed them to sit. "Would either of you care for something to drink?"

"No, thank you," Annabelle replied as she took a seat.

Quinn shook his head.

"I guess you heard about what happened to Kendall," Quinn said, standing face-to-face with Griffin.

"Oh, yes," Griffin replied. "It's already on the local TV news and I'm sure her murder will make the front-page headlines in tomorrow's *Commercial Appeal.*"

"Before you ask—no, I didn't kill her."

Clenching his teeth, Griffin glowered at Quinn. "It looks bad for you. Two of your lovers have been murdered in the span of seventy-two hours. I imagine that, as with Lulu's murder, you're the number one suspect in this one, too. How does that make you feel?"

Annabelle held her breath as she studied the two powerful men, gazes melded, bodies battle-station ready. *Don't do this to him,* she wanted to tell Griffin, but remained silent. She instinctively knew that Quinn wouldn't appreciate her coming to his defense. Not in this situation.

"How the hell do you think it makes me feel?" Quinn's gaze became glassy. Although he was looking right at Griffin, it was as if he didn't really see him. "How can I defend myself against something like this when I can't prove I didn't kill anyone? That's why I need you. We have to find another suspect." Quinn glanced at Annabelle and then, with clear eyes, he glared at Griffin. "Two women I cared about are dead and I can't even mourn them because I'm too wrapped up in trying to figure out a way to keep from being arrested for their murders."

"Do you have an alibi for tonight?" Griffin asked point-blank.

Not replying immediately, Quinn sucked in his breath. Annabelle suddenly felt queasy. *Please, God, please let him have an alibi.*

"I don't know exactly when Kendall was murdered," Quinn said. "But my guess is that I was alone in my car, on my way to her house, when it happened."

Griffin blew out a disgusted breath. "This isn't good. First you're the one who discovered Lulu's body, and now you don't have an alibi for when Kendall Wells was killed. You were involved with both women and they're both dead. And it's only a matter of time before the police discover what happened to Joy Ellis down in New Orleans."

Visibly tensing, Quinn glowered at Griffin. "Joy Ellis?"

"Yeah, you know the lounge singer you hooked up with when you went down to New Orleans about this time last year, not long after Mardi Gras."

Huffing, Quinn stomped loudly toward Griffin, stopping when they were less than two feet apart. "I know who Joy is, but I don't know what you mean about something happening to her."

Griffin nodded. Annabelle noted what she thought was an expression of relief settle over his features.

"When's the last time you either saw or were in contact with Joy Ellis?" Griffin asked.

"Last year right before I left New Orleans," Quinn replied. "Our little fling was very private and very brief. How did you find out about it?"

"Good investigative work on the part of my detectives. And actually, your name wasn't mentioned, but by putting two and two together, my guys came up with the inevitable four. Seems Joy mentioned you—by reputation only—to a girlfriend. The girlfriend told the police, but she couldn't give them a name and their ability to add two and two apparently wasn't that great. Nobody in the NOPD ever came up with your identity."

"Just what the hell are you talking about?" Quinn all but growled the question.

"Somebody murdered Joy Ellis and the crime is still unsolved. It's not common knowledge, but the lady was smothered with a pillow, just as Lulu was, and her right index finger was hacked off. What do you want to bet that Kendall Wells was smothered and she's missing her right index finger?"

"Why did you bother bringing the guy down here?" Chad George tramped across the room and glared at Jim. "We can question Kendall Wells's ex-husband all night and what good will it do? You let the real murderer walk off—no, drive off with Annabelle Vanderley at the scene of the crime. We both know Cortez is guilty. He's killed two women here in Memphis in the past seventy-two hours and he's walking around scot-free."

"Calm down and lower your voice," Jim Norton advised. "We have no evidence against Cortez. Just because he knew both women—"

"He was intimately involved with both women."

"Okay, so what if he was sexually involved with Lulu and Kendall. How does that fact make him their killer?"

"There's a link there somewhere. Something we haven't discovered yet. But we have a motive for the Lulu Vanderley murder. She was pregnant by Cortez, wanted him to marry her and when he refused, things got ugly and in a fit of rage, he killed her. And who knows what set him off with Kendall Wells. Maybe Ms. Wells was blackmailing him. Or maybe she threatened him in some way. What we need to be doing is grilling the guy. Give me ten minutes alone with him and I'll—"

"If you got those ten minutes alone with an uncuffed Cortez, my money would be on him. He'd either outsmart you or knock your lights out. The guy would tear you apart in no time flat." Jim chuckled. "You haven't read the report on Cortez, have you? He's smarter than you are. And besides that, the guy's not only a karate black belt—and I believe you're not, are you Chad?—but one of his hobbies is skeet shooting. He's a crack shot."

Chad swallowed hard. "Damn, Jim, he's dangerous and we shouldn't have allowed Annabelle to go off with him that way."

"That's what's really bothering you, isn't it—that Annabelle Vanderley stepped between you two and walked away with him?"

"Are you implying that there's something personal going on between them?"

"You don't think she intervened in order to stop Cortez from whipping your butt, do you? Hell, man, she didn't want him getting in more trouble with the law. If he'd knocked you on your ass, I'd have had to arrest him, even if you did provoke him."

Chad's face turned red. He stood there and glared at Jim, but didn't say anything for several minutes. "I'm phoning Purser. Instead of wasting our time looking for other suspects in these two murders, we should concentrate all our energy on Cortez. I'm going to try to make the inspector see things my way. And if I can't bring him around, I'll go straight to Director Danley."

"Go right ahead, but keep one thing in mind—if you arrest an innocent man, it won't look good on your record."

Chad didn't bother replying, but he did give Jim a scurrilous glare as he headed toward his desk.

Idiot. Cocky, hotheaded idiot.

Jim entered the interview room where Dr. Jonathan Miles sat with Officer Dobbs. The man's hand trembled as he lifted a cup of black coffee to his lips. *Poor guy,* Jim thought. When he'd arrived at the Wells home and taken over from the patrolman who'd been the first officer on the scene, he'd gotten a firsthand glimpse at what bad shape Dr. Miles was in. The man had been crying. And every time he said his ex-wife's name, he broke down all over again. Unless the man was an Academy Award–winning actor, he was genuinely torn up by his ex-wife's death.

"I'm sorry to have kept you waiting, Dr. Miles." Jim closed the door behind him, then motioned for Officer Dobbs to stay put. Jim sat across the table from Miles. "It must have been terrible for you to have found your wife—your ex-wife's dead body."

Fresh tears pooled in Dr. Miles's eyes. "Who could have done something like that? I can't believe she's dead."

"We don't have any suspects, but rest assured we'll do our best to find Ms. Wells's murderer."

"She was lying there, with the pillow over her face," Dr. Miles said, his voice raspy with emotion. "I thought it was odd, but at first I didn't realize she was . . . then I noticed the blood . . . and her finger—" His voice broke. "Kendall . . . Kendall . . ." He hung his head, covered his face with his hands and wept.

Never being one to deal well with emotions—his own or other people's—Jim certainly wasn't comfortable witnessing another man falling apart before his very eyes. But how would he react if he were in Dr. Miles's shoes and he had discovered Mary Lee's body shortly after she'd been murdered? He might hurt like hell inside, but no way would he crumble to pieces in front of an audience. Alone, he might smash his fist through a wall. But first and foremost, he'd hunt down the person who'd killed her.

The odd thing was, a part of Jim actually envied Dr. Miles's ability to cry like a baby. Mary Lee had accused him more than once of being an unfeeling bastard. She'd never understood him. It wasn't that he didn't feel. He did. He just couldn't verbalize his feelings or show his emotions.

Jim motioned to Officer Dobbs, who got up and came over to him. "Yes, sir?"

"See that Dr. Miles gets home safely and have somebody take his car to his house first thing tomorrow."

"Yes, sir. Are we finished here?" Dobbs asked.

Jim glanced at Miles, whose shoulders shook as he continued weeping quietly. "Yeah, we're through."

After Officer Dobbs escorted Jonathan Miles out of the interview room, Jim sat down and rubbed the back of his neck. He mulled over everything he knew about Lulu Vanderley's murder. Then he compared those facts to what little he knew about Kendall Well's murder tonight. The killer's MO seemed identical; however that didn't necessarily mean the same person killed both women. But all the facts about Lulu's murder hadn't been made public, so there shouldn't be any way that a copycat killer would know the details.

Quinn Cortez was the only common denominator, the only connection—that they knew of—between Lulu and Kendall. That fact alone would be enough for some people to condemn Cortez. Chad seemed dead certain that Cortez was a killer.

Hell, maybe I'm wrong. Maybe in this case, Chad's right.

When the door behind Jim opened, he pivoted his head just enough to catch a glimpse of Chad charging into the room. He groaned inwardly.

"Inspector Purser wants Quinn Cortez brought in first thing in the morning," Chad said triumphantly.

"For questioning in the Kendall Wells murder?"

"Of course in the Kendall Wells murder. If the guy doesn't have an alibi and we can come up with a motive, then the inspector says the next step could be an arrest warrant."

Jim nodded.

If Cortez didn't have an alibi. *If* he had a motive.

Jim figured that Ted had been trying to pacify Chad, understanding the need to placate Congressman Harte's nephew and at the same time keep the boy under control. In the end, they might wind up arresting Cortez, but not without some rock solid evidence. Right now, they didn't even have enough circumstantial evidence to indict the man. And so far all their leads in the Vanderley case hadn't given them a suspect they could arrest. He'd rather arrest Randall "Randy" Miller for killing Lulu than arrest Cortez. But that wasn't likely to happen. As much as he personally disliked Miller, he knew they didn't have any evidence against the guy. Besides, Chad was dying to put the cuffs on Cortez.

If Ted Purser thought he could pin both or either of the crimes on Cortez, he'd have already contacted DA Campbell and ordered Cortez's arrest.

"Cortez will have to get a new lawyer," Jim said. "Considering what's happened, I'm really curious about who he'll hire."

"It doesn't matter who he hires. The guy's as guilty as sin and I'm going to bring him down."

Nodding, Jim grinned. *Yeah, boy, you do that. And do it single-handedly. Hell, I don't know why they bothered to give you a partner since you obviously don't need one.*

"I'm heading home soon." Jim rose languidly from the chair. "I suggest you do the same. We both could use a few hours of sleep. Tomorrow's going to be a real bitch."

"Yeah, you're right, but I thought on my way home, I'd stop by the Peabody and check on Annabelle, make sure she got home okay."

Jim laid his hand on Chad's shoulder. "I wouldn't do that if I were you."

"Why not?" Chad frowned. "Are you suggesting she might not be alone?"

"I'm not suggesting anything other than the obvious facts. Not only is the lady way out of your league, but it's also apparent you're not the man she's interested in." When Jim felt Chad bristle, he patted him on the back. "Why don't you stick to a sure thing?" Jim walked to the door, opened it and then with his back to Chad, added, "If you need a woman tonight, why don't you give my ex-wife a call?"

Jim shut the door and walked away, not waiting for his partner's reaction.

Chapter 15

Aaron turned out the lights throughout the house, locked the doors and headed down the hall to his room. When they traveled with Quinn, Marcy always rented a three- or four-bedroom house, apartment or condo and when necessary, a hotel suite that would accommodate four people. Although he preferred having his own room, he didn't mind sharing quarters with Jace. The kid was neat as a pin, almost fanatically so, and he wasn't much of a talker. They weren't exactly best buds, but they had formed a comfortable friendship in the year since Jace had joined the team. The guy who'd been Quinn's other gofer, before Jace Morgan, was now in the army, serving in Iraq. Bobby Joe Kirby had been another Judge Harwood Brown Boys' Ranch alumnus, another of Quinn's projects. Yeah, that's what they all were in one way or another. Do-gooder projects. Aaron figured the outside world saw them as nothing but charity cases and assumed a guy like Quinn supported the ranch and tried to reform bad seeds for the good publicity it got him. But those were people who didn't really know Quinn. He didn't make a big show of helping a troubled kid turn his life around; he just did it. Word was that Quinn had been a wild teenager who'd gotten in trouble with the law and the man who kept him from a life of crime was old Harwood Brown, a judge who'd had his own methods of dealing with delinquents.

Making his way down the hall, he wondered how long they'd be in Memphis. A week or two at the very least—or however long it took Quinn to clear up this mess with the two murders.

If Quinn showed up later tonight, he had a key and could let himself in, so there was no need for any of them to wait up for the boss. Knowing the guy as he did, Aaron figured Quinn was off somewhere licking his wounds, maybe getting drunk and possibly even getting laid. Things had looked pretty dark for Quinn with the police because of Lulu's murder, but now that Kendall Wells was dead, things looked downright pitch-black.

As Aaron passed Marcy's closed bedroom door, he paused. What would she do if he knocked on her door? Would she tell him to get lost or would she invite him in?

Move on, buddy, he told himself. *That gal doesn't want you.*

The door to Jace's room stood partially open, enough to reveal the kid lying atop the covers, earphones in place, listening to music on his portable CD player. Jace was an odd kid, a real loner. And as far as Aaron knew the boy didn't have a sex life. He'd never known of him having a girlfriend. Or a boyfriend for that matter. And he didn't talk about his past, about his family or where he came from, nothing the least bit personal. But then again, neither he nor Marcy ever mentioned their lives before coming to work for Quinn. Sometimes it felt as if they had all been reborn the day they became a part of the Quinn Cortez entourage.

Aaron entered his own bedroom, lifted his suitcase off the floor and onto the bed, then began unpacking. He yanked open a dresser drawer and tossed handfuls of his stuff inside, caring less that his things were scattered and jumbled. Grabbing a pair of PJ bottoms, a clean T-shirt and his shave kit, he shoved the drawer closed. As he passed by Jace's room on his way to their shared bathroom, he glanced in at the teenager again, intending to tell him he was on his way to take a shower and say good night. But Jace had his eyes closed and was bouncing his head gently to the rhythm of the music.

Fifteen minutes later, showered, shaved and ready for bed, Aaron came out of the bathroom and headed back toward his bedroom. What was that odd sound? He stopped in the middle of the hallway and listened. Crying? Somebody was crying. He crept closer to Marcy's door. Sure enough, the noise was coming from her room.

Should I or shouldn't I?

He knocked softly.

No response, but the crying stopped.

"Marcy," he called her name quietly.

The door opened just enough for her to peek at him through the narrow crack.

"Are you all right?" he asked. "I thought I heard you crying."

"I'm okay."

He could see her eyes were swollen and red. "Want to talk about it?"

"There's nothing to talk about."

He laid his hand on the door and shoved gently, inching it halfway open. Marcy jumped backward and glared at him. His gaze skimmed her from head to toe. Her curly blond hair was slightly disheveled as if she'd been tossing and turning. She wore a pair of blue and white striped pajamas and was barefoot. He noticed that her toenails were painted bright coral.

Grinning, he leaned into the open space and braced himself by resting his left arm against the door facing. "Anybody ever tell you that you're darn cute without makeup, your hair a mess and wearing baggy pajamas?"

She stared at him questioningly. "What are you trying to do, imitate Quinn's smooth technique?"

"Is that who I sounded like?" His smiled widened. "Maybe just being around the guy has rubbed off on me."

"Maybe it has."

Aaron reached out and ran his index finger across and down her cheek, then circled it under her chin. "I'm not the great man himself, but if you're willing to settle for a substitute, I'm your guy."

"Are you propositioning me?"

"I'm a man, you're a woman and we both have needs." Just looking at Marcy had given him a hard-on. He wanted her. She needed him. Why shouldn't they ease each other's pain?

"Look, honey"—he used Quinn's pet name for every woman he met, hoping it might affect Marcy in a favorable way—"if you're saving it all up for Quinn Cortez, you're making a big mistake. You're his friend and his valued assistant. He's not going to screw that up by taking you to bed, then dumping you. If he'd had plans to bonk you, he'd have done it years ago."

Tossing back her head, Marcy closed her eyes and sniffled. Tears slipped from the corners of her eyes and trickled down her cheeks.

"Ah, honey . . . Marcy, don't." He shoved the door all the way open, walked into her bedroom and pushed the door closed with his foot. "He's not the only man in the world, you know."

Opening her teary eyes, she nodded, then said, "He's with Annabelle Vanderley. Can you believe that? The police suspect him of murdering the woman's cousin and she's probably in bed with him right now."

After tossing his shave kit onto her bed, Aaron slid his hand behind Marcy's neck, gripped tightly and yanked her to him. Gasping, her eyes wide and her mouth open, she stared up at him, but didn't try to jerk away or protest in any way. When he lowered his head, she stood on tiptoe and met him halfway. Forcing her mouth against his, he kissed her. Kissed her hard. When her mouth gaped wide open, he took advantage of the situation and rammed his tongue inside, deepening the kiss.

His erection strained against his cotton PJ bottoms and

pressed into her belly. Marcy lifted her arms and flung them around his neck, prompting him to make the next move. Sliding his hands down inside the back of her pajamas, he cupped her small, firm buttocks.

Moaning, she ran her hands underneath the back of his T-shirt and caressed his waist before moving all the way up to his shoulder blades.

"I want to make love to you," he whispered in her ear as he maneuvered one hand up and around to cover her left breast. "I've wanted that for a long time."

"I—I think I want that, too," she said breathlessly between kisses. "But you have to know that I don't love you . . . that it's Quinn I really want."

"Yeah, I figured that out already."

He eased her pajama bottoms down over her hips and legs. When they pooled around her feet, she kicked them aside and inserted her fingers inside the waistband of his pajamas.

"I haven't been with anybody," she said. "I mean . . . I'm not a virgin, but I'm not experienced."

"If I do anything you don't like, just tell me." He removed his pajama bottoms, then bent down and lifted her up by her waist. She wrapped her legs around his hips as he walked them over to her bed.

"Aaron?"

"Huh?" He lowered her slowly, easing over her, his knees straddling her hips.

"I really do want *you*." She emphasized the word *you*.

"It's okay, honey. If you want to pretend I'm Quinn, I won't mind. Not this first time."

And before she could respond, he inserted a couple of fingers into her, testing her readiness. She wasn't gushing, but she was wet. Wet enough. Hurriedly, he licked one nipple and then the other, smiling when both instantly went pebble hard.

He quickly reached out and yanked his shaving kit toward him, then unzipped the pouch and removed a condom. He couldn't remember the last time he'd been so eager. In seconds, he was ready. God, was he ready!

Grasping her hips, he lifted her up and forcefully thrust into her. She was tight and hot, her body gripping him. A humming sound vibrated in the back of her throat. He waited, making sure she was all right with what had happened and when she began moving, pushing herself upward, urging him into movement, he retreated, then lunged again. And again. She caught on fast, her upward and his downward thrusts in perfect unison.

For a fairly inexperienced woman, she was wild, as if she couldn't get enough of him. Somewhere in the back of his mind, he remembered that it wasn't him she was fucking; it was Quinn. And when she came, moaning, groaning and crying softly, it was Quinn's name she whispered in his ear. But he didn't care. Not now. Not when release was so close.

And then he came, his juice shooting out and filling the condom. No matter what name she called out this time, next time the only man on her mind and in her heart—the only name on her lips—would be Aaron Tully.

Shocked at the news of Joy Ellis's murder, Quinn felt as if he'd been hit in the head with a sledgehammer. He and Joy had spent only a few days together—wild, fun hours similar to ones he'd spent with dozens of other women. Nothing more. Nothing less. When he met her at the club where she worked, she had told him that she had recently ended a two-year relationship and wasn't looking for anything more than a few laughs and some hot sex. Now nearly a year since he'd been with her, he remembered little about her, except she'd been a bosomy redhead with a loud laugh.

"You're telling me that three women with whom I've had affairs are dead, all three murdered in the same way." Quinn's stomach knotted and sour bile burned his throat. "And Joy's and Lulu's right index fingers were cut off."

Something odd was going on, something he didn't understand. He hadn't killed Lulu or Kendall and he'd had no idea that Joy was dead.

"Exactly when was Joy murdered?" he asked.

"The day you left town," Griffin said. "According to what my detectives found out, her estimated time of death was actually a couple of hours before you flew out of New Orleans that morning, so unless you have an alibi for those few hours . . ."

"I don't remember right offhand," Quinn said. "Hell, man, that was nearly a year ago. And I was on vacation. I drank more than usual, partied more than usual and to be honest, I kept a perpetual hangover for days, something I seldom allow to happen."

"If you were drunk, is it possible that you could have done something and not remembered it?" Griffin looked right at Quinn as if daring him to lie.

"Anything's possible, but I'm telling you that I didn't kill Joy. Yes, I did spend some time with her the night before I flew back to Houston, but I left her apartment around dawn. I took a cab back to my hotel and grabbed a few hours of sleep before going to the airport. I remember that much."

"Were you alone in your hotel room?"

"Yes."

"And Joy Ellis was still alive when you left her?"

"Of course she was." Quinn glanced at Annabelle who sat perfectly still and quiet, her face pale, her expression strained. Did she believe he was a murderer? Had learning about Joy Ellis's death given her second thoughts about his innocence in Lulu's and Kendall's murders?

Please, honey, please don't lose faith in me.

Griffin turned to Annabelle. "Do you still want to be partners with Quinn? I've put half a dozen investigators on this case and that's going to cost a lot of money. Are you willing to split the tab with him or do you want to pull out now?"

"I'll pay for everything," Quinn said. "You keep digging, keep looking for the person or persons who killed Lulu and Kendall. And Joy."

"Cortez, you're either an innocent man or you've got a split personality. Or you're doing your best to play me like a fiddle." Griffin studied Quinn, apparently trying to figure out which scenario fit.

"I don't want out," Annabelle said, her voice raspy soft as if she were on the verge of crying. "Do whatever it takes, spend as much as necessary, but find out who killed Lulu."

Griffin nodded. "I think we have one killer, not two or three. From what we can find out, the MO is the same. All three women were smothered with a pillow and we know two had their right index fingers removed, postmortem. There was no evidence of sexual assault and no signs of other injuries. It's as if the killer didn't want to hurt these women. He just wanted to kill them gently. Their physical appearances varied, as did their backgrounds and ages. Lulu was only twenty-seven, never married, a slender blonde and a filthy rich heiress who hadn't done an honest day's work in her life. Kendall was in her mid-forties, a trim brunette, divorced and a partner in a Memphis law firm. Joy Ellis was thirty-six, a buxom red-headed nightclub singer, divorced, and had a thirteen-year-old daughter living with her father. The only apparent connection among the three women is you, Cortez. You seem to be the common denominator."

"I didn't know Joy had a child." Quinn rubbed the back of his neck as he paced about in the lounge area. In retrospect, he realized that he usually didn't waste time getting acquainted with most of the women he screwed. Kendall had been different only because they'd known each other for years.

"I work for you, Cortez," Griffin said. "And as a general rule, I don't volunteer information about my clients to anyone else, including the police. But in this case, I also work for Annabelle." He focused on her. "Do you want me to contact the police and tell them what I know about Joy Ellis?"

Quinn felt as if an invisible noose had just been draped around his neck and Annabelle alone could decide whether to keep the rope loose or to hang him with it.

"Don't put her in that position," Quinn said. "Call Lieutenant Norton and tell him everything."

"No!" Annabelle shot up off the sofa and looked back and forth between Quinn and Griffin. "Not yet. You know that once the police learn another woman Quinn knew was murdered, they're going to think he's guilty of all three crimes."

"And you don't think he is?" Griffin asked.

Quinn held his breath, waiting for her response. He couldn't remember the last time a woman's answer to any question had meant so much to him. But this was no ordinary question and Annabelle Vanderley was definitely no ordinary woman. He couldn't explain even to himself what it was about her that affected him so strongly. Yes, he wanted to screw her. But there was more to it than that. Exactly what, he wasn't sure. But he did know one thing—he desperately wanted her to believe in him.

"No, I don't think he killed Lulu or either of the other women." With tears in her eyes, she looked at Quinn and their gazes melded together.

"I agree with you," Griffin said. "Going strictly by my gut instinct, I don't think he killed any of them. And my instinct and experience also tells me that these three women might not be the only three."

"What?" The question came simultaneously from Annabelle and Quinn.

"That's one reason I've put extra personnel on this case," Griffin told them. "I have a feeling we might be dealing with a serial killer."

"Then maybe you should tell the police." Annabelle moved toward Quinn.

"Not yet. It's just a theory," Griffin said. "I need evidence. And we want something that will point the finger away from Quinn, not toward him. No pun intended."

Relief washed over Quinn in gentle, soothing waves. Not only did Annabelle believe him, but so did Griffin. Together they could fight the accusations with the truth, whatever that truth might be. All that mattered was that someone else had killed those women—three of his lovers—and they had to find this person and prove what he'd done.

Quinn took Annabelle's hand in his. Standing at his side, the two of them facing Griffin together, she squeezed Quinn's hand.

"If your theory is right and there have been more women murdered by this one person, what are the odds that it'll turn out to be a coincidence that three of them were my former lovers?" Quinn asked.

"If my theory is correct, then every murder victim—be it three or thirty—will have been one of your former lovers."

"You think someone is killing women who have been sexually involved with Quinn?" Annabelle frowned. "But why would—"

"At this point, it's only a theory," Griffin said. "The killer could be female, someone wanting to eliminate what she perceives as the competition. Or if the killer is male, and serial killers usually are, he could be motivated by some warped sense of jealousy or revenge."

"We won't go to the police with any information until you can either prove or disprove your theory, right?" Annabelle's question sounded more like a command.

"Right." Griffin looked directly at Quinn. "It would help if you could give me a list of the women you've been involved with in the past couple of years. We'll start with the most recent and work our way back. If my theory is correct, there will be a starting point somewhere. A year ago . . . two years ago . . . five years ago."

Five years ago? Surely not. That could mean countless women. No, if that many of his former lovers had been murdered, that fact would have surfaced before now. As far as reciting a list of his former lovers' names in front of Annabelle—that was the last thing Quinn wanted to do. Besides, if he had to go back further than a couple of years, he doubted he'd remember most of them by name. Calculating quickly in his mind, he counted two women this year. Only two. Lulu and Kendall. And last year? Joy Ellis, then the Parisian model,

Claudette, when he'd gone to France in May. After that came Carla, an interior designer from Houston. He'd met Lulu at Thanksgiving last year and began an on-again/off-again affair. Only four women last year. He was slowing down. There had been a time when he easily went through at least a dozen or more in a year.

Not wanting to name names in front of Annabelle, Quinn gave Griffin a help-me-out-here look, which prompted Griffin to say, "Why don't you go over to the desk and write down the names for me. In the meantime, I'll make a phone call to a friend of mine, a Chattanooga lawyer who will probably be willing to come to Memphis to represent you as a favor to me."

Quinn stared quizzically at Griffin. "Who's your Chattanooga lawyer friend?"

"Judd Walker."

"I figured as much. He and I locked horns several years ago when he worked in the Chattanooga DA's office. He's not going to want to represent me. I actually thought of Judd, then I decided I needed a Memphis lawyer ASAP and called Kendall."

"He's the best Tennessee has to offer," Griffin said. "And he owes me a favor."

"And you're willing to call in that favor for me?"

Griffin chuckled. "Not only that, but I'm going to contact an old buddy of mine who just happens to be on the Memphis police force and is the lead detective on the two murder cases. Jimmy Norton and I played ball together at UT."

"Lieutenant Norton is an old teammate of yours?" Annabelle released a delayed gasp of surprise.

"When this is all over, I'm going to owe you big time," Quinn said.

"Yeah, you will," Griffin replied. "And someday I may call in that marker. But for now, write down those names for me while I make a couple of phone calls."

Quinn knew what he had to do. The honorable thing where Annabelle was concerned. "While we're both busy, how about giving Annabelle that basic report you had compiled on me," Quinn said.

"You want her to read that report?"

Quinn nodded.

"Are you sure?"

"I'm sure." He squeezed Annabelle's hand, then released it and walked away from her, toward the desk.

"I'll get the report for you," Griffin told her, then left the room.

Annabelle laid the file folder on the coffee table in front of the sofa. Taking a deep breath, she leaned her head back and closed her eyes. Although the Powell Agency's report was brief—only three pages—it was a precise, condensed version of Quinn Cortez's life from birth to the present. A poor kid who grew up on the streets of San Antonio, a half-Mexican delinquent who stayed in trouble from the age of ten until he wound up in Houston and was arrested for vagrancy. He'd been sixteen at the time. A runaway with no place to go. A renowned Houston judge, Harwood Brown, who had a reputation for saving teens in trouble, had helped Quinn turn his life around in a few short years. After law school and passing the bar, he'd been a street-smart, power and money hungry young lawyer, willing to do whatever it took to succeed. And succeed he had. He was considered one of the top criminal lawyers in the country and his astronomical fees had made him a multimillionaire.

Quinn had won ninety-five percent of his cases and had a reputation that made other lawyers quake in their boots. And on a personal level, he was known as a Latin lover, a lady-killer, a love-'em-and-leave-'em kind of guy. He'd never been married or engaged. Not even close.

So this was the man she had chosen to believe in, to trust, to stand by his side against all odds. What made her think that he wasn't using her as he had used so many other women?

"Are you okay?" Quinn asked as he rose from the chair

across the room and laid the list he'd written out for Griffin on the desk.

She opened her eyes and looked at him. "How many women are there on that list?"

He picked it up, walked across the room and handed it to her. When she took the list, her hand quivered just the slightest bit.

She glanced at the sheet of paper. Five names in all. Five lovers since January of last year. A hysterical giggle bubbled up inside her. She'd had three lovers in the past eleven years. Hell, she'd had a total of three lovers in her whole life and one of those—the only one who had counted—had been her fiancé, a man she had dearly loved. That giddy chuckle inside her erupted suddenly, vocalizing as a squeaky laugh.

"Annabelle . . . honey . . . ?"

"You don't owe me any explanations. You've been completely honest with me and I appreciate that fact." After handing the list back to him, she clasped her hands together and held them in her lap, then stared downward, avoiding making direct eye contact with him. "I'm going to return the favor. You need to understand something about me." She paused, gathering up her courage. "I hate myself for being attracted to you. You're not the type of man I would choose to become involved with and even though I do believe you didn't kill Lulu, I don't entirely trust you. You could very easily break my heart."

Quinn knelt in front of her and grasped her hands. "Look at me, honey."

She forced herself to do as he'd requested. When their gazes met, she clenched her teeth tightly and willed herself not to cry. Right now she wanted him to hold her, to swear to her that she had nothing to fear from him, that what he felt for her was different from anything he'd ever felt before for any other woman.

"You're right. I could break your heart. And I don't want to do that." He laughed, the sound hollow and anguished.

"You can't imagine how much I want you. But I've wanted a lot of women and I've had just about every woman I've ever wanted."

"Are you trying to warn me off again?"

"I'm telling you that you should run from me. Run like hell."

Griffin Powell cleared his throat when he entered the room. Quinn released Annabelle's hands and rose to his feet to face the other man.

"I've got Judd on the phone," Griffin said. "He wants to speak to you."

"I suppose he wants to hear me beg a little before he agrees to become my lawyer."

Griffin grunted. "Yeah, something like that."

"While I'm on the phone with Judd, would you mind seeing Annabelle to her suite?" Quinn asked.

"Sure thing."

When Quinn disappeared inside Griffin's bedroom and closed the door behind him, Griffin turned to Annabelle. "If you're ready . . ."

"I'm ready."

She wanted and needed a straightforward, uncomplicated relationship with a man. Annabelle Vanderley was a marriage, children and ever-after kind of woman. Even if she was certain of nothing else in her life right now, she was certain of that.

"You'll do all you can to help him, won't you?" Annabelle stood.

"You sound as if you're walking away from this situation, away from him."

"I am. I have to." She followed Griffin to the door.

"So you'll be going home then, back to Mississippi?" he asked as he opened the door for her.

"Yes, as soon as they release Lulu's body, I'll take her home to Uncle Louis. He needs to see that she has a proper funeral and a burial in the family cemetery."

"And will you come back to Memphis after the funeral?"

"If it's necessary, yes, I'll come back. But in the meantime, I expect you to keep in touch with me. I'll want full reports on whatever you find out about Lulu's murder. And I want you to do whatever is necessary, regardless of the cost, to prove Quinn is innocent."

Chapter 16

He had spent a lifetime trying to forget, praying that God would erase the horrible memories. But he had learned that there was no escape, no way to stop the nightmares that plagued him—awake or asleep—no way to control the need to end not only his misery, but hers, too. Although he had suffered unbearably, so had she. And in her own cruel, tormented way, she had loved him. Hadn't she?

The sound of her voice reverberated inside his head. He covered his ears with his hands, trying to block out the condemning words. But it was useless. He was doomed to relive the memories of his tortured childhood again and again.

"Don't hide from me, you little devil you!"

Lying flat of his stomach under his bed, his body shaking uncontrollably, he held his breath. If he could stay very still and very quiet, maybe she would go away. *God, please, make her leave me alone.* Breaking her favorite ashtray had been an accident. After he'd dumped the ashes and cigarette butts in the garbage can, he had wiped the tray clean with a wet cloth. He didn't know how it had happened. One minute he was holding it and the next it had slipped through his fingers.

She had heard the shattering glass the minute the tray hit

the kitchen floor and had jumped up from the table where she'd been sitting drinking a beer.

"What the hell have you done now, you stupid little fuck-up?"

He'd looked up at her, seen the fury in her hazel eyes and without thinking of the consequences, ran past her and through the house, straight to his room.

The sound of the breaking glass clattered inside his head. He kept hearing it over and over again, like background music that he couldn't shut off.

"I thought you knew better than to hide from me," she called to him. "You know that when I find you, I'll have to punish you twice. Once for breaking my favorite ashtray and again for running and hiding."

He held his breath for as long as he could, then finally sucked in air as quietly as possible. Lying there against the cold wooden floor, he listened while she tore his room apart in her rage. Lifting his head just a fraction, he peered out from under the bed and watched while she ripped the curtains from the windows, yanked all the drawers out of the dresser and then jerked open the closet door.

"If you're not in the closet, then where are you?"

He couldn't see her evil smile, but he knew she was smiling. Whenever she punished him, she smiled. He couldn't understand how hurting him could make her so happy.

When she walked toward the bed, he clenched his teeth tightly together and held his breath again. *No, please, no. Don't hurt me. Not again.*

His heart beat so fast he thought it was going to jump out of his chest as she knelt down beside the bed and looked underneath it. He scooted as far back against the wall as he could. She was so big; and he was so very small. She had all the power; he had none. He tried so hard to be good, to please her, to prove to her that he did love her, but it was never enough.

"If I have to come under there and drag you out, you'll be sorry."

He froze with fear.

She got down on her belly and inched her way beneath the bed, just far enough so that she could reach out and grab his ankles. The minute she touched him, he peed his pants.

Oh, no. She'd punish him for that, too, for wetting his pants.

She dragged him out from under the bed, then rose to her feet and stood over him like a menacing giant, glaring at him. "Why do you do these things?" she asked him as if genuinely puzzled. "Why can't you be a good boy?"

He opened his mouth to tell her that he tried, tried so very hard to be good. But the words lodged in his throat.

With him lying at her feet, she slid her hand into her shirt pocket, pulled out a pack of cigarettes and a lighter. Then she sat down on the edge of his bed and lit one of the cigarettes. After placing the pack and the lighter back in her pocket, she took a long draw on the freshly lit cigarette.

"Look at you, all wet and nasty. You pissed in your pants again, didn't you? You think just because you're so damn good-looking the rules don't apply to you? You think because I love you, I'll let you treat me any way you want to? Well, you're wrong. Damn wrong!" She lifted her foot and kicked him in the ribs.

The pain radiated through his whole body, but he kept quiet, enduring in silence. She liked to hear him cry, but he wouldn't cry for her. Not this time. He wouldn't!

Leaning down, she stuck the cigarette in her mouth before she grabbed his wrists and yanked him off the floor. She spread her legs, forced him between her thighs and then closed them, holding him in place.

He watched helplessly, completely terrified, as she removed the cigarette from her mouth and brought it down to his arm. When the burning tip pressed into his skin, he keened quietly, but he didn't cry. She lifted the cigarette and moved it up his arm a couple of inches, then pressed it into his skin again. Tears welled up in his eyes. He clenched his teeth as tight as he could. She repeated the torture again and again until she had inflicted eight burn spots—four on each arm.

"Damn, you. Cry. Any normal kid would cry when he's being punished."

She yanked his unbelted jeans down, taking his cotton briefs with them.

"Don't, please, don't. I'll cry for you, Mama. I'll cry."

"Too late, you little shit."

When he tried to escape her tenacious hold, she grabbed him by the shoulders, lifted him off his feet and flung him onto the bed.

He cried then, cried as loud and as hard as he could.

But it didn't matter. She was going to do what she was going to do no matter what. When he tried to cover himself with his hands, she prized his hands away and while he struggled fruitlessly, she stuck the red-hot end of her cigarette to the tip of his little penis.

Valerie Miller waited until their housekeeper, Eula, placed her breakfast plate in front of her, poured her coffee and returned to the kitchen, before she spoke to her husband. Randall sat at the far end of the dining room table, this morning's *Commercial Appeal* in his hand, his gaze riveted to the front-page.

"Something interesting in the news this morning?" she asked.

Randall folded the paper and laid it beside his plate. "Another woman has been murdered. Kendall Wells. She was Quinn Cortez's lawyer."

"Interesting. He's one of the other suspects in Lulu's murder, isn't he?"

"Damn it, Val, I'm not a suspect. The police simply questioned me because my name was in Lulu's date book several times."

"You would be a suspect, my darling, if the police knew you didn't have an alibi for the time Lulu was murdered."

She loved the fact that she held her husband's fate in her hands. If she told the police the truth—that he hadn't been with her during the time he said he was—he would be in terrible trouble. She didn't know if Randall had killed Lulu Vanderley and really didn't care. The woman had been trash. Rich trash, but trash all the same.

Randall picked up the newspaper and held it out to her. "You should take a look at this. The reporter all but accuses Quinn Cortez of killing both Lulu and Kendall Wells. My name isn't even mentioned in the article. That should please you."

"Don't get too smug, darling. Until they make an arrest in the case and actually convict someone of Lulu's murder, you don't dare breathe a sigh of relief."

His facial muscles tensed. *There, that's better,* she thought. She wanted him to worry, wanted him to suffer. Privately, of course.

"You're enjoying this, aren't you?" He glowered at her, pure hatred in his eyes.

"Am I enjoying watching you sweat? Yes, I am. As long as your involvement in this affair doesn't become public knowledge, I'll stand by you and pose as the supportive, loving wife. However, if you were to be charged with Lulu's murder, I would play the wronged, martyred wife who couldn't believe her husband was such a monster."

"I didn't kill Lulu. How many times do I have to tell you?" He slapped the paper against his open palm. "This article implies that the two murders are connected and that connection is Quinn Cortez. For God's sake, Val, I didn't know Kendall Wells. There's no way I can be involved."

"For your sake, I hope the police believe you."

"Read the article." Randall threw the folded newspaper across the table.

When it landed a few inches short of her plate, Valerie glanced at it, then lifted her Haviland china cup and sipped on her morning coffee. Eyeing her husband over the rim of the cup, she said, "Do you have an alibi for the time when

Kendall Wells was murdered? If not, perhaps you'd like for me to lie for you again."

He stared at her, a puzzled look on his face. "Why would I need an alibi?"

"Because it's possible the police will find out that you actually did know Ms. Wells, that her law firm represented your friend, Tom Wilson, six months ago, when he was charged with manslaughter in a hit-and-run case."

Randall's face paled. "I—I'd forgotten all about that. But just because she was one of Tom's lawyers, doesn't mean—"

"It means you did know her. You testified as a character witness for Tom, didn't you?"

"Yes, I did, but—"

"Perhaps you and Ms. Wells became acquainted. Very well acquainted. For all I know you could have had an affair with the woman. A man who's been unfaithful once could easily have been unfaithful twice."

Randall gasped.

Valerie smiled. "Of course, I'd never suggest such a thing to the police. Unless . . ."

"Whatever you want," he said. "Just name your price."

"My price?" She laughed softly. "Whenever I say jump, you'll ask me how high."

Quinn felt like crap. He'd gotten home around midnight, undressed and fallen into bed; but he'd slept fitfully and finally gotten up at six. His life hadn't been so messed up since he'd been a kid, fending for himself and trying his best to stay out of his mother's way. Back then, he hadn't been able to do anything right and that bad karma had followed him around until he'd met Judge Harwood Brown. From that day forward, his luck had changed and he had fought his way to the top. No easy task when you started at rock bottom.

He'd never been an emotional man, having learned at an early age that if you cared too much about somebody they'd just wind up hurting you. But in his own way, he had cared about Lulu. He'd miss her. Miss all that wild exuberance. Why the hell would anybody want to kill her?

And Kendall. He couldn't honestly say he'd loved her, but he had respected her brilliance as a lawyer and her loyalty as a friend. He still couldn't believe she was dead. But she was gone, murdered just as Lulu had been, and if Griffin Powell's theory turned out to be right, then both women had died because they'd been involved with him. Because they had been Quinn Cortez's lovers.

After showering and shaving, Quinn dressed in casual khaki slacks and a button-down light blue shirt. He'd learned early on how important appearances were. Only at the ranch did he ever dress just to suit himself. At all other times, he was aware, even subconsciously, that he needed to project the Quinn Cortez image he had worked so long and hard to obtain. Judd Walker was driving in from Chattanooga this morning, and when meeting with friends, clients, business associates and rivals, Quinn always put his best foot forward. Dress for success was his motto, even in an informal situation.

Judd had told Quinn last night that he'd see him around eight this morning. As Quinn lifted the glass pot from the coffeemaker, he eyed the wall clock. Seven forty-five.

Just as Quinn pulled out a chair from the table, Jace came through the back door, today's newspaper in his hand. He had sent Jace out ten minutes ago to find the morning edition of the *Commercial Appeal*. There was bound to be a big spread about Kendall's murder and he'd bet his last dime that the reporters would connect her death not only to Lulu's recent murder, but to him. After all, as everyone kept reminding him, he was the common denominator, the only link between the two women.

"Marcy and Aaron not up yet?" Jace asked as he laid the newspaper down on the table.

"I haven't heard a peep out of either of them," Quinn said.

Usually Marcy was up by seven at the latest and ordinarily would have had breakfast prepared. Aaron, on the other hand, would sleep until noon, unless told to set his alarm.

"Want me to wake them?"

"Yeah, if they're not up in the next five minutes. I'm expecting Judd Walker, a lawyer from Chattanooga, to show up around eight. We spoke on the phone last night and I may be hiring him to take Kendall's place."

"It's awful about Ms. Wells. I know you liked her a lot, that you two were friends as well as . . ." Jace cleared his throat. "Do the police think you killed her? If they do, they're crazy."

Yes, Kendall had been his friend. And his lover. And a basically good person. Lulu's death had been tragic and had gotten him into a heap of trouble. It seemed impossible to believe someone so vibrant and alive was gone. He'd cared about Lulu, but not in the same way he'd cared for Kendall. In time, Lulu would have been nothing more than an old lover, but Kendall would have always been his friend.

"I'm sure I'll wind up being a suspect in Kendall's murder just as I am in Lulu's, since I don't actually have an alibi for a couple of hours yesterday evening."

"How come you don't have an alibi? You were here with Aaron and Marcy until you left for Ms. Wells's house. There couldn't have been more than thirty minutes while you were driving over there that you were alone."

"I made a stop along the way," Quinn said, but didn't elaborate. He didn't want anyone to know about the odd spells he'd had the night of both murders. Not exactly blackout spells, but something similar. Once things were cleared up about Lulu's and Kendall's deaths and he was allowed to return to Houston, he intended to make an appointment with his personal physician and find out if something was physically wrong with him. The thought had crossed his mind that maybe he had a brain tumor, but he'd dismissed the notion. Quinn Cortez was invincible, wasn't he? He'd spent the past twenty years proving to the world that nothing could con-

quer him, that no matter what the situation, he was the kind
of man who came out on top.

"Didn't anybody see you wherever it was you stopped?"
Jace asked.

Quinn shook his head, put his coffee mug on the table and
then sat. He eyed the newspaper. "Did you take a look at it?"

"Yeah."

Quinn could tell by the tone of Jace's voice that the news
was bad. He picked up the *Commercial Appeal* and flipped it
open so that the entire front-page was visible. Holy shit! It
was a lot worse than he'd imagined. There on the front-page
were three photographs. Kendall on the left. Lulu on the right.
And smack dab in the middle was a picture of him. The
headline read: CORTEZ REAL LADY-KILLER.

"You can sue them for slander, can't you?" Jace's voice
quivered with outrage.

"Probably not," Quinn replied. "My guess is that they
stopped just short of calling me a murderer. There's a thin
line between journalistic freedom and slander."

Quinn scanned the article. Just as he'd thought. The im-
plication was that he was a suspect since the only connection
between the two women was the fact that they had both been
personally involved with Quinn Cortez. Although the expression lady-killer could be taken more than one way, its
use in the headlines would be viewed in the worst possible
light, whereas in the article, the reporter referred to Quinn as
having a reputation as a charming, playboy-type lady-killer.

Quinn's gaze paused on one particular line in the article.
*Although the police are not free to give out the exact details
of either murder, we have discovered that both women were
murdered in the same way, leaving the police to believe the
same person killed both Kendall Wells and Lulu Vanderley.*

"When Judd Walker arrives, I want to see him alone, so
after you wake Aaron and Marcy, tell them I'd like all three
of you to go out for breakfast. On me, of course." Quinn
folded the newspaper, laid it aside and lifted his coffee mug
to his lips.

"Don't you trust us?" Jace asked, a hurt expression on his face. "You think there are things you can tell your lawyer that you can't tell us. Is that why you want us to leave?"

"You shouldn't take my request personally. Stop and think for a minute. What I tell my lawyer is privileged information."

"Oh, yeah, you're right. Sorry. I wasn't thinking."

Quinn reached up and patted Jace on the arm. The boy had little self-esteem and was one of the most sensitive people Quinn had ever known. He seemed to thrive on the attention Quinn gave him. Aaron said that Jace hero-worshiped Quinn. God, he hoped not. Being a professional role model to boys like Jace was one thing, but he sure as hell didn't want anybody imitating his actions in his personal life. He'd never done anything purposefully to harm another person and he'd always tried to be up-front with the parade of women who came and went in his life. But here he was nearly forty and he had no one truly special in his life. No wife. No children. No real family. And until recently, those things hadn't really mattered to him.

He could easily continue being a lady-killer, going from one lovely, entertaining woman to another. Why not? Other men envied him, didn't they? What guy wouldn't want to have his life?

He could tell himself that Lulu's murder, followed by Kendall being killed, had affected his way of thinking about life in general. And although that was true enough, their deaths alone hadn't made him question his personal values. He'd been restless for a couple of years, but especially the past few months. Neither his work nor his love life gave him the pleasure they once had. And then there was Annabelle Vanderley, a lady who'd gotten to him in a way no other woman ever had. They were all wrong for each other, even on a temporary basis. The lady was a class act in every way. He on the other hand had been called a wetback, a bastard (although his birth certificate stated his parents had been married), a son of a bitch, a lady-killer, a womanizer and even a shyster. He had made something of himself, become rich and powerful despite his humble beginnings, but all the money in the world couldn't buy him what Annabelle possessed. Class. Real class. And it had nothing to do with how wealthy she was.

He'd done the lady a big favor last night by allowing her to read Griffin Powell's report on him. Even after learning the truth about him, she would have still given him the benefit of the doubt if he hadn't warned her to run like hell.

You implied that you wanted her the way you'd wanted and had countless other women. You lied to her. She's nothing like any other woman you've ever known. And the way you want her is different because she's different.

"I'll go get Aaron and Marcy up and herd them out of here before your lawyer comes," Jace said. "Is there anything I can do for you before we leave?"

"I can't think of anything," Quinn told him. "Y'all give me about an hour alone with Judd Walker and if I'm not here when y'all get back, I'll leave a note. I figure the police will want to question me sometime today."

Marcy heard a loud gasp. Her eyelids flew open and she shot straight up in bed. Only then did she realize she was completely naked and she wasn't alone. After grabbing the sheet up to cover her breasts, she cut her eyes toward the open door. Jace stood in the doorway, his hazel eyes wide and round behind his glasses, an expression of pure shock on his face.

"What do you think you're doing?" Jace asked in a trembling, wispy voice. "You slept with Aaron? I thought you loved Quinn. How could you—"

"Put a lid on it, will you?" Aaron rolled over, yawned and draped his arm across Marcy's belly. "It's none of your damn business who Marcy sleeps with. And hell, man, we all love Quinn, don't we? But none of us are screwing him, so we gotta look elsewhere for our fun."

Marcy jabbed Aaron in the ribs. Clutching his side and moaning, he scooted away from her and got out of bed. Standing there totally naked, with a morning erection, he winked at her when she glared at him.

"You're vulgar, you know that, Aaron?" Jace frowned, the action scrunching his facial features.

Aaron grabbed his discarded pajama bottoms and slipped into them. "Yeah, so what else is new? What are you doing coming into Marcy's room without knocking?"

"I did knock," Jace said. "But when she didn't say anything, I came in to wake her. Quinn wants us out of the house for an hour or so. He's expecting some lawyer in from Chattanooga anytime now and they'll need some privacy."

Marcy wanted to get up and run, to escape from this embarrassing moment and from having to talk to Aaron after spending the night having sex with him. Three times. The first time, she had pretended he was Quinn, but the next two times, she'd known exactly who was giving her so much pleasure. But that didn't change the fact that she wasn't in love with Aaron. Not the way she was in love with Quinn.

"What's the lawyer's name?" Marcy asked, trying her best to act nonchalantly as she sat up in bed and pulled the sheet up to her neck.

"Judd Walker," Jace said. "Ever heard of him?"

"Judd Walker? Yeah. One of the only cases Quinn ever lost was in Chattanooga, about seven years ago," Marcy said. "Walker was with the DA's office back then. The man's good. I mean if he can beat Quinn . . ."

"He may be good and he might have won that case, but he'll never be as good as Quinn," Jace said adamantly.

"No, of course not." Aaron rolled his eyes toward the ceiling. "Jace, there's something you've got to realize—Quinn Cortez ain't God!"

Jace blushed. "Just get ready, will you? Quinn said for us to go out for breakfast." Just as Jace turned around so that his back was to Marcy and Aaron, the doorbell chimed. "Hurry up, will y'all? That's probably Mr. Walker now."

"Why don't you go let Mr. Walker in," Marcy said. "Aaron and I will be ready to go in just a few minutes."

When Jace disappeared down the hall, Marcy slid out of bed, dragging the top sheet off the bed and wrapping herself in it.

"What the hell are you doing?" Aaron laughed. "Honey, I've already seen it all. And touched it . . . and tasted it."

"Jace is right. You are vulgar." But the way he'd called her honey reminded her so much of the way Quinn called her—and every other woman on earth—honey. Aaron's voice had even sounded a lot like Quinn's.

"I think the kid's a virgin. And probably asexual. I've never seen him ogling a girl or another guy. And if he's ever had a hard-on, I've never noticed it."

"Are you in the habit of noticing other men's hard-ons?"

Aaron laughed. "Hey, the guy and I share a room sometimes. And most guys, especially nineteen-year-olds like Jace wake up with a woody. He doesn't. That kind of thing you notice."

"Whatever you do, don't ever say anything to him about it. He's a sweet kid. A little strange, but sweet."

Aaron came up behind her, grabbed the edge of the sheet and whipped it off her. Standing there naked, Marcy groaned. "Forget it. It's not going to happen," she told him.

"Is that a not now or not ever?"

Good question. Did she want a repeat of last night? What if Jace told Quinn that she and Aaron were sleeping together? So what if he did? Quinn wouldn't give a rat's ass.

She hurriedly picked her clothes up off the floor. "It's a not now."

Aaron popped her on her naked butt. "I'm grabbing a quick shower. Are you sure you don't want to join me?"

Pulling on her pajama bottoms, she turned and glared at him. "Quit wasting time. You heard Jace. Quinn wants us out of here pronto."

"Quinn, Quinn, Quinn. I'm beginning to hate hearing the

man's name. You know you called it out last night, the first time you came."

Marcy blushed. Her fingers stopped in their task of buttoning her pajama top. "I'm sorry."

"Don't sweat it," Aaron said. "I knew you were pretending I was him."

Only the first time, she wanted to tell him, but didn't. It wouldn't be fair to let Aaron think there could ever be more to their relationship than sex. Maybe Quinn could never be hers, but that didn't mean she'd ever stop loving him.

Annabelle nibbled at the whole wheat toast she'd ordered from room service. In between thoughts of Quinn and trying to stop thinking about Quinn, she'd gotten perhaps a total of three hours sleep last night. She'd never obsessed over a man the way she was doing with Quinn Cortez. It was as if the man had somehow infiltrated her mind and had taken possession of her heart. She didn't love him. How could she? But she felt something for him. Something powerful and all-consuming.

He was not the kind of man she wanted or needed. He was nothing like Chris, who'd been kind and gentle, trustworthy and honorable. But what she had felt for Chris bore little resemblance to the raw emotions Quinn evoked in her. There was something primitive and wild in the way she felt about Quinn, a hunger that went soul-deep. The tender emotion called love that she'd shared with Chris had absolutely nothing to do with the savage desire she felt for Quinn.

Unease quivered in her stomach. She dropped the toast to her plate, scooted back her chair and stood. Crossing her arms over her waist, she clasped her elbows and hugged herself.

Pick up the phone, call Griffin and ask him for Quinn's cell phone number. Then call Quinn. Tell him you don't care about all the other women. Tell him that you want him, that you're willing to have an affair.

No! You can't do that. You aren't that kind of woman. If you appease your sexual desire by becoming just one more of Quinn Cortez's women, you'll regret it for the rest of your life.

She had spent most of the nine and a half years that Chris had lived after his car accident completely celibate. They had shared kisses and hugs and even intimate touches, but sex hadn't been possible for Chris. Aunt Perdita had encouraged her to have an affair and even Chris had told her that he would understand if she turned to another man for what he couldn't give her. She had waited five years before having a one-night stand with an old friend, someone she reconnected with on a business trip and had seen only rarely since then. Afterward, the guilt had eaten her alive. Only Aunt Perdita's warning that if she told Chris it would serve no purpose and would hurt him terribly had kept her from confessing her sin. After that one infidelity, she had returned to her nunlike existence until she'd met Lance Holt two years later. Lance's wife had been a paraplegic for three years at that time and he had been completely faithful to her. Annabelle and Lance had met through her work with the Christopher Knox Threadgill Foundation and they had become instant friends. They'd had so much in common, shared the same grief and carried a similar emotional burden. Mutual admiration had fired their passion, never love. Each had understood the other's need for physical gratification without the complications of romance. Their on-again-off-again, six-month affair had ended amicably when Lance's wife died. Her death had set Lance free to live again. And to love again.

Annabelle hadn't been with anyone in four years. She could tell herself that it wasn't Quinn she wanted, it was just sex. That any man would do. But that wasn't true. She'd had numerous chances for one-night stands and brief affairs. And if she'd wanted a serious relationship, even marriage, she could have had her pick of men.

Face, it—you want Quinn Cortez. And only Quinn Cortez.

Why him? Of all the men on earth, why did her body yearn for him? Why did her heart cry out for him?

The police think he could have killed Lulu, she reminded herself.

He didn't kill anyone. Not Lulu. Not Kendall. Not Joy Ellis.

That's what she wanted to believe, that he was incapable of murder, that he was innocent. If he was a murderer, she'd know. On some deep, purely instinctive level, she'd sense it, wouldn't she?

Not necessarily. He's a high-priced lawyer who has gotten filthy rich by using his silver tongue to influence juries. He's a charming womanizer. A real lady-killer.

Annabelle's gaze fell on the newspaper lying beside her breakfast plate. She had read every word of the article and felt heartsick about the ugly picture the reporter had painted, not only of Lulu, but of Kendall and of Quinn. He hadn't stepped over the line between truth and slander, but he'd certainly stretched that line as far as he possibly could. In the hopes of protecting Uncle Louis, she had phoned his house and given instructions to the servants and his nurse to continue making sure her uncle never got his hands on a copy of the *Commercial Appeal.* Especially not this morning's edition.

Annabelle tensed when she heard someone knocking at the door. Her first thought was that her early morning visitor was Quinn. She wanted it to be Quinn.

Please, God, let it be Quinn.

Pulling the lapels of her lavender silk robe together and tying the fabric belt, she hurried to the door and peered through the viewfinder. Her heart sank when she saw Chad George on the other side.

Putting on a happy face, she unlocked and opened the door. "Good morning, sergeant. Won't you come in?"

Before entering, he studied her carefully, as if searching for any sign that she had been contaminated by Quinn Cortez.

Was Chad wondering if Quinn had spent the night, if he might still be here with her?

"Are you all right?" he asked.

"Yes, of course. Why shouldn't I be?"

When Chad walked in, she closed the door and came up beside him.

"I was concerned when you left with Quinn Cortez last night. I wanted to come after you, but . . ." He shrugged. "What you did was dangerous and foolish, Annabelle. You realize that, don't you? Quinn Cortez may have killed two women and you went off alone with him."

Three women, Annabelle thought. *Three of Quinn's former lovers are dead. But he didn't kill them. I know he didn't.*

"I was perfectly safe. Quinn and I went to see Griffin Powell, the investigator we hired to look into Lulu's murder."

"You don't have much faith in the Memphis PD, do you? Do you have any idea how that makes me feel—to know you don't believe I'll bring in Lulu's murderer without any outside help."

He would bring in Lulu's murderer? Chad had said that as if he thought he and he alone would apprehend the person who had killed Lulu and Kendall. It had been an arrogant statement made by an overly confident young man.

"Chad, I'm sorry if I have offended you by leaving with Quinn the way I did last night. It was a spur-of-the-moment decision." She didn't owe Chad any explanations, but there was no point in antagonizing him. "As for hiring Griffin Powell—"

"I can't understand what possessed you to go into partnership with Cortez to hire a private investigator."

Annabelle sighed. "Both Quinn and I had contacted Mr. Powell and he refused to take the case unless it was a joint effort. Since we both want the same thing—to find out who murdered Lulu—we saw no reason not to join forces."

When Chad reached out and gently grasped her shoulders, she tensed; and when he smiled, her muscles tightened even more. "Annabelle, Annabelle, you're far too trusting. Don't you think that Cortez would use you if he thought it would help him? You can't trust him. You don't dare. Everything points to him as the man who killed both Lulu and Kendall Wells."

"What do you mean everything points to him?"

Chad eased his hands down her arms, all the way to her wrists, then grabbed her hands and held them. "I'm not at liberty to discuss details. Just believe me when I tell you that he's a dangerous man and you have to stay away from him."

Annabelle's mind weighed everything Chad had said and came to the conclusion that there weren't really any details he wasn't at liberty to discuss concerning evidence against Quinn. That meant Chad had lied to her. But why?

He's jealous!

She pulled her hands from his grasp. "I won't be seeing Quinn again, unless it's absolutely necessary."

Chad's smile spread from ear to ear, his expression like a little kid's, one who had just been told he was being given the toy he'd always wanted but thought he'd never have. A sense of uneasiness settled over Annabelle. Chad saw her as that toy, as a prize, something to be won or lost. And he instinctively knew that Quinn Cortez was his greatest competition.

The only problem with his reasoning was that she was no man's prize. He could neither win nor lose her. There was no competition. No decision to be made as to who the better man was.

Annabelle's heart had already decided for her.

Chapter 17

Jim Norton hadn't seen Griffin Powell in several years, not since Powell's agency represented a local art dealer, Monty Addis, whose gallery had been robbed of several million in paintings and sculptures. On that case, he and Griffin had become the buffers between Addis and the police department. Neither had trusted the other. The police had suspected an inside job and all but accused Addis of stealing his own paintings. Addis had been very vocal about how inept he thought the police were and had told the press and everyone who would listen that that was the reason he'd hired renowned investigator Griffin Powell to find out who had actually stolen his property. As it turned out, Jim and Griffin figured out that Addis's wife and her current boyfriend were the culprits.

When Griffin had phoned Jim yesterday, he'd hadn't been surprised. He knew his old UT teammate was representing Quinn Cortez and Annabelle Vanderley. Now, those two were a real odd couple, if they actually were a couple. Being a fairly good judge of character—despite his judgment failing him when he'd married Mary Lee—he pegged Ms. Vanderley to be exactly what she seemed to be: a rich, cultured blue blood. And Quinn Cortez might be rich and powerful and feared by his opponents in a court of law, but the man was, by nature, a ruffian. A more generous way to describe him might be as a diamond in the rough. All the fancy clothes, Rolex watches, Porsches and manicures would never turn Cortez into a gentleman.

Griffin's assistant, Sanders, opened the door to the suite and ushered Jim into the lounge. "Lieutenant Norton," Sanders announced, then disappeared into one of the two adjoining rooms.

Griffin sat at the dining table, a cup of coffee in one hand and a folded copy of this morning's *Commercial Appeal* in the other. When he glanced at Jim, he tossed the paper down on the table and invited him over with a wave of his hand.

"Join me for breakfast," Griffin said. "I ordered a couple of Western omelettes and buttermilk biscuits. I seem to recall that's what you had the last time we ate breakfast together."

"You have a good memory." Jim walked over to the table, lifted the coffee pot and poured the cup sitting by his plate full of the hot black brew.

"I appreciate your meeting with me," Griffin said. "I assume you know I'm representing Quinn Cortez."

Jim pulled out a chair and sat. "And Annabelle Vanderley as well."

Griffin nodded. "Yes, and Ms. Vanderley."

"Those two are an odd combination, don't you think? For her it has to be kind of like sleeping with the enemy." Jim lifted his cup to his lips.

Griffin eyed him speculatively. "I wouldn't put it that way. Not exactly."

"Then there's nothing personal between them?"

"I didn't say that." Griffin removed the cover from his plate and set it aside, then picked up his fork and sliced into his omelette. "Whether or not there's anything of a personal nature taking place between Quinn and Annabelle is nobody's business, but theirs, is it? As for my working for both of them—it's a compromise. Since they contacted me practically simultaneously, it was either say no to both of them or ask them to join forces."

"I'm surprised they agreed. Especially Ms. Vanderley. She doesn't seem the type who would be easily charmed by Cortez's Latin charisma."

"Why not? She's a woman."

Jim chuckled. "Shot you down, did she, Griff?"

"I'll never tell." Grinning, Griffin speared a slice of omelette and brought it to his mouth.

After removing the lid from his plate, Jim split open a biscuit, buttered it and then smeared it with blackberry jam. How the hell had Griffin remembered blackberry was his favorite? The guy had a mind like a steel trap. Back in their days at UT, he'd been one of those rare athletes who'd starred academically as well as in the sports arena. The big guy had graduated summa cum laude. Of course, Jim hadn't done too badly himself, graduating cum laude. But on the field and in the classroom, Griffin Powell had been The Star. Funny thing was, Jim had never minded being a runner-up; after all, every other guy at UT had been, too.

The whole world knew why Jimmy Norton hadn't turned pro. A running back with a couple of bum knees wasn't worth two cents to a pro team, even if he was otherwise in top physical shape. But no one knew why Griffin Powell hadn't gone on to pro-football stardom. The first time Jim had met up with Griffin again, a good eight years ago, he'd wanted to ask him what had happened to him. But a couple of subtle statements his old buddy made let him know right away that those mysterious ten years of Griffin's life when he'd disappeared from the face of the earth was an off-limits subject.

The two men shared their meal, occasionally talking about sports, the Memphis night life, Elvis, and the cool March weather. When they finished their omelettes and both were on their third cup of coffee, Griffin turned to Jim and narrowed his gaze.

Serious talk now, Jim thought.

"I'm not asking for any favors," Griffin said. "And I certainly wouldn't expect you to reveal any confidential information. It's not my style to try to take advantage of an old friendship, so rest assured I'm not going to test your integrity."

"That's good because my integrity is about all I've got left and some people question whether I've still got that."

Griffin nodded. "A nasty divorce, alimony and child support payments, a kid you see only when your ex says you can, a career going nowhere and just enough money to get by."

"Humph." Smiling, Jim shook his head. "What'd you do, run a check on me?" He threw up a hand in a forget-I-asked gesture. "Sure you did."

"If you ever get tired of spinning your wheels with the Memphis PD, give me a call. The Powell Agency can always use a top-notch investigator."

"Is that what you think I am?" It had been a long time since anyone had praised Jim in any way, on the job or in his personal life.

"I know that's what you are."

"You heard about my breakdown a few years ago, didn't you? And the rumors about what some people think I did?"

Griffin nodded. "Yeah, I heard. We all have our breaking points. And what you did or didn't do—" Griffin shrugged.

"I'll keep the job offer in mind."

"It's an open-ended offer. No time limit."

Something to think about, Jim told himself. Of course accepting a job with Griffin's PI agency would take him away from Memphis a lot and that meant taking him away from Kevin.

"Right now, this morning, what is it you want from me?" Jim asked.

After placing his empty cup on the table, Griffin turned all the way around in his chair and focused on Jim. "I want your opinion."

Scrunching his face, Jim stared at Griffin inquisitively. "My opinion?"

"I know y'all will be questioning Quinn Cortez this morning about Kendall Wells's murder. Right now, it seems the only person with any connection to both women was Cortez."

"Yeah, it seems that way."

"Do you think Cortez killed Lulu and Kendall?"

"Ah, that's it, is it? You've already decided what you think, haven't you? But you're not a hundred percent sure you're right. Are you going by instinct alone or do you have evidence to back up your opinion?"

"We aren't exchanging confidences, remember? Not yet anyway."

Jim flicked his tongue over his front teeth. "Okay. You want my opinion on Cortez, I'll give it to you. He may be a womanizer and a shyster and under the right circumstances is probably capable of murder, but I don't think he killed either woman. The way I see it, he just didn't have a strong enough motive to kill Lulu, not even if she was carrying his baby. And what possible motive could he have had to kill his lawyer?"

"Thanks, Jim. I agree. I don't think Cortez killed Lulu or Kendall, but I do think his relationship with both women is what got them killed."

Uh-oh. A red warning light went off in Jim's brain. "You know something we don't know, don't you?"

"Maybe."

"Withholding evidence is—"

"I'm working on a theory," Griffin said. "If it pans out, I'll inform Cortez and Annabelle first and then call you. In the meantime, do what you can to keep the DA and Director Danley from railroading Quinn." When Jim gave Griffin a that's-asking-for-a-favor look, Griffin chuckled. "Hey, if y'all arrest the wrong man, how's it going to look to the press when we nail the real killer and prove Cortez innocent?"

*   *   *

Not in a million years had Quinn ever thought the day would come when he'd hire Judd Walker as his lawyer. If only a week ago someone had painted this peculiar scenario—the two of them sitting across the table from each other, sharing a pot of coffee and discussing Quinn's legal problems—he would have laughed in their face. Actually, he'd have said that it would be a cold day in hell before he'd ever hire Walker to be his lawyer.

Undoubtedly, hell had frozen over. One thing he knew for sure, his life had turned into hell now that he was under suspicion for two murders.

"Let's get one thing straight up front," Walker said. "You and I don't have to like each other for me to represent you and for me to do my very best for you."

Quinn grinned. "That's always my sentiments when I take on a new client."

"There's one difference, Cortez."

Quinn cocked an inquisitive brow.

"You've probably represented more than one person you didn't think was innocent, as most lawyers have. I'm not one of those lawyers. If I don't believe in a client's innocence, I don't take the case."

"Every person deserves the right to an attorney, even the guilty."

"I agree. But I don't have to be the lawyer to defend them."

"You're a man with scruples, high moral values and a trust fund from granddaddy moneybags."

Not seeming at all offended by Quinn's last comment, Walker laughed. "And here all this time I thought you didn't like me because I was one of only a few opponents who ever beat your pants off in a court of law. But actually you hate me because I was born with a silver spoon in my mouth and you weren't."

"Like you said, we don't have to like each other. So,

what's it going to be? Will you represent me or not? Am I innocent or guilty?"

"I'm here, aren't I?"

"Meaning?"

"Meaning Griffin Powell thinks you're innocent and the man has unerring instinct."

"It's good to know that Powell believes I didn't kill Lulu or Kendall. But what do you think?"

"I think you're a very smart man and if you wanted to kill somebody, you'd do it in a way where no one would ever suspect you. Either you have no connection whatsoever to the two murders or you're living a double life. Or maybe somebody's setting you up."

Quinn's body instantly tensed at the thought that someone might be setting him up. Had someone killed three women in order to try to pin the rap on him? If so, who and why? "Powell told you about the third woman, didn't he?"

"Joy Ellis? Yes, he told me. He also told me that he thinks there's a possibility that he'll find others. Other murdered women who were once your lovers. He'll have to turn the information over to the police if they haven't already acquired it from their own sources by that time. Since he's representing Ms. Vanderley as well as you, all information he acquires will be shared by the two of you. Anyway, if Griffin discovers that there are other former lovers of yours who have been murdered, it may or may not work in your favor. The police may think you've killed all of them or they could start looking for another suspect, someone with a reason to want to frame you."

"God, I hope there haven't been any others."

"We'll face that problem if and when the time comes. For now, we need to concentrate on the two murders in which you are a suspect. Let's go over every minute of your time from when you left here yesterday until you arrived at Kendall Wells's house. Then I want you to tell me everything about your trip from Nashville to Memphis the night Lulu Vanderley was murdered."

Quinn nodded. "I can give you details if you want them, but the bottom line is that I don't have an alibi for the time when either murder occurred. I was on the road from Nashville to Memphis when Lulu was killed, but I can't prove I didn't arrive earlier than I said. The same thing for Kendall's murder. I was driving from here to her house when she was murdered, but I could have gotten there earlier, killed her, left and then went back to make it look as if I was innocent."

Walker frowned. "What I'm hearing, but you're not saying, is that there's a period of time you can't account for in each instance. Want to tell me what you were doing each time?"

Quinn tensed. No, he didn't want to tell anyone about his odd blackout spells, not even his new lawyer. Especially not his new lawyer. Appearing weak or vulnerable in any way before Judd Walker was the last thing Quinn wanted. Besides, admitting to having experienced strange sleepy spells that had compelled him to stop driving on both occasions, when he was on his way to Lulu's and Kendall's homes, wouldn't help prove his innocence. On the contrary—if he couldn't account for an hour or more of his time during which each murder occurred, it could actually make him look guilty.

But a client should be completely honest with his lawyer, otherwise if a secret came out later on, it could cause immeasurable harm to the case. But Quinn hadn't been arrested and charged with a crime. Not yet. If that happened, there would be time enough to confess his secrets to Walker.

"He's got to be the luckiest damn son of a bitch in the world." Chad George stood outside the interview room and glared at the two men inside sitting side by side and talking quietly to each other.

"Why do you say that?" Jim knew full well Chad was referring to the fact that Quinn Cortez had—overnight—hired himself the best damn lawyer in the state of Tennessee.

"How did he pull that off, I wonder." Chad huffed. "Rumor

is those two hate each other and have ever since they butted heads in court years ago and Cortez lost the case."

"It took balls for Cortez to contact Judd Walker," Jim said.

"Yeah, well, I hear the guy has a set of big brass ones."

"Come on. We might as well get this over with. I think we're wasting our time trying to pin this on Cortez when we don't have any evidence."

"We'll find some. It's out there somewhere."

"And if it isn't, then what? We'll have wasted a lot of valuable time that we should have been using to track down the real killer."

Chad focused his hard gaze on Jim. "What's with you? Did Griffin Powell persuade you to go easy on Cortez? Is that it? Your old teammate, the former UT god, told you Cortez is innocent so naturally if Griffin Powell says it, then it has to be so."

Jim took a deep breath. "Don't push me too far, boy."

Chad's cheeks flushed. Without saying another word, he entered the interview room and introduced himself to Judd Walker. Jim followed a couple of minutes later and closed the door.

"This is my partner, Lieutenant Norton," Chad introduced him to Walker.

"Is my client being charged with a crime?" Walker asked, forgoing any pleasantries.

"No," Jim said.

"Then why are we here?" Walker looked right at Jim, completely ignoring Chad.

"We just need to ask him a few questions because of his involvement with Kendall Wells, both professionally and personally. And because Mr. Cortez is already connected to another murder that has certain similarities to Ms. Wells's murder."

"Mr. Cortez has no information that can help you with your investigation into the Kendall Wells murder," Walker said.

Chad's lips curved into a hint of a smile, as if he were amused by something only he knew. He zeroed in on Cortez. Their gazes clashed.

"Where were you yesterday evening between four and seven?" Chad asked.

"I was at the condo I've leased here in Memphis until a little after four," Cortez said. "I phoned Kendall's office and was told she'd left early to have drinks with someone and then was heading home. You can check with my assistant, Marcy Sims, about the time. I drove from my condo across town, made one stop—and no, I don't think anyone can collaborate that—then I drove straight to Kendall's. The police were already on the scene when I arrived."

"Are you saying it took you more than two hours to drive from your condo to Kendall Wells's home?" Jim asked, already aware that the trip, even in late afternoon traffic shouldn't have taken more than thirty minutes, if that.

"No," Cortez replied. "I stopped before arriving at Kendall's. I wasn't feeling well. It was probably something I'd eaten for lunch. I pulled over into a parking area and found a bathroom. I sat there in the car for quite a while, waiting to make sure I wasn't going to be sick again."

Jim didn't believe Cortez. There was something off about his story, but he couldn't quite put his finger on what it was. While Jim was contemplating his next question, Chad leaned over the desk, planted both hands palms down and got right up in Cortez's face. He jumped in and rattled off a series of aggressive, accusatory questions in rapid succession. Jim had seen his partner use the machine-gun barrage of questioning before to unnerve a suspect. But Cortez appeared as cool as a cucumber. With his black eyes constricted into narrow slits, he sat there staring at Chad, not responding by word or mannerism.

When Chad paused, backed off and stood up straight, Judd Walker rose from his chair and said, "The next time you request my client's presence, I suggest you read him his rights and be prepared to arrest him. Sergeant George, you walked a fine line between interviewing and interrogating."

Quinn Cortez stood.

"We're through here," Walker said.

And without another word from anyone, Cortez and Walker left the interview room, neither of them so much as glancing back at Jim and his partner. When Chad made a move to go after them, Jim called to him.

"Let 'em go."

Chad whipped around and with most of the other detectives stopping whatever they were doing to stare at them, he glared at Jim. "Are you going to let him go, just like that?"

"We can't arrest him." Jim crossed the distance that separated him from his partner, not wanting to share their disagreement with all the other on-duty officers. "Cortez answered our questions—"

"He damn well didn't answer all of *my* questions."

"Did you expect him to? No, you didn't. Walker saw through what you were trying to do and so did Cortez." Jim grabbed Chad's arm and pulled him into a private corner. "Did you forget that you were dealing with two brilliant and experienced lawyers? The kind of scare tactics that work on some punk are wasted on guys like Cortez and Walker."

"If you know so damn much, then what do you suggest?"

"I suggest we do our jobs and continue investigating two murder cases," Jim said. "And until we have some real evidence against Cortez, we can't rule out the possibility that he's innocent, that someone else killed Lulu and Kendall."

Annabelle replaced the telephone receiver, her hand slightly unsteady. The coroner's office had just called. They would be releasing Lulu's body tomorrow afternoon. She could make arrangements to take her cousin home, back to Austinville, Mississippi, where the Vanderley roots grew deep in the rich, fertile, Deep South soil.

She had spent the better part of the afternoon finalizing the preliminary arrangements, which was all she'd been able to do until a definite date could be set. Now, she could set the date. Everything had already been put in motion, every detail planned. Uncle Louis had made it clear that no expense was to be spared, that he wanted and expected this last farewell to be done with pomp and ceremony. A funeral done in true Vanderley style.

There had been too many funerals in the past few years. She had lost too many people she loved. Her parents. Her Aunt Meta Anne. Her fiancé. And now her cousin. Unless he was far stronger physically than Annabelle thought, it would be only a matter of time before she lost Uncle Louis, too. Lulu's death had been the final blow to his failing health. Knowing that her uncle's days were numbered had given Annabelle an even greater incentive to follow his wishes when she planned Lulu's funeral.

A part of her wished she could skip these next few days. Of course, she couldn't. She would do what she always did— be the strong, in-charge, in-control member of the family. Others depended on her. She couldn't let them down, certainly not now.

If only she didn't have to go through this ordeal alone. Even with Aunt Perdita at her side, she would have to be the tower of strength for everyone else, including the feisty Perdita.

Images of Quinn Cortez suddenly flashed through her mind. What was it about the man that made her overlook his obvious flaws? Not since her father died had there been a big, strong man in her life, someone with broad shoulders she could lean on and loving arms to comfort her. If only she could rely on Quinn right now. If only she could turn to him and ask him to stand at her side and see her through the difficult days ahead. In a perfect world, it would be possible. But not in the real world.

Chapter 18

Annabelle had wanted to stay in her own home, surrounded by wonderful memories of her parents and the life she had shared with them. What a comfort it would have been to settle back into her normal routine, with her own four-poster bed, her own worn and comfy leather chair in the library and her own staff, who helped simplify her life. But Uncle Louis had insisted she stay here, at Vanderley Hall, giving her little choice since she knew how badly he needed her. Wythe would be of little help to his father or anyone else. And the thought of possibly having to fight off her cousin's unwanted advances both nauseated and unnerved her. Thank God her aunt Perdita had arrived back in Austinville this evening and had agreed to come with her to Vanderley Hall.

Dinner had been a solemn affair, with Uncle Louis sitting at the head of the table, picking at his food and wiping the tears from his eyes as he talked about his daughter. When they left the dining room, Wythe aiding his fragile father, and went into the front parlor, Hiram and one of the maids followed. Once Wythe helped ease Louis down onto the antique Victorian rosewood settee, he stood vigil directly behind his father. The servants set up the silver service and poured after-dinner coffee from a hundred-and-fifty-year-old silver coffeepot into hundred-and-fifty-year-old china cups.

When Uncle Louis accepted his coffee, his hands trembled, sloshing the black liquid from the cup onto the saucer. Wythe quickly took the cup and saucer from him and handed them back to Hiram.

"Please give Daddy another cup, one not quite so full," Wythe said, his tone critical.

Without saying a word, Hiram did as he was told.

"You have contacted everyone, haven't you?" Louis looked directly at Annabelle. "The governor, Senator Johnson, Senator—"

"Now, don't fret. I have everything under control," Annabelle said as she accepted the cup of coffee the maid offered her. "Everyone will be there Friday for the funeral and most folks will show up tomorrow evening for visitation."

"I want her here, not at the funeral home." Louis cleared his throat in a wheezing cough.

"I've already arranged for Mr. Turberville to set everything up right here in the front parlor. Lulu will be brought home, here to Vanderley Hall, for visitation tomorrow evening."

"You'll take her things over to the funeral home in the morning." Louis glanced up at the portrait hanging over the mantel. "I want her to wear that dress. The one she wore for her debutante ball."

"Yes, I know." Annabelle set her untouched coffee aside, got up and walked over to her uncle. After sitting beside him, she reached over and took his trembling, age-spotted hands into her gentle grasp. "Naturally, you'll want her to wear Grandmother's pearls, the necklace and matching earrings. And I've already arranged with Marty to do Lulu's hair and makeup. And Jayne, at Austinville Flowers, has made certain that a hundred orchids will be available to form the blanket for the casket."

Uncle Louis gave her hand a frail squeeze. "I should have known you would handle everything to perfection."

"Yes, I've done my best to think of everything that you'd want, everything that will make tomorrow and Friday wonderful tributes to Lulu. I've arranged for a string quartet for tomorrow evening. A bagpiper will play before and after Friday's service and the quartet will accompany Marcella Casale when she sings at the funeral."

Louis sighed. "You have thought of everything, my dear Annabelle."

"Doesn't she always?" Wythe said, his voice pleasant, but the look he gave Annabelle chilled her.

Ignoring Wythe completely, she smiled at her uncle. "You look tired. Don't you think you should let Hiram see you upstairs to bed?"

Louis nodded. "I am weary, but all I've done for days is stay in bed and rest."

"That's exactly what you should be doing," Perdita told him. "The only way you'll make it through these next couple of days is if you take care of yourself."

"I'm not ready to die yet," Louis said adamantly. "I'll get through tomorrow and the day after by concentrating on living to see Lulu's murderer caught and brought to justice."

Pivoting slightly to his right, Louis glanced up at his son. "Wythe told me that the Memphis police have a suspect, someone they believe killed my Lulu. A man named Quinn Cortez, some Texas lawyer who was romancing my little girl. They're on the verge of arresting the man, aren't they? When they do, I want to go to Memphis and see this animal face-to-face."

Annabelle tensed, her grasp inadvertently tightening on her uncle's hand. "I'm afraid Wythe misinformed you, Uncle Louis. Mr. Cortez is only one of several people the police have questioned. He had a date with Lulu the night she was murdered. He . . . he was the person who found her body. But he didn't kill her."

Louis glared at Wythe. "Is that true? Did you lie to me about this man?"

Wythe's cheeks flushed just enough to be noticeable.

"No, I didn't lie. I just gave you my opinion and the opinion of Sergeant George, one of the detectives investigating Lulu's murder. Annabelle has chosen to believe Mr. Quinn is innocent."

"A man is innocent until proven guilty," Louis said. "No one wants Lulu's killer caught more than I do, but we must make certain the police arrest the right man."

"And they will," Annabelle squeezed her uncle's hand again. "Now, enough talk for this evening. I insist Hiram see you upstairs, after which your nurse can take over."

"She'll just give me another one of those damn sleeping pills," Louis grumbled, but didn't protest when Hiram came forward and assisted Annabelle in getting him up on his feet. Standing there, a bit shaky, he turned to Perdita and said, "I don't want to go to sleep yet. It's not even nine o'clock. Why don't you come up with me and regale me with tales of your recent trips. You've always been an entertaining storyteller."

Perdita looked to Annabelle for approval and when she offered her aunt a yes-please-go-with-him nod, Perdita got up, walked over and slipped her arm through Louis's. "Let me tell you about the English earl I met at Joyce and Whit Morris's daughter's wedding recently. The man was simply mad for me. And to be honest, if he'd been single, I might have accepted his offer to fly away to Barbados with him."

Louis chuckled lightly as Hiram and Perdita led him from the parlor. Annabelle sighed, grateful to her aunt for putting even a faint smile on Uncle Louis's face.

"You should be grateful to me for not telling Daddy just how involved you are with the man who killed Lulu," Wythe said, smiling wickedly. "And if you'd like for me to keep your secret, I can think of numerous ways you can persuade me."

Annabelle spun around and pinned her cousin with a sharp glare. "Don't you dare threaten me, you spineless weasel. I'm not the one who needs to be concerned about Uncle Louis discovering my secrets—you are."

Wythe's smile vanished. "Whatever you think you know, you have no proof."

"You think not?"

Studying her as if trying to probe her mind, Wythe focused on Annabelle's face. A sheen of perspiration dampened his upper lip. "You'd never tell Daddy, never give him any proof of my sins, now would you? You care too much about the old man to hurt him that way."

"You're right. Up to a point. I love Uncle Louis and I'd never want to hurt him, especially not now that he's lost Lulu. But be warned, cousin dear, the day will come when no one will be able to protect you."

The tension drained away from Wythe, his sudden relaxation quite visible as his mouth curved in a hint of a smile. "Has any man ever told you how extremely sexy you are when you're being strong and assertive?"

"You're beneath contempt."

When Wythe walked toward her, his movements slow and threatening, Annabelle forced herself to stand her ground. When he came right up to her, she titled her chin and locked gazes with him.

"What kind of lover is Cortez?" Wythe asked, standing so close that she could smell the wine he'd drunk with supper on his breath. "Does he like it rough? His type usually does. Has he done really bad things to you? And did you enjoy it? I'll bet you did, didn't you?"

Annabelle slapped Wythe. No thought went into the action, only reflex.

Gasping, he put his hand to his red cheek and stared at her, obviously stupefied by what she'd done. Wide-eyed, his body taut, he caressed the spot where she'd hit him. "Vicious little bitch, aren't you? Now that I know you like to play rough—"

"You will keep your distance from me or you'll be sorry. Do you hear me?"

"And if I don't, what will you do, sic Cortez on me?" He

made the comment sarcastically, with a wavering smile on his lips.

She smiled back at Wythe and, hoping to unnerve him, said, "Perhaps I will tell Quinn that you've been sexually harassing me. Wonder what he'd do to you?"

While Wythe stood there with his mouth agape and his eyes big as saucers, Annabelle turned around and walked out of the front parlor. Once in the foyer, she hurried to the staircase and flew upstairs to the guest bedroom that had been prepared for her. Not until she was inside her room, with the door locked, did she feel safe. Pressing her back against the door, her breathing erratic, she sucked in huge gulps of air.

Wythe was a pervert, a sexual predator who should have been sent to prison years ago, but the Vanderley power, money and prestige had protected him. Even she had protected his vile secrets. For Uncle Louis's sake. For the sake of the Vanderley name. And because Lulu had begged her to never tell anyone. But how much longer could she hide the ugly truth?

The visitation reception held at Vanderley Hall for Lulu had been a grand affair, with everyone who was anyone within their social circle in attendance. Uncle Louis had told Annabelle several times how pleased he was with the turnout and with how beautifully she had planned the event, which had been executed to perfection. As the evening wound down and the huge crowd dissipated, Annabelle sought her aunt and found her in the dining room, a small plate of boiled shrimp in her hand.

"I think Uncle Louis held up quite well, don't you?"

"His nurse had him so doped up he barely knew where he was," Perdita replied as she dipped a shrimp into the cocktail sauce. "But that's good. God knows how he'd get through this otherwise. I thought my heart would break when he leaned over and kissed Lulu good-bye." She dropped the sauce-coated shrimp into her mouth.

"I wish he would let Mr. Turberville take her back to the funeral home tonight. But he gave me strict instructions to keep her here until time to move the coffin to the church tomorrow afternoon."

"Maybe you should disregard his instructions just this once. After all, if Lulu's still here in the morning, you know he'll want to see her again . . . to say good-bye again."

Hugging herself, Annabelle huffed softly. "Oh, God. I wish this was all over."

Perdita set her plate down on the nearby table, then put her arm around Annabelle's shoulders. "I haven't been much help, have I? It's just not right that you bear all the burden. That worthless Wythe should be helping you."

"I don't want Wythe anywhere near me," Annabelle said without thinking.

Perdita eyed her curiously. "Has that creature done something—"

"Shh . . ." Annabelle cautioned her aunt when several members of the catering staff entered the dining room.

"Is it all right for us to begin clearing away now, Ms. Vanderley?" Joanna McIntyre asked. Joanna was the caterer from Jackson that the Vanderley and Austin families always used.

"Yes, certainly. I believe just about everyone has left now."

"Why don't you and I say good night to the few stragglers, send them on their way and then go upstairs?" Perdita urged Annabelle toward the foyer. "After we get ready for bed, I think we should talk, don't you?"

Annabelle sighed. Her aunt was the only person she could trust with her secrets, the only person who knew that Wythe had once tried to rape her.

"Yes, we need to talk." Annabelle grunted. "I need to talk.

I need someone trustworthy who'll listen and tell me what to do."

Perdita slipped her arm around Annabelle's waist and herded her out of the dining room. Pausing in the doorway, she looked at Joanna McIntyre. "Prepare two plates with a variety of food and send them upstairs to Miss Annabelle's room in about twenty minutes, along with a bottle of wine."

"Yes, ma'am," Joanna replied.

"I don't think I can eat a bite," Annabelle said. "I seem to have lost my appetite."

"Nonsense. A decent meal is just what you need, along with a trustworthy confidante."

When Perdita winked at her, Annabelle couldn't help smiling. Pausing in the foyer, she put her arms around her aunt and hugged her. "You just don't know how glad I am that you're here."

I must be very careful. Locking my door and turning off the lights should be enough to deter anyone from bothering me. If they knew, they wouldn't understand. No one understood. Sometimes, even I don't understand why I do the things I do.

But I'm not crazy. And I'm not bad. She was wrong about my being a bad boy. I tried to tell her, but she wouldn't listen. It was her fault. All her fault.

"I'm sorry, Mama. I'm so sorry."

Why should I be sorry? I don't have to justify myself to her. Not any longer. I will never again have to plead for mercy. I have all the power now. The power of life and death.

You'd be so proud of me, Mama. I put them out of their misery, just as I did you. I kill them softly. Gently. No pain. It's so much better for them to die than to suffer the way you did for so many years. Didn't you tell me that over and over again? Didn't you say that you'd rather be dead than to live in such agony?

I can see moonlight coming in through the windows now that my eyes have adjusted to the dark. But if I get out my case and look at my souvenirs, I'll need to use a flashlight. And I'll have to be very quiet. I don't want anyone to pass by my room and think I'm still awake.

Maybe I shouldn't take the case from where I've hidden it. After all, it's been only three days since I looked at it, when I placed the latest addition with the others in my collection.

But you want to look at them again. You know you do, that haunting inner voice said. After all, that's the reason you carry the case with you, isn't it? So you'll have them with you, so you can look at them whenever you'd like.

Yes. Yes, of course. I can do whatever I want to do. No one can tell me that I can't take the case from its hiding place, open it and look at the contents.

That's it. Go over there and get the carryall, then lift up the bottom flap.

It's so simple. I can see the carryall lying on the floor be-side the TV, just where I left it.

Pick it up.

Yes, I will.

Lay it on the bed.

I am.

Lift up the bottom flap.

I need a flashlight.

You left the flashlight on the TV stand. Just reach out and get it.

Yes, of course.

The light shone brightly, focusing on the hidden compartment in the carryall.

Just look at those five small glass bottles glistening in the yellow-white glow. Lined up, side-by-side, they are a beauti-ful sight.

My souvenirs.

After what I did for Mama and those other women, killing

*them in the kindest way possible and ending their torment, I
deserved to take some small token, didn't I? Something to
remember them by.*

*I wait until they're dead, until they can't feel any pain, be-
fore I do it. I'd never want to hurt someone because I know
how it feels to hurt. To hurt really bad.*

Inside the case were his prizes. Five identical clear glass
bottles, filled with formaldehyde. Each one containing an
index finger.

Aren't they beautiful?

*Touch them gently. Remember to show the proper rever-
ence. Trace your finger up and down each bottle, the last one
first.*

Kendall.

Her fingernails had been painted a bright red.

Now the next to last.

Lulu.

Her finger was long and slender, just as she was.

What's that sound? Is there someone outside my door?

*I have to put my prizes away. I can't let anyone else see
them. No one would understand.*

Hide them. Do it quickly. Now!

Wearing a bright turquoise kaftan trimmed in heavy beige
lace, Perdita Austin sprawled out on the chaise lounge in
Annabelle's bedroom. With her stylishly short, salt-and-pepper
hair swept away from her face and all her makeup removed,
Perdita still didn't look her age. Anyone would guess her to
be at least ten years younger than the age on her birth certificate, which Annabelle knew was fifty-seven.

Perdita balanced a plate, piled high with edible delights,
in her lap and held the crystal wineglass with her right hand.
"If you don't eat at least half the things on your plate, I shall
be very cross with you, Annie Belly."

Sitting at the antique desk by the windows, Annabelle

chuckled softly as she glanced at her aunt. "It's been years since you called me Annie Belly."

"Oh, my sweet girl, you're like my own daughter and I'm afraid I've neglected you lately, ever since Christopher died." Perdita shook her head sadly. "I suppose I thought that once he was gone, you'd be too busy living and loving to need me. But I was wrong, wasn't I? There hasn't been anyone since . . . well, since Christopher died, has there?"

"No, no one."

"Why ever not?" Perdita popped a chocolate-dipped strawberry into her mouth.

Annabelle shrugged. "I haven't met anyone."

Perdita eyed her contemplatively. "That's nonsense. The world is full of gorgeous, eligible men." Squinting, Perdita scrutinized Annabelle pensively. "You haven't let that nasty incident with Wythe turn you off men, have you?"

Annabelle gasped. "Good God, no."

"You should have called the police that night and had the scoundrel arrested. It makes my blood run cold to think what might have happened if he hadn't been drunk and you were able to coldcock him with that marble statue." Perdita tsk-tsked. "Damn shame about that lovely statue. I brought it back to you from Venice."

"Exposing Wythe for what he is would kill Uncle Louis."

"If he ever tries anything like that with you again, I'll cut off his pecker with a dull knife."

Annabelle smiled. "And you would, wouldn't you?"

"Most definitely."

"I don't think that will be necessary. I'm perfectly capable of dealing with Wythe. He's made numerous overtures since that night, but he never puts his words into action. I actually think that after I knocked him out and he had to get stitches in his head at the ER, he's just a little bit afraid of me."

Perdita giggled. "I love the thought of Wythe being afraid

of you." She sliced into a piece of prime rib, speared it with her fork and lifted it to her mouth.

Annabelle's cell phone, tucked away in her purse, jingled the distinctive Mozart tune she had programed into it.

"Is that your phone?" Perdita asked, her mouth half full.

"It's my cell phone." Annabelle shoved back the chair, hurried across the room to the nightstand where she'd laid her purse earlier in the day. After unzipping the side compartment, she retrieved the phone, flipped it open and placed it to her ear. Surely this wasn't a business call. Not at ten in the evening, the day before Lulu's funeral.

"Hello."

"Annabelle?"

Her heart skipped a beat when she recognized the voice of her caller. "Yes."

"You probably don't want to talk to me, but I had to call," Quinn Cortez said. "If you want me to hang up, I will."

"No, don't. It's all right. Really." Annabelle glanced across the room at her aunt Perdita who was watching her like a hawk.

"I've been worrying about you," Quinn told her. "Under different circumstances, I'd be there tomorrow. I would give anything if I could be there for you."

"I wish—I wish the same thing."

"How are you? Really."

"I'm all right."

"You don't sound all right."

How could this man who barely knew her, whom she'd met less than a week ago, conclude only from the sound of her voice that she was barely holding on, barely managing to put up a brave front and keep her emotions in check?

"You're very perceptive."

"Annabelle . . . honey . . ."

"It was very kind of you to be concerned, but I'll be fine. My aunt Perdita Austin is here with me, so I won't be facing Lulu's funeral alone."

"I'm glad you have someone there with you."

"Is everything all right there?" she asked, doing nothing more than making idle conversation, but reluctant to say good-bye. The sound of his voice soothed her, reassured her. But she didn't understand why.

"Things here in Memphis are about the same. No updates from Griffin, yet. And the police have stopped harassing me, at least for the time being."

"So the police don't have any new leads, no other suspects?"

"No new leads. No new suspects. Just me."

Annabelle sighed. "I—I really should go . . ."

"I miss you."

Her breath caught in her throat. *Oh, Quinn, I miss you, too.* "Thank you for calling."

"Annabelle?"

She hit the OFF button and closed her cell phone, then tossed it on the bed. Nothing Quinn could say or do would change the basic facts. One: He was a suspect in Lulu's murder. And two: She couldn't trust him, no matter how much she wanted to.

"Who was that dear?" Perdita asked.

"A friend."

Lifting a questioning eyebrow, Perdita studied Annabelle. "Your cheeks are flushed and you look like a woman who's been talking to her lover. Who was that? And don't lie to me. I've been able to tell when you're lying ever since you were a little girl."

"It was Quinn Cortez."

"The man who might be a suspect in Lulu's murder?"

"He didn't kill Lulu."

Perdita's eyes widened in speculation. "You met him in Memphis, after Lulu's death, right?"

Annabelle nodded.

"You've known him for how long? Five or six days?"

"Yes."

"Oh, my dear girl, you've fallen in love with this man, haven't you."

"No, I . . ." Tears misted her eyes. "I don't know. Maybe I have."

"Oh, my . . . my . . ."

"Nothing will ever come of it. We aren't going to see each other again."

"That's where you're wrong, Annie Belly. You might have the best intentions, but in the end, you won't be able to stay away from him. I know all about loving a man that you don't want to love, a man who's nothing but trouble. I just pray to God that he doesn't wind up breaking your heart."

Chapter 19

Friday dawned warm and bright, not a cloud in the brilliant blue sky. Springtime birds chirped happily and all along the winding brick walkway leading to the front portico of Vanderley Hall, dew-kissed yellow daffodils glistened in the morning sunlight. Annabelle opened the double French doors leading to the balcony and stepped outside for a closer look at this momentous day—the day Louisa Margaret Vanderley would be laid to rest alongside generations of her ancestors in the private family cemetery. But the burial wouldn't take place until after a lengthy and heart-wrenching funeral at the Austinville Presbyterian Church on High Street.

Today would be a day for remembering the good times, the happy moments of Lulu's life. Uncle Louis had asked Annabelle to give the eulogy. She had known he would—had dreaded that he would—but after her father's death, she had accepted the fact that it fell to her to take over his role of family caretaker. Caretaker of the Vanderley name, the Vanderley fortune and the members of the Vanderley family.

Long after Aunt Perdita went to her own room last night, Annabelle had stayed up working on the eulogy. She hoped that her words did justice to Louisa Vanderley, to the person she could have been, should have been, to the beautiful, wide-eyed child who had embraced life with such exuberance. That Lulu Annabelle remembered so well. That Lulu Annabelle had loved.

As she looked out over the vast lawn of Vanderley Hall, kept in immaculate condition by a crew of hardworking gardeners, Annabelle thought about how much of her childhood had been spent here at her ancestral estate. Although several years older than her young cousin, she and Lulu had played together as if they were sisters. And indeed there had been a time when she'd loved Lulu as if she were her own sibling. They had hunted Easter eggs out there in the yard every year at the annual Easter celebration the family hosted for their friends. They had trapped lightning bugs in vented jars on warm summer nights after frolicking in the backyard pool all day. Although both of them had fair complexions, Lulu had tanned as brown as a little gingerbread girl, where Annabelle had often blistered. And they had played hide-and-seek countless times, finding numerous hiding places within the gated walls. Always happy. Always safe. Or so Annabelle had thought.

If only Lulu had told someone what was happening to her. If she'd gone to Uncle Louis or to Aunt Meta Anne or to Annabelle's parents. Or even if she'd come to Annabelle and told her. But she had kept the horrible secret, lived with it, endured it and let it change her from a sweet, innocent child into a wild creature with no morals.

She had finally told Annabelle, confessed her secret shame, only a few years ago, on one of those occasions when Annabelle had tried to persuade her cousin to do something meaningful with her life. And perhaps the truly awful thing about it all was that Annabelle hadn't been surprised. Shocked? Yes. Surprised? No.

If only things could have been different for Lulu. If only . . .

It was too late for if only. There would be no tomorrow for Lulu, no future. At least not here on this earth.

Breathing in the fresh springtime air, Annabelle gripped the wrought-iron railing around the balcony and rejoiced in being alive as only a person who had recently lost a loved one could rejoice. A death in the family reminded her how very fragile mortality is, how quickly a life could end.

A ringing telephone caught Annabelle's attention. Listening for a couple of seconds, she realized that it was her cell phone. Could it be Quinn calling her again? Leaving the French doors wide open, she rushed into the bedroom and to the nightstand where her phone lay. She picked the phone up, flipped it open and held her breath.

"Hello."

"Annabelle."

It was Quinn. She released her suppressed breath.

"How are you this morning?" he asked.

"Weepy. Nervous. Dreading giving Lulu's eulogy."

"It'll be okay. You'll say all the right things."

"Will I?"

"You'll tell everyone what a wonderful person she was, how much you loved her, how close you two were as children." Quinn paused, apparently giving her time to respond, but when she didn't say anything, he continued, "Lulu had a hunger for life. She wanted to do everything, try anything, take risks."

"There was another side to her, you know."

"No, I'm sorry to say I didn't know," Quinn admitted. "We didn't share intimacies. We seldom talked about our personal lives. Our childhoods, our families."

"How odd that you can say you and Lulu didn't share intimacies when you were lovers. I can't think of anything more intimate than that."

After a long pause, he replied, "Lulu and I had sex. We didn't make love. We didn't love each other. Sometimes sex isn't all that intimate."

Have you ever loved a woman? she wanted to ask, but didn't. "I understand."

"Do you?"

"Yes, I do." A fluttering sensation swept through her stomach.

"If we ever had sex, it would be intimate," he said, his voice low and deep. Seductive.

Sensual heat flushed her body, from head to toe. Feminine moisture gathered between her thighs. "Please, don't . . ."

"Should I apologize for wanting you?"

"No. But I can't . . . we can't. You told me yourself that you want me the way you've wanted countless other women."

"I lied. I've never wanted another woman the way I want you."

Her accelerated heartbeat drummed in her ears. The muscles in her belly tightened. "You told me that you'd wind up breaking my heart."

Deny that, too, she pleaded silently. *Tell me that you'd never hurt me, never break my heart. Swear to me that I can trust you.*

He didn't say a word.

"Quinn?"

"After the funeral, after you've done what you need to do there, come back to Memphis."

"I'll think about it. But I have to go now."

"I'll be thinking about you today."

And I'll be thinking about you, too, wishing you were here.

"Good-bye, Quinn." She hung up the phone before she said something she would regret, before she made a promise she shouldn't.

Afternoon sunlight, warm and pure, shimmered across the white casket and sparkled against the heavy gold trim. A gentle, barely there springtime breeze whispered through the treetops and caressed bare skin. The aroma of freshly shoveled earth, piled high on the far side of the grave mingled with the scent of newly mowed grass. As Dr. Porter, the Presbyterian minister, quoted scripture at the end of his brief graveside speech, Annabelle glanced at Uncle Louis, who

sat on her right side. He looked very old, very weak and unbearably sad. To his credit, Wythe stood behind his father,
his hands resting protectively on Louis's shoulders. He'd
been a good son today, ever mindful of his father's poor
health and delicate emotional state. Although she despised
her cousin with a passion, she forced herself to pretend that,
only for today, he was the man he should have been instead
of the man he was. When giving Lulu's eulogy, she had done
the same. Both of Uncle Louis's children had turned out
badly, the younger's fate sealed by the actions of the elder.
Lulu could be forgiven. Wythe could not.

After Dr. Porter ended with a prayer, the bagpiper played
"Amazing Grace" and the small crowd gathered at the family cemetery began to disperse, most of them preparing to go
on up to the house. Last night's visitation at the mansion and
today's funeral at the downtown Austinville church had been
public affairs, a chance for one and all to pay homage and
say good-bye to Lulu. The graveside service had been a private affair, for close friends and family only. And it would be
those few who would return to the house this afternoon to
share their grief.

When leaving the church over an hour ago, Annabelle
had seen Sergeant George in the crowd outside and had gone
over to thank him for driving in from Memphis for the funeral. He'd been sympathetic and caring, offering to do anything he could for her. She'd found herself inviting him to
come to the cemetery for the burial. It wasn't that she had
actually wanted Chad George at her side today, but he had
been there, available and willing. Whereas the man she truly
wanted—here today and in every way a woman can want a
man—couldn't be with her, even though he wanted to be.

When she rose from her seat, she helped Wythe get Uncle
Louis to his feet. With the two of them flanking him, they
walked him to the limousine and placed him in the backseat.
Then she turned to Chad, who stood off to the side of the
others, obviously waiting for her.

"Come back to the house with me," she said.

"Are you sure you want me there?" he asked.

"I'm sure. If I didn't want you to stay with me this afternoon, I wouldn't have invited you." She held out her hand.

Chad grasped her hand gently. "You know I'd do anything for you, Annabelle. Anything at all."

She smiled at him. "Be my friend today. My caring, supportive friend."

"It would be my honor."

When they walked over to her Cadillac, he offered to drive and she readily tossed him the keys. It felt good to turn over even this small, insignificant job to someone else. Someone she could count on without reservations.

Chad was the type of man who should appeal to her. In some ways, he reminded her of Chris. Boyishly handsome. Almost too pretty to be masculine and yet all man. And Chad was a police detective, the nephew of a congressman. From a good family would be her guess. Not wealthy by Vanderley standards, but respectable. She could trust Chad. He wouldn't lie to her. And he wouldn't break her heart if she had an affair with him.

He wouldn't break your heart because you don't love him. You like him. You respect him because of his profession. And you wish you could feel for him what you feel for Quinn. But you don't.

No, I don't, but maybe I could if I tried.

After attending to both of his employer's guests, Sanders handed Griffin a glass of bourbon. Quinn swirled the liquor around inside the glass, then lifted it to his lips and sipped. Perfection. Of course, he had expected Griffin Powell would serve only the best. Powell possessed a sophisticated polish that went beyond the surface, whereas Quinn's was simply a thin veneer that barely disguised the roughneck beneath. Quinn wasn't a connoisseur of fine wines or distinguished hard liquor. When he drank liquor of any kind, except for social occasions, he usually drank beer, but for the most part he preferred iced tea. Maybe having a mother who fell into a whiskey bottle when he was a small kid, and never managed to drag herself out of it had turned Quinn against booze at an early age. Sheila Cortez, God rest her soul, had never met a bottle of whiskey she didn't like. But whiskey had sure enough hated her. It had aged her before her time, ruined her health and eventually helped kill her.

"I've ordered room service for dinner," Griffin said. "I took the liberty of ordering for all of us. If you don't mind, Sanders will join us."

"Fine with me," Quinn said. His gut instincts told him that there was more than an employer/employee relationship between Powell and Sanders.

"Certainly," Judd Walker added.

"But business before the pleasure of a good meal." Griffin set his bourbon glass on the desk, then picked up a piece of standard eight-by-eleven paper. "I just received information this afternoon that strengthens my theory that someone is murdering Quinn's lovers."

Quinn's gut tightened. "Please tell me that another of my former lovers wasn't killed."

"Do you remember Carla Millican?" Griffin asked.

"Carla's an interior designer," Quinn said. "We met late last summer at a party given by a mutual friend, someone whose apartment she'd decorated."

"Did you know that Carla was murdered four months ago?"

Nausea churned in Quinn's stomach. His pulse rate increased, creating a buzzing hum inside his head. "No, I had no idea."

"You two had an affair." Griffin probed Quinn's face, focusing on his eyes.

What was he trying to do—figure out whether of not he can trust me to tell him the truth? Is he searching for a sign that will tell him I wouldn't lie to him?

"If Carla was murdered in Houston four months ago, I'd have read about it in the newspaper and I don't remember—"

"She had moved to Dallas two months before her death."

"Was her killer caught?" Judd asked.

Griffin shook his head.

"Was her killer's MO the same as the person who killed Lulu Vanderley and Kendall Wells?" Judd asked.

"Yes. Carla was smothered. And her right index finger was cut off."

"Goddamn!" Quinn set his glass on the coffee table, then bounded up off the sofa. "I can't believe this." Suddenly something hit him, a memory flashing through his mind. "I was in Dallas four months ago. Briefly. I flew there one day and back to Houston the next."

"You flew in on November twentieth and back to Houston on the twenty-first," Griffin said. "You were called in as a consultant. An old law school buddy was trying a big case and he wanted to pick your brain."

"Don't tell me—Carla was murdered on November twentieth."

"You got it. She was murdered while you were there in Dallas. Do you happen to remember what you were doing between ten P.M. and one A.M. that night?"

"I was in my hotel room, asleep."

"Can you prove it?" Judd and Griffin asked practically simultaneously.

"No, damn it, I can't prove it. I was alone."

"Someone has gone to a great deal of trouble to frame you," Judd said. "Unless you're Jekyll and Hyde and are murdering these women without one part of your personality knowing what the other is doing."

"Don't joke about something like this," Quinn told his lawyer.

God, did I have one of those peculiar blackout spells while I was Dallas? Think, damn it, think. Try to remember.

The first odd sleepy spell hit me in New Orleans nearly a year ago. Did the second one occur in Dallas? Yes. Oh, God, yes, it did. And both times a woman was murdered. Just like here in Memphis when Lulu and Kendall were killed. Is it possible that I actually killed those women? No. No way in hell. I'm not a murderer. I had no reason to kill Joy or Carla or Lulu or Kendall.

"Four women with whom you've had affairs are dead," Griffin said. "All four murdered in the same way—smothered. And each woman had her right index finger cut off. I'd say we have a serial killer on our hands."

"A serial killer who is somehow connected to Quinn," Judd added.

Anger combined with guilt built up within Quinn. Rage screamed inside him. He stomped across the room, adrenaline surging through his body. He wanted to lash out, hit something, rip something apart with his bare hands.

"Take some deep breaths and calm down," Griffin advised. "You're about to blow a gasket and that's not going to help you."

"Someone has killed four of my lovers and made sure I was in a position to be blamed for each one. How the hell can you expect me to calm down? Four women are dead because of me."

"Griffin's right. You need to control that temper of yours or it's going to wind up hurting you," Judd said, and his lawyer's cool and collected demeanor enraged Quinn all the more. "If some psycho has targeted women you've had affairs with, that's not your fault. If you're his real target, then why didn't he just come after you?"

Halting in midpacing, Quinn glared at Judd. "What?"

"Whoever killed these women apparently doesn't want you dead, at least not yet. He wants you to suffer," Griffin told Quinn. "He wants you to realize what he's done and feel guilty and remorseful, just as you're doing now."

Judd said, "It's possible that his plan all along was to frame you for these murders. He's gone to a great deal of trouble to make sure you didn't have an alibi for when any of these murders took place."

What if he also went to a lot of trouble to make sure I blacked out, that I couldn't account for a couple of hours of my time when each murder occurred? Maybe my peculiar sleepy spells were orchestrated by someone else. But how? By whom? The only people close enough to him, who could have slipped him a mickey, were Marcy, Aaron and Jace, three people he trusted implicitly. Besides they hadn't been in New Orleans or in Dallas with him. Or could one of them have followed him? No, God no!

"I'll have to inform Annabelle Vanderley," Griffin said. "You realize that, don't you?"

"What?" Quinn had been only halfway listening. *Tell Annabelle, is that what Griffin had said?* "Yeah, I know. We'll have to tell Annabelle and the police."

"They might not buy my theory," Griffin said. "The police might see this as evidence that you're the serial killer. But it's better for you if we tell them before they unearth the facts about Joy Ellis and Carla Millican themselves."

"And you think that's likely to happen?" Quinn asked.

Griffin nodded. "Jim Norton is a damn good detective. My guess is that he'll keep digging until he finds out everything he can about you and anyone he suspects might have killed Lulu Vanderley."

"Yeah, I guess you're right." Quinn took those deep breaths Griffin had suggested, then said, "I need to talk to Judd alone. Do you mind?"

Griffin shook his head. "Client/attorney privileged information?"

"Right."

Griffin left the lounge area without any further comment. As soon as he closed the bedroom door behind him, Quinn sat down across from Judd Walker and looked him square in the eyes.

"Almost a year ago, when I was in New Orleans, I had an odd sleepy spell. I didn't think much about it at the time. I thought I'd been drinking too much, something I seldom do, and maybe exhausting myself with a certain lady. Joy Ellis. I remember getting really sleepy all of a sudden, tired and lethargic. I fell asleep in my hotel room and woke up a couple of hours later with a headache."

When Judd opened his mouth to speak, possibly to ask a question, Quinn made a wait-I'm-not-finished hand gesture. Judd nodded.

"I'd pretty much forgotten about it when it happened again months later. In Dallas. The same night Griffin just told us that Carla was murdered."

"Let me guess," Judd said. "You had the same kind of sleepy spells on the night Lulu was killed and again when Kendall was murdered."

"Yes. I had to pull off the side of the road for a nap on my way from Nashville the night Lulu died. And then on my way to Kendall's this past Monday evening, the same thing happened. I left the highway, pulled into a parking lot and went to sleep."

"Why haven't you seen a doctor about these sleepy spells?"

"Because until recently, I'd had only two. And they'd been months apart. After the two I've had here in Memphis, I started thinking maybe there was something physically wrong with me and I'd planned to see a doctor when I went back to Houston."

"You're well aware of how the police might interpret this information."

"If they believed me, they'd think I was crazy and that when I thought I was sleeping, I wasn't, but instead was out there killing those women. They'll think I smothered four of my lovers."

"Is it possible that you did kill them?" Judd asked.

"No! No, I couldn't have. I had no reason to kill them."

Chapter 20

Jim Norton glanced down at the folders on his desk containing info on the two murder cases the department was working on at present. Being the lead detective on both cases, since it was assumed they were definitely connected and more than likely committed by the same person, the responsibility weighed heavily on his shoulders. While Chad was off trying to score brownie points with Annabelle Vanderley, Jim had been left to do the work. When Chad had told him this morning that he was taking off to Mississippi for Lulu's funeral, he'd wanted to ask him why. But he knew why. The guy actually thought he still had a chance with Ms. Vanderley. Talk about being overly confident. But Jim had decided there was little use in trying to talk sense to his partner. It was only a matter of time before the lady herself burst his bubble. He probably thought that when Cortez was arrested for Lulu's and Kendall's murders, Annabelle would need a shoulder to cry on. Chad was counting on those DNA results proving Cortez had fathered Lulu's baby.

Jim looked over the DNA results, which had just come in less than an hour ago, once again, just to make sure he hadn't misread the notation from the lab. Son of a bitch! It took all kinds, didn't it? In his line of work, he'd run across every type of scumbag walking the face of the earth and supposed he was somewhat jaded. Although little surprised him, some things still made him sick to his stomach. Like these test results.

He'd wait until Chad got back from Austinville to share the information with him. He was going to be pissed enough as it was. Maybe he should just tell Chad the results would be in first thing tomorrow, after all, it was past six already, and it was highly unlikely they could round up all the major players before morning.

"You planning on spending the night here, Norton?" Lieutenant Ed Palmer, an old pro like himself, slipped into his jacket as he walked past Jim's cubicle.

Jim shook his head. "Nah, I'm heading out in a few minutes. I'm going over to my ex-wife's to see my kid. He called me and invited me for supper."

"Watch out," Ed said. "When an ex-wife starts cooking for you, she's either wanting to ask for more alimony and child support or she's looking to reconcile."

"Knowing Mary Lee the way I do, I'd say it's definitely the former. And I doubt she's done any cooking. She probably ordered pizza or went by KFC."

Ed guffawed. "If you ever get to hankering for some home cooking, come home with me. Betty Jean feeds me too well." Ed patted his round belly.

Jim sat there for several minutes after Ed left, his mind absorbed in thoughts of what he'd expected his life would be like and what it actually was. He was one of those old-fashioned guys who'd thought he'd have a stay-at-home wife, the kind his mother had been. Divorce hadn't been a word in his vocabulary. If things had been different . . . if Mary Lee had been different . . . if he had been different.

Damn it, don't look back. No use torturing yourself.

He picked up the phone and dialed Chad's cell number. He let it ring repeatedly. No answer. He'd try Chad later, on his drive over to Mary Lee's.

"Hey, Norton," Sandra Holmes, one of two female detectives on the force paused at his cubicle. "How's it going?"

Sandra had a pair of eye-catching knockers. Being a guy, it was the first thing he noticed about her. But her only claim to fame wasn't just her big boobs. Sandra had graduated first in her class at John D. Holt and after eight years on the force, she'd proven what a good cop she was.

"It's going," Jim replied. He'd thought about asking Sandra out, but wasn't sure she'd be interested. Since her divorce became final three months ago, every single guy on the force and a couple of married ones had asked her out. She'd shot all of them down. Even Chad.

She held out a sheet of paper. "I filled in the VICAP form with the information on the Vanderley and Wells murders, per your request, and here's what I got. I think you'll find this very interesting."

The department had a special computer program that generated a request form with all pertinent information about a crime that linked to the FBI's Violent Crime Apprehension Program. At the time of Lulu's death, they hadn't figured it was connected to any other murders, believing that someone who knew Lulu personally had committed the crime. But after Kendall Wells's murder, the scenario changed. Although Chad and the department as a whole believed Quinn Cortez was the guilty party, Jim's gut instincts told him something different.

What if both women had been murdered by a serial killer, someone who had killed before and would kill again? He'd put in calls to the Bureau of Investigation in several surrounding states these past couple of days, hoping to connect his two murders with other murders. No luck. Not in Alabama, Mississippi, Georgia, Arkansas and his home state of Tennessee. Chad was supposed to check the VICAP today, but since he was in Austinville playing love-sick fool, Jim had asked Sandra if she'd do it for him. Now that he'd taken a look at the DNA results on Lulu Vanderley's fetus, he felt all the more certain that they were dealing with a serial killer, not a crime of passion.

"Thanks. I appreciate it." He took the e-mail message from her hand. After he'd read it, he let out a long, low whistle.

"Three murders with the exact same MO as ours showed up," Sandra said.

He noted the names of the police departments and the investigators involved in each case. "One in Louisiana nearly a year ago and two in Texas. One four months ago and the other . . . nearly two years ago."

"Quinn Cortez is from Houston, Texas, isn't he? One of those murders took place in Dallas and the other in Baytown, which is practically a suburb of Houston."

"Hmm . . ." Jim read the names of the three victims: Joy Ellis in New Orleans; Carla Millican in Dallas; and Kelley Fleming in Baytown, Texas.

"Want me to get in touch with each department tonight and see what I can find out?" Sandra asked.

"Don't you have any plans for this evening?" he asked.

"Not tonight. I'm just going home, taking a hot bath and curling up with a good book. I don't mind staying and placing those calls. I can give them my cell number."

"You can give them mine," Jim told her.

"You don't want to be disturbed while you're having dinner with Kevin, do you?"

When he looked at her questioningly, she smiled. Sandra had a downright pretty smile, although she wasn't a pretty woman. But she was attractive in a rough, earthy way.

"I heard you telling Ed," she explained. "About having dinner with your kid and ex-wife. So, let me make those calls, give them my cell number and then later tonight, on your way home, drop by my apartment and I'll give you whatever info I get."

Was Sandra inviting him for more than sharing information or was he reading her all wrong? "I can do that," he heard himself saying.

Her smile broadened. "I live on Union Avenue in midtown. It's a quaint old apartment complex called the Georgian Woods." She picked up a pad and pen from his desk and jotted down something on the pad, then tore off the top sheet and handed it to him. "My address and phone number. Come by anytime tonight. It doesn't matter how late."

Jim suddenly felt warm, all the way from his dry mouth to his twitching dick. "Yeah, sure. I'll see you later then."

He waited a few minutes after she left before he stood up, needing time for his erection to deflate. God, he was bad off if just the thought of getting laid could give him a chunky.

Once he could get up without embarrassing himself, he stood, removed his jacket from the back of his chair, put it on and headed out of the office. First things first. And his son always came first with Jim. When Kevin had called and invited him to supper at seven, he'd asked if Kevin had checked with his mother before issuing the invitation. "It was her idea, Dad." Whenever Mary Lee was nice to him—and inviting him to dinner was being nice—he got suspicious. Since their divorce, Mary Lee went out of her way to make his life miserable every chance she got, so she had to have an ulterior motive for inviting him to supper and allowing him extra time with Kevin.

Watch your back, Norton. Mary Lee's liable to stick a knife in it when you least expect it.

Annabelle walked Chad to the door, then went out onto the veranda with him. The sky was clear, stars bright and twinkling, the half moon creamy yellow against the inky black backdrop. When the sun went down, temperatures dropped rapidly and she imagined it wasn't much more than sixty degrees right now and would probably drop into the low fifties by dawn. The black silk suit she'd worn today, though long-sleeved, did little to protect her from the chilly evening breeze.

"I can't tell you how much I appreciate your coming

down for the funeral and staying on until after everyone left," Annabelle said. Although he wasn't the man she'd wanted at her side, not the guardian she'd longed to see her through this unhappy day, Chad had been a godsend to all of them, even Uncle Louis, who had been genuinely pleased to meet one of the detectives working to solve Lulu's murder.

"I'm just glad I could be of help in some small way." Chad took her hand in his. "Annabelle, I hope you know how special you are to me."

She resisted her first instinct—to jerk her hand away—and instead offered him a forced smile. "I don't quite know how to respond to that. We met only a week ago and under very trying circumstances. It would be unwise for us to—"

"Say no more." He squeezed her hand gently. "I simply wanted you to know how I felt. I only hope that you would like for us to become better acquainted."

"Yes, certainly."

Tugging on her hand, he pulled her to him. And then unexpectedly, he kissed her on the lips. Quickly, but thoroughly. Startled by his actions, Annabelle was speechless. It was wrong of her to lead Chad on, to let him think there could be more between them than friendship. But how could she explain? She could hardly say, "I like you, Chad, but I think I've done the unforgivable and fallen in love with Quinn Cortez. And yes, I've known him for only a week and yes, I know he's a notorious womanizer and a possible suspect in Lulu's murder. And yes, a thousand times yes, you would be so much better for me than he would. But the heart doesn't act on reason, only on emotion."

The sudden ringing of Chad's cell phone startled her. She gasped aloud.

He shoved back his jacket on the left side and retrieved his phone from the belt clip. "Sorry about this. I've had it turned off most of the afternoon and just turned it back on a few minutes ago." He hit the ON button and put the phone to his ear. "Sergeant George here."

Annabelle rubbed her hands up and down her arms in an

effort to warm herself. The cool springtime breeze had picked up considerably in the last few minutes.

"Yeah, that's good. Tomorrow morning. Sure, I'll inform Ms. Vanderley," Chad said to the caller. "And yes, I'm coming back to Memphis tonight. See you in the morning." Chad returned his phone to the belt clip.

"What was that all about?"

"That was Jim. He said the DNA report on Lulu's fetus would be available in the morning."

"This soon?"

"I asked for a rush job."

"You think the child was Quinn Cortez's, don't you?"

"Yes, I do. And tomorrow morning we'll find out for sure." He looked at her longingly. "I'll call you as soon as I can in the morning and tell you the results."

She nodded. "Thank you."

He acted as if he wanted to kiss her again, so she took several steps back, toward the closed front door. "Drive carefully. And again, thank you for . . . for today."

"Take care of yourself, Annabelle. And if you need me, I'm just a phone call away."

She waited on the veranda and watched him until he got in his car, then she turned and went back into the house. Warmth greeted her inside the mansion, as did Aunt Perdita.

"A rather interesting young man," Perdita said. "He's quite taken with you, my dear."

"I like Chad. He's a nice person."

"A suitable suitor." Perdita grinned as she laced her arm through Annabelle's. "I have coffee waiting in the back parlor."

"Is it just the two of us?" Annabelle asked.

"Yes. Isn't that nice? Wythe went out the back door an hour ago, got in his car and drove off. At least that's what Hiram told me. Once he'd put on a show of tortured mourning for Louis and the rest of our family and friends, he hightailed it out of here."

"He can stay gone for all I care."

Annabelle followed her aunt down the hall and into the back parlor, which had been, in times past, the ladies' parlor. Decorated in light shades of blue and green and filled with priceless antiques, this was Annabelle's favorite room in the mansion. She remembered playing dominoes and checkers in this room with her Grandmother Vanderley, a notorious cheat who wanted to win at all costs. Once this house had been filled with laughter and love. Now only sadness dwelled within these ancient walls.

"You should go home, to your own house," Perdita said as she poured their coffee from the silver pot atop the silver tray on the tea table. "Why don't we pack first thing in the morning and—"

"I'm going back to Memphis in the morning," Annabelle said as she accepted a cup from her aunt.

Perdita eyed her inquiringly. "I thought you didn't intend to return to Memphis for the time being, not until you'd worked through whatever feelings you have for the Cortez man."

Annabelle sat in one of the two chairs flanking the tea table. After pouring herself another cup of coffee, Perdita took the opposite chair.

"There's something I didn't tell Uncle Louis and I made Wythe promise not to tell him," Annabelle said. "You see, Lulu was pregnant. Approximately six weeks."

Perdita's mouth opened on a silent ah-ha. "Was Quinn Cortez the father?"

"He says not, but . . . she did have other lovers who could have fathered the child. Three men gave DNA samples to be compared to the fetus's DNA. Chad received a call right before he left telling him the results of the DNA testing would be in tomorrow morning."

"You don't have to go back to Memphis just for that." When Perdita lifted her cup to her lips, she looked right at Annabelle and then said, "Ah . . ." She took a sip of the coffee. "It's such a pity you didn't meet Mr. Cortez under different circumstances."

Annabelle gazed down into the cup and sighed. "Go ahead and call me a fool. I am, you know. I want to be there with him when we find out if he was the baby's father."

"Oh, my poor Annabelle. Life plays cruel tricks on us sometimes, doesn't it?"

Kevin paused in the doorway between the living room and hall. "Ah, Mom, why can't I stay up just a little while longer. It's not like Dad's here every night."

"I said no." Mary Lee pointed her finger toward the corridor leading to the bathroom. "Go brush your teeth and get ready for bed. It's ten-thirty. I let you stay up thirty minutes later than usual."

When Kevin gave her a pleading look, she frowned. "Your dad will come in and say good night before he leaves."

"Go on, pal. Do what your mother says." Jim could fault Mary Lee on many issues and she might not be the ideal mother, but she tried her best. When she set rules for Kevin, Jim did what he could to support her.

When Kevin reluctantly disappeared down the hall, Mary Lee turned to Jim. "Want another beer?"

"No, thanks."

Just as he'd predicted, Mary Lee had ordered pizza and served them cold beer and their son iced cola. They'd eaten store-bought chocolate chip cookies for dessert and then Jim had helped Kevin with his homework while Mary Lee cleaned up. It wasn't fair to compare his ex-wife to his mom, who'd baked homemade cookies on a regular basis. And who had been a loving, supportive and faithful wife until her dying day.

You're not the man your dad was either, he reminded himself. *If you'd been a better husband, maybe Mary Lee would have been a better wife.*

"How are those murder cases going?" Mary Lee asked. "You haven't arrested that big shot lawyer from Texas, have you? Quinn Cortez. God, even the guy's name sounds sexy."

Mary Lee would think a name could sound sexy. Bet she'd jump Cortez's bones in a New York minute if given half the chance.

"No, we haven't made an arrest yet."

"Want to sit down?" she asked.

He shook his head. "I'll just go say good night to Kevin and then leave."

Mary Lee came up to him. "Look, let's lay our cards on the table, okay?"

Here it comes. Whatever reason she invited me to dinner and let me have this extra time with Kevin. "Sure thing."

"I know that you know I've been having a thing with Chad."

Was that it? Was that what the invitation to dinner had been about? Did she honestly think he'd give a damn? Had she been concerned about how he would react when he found out? "Yeah. So?"

"Don't you care?" She inched closer, so close that her breasts almost touched his chest.

There had been a time that whenever Mary Lee just walked into a room, he got hard. "Why should I care?"

With her body leaning into his, she lifted her arms and placed them around his neck. "Aren't you just the least bit jealous? Don't you wish you were getting some from me instead of him? The sex was always good for us, wasn't it, Jimmy?"

His dick twitched as old memories flickered through his mind. "Yeah, babe, the sex was always good." He clasped his fingers around her arms and removed them from his neck, then took a step backward, putting some breathing room between them.

She glanced down at his crotch and smiled when she noted his partially aroused state. "Why don't you stick around and after Kevin goes to sleep—"

"I can't," he said. Damn, he was tempted to stay. A part of him still wanted her. Yeah, the part that didn't have a lick of sense. "I've got a late night date." He wasn't lying. Not exactly. Sandra had suggested he drop by tonight and she'd all but told him he'd be welcome to spend the night.

Mary Lee's nostrils flared as she took in several quick, sharp breaths. He knew that look. She was pissed.

"This was a one-time-only offer," she told him. "Take it or leave it, but know this—I won't ask you again."

Yeah, she would. In the years since their divorce, she'd made the offer at least once every six months and every time he rejected her she swore it would be the last time.

"Hey, Dad, I'm ready for bed," Kevin called from down the hall.

"I'll go say good night to Kevin." Jim glanced at his ex-wife briefly, then left her standing there fuming.

"Be right there," Jim told Kevin as he walked out of the living room, halfway expecting Mary Lee to start screaming at him.

But she didn't. And when he came out of Kevin's room ten minutes later, she was sitting in front of the TV and didn't even acknowledge his presence when he said good night.

Annabelle had soaked in the tub for nearly an hour after coming upstairs to her room at Vanderley Hall, hoping it would relax her enough so that she could sleep. But as she lay in bed, her eyes wide open and staring up at the twelve-foot ceiling, she realized that she probably should have asked Aunt Perdita for one of her sleeping pills.

Her aunt was a walking drugstore, keeping a large variety of prescription and nonprescription medication with her at all times.

"You never know when you or a friend will need something for pain or to sleep or to pep you up," Perdita had once told Annabelle.

Maybe she should go down the hall and knock on her aunt's door. What would it hurt to take a sleeping pill tonight since she so rarely used anything stronger than an aspirin? Just as Annabelle flung the covers back and slid to the edge of the bed, her cell phone rang. Knowing before she lifted the phone from the nightstand who the caller was, she snatched the phone up, flipped it open and said, "Hello."

"Are you all right?" Quinn asked.

"I am now," she replied honestly.

"Rough day, huh?"

"A really bad one."

"I guess you know the Memphis PD will have the DNA test results tomorrow morning."

"Yes, I know," she said.

"Did Jim Norton call you?"

"He called Sergeant George, who in turn told me."

Silence.

"Quinn?"

"Chad George was at Lulu's funeral? He was there with you this evening?"

"Yes."

"He's got a thing for you, doesn't he?"

"Yes, I believe he does."

"How do you feel about him?" Quinn asked.

"I should tell you that it's none of your business how I feel about him, but . . . He's what my parents would have referred to as a very suitable young man."

"Meaning he's a white Anglo-Saxon Protestant from a respectable middle-class background and is an up-and-coming member of a time-honored profession."

"Yes."

"He's much better for you than I am. You'd be a fool to reject him in favor of me, considering I have none of his attributes to recommend me."

Tell him. Admit the truth. You can't keep lying to yourself, so why lie to Quinn?

"You're assuming it's an either/or situation," she said.

Quinn laughed quietly, a low rumbling chuckle. "Yeah, I guess I did narrow down the field and limit your choices, didn't I?"

"Quinn, I'm coming back to Memphis in the morning," she told him. "I want to be there when you find out the DNA results."

"I should tell you not to come, to stay as far away from me as possible, but I can't do that. You see, honey, I'm a selfish bastard. I want you to want to be with me."

"I'll see you in the morning and afterward . . . after we leave the police station, we should go somewhere and talk. I'll stay at the Peabody again, so—"

"There's something you should know."

"What?" Her heart skipped a beat.

"Griffin has found out that another woman I used to know—Carla Millican—was murdered in Dallas four months ago, on the same day I was there. But I swear to you, Annabelle, I didn't kill her any more than I killed Lulu or Kendall or Joy Ellis."

A fourth victim! Four of Quinn's lovers had been murdered. There was no way their murders could have been coincidental. "Was she . . . was Carla killed the same way the others were?"

"She was smothered and her right index finger removed after she was dead."

"Someone is trying to frame you," Annabelle said. "That's it, isn't it?"

"Possibly. Griffin and Judd believe we have a psychopath on our hands. A serial killer. And with the evidence Griffin has acquired so far, it appears the first murder was a year ago."

"You'll have to share this information with the police. Surely then they'll realize you're completely innocent."

"Maybe. But there's a chance that since I was in the same city at the time of each murder and have no alibi any of the four times, the police could figure that I killed all four women."

"But you didn't. I know you didn't." How did she know? How could she be so sure? It wasn't as if she had any past experience with Quinn on which to base her conviction. Just because she was infatuated with Quinn—possibly in love with him—didn't mean he was innocent.

"I couldn't blame you if you had some doubts. Hell, if I didn't know better, I might think I was guilty."

"Maybe my head has some lingering doubts," she admitted. "But my heart doesn't."

"Ah, Annabelle. Honey." Genuine anguish saturated his speech. "Please, please don't let me hurt you."

At eleven-fifteen, Jim Norton stood outside Sandra Holmes's apartment. He rapped on the door only a few times and as quietly as possible, not wanting to disturb her neighbors. He waited. Knocked again. Then waited. And just when he'd given up on her responding and turned to leave, the door opened.

"Jim?"

He did an about-face. Sandra wore a pair of cotton shorts and an oversized T-shirt, her pointed nipples pressing against the material. "Hi," he said. "Is it too late to—?"

She reached out, grabbed the lapels of his jacket and tugged him toward her. "It's not too late for you, Jimmy Norton. It would never be too late."

When she slid her arms around his waist and dropped her hands to cup his buttocks, Jim's body reacted immediately. She stood on tiptoe, lifted her face and kissed him. Responding to her advances, he grabbed the back of her neck and deepened the kiss. She thrust her tongue into his mouth and moaned when their tongues did a wicked tango.

Sandra practically dragged him into her apartment. Once inside, he kicked the door closed behind them, not even bothering to lock it. Within two minutes flat, she was naked from the waist down and had unzipped his fly and freed his rock-hard penis. He toppled her over and down onto the couch in the living room, then just before he lost it completely, he paused.

"Wait just a second." He lifted himself up and off her just long enough to remove a condom from his pants pocket and hurriedly slid it down over his erection.

Chapter 21

Jim woke to the sound of humming and the smell of coffee perking. He rolled over, rooted his head against the pillow and opened his eyes. This wasn't his bed and this wasn't his apartment in the Exchange Building. He'd been living on Second Street, three blocks from the Criminal Justice Center, for the past five years and this definitely wasn't the bedroom in his place. For one thing, his room wasn't painted pale yellow and for another—he rubbed the sheet covering him between his thumb and forefinger—he didn't own any yellow satin sheets.

"Don't panic," a female voice said. "It's only six-thirty."

He rolled over, stretched and looked up at Sandra Holmes standing over him at the side of the bed, a bright red cup in her hands and a smug smile on her face.

Now it was all coming back to him. Sandra. Sex. Satisfaction. Jim smiled. "Good morning."

"Yes, it is a good morning. And it was an incredible night." When Sandra sat down on the edge of the bed and held out the red mug to him, her oversized T-shirt rode up high enough to give him a glimpse of her naked thighs and bare hips. It was obvious that she wasn't wearing any panties.

Yeah, it had been a rather incredible night. Sandra was a

top-notch officer, as good as any man on the force, but in the bedroom she was all woman. And his two performances last night—or rather early this morning—hadn't been too shabby, if he did say so himself. From the way Sandra had acted when she came both times, he figured he must have done something right.

As he sat up in bed, the sheet dropped to his hips. He reached out and took the mug from Sandra. "I hope this is coffee."

"Hot and black."

"Just the way I like it." Taking a sip, he focused on the mug in order to avoid prolonged eye contact with the woman sitting beside him.

Jim wasn't sure what to say now. He'd never been much good at mornings after and this time, things were a bit more awkward than usual. This was a first for him—the first time he'd ever slept with a fellow police officer.

"I'm glad you stopped by last night," she told him.

"Yeah, me, too." He took another sip of coffee.

She chuckled, the sound deep throated. "It's okay, Jim, I don't expect anything from you this morning. Last night, I wanted you and you wanted me. We had some fantastic sex— twice—but we didn't make any promises or declare our undying love. If this turns out to have been a one-night stand, I'm okay with it. And if we decide we want to see each other again, that's fine with me, too."

Jim heaved a huge internal sigh, although outwardly he simply looked at Sandra and grinned. He took another swig from the mug, then handed it back to her and said, "I'd better get going. I need to run by my apartment to shower, shave and change clothes before heading to the office."

Sandra stood, then keeping her back to him, responded, "I'm off duty this weekend, so I'll see you Monday." Not waiting for him to comment, she walked out of the bedroom, into the adjoining bath and closed the door behind her.

Jim jumped out of bed, picked up his discarded clothing and dressed as quickly as he could. But he felt he needed to say something to Sandra before he left, even if it was just good-bye. He walked over and knocked on the bathroom door.

"Yeah?" Sandra called.

"I'm leaving now."

She eased the door open no more than three inches, just enough for him to get a glimpse of her naked body. Her hot body. The lady was stacked.

"Come back anytime."

Jim swallowed hard. "Yeah, I just might. Thanks."

"Thank you." She winked at him, then closed the door.

Get going while you still can. If you don't leave now, you'll be humping her in the shower in three minutes flat.

Jim all but ran to the front door and out into the hall. As he headed downstairs, he slowed his pace and started whistling.

Chad George met Annabelle when she entered the tenth floor of the Criminal Justice Center. She'd called his cell phone on her drive into Memphis to tell him she had decided she wanted to be there this morning when the DNA results came in. After all, she felt she owed him the courtesy of telling him beforehand and not just showing up unannounced.

"There's really no need for you to be here," he told her. "I would have phoned you with the information." He slipped his arm through hers and led her straight to the interview room, which was empty. "Let me get you some coffee."

"No, thank you." She glanced around the room and out into the office through the open door. "Am I the first to arrive?"

"We're expecting Cortez and Aaron Tully, along with Cortez's lawyer, any minute now, and Randall Miller's bringing his lawyer with him, too."

"Have you seen the DNA report?"

"No, I just arrived a few minutes ago. I'm sure my partner has the report by now."

Annabelle noted something in Chad's voice and in the expression on his face. Anger? Yes, that was it—disguised anger, but anger nonetheless. Was he upset that his partner, the senior detective on the case, would see the report first?

"Will you be staying in Memphis overnight?" Chad asked. "If you are, I'd like to take you to dinner."

"I'm staying, but I have to decline your offer. I've already made plans for this evening." She had no intention of telling him that she planned to spend the evening with Quinn.

"Oh." A combination of irritation and disappointment etched his features. "Another time then."

When Chad started to say something else, she just knew he was going to ask her with whom she'd made plans for this evening. But Jim Norton breezed into the room whistling, unwittingly coming to her rescue.

The minute Lieutenant Norton saw Annabelle, he nodded to her and said, "Good morning, Ms. Vanderley. I didn't expect to see you today."

"I decided I should be here to represent the family." *And to be with Quinn when he finds out whether or not he fathered Lulu's baby.*

"You're certainly welcome," Norton said. "The Memphis police department wants to do everything possible to assist you and the Vanderley family."

Jim Norton held a file folder securely tucked beneath his arm. The DNA report? As he laid the folder on the table and pulled out a chair, Annabelle studied the police lieutenant. Broad shouldered, lean hipped, washboard flat belly. His dark brown hair was cut conservatively short. His clothes were neat, but inexpensive, probably several years old and purchased off the rack. He appeared to have freshly shaved this morning and there was a twinkle in his eyes. She sensed that he was happy about something. Something personal.

"Have you read the report?" Chad eyed the folder, then reached for it.

After sitting down, Jim slammed his big hand down on

top of the folder, preventing Chad from picking it up. "Yeah, I've read it. And as soon as everyone involved gets here, I'll reveal the results."

Chad glowered at his partner.

Voices outside the open door gained Annabelle's attention. A silver-haired man in his fifties and a forty-something, partially bald man entered the room. Pleasantries were exchanged between Chad and the silver-haired man whom Chad called Mr. Miller. So that was one of Lulu's other lovers, the one she referred to as Randy. The man was twice Lulu's age, but that was no surprise. Lulu loved older men. Especially rich and powerful older men.

"Let's get this over with," Randall Miller said.

"We're waiting for Mr. Cortez and Mr. Tully," Chad explained.

"Who's this Tully?" Miller asked.

"Another man who had sex with Lulu Vanderley in the past two months," Lieutenant Norton said. "Another daddy candidate."

Miller's face pinched into a displeased expression.

"Won't you sit down, Mr. Miller? And you, too, Mr. Baldwin." Chad pulled out a chair for Miller.

Annabelle couldn't help noticing the differential way in which Chad treated Randall Miller and his lawyer. The expression "kissing up" immediately came to mind. It had become quite apparent to her that Chad aligned himself with people he thought could benefit him in some way. What did he think real estate czar Miller could do for him? Just what *were* Chad's plans for his future?

Suddenly, she realized that Quinn had arrived, sensing his presence first, several minutes before she actually saw him. Like an odd sort of feminine radar, she knew the moment he entered the homicide department. Her stomach fluttered; her heartbeat accelerated.

Annabelle glanced at the door just as Quinn approached the interview room. Their gazes met, connected and separated in the span of half a second. Warmth originated deep inside her and quickly spread through her entire body. Sensual fire ignited by her close proximity to Quinn Cortez.

"If everybody will take a seat, we'll get this done quickly," Jim Norton said as he stood and indicated the empty chairs.

Chad pulled out the chair to Annabelle's left and sat down beside her. When he placed his hand on the back of her chair, she glanced over her shoulder and frowned. He removed his hand instantly.

Annabelle looked at the two men with Quinn. She assumed the younger was Aaron Tully. He was about the same height as Quinn, only youthfully lanky, and possessed the same dark coloring as his employer. The other man with Quinn, his lawyer Judd Walker, looked familiar to her. He was an inch or two taller than Quinn and had the most fascinating golden eyes, a few shades lighter than his honey brown hair. When she'd first heard his name mentioned, she'd thought she should know him and believed that they had met at some time. But when and where?

When he walked past her, Mr. Walker nodded and smiled. "How are you, Ms. Vanderley? I'd like to extend my condolences on the loss of your cousin."

She returned his smile. "Thank you, Mr. Walker."

Studying his face for the sixty seconds of their exchange, Annabelle remembered where she had met this man. At the same charity event in Chattanooga where she'd met Griffin Powell a few years ago.

Quinn sat across the table from Annabelle, but didn't glance her way. His lawyer remained standing, as did Randall Miller's lawyer. With her hands folded in her lap and one foot placed partly behind the other, Annabelle looked directly at Lieutenant Norton and said a silent prayer that the DNA results would show that either Aaron Tully or Randall Miller had fathered Lulu's baby. For Quinn's sake, she hoped the child hadn't been his.

Norton opened the file folder, glanced at the report, then

swept his gaze around the room, looking briefly at each person. "The DNA report proves conclusively that Randall Miller couldn't have fathered Lulu's baby."

Miller released a loud sigh. "Am I free to go?"

"Certainly," Norton said. "But we may need to question you again in the course of this investigation."

"My client will be at your disposal," Mr. Baldwin said as he followed his client, who was already opening the door in his eagerness to leave.

"Aaron Tully wasn't the father, either," Norton said.

Annabelle's stomach muscles knotted. She hazarded a quick glance at Quinn, who sat there stoic, his expression showing no emotion whatsoever.

She turned and glanced at Chad. He was smiling, damn him.

"And Mr. Cortez," Jim looked right at Quinn. "You were not the father."

"What?" Chad shouted.

Annabelle's and Quinn's gazes met and held. Relief washed over her like a cleansing rain. And she felt Quinn's relief in every fiber of her being.

"Mr. Tully, you are free to go, but just as with Mr. Miller, we may need to question you further at a later time," Norton said.

"Wait a minute." Chad shot up out of his chair. "If Cortez, Miller or Tully wasn't the father—"

Cutting his partner off midsentence, Norton turned to Annabelle and said, "Ms. Vanderley, would you stay, please. I'd like to talk to you about the DNA results."

"Yes, certainly." Chill bumps broke out on her arms. *Please, God, don't let him tell me what I fear the most.*

"Lieutenant Norton, Mr. Cortez and I would like to meet with you when you've finished here." Judd Walker glanced at Annabelle. "Ms. Vanderley, if you'd like to join us, you're quite welcome."

"As a matter of fact, I have a few more questions for Mr.

Cortez, so if y'all will wait outside, this shouldn't take long with Ms. Vanderley," Norton said. "Then we'll hear what y'all have to say."

Quinn didn't speak to her as he followed Aaron Tully to the door. After Aaron went into the outer office, Quinn paused before leaving and looked at her. She knew he was telling her that he would wait for her, that he wouldn't leave without her. When she nodded, telling him she understood his telepathic message, Quinn left the interview room quietly, followed by Judd Walker.

"Just what the hell is going on?" Chad asked Jim. "You should have allowed me to read that DNA report before announcing the results. And what's with Cortez's lawyer wanting a private meeting?"

"You were late getting in this morning," Jim said. "You didn't get here in time to do more than meet and greet Ms. Vanderley before the others arrived. As for why Cortez's lawyer wants to talk to me, I don't know, but since he invited Ms. Vanderley to join us, I wouldn't call it a private meeting."

"Why did you ask Annabelle to stay? Surely you don't think she knew that Lulu had another lover and didn't tell us."

Lieutenant Norton zeroed in on Annabelle, a sympathetic expression in his timber wolf blue-gray eyes. "The DNA results on the fetus showed that the child was fathered by . . ." Norton cleared his throat. "By a close male relative of Annabelle's."

Tears pooled in Annabelle's eyes.

"My God! Are you saying that—" Chad leaned over and stared directly into Annabelle's face. "You didn't know about this, did you?"

Norton clamped his hand onto Chad's shoulder and jerked him away from Annabelle. Chad bristled, giving Norton a half-crazed look, but he moved away and kept his distance. "I'm sorry, Ms. Vanderley, to have to tell you about the paternity of the child Lulu was carrying, but I suspect you already knew that Lulu had been having an intimate relationship with her half brother, didn't you?"

Annabelle clenched her teeth. When she closed her eyes momentarily, tears dampened her eyelashes. "Yes, I knew."

"Why didn't you tell us?" Chad asked.

"Because I had prayed there would be no need. Wythe didn't kill Lulu. He was in Austinville at the time of her murder. And my uncle Louis has no idea that . . . It would kill him if he found out. The relationship between Lulu and Wythe is our family's dirty little secret, one that I had hoped was buried with my cousin."

"How did you find out about their relationship?" Norton asked.

"Lulu admitted it to me several years ago." She would not tell these police officers more than they already knew. What difference did it make now what they thought of Lulu? Would it absolve Lulu of her sins if these men knew that Wythe had begun molesting Lulu when she was just a child? The fact that by the time she was fifteen, Lulu thought herself in love with her own half brother was no one's business. Nor was the fact that long after her infatuation with Wythe ended, their sexual relationship continued.

"I promise you that I will do everything I can to keep this information under wraps," Norton said. "Of course, if and when Lulu's murder case goes to trial . . ."

"I understand." Annabelle stood and held out her hand to the lieutenant. "Thank you. I appreciate your not sharing the DNA results with everyone else."

"No one else needed to know."

"I'd like to go to the restroom and freshen up." She wiped away her tears with her fingertips. "And since Mr. Walker invited me to join y'all, I'll be right back."

As soon as Lieutenant Norton gave her directions to the ladies' room, she escaped quickly into the outer office before Chad offered to escort her. She searched for Quinn, but didn't see him anywhere. Then just as she'd given up hope of finding him, she caught a glimpse of him and Judd Walker near the men's room. Glancing around to see if anyone was watching her, she waited nervously while Quinn walked toward her.

When he reached her, he left at least two feet between them. "You've been crying. Want to tell me what happened?"

"I will. Later. Once we're out of here and alone."

Quinn nodded. "You know why we've asked for a meeting with the detectives on Lulu's case, don't you?"

"You're going to give them the information about Joy Ellis and Carla Millican."

"Once they know, this thing could go one of two ways—they'll either think I killed all four women or they'll know I'm innocent and start looking for a serial killer."

She longed to touch him, to take his hand into hers and say something comforting. And by the way he was looking at her, she knew he felt the same.

Judd Walker, who had stayed at a discreet distance, came over and put his hand on Quinn's shoulder. "Lieutenant Norton is motioning to us. I think they're ready to hear what we have to say."

Chapter 22

With a look that could kill, Jim Norton scowled at his partner, daring him to open his mouth. Chad clenched his teeth and gave Jim a withering glare, but he kept quiet.

"We didn't have to come forward with this information," Judd Walker said. "But we felt it in the best interest of my client to make you aware of these facts."

"You say there were two other women, both murdered the way Lulu Vanderley and Kendall Wells were murdered and both were former lovers of Mr. Cortez." Although his question was directed at Judd Walker, Jim studied Quinn Cortez's reaction. Jim couldn't quite peg Cortez. Not even the infamous Houston lawyer himself thought he was one of the good guys. But being a cutthroat criminal lawyer didn't mean the man was capable of murder.

"Yes," Judd replied, then glanced at the file folder he had laid on the table. "All the information that the Powell agency unearthed is in there."

"Four murders, same MO, all four women connected by one thing—Mr. Cortez." Jim reached out, put his hand on the folder and slid the file across the table toward him, but didn't open it. "I suppose you want me to believe that some mystery killer is responsible for these crimes."

"We've hired a former FBI profiler to work up a profile of the killer," Judd said. "But it seems apparent to me that we're dealing with a serial killer in all four murders."

Although he remained standing in a far corner, Chad spoke up, apparently unable to hold himself back any longer. "Yeah, and that serial killer is Quinn Cortez."

"That's ludicrous," Judd replied. "Mr. Cortez is no more a serial killer than you or I. If you continue your persecution of my client, I'll be forced to—"

"No one is persecuting Mr. Cortez." Jim cut his eyes menacingly at Chad, then looked at Judd. "And although I tend to agree with you about a serial killer having committed these crimes, I'm not a hundred percent sure we can automatically rule out your client."

"Damn right about that," Chad said.

Jim huffed loudly. He'd like nothing better than to backhand his partner, whose show of machismo was lost on Annabelle Vanderley. If Chad thought that by acting tough, by hammering away at Cortez, he would impress the lady, then the guy was an idiot. Ms. Vanderley sat at the far end of the table, as far away from Cortez as possible with the two of them still in the same room, but Jim hadn't missed the subtle way she watched the man, concern in her gaze.

"I appreciate your coming to us with this information," Jim said. "I figured it was only a matter of time before Griffin found out the same info we did, but I didn't expect him to get hold of it first."

Chad snapped his head around and shot Jim a what-the-hell-are-you-talking-about? look.

"Are you saying you already had this information, that you knew about Joy Ellis and Carla Millican?" Judd asked.

"Yes, as a matter of fact, we did. I actually spoke to the lead detective on one of the murder cases this morning," Jim told them. Thanks to Sandra Holmes, Jim had come in to work today with the names of the lead detective in all of the other murder cases identical to Lulu's and Kendall's. "Conrad

McCaffery, out in Dallas, was in charge of the Carla Millican case. And I have calls in to the New Orleans PD and . . . I take it Griffin hasn't gone further back with the investigation than this past year."

"His agents are continuing the search," Judd said.

"He'll come up with one more name—Kelley Fleming. She was murdered two years ago in Baytown, Texas."

"Was this woman another of your lovers?" Chad asked as he came out of the corner and stood across the table from Cortez and his lawyer.

"I don't recognize the name," Quinn replied, but he was looking at Judd Walker, not Chad.

"Maybe you just forgot her. After all, it was two years ago." Chad cast a quick glance at Annabelle, then returned his attention to Quinn. "Love 'em, kill 'em, and forget 'em. Is that the way it is for you, Cortez?"

Quinn rose halfway out of his seat, pure rage exhibited in his taut body and ferocious facial features. Judd grasped his arm. Quinn threw off his lawyer's hold as he stood and zeroed in on Chad.

"Sit down," Judd Walker told his client, but Quinn ignored him.

Just as Quinn leaned across the table as if ready to pounce on Chad, Annabelle spoke in a quiet, soothing voice that startled all four men in the room.

"Quinn didn't kill any of those women, including my cousin, Lulu."

Her words diffused the Cortez/George time bomb on the verge of exploding. As if she'd reached out and physically touched him, Quinn relaxed instantly, stood up straight and backed away from the table. Chad turned and stared at Annabelle, his gaze plainly telling her that he couldn't believe she'd so readily come to Quinn's defense.

"Let's everybody calm down," Jim added. "Mr. Walker, remind your client that if he's wise, he'll control his temper." Jim glanced at his partner. "And Sergeant George, remember you represent the Memphis Police Department and your actions can reflect badly on all of us if you conduct yourself in an unprofessional manner."

"Yes, sir," Chad replied through clenched teeth.

"Now, Mr. Cortez, you said you didn't recognize the name Kelley Fleming. Is that right?"

Quinn nodded. "If she was someone I knew a couple of years ago, I would remember her name. I didn't know a Kelley Fleming."

"I assume Ms. Fleming was murdered the same way the other victims were?" Judd Walker asked.

"That's confidential—" Chad said.

"The Powell Agency will have the info today or tomorrow," Jim reminded his partner, then replied to Judd, "Yes, the MO is the same."

"I'd say that this fifth murder, and of a woman my client didn't even know, adds credence to our theory that these women were murdered by a serial killer, not by Quinn Cortez," Judd said.

"Possibly." Jim glanced from Quinn to Judd. "If Mr. Cortez didn't know Ms. Fleming and if he was not in New Orleans or Dallas or Baytown when each woman was murdered, then I agree with you."

Silence.

Jim glanced from Cortez to Walker to Annabelle Vanderley and realized that all three of them knew something he didn't know. Not yet. And they sure as hell weren't rushing to reveal anything more. His bet was Cortez had been in either Dallas or New Orleans when the murders occurred, but if he went much further with his questioning, Judd Walker wouldn't allow his client to cooperate. He'd leave it alone, for now.

"If that's all . . ." Judd looked inquiringly at Jim.

He nodded. "Yeah . . . for now." He cast Chad a keep-your-mouth-shut glare.

Judd and Quinn rose simultaneously, then Quinn went straight to Annabelle, pulled out her chair and held out his hand to her.

"Annabelle," Chad called.

But she didn't answer him, didn't even glance his way. Instead she took Quinn's hand, got up and walked out of the room with him.

As soon as they were alone in the interview room, Chad cursed under his breath. "Goddamn son of a bitch."

"Cool off," Jim advised.

"Yeah, how the hell do I do that? Annabelle just walked out of here with that man. She has no idea what he's capable of doing. She thinks he's innocent. Goddamn it, Jim, the guy could kill her. She could be his next victim."

"Since you're so concerned about Ms. Vanderley and equally convinced that Cortez is guilty, then find us some proof. Something the DA can take to a grand jury, something that will prove to the lady you're so worried about that she's putting her trust in a killer."

"That's just what I intend to do."

"You might want to start by finding out if Cortez was in Dallas when Carla Millican was murdered and if he was in New Orleans when Joy Ellis died."

Annabelle and Quinn walked out of Griffin's suite shortly after one that afternoon, leaving Judd and Griffin to ponder the next move in Quinn's defense. Griffin intended to give the name Kelley Fleming to one of his top agents and send the guy to Baytown, Texas, to dig up as much information about that particular victim as possible. If her death was connected to the other four, that meant these murders hadn't begun only a year ago as they had first thought. And if there was no connection between Quinn and Ms. Fleming, then did that mean his having been a friend and lover to the other four was nothing more than mere coincidence?

"Still think he's innocent?" Judd asked.

Griffin nodded. "Yes, I do. But what about you, Judd? Are Annabelle and I the only two people who believe Quinn didn't kill any of those women?"

"I agreed to take this case because you convinced me he's innocent. But I have to admit that I have a few unsettling doubts. Something about this case isn't right. I thought I had it all figured out—that somebody was killing Quinn's lovers either to pin the rap on him or to punish him in some way. But now the police have discovered another victim—one Quinn claims he doesn't know. If Kelley Fleming was killed by the same person as the other four, then it doesn't make sense. Any of it."

"Maybe Quinn did know Kelley Fleming," Griffin said. "Maybe he knew her by another name or maybe he never knew her name. I'll see if Sullivan can e-mail us a photo of the woman ASAP. It's possible Quinn will recognize her, even if her name didn't mean anything to him."

Judd's cell phone rang, interrupting their discussion. "Excuse me," Judd said as he answered the distinctive Beethoven's Fifth ring. "Walker here." Judd's features softened. "No, it's all right. I'm glad you called, honey. Give me a minute, will you?" Smiling, he glanced at Griffin as he held the phone away from his mouth. "I need to take this call. It's personal. My fiancée."

Griffin gave Judd a how-about-that grin. "I'll use the phone in my bedroom to call Sullivan and give you a little privacy."

"Thanks."

As Griffin headed out of the lounge, he paused and looked back at Judd. "Who's the lucky lady?"

"Jennifer Mobley."

"Former Miss Tennessee, Jennifer Mobley?"

"One and the same," Judd said proudly.

"Wasn't she in some sort of freak accident the year after she was a runner-up in the Miss America pageant?"

"During an ice storm, her car skidded off Lookout Mountain. She nearly died. But after plastic surgery and a year of therapy, she recovered fully. She's as beautiful as ever and come May, she'll receive her doctorate degree from UT in child psychology. And in June we're having the biggest, fanciest wedding Chattanooga has ever seen."

"Congratulations," Griffin said. "And by the way, tell the lady that I think she's way too good for the likes of you."

"I've already told her, but she's going to marry me anyway."

"Then you're the lucky one."

"Don't I know it."

Griffin closed the door behind him after he went into his bedroom. So Judd Walker was getting married. Every marriage-minded woman in Chattanooga must be heartbroken. The heir to the Walker fortune, old money that went all the way back to reconstruction days in Tennessee, was considered the number one eligible bachelor in the city, if not in the state.

Griffin sat down on the side of his bed and pulled the telephone to the edge of the nightstand. Of course, he was considered quite a catch himself, another sought-after bachelor. But where men like Judd could and would marry and live normal lives, with wives, children and a shot at real happiness, Griffin would never have any of these things. Destiny had dictated his future years ago.

He lifted the receiver and dialed Sullivan's cell number. Ben answered on the second ring. "This is Griffin. I need for you to fly to Baytown, Texas, right away. Track down all the info you can on a woman named Kelley Fleming." He spelled both the first and last name. "According to the Memphis PD, she was murdered in Baytown approximately two years ago. The lead detective on the case was a guy named Lieutenant Stovall. I need to know everything there is to know about this woman as soon as possible. Find out if the lady knew Quinn Cortez or had any kind of connection to him. And send me a recent photograph just as soon as you get hold of one."

* * *

Quinn entered Annabelle's suite with no expectations. He was just grateful that she had returned to Memphis, that she wanted to be with him. During the days she'd been gone, back to Austinville for Lulu's funeral, he had missed her. When had he ever missed anybody, least of all a woman? Under different circumstances, he would have gone to Mississippi to attend Lulu's funeral. And yes, it would have been for Annabelle's sake far more than to show his respects to Lulu, although he would have liked to do that, too.

He and Annabelle hadn't so much as held hands during the elevator ride, hadn't touched at all during the short flight down from one floor to another at the Peabody. And they had glanced at each other only once. When she had smiled at him, he'd felt as if he'd been awarded the grand prize in a very important contest.

God, he was acting like a lovesick teenager. And he was nervous. Quinn Cortez, nervous? Unheard of. He had nerves of steel and balls of brass. He didn't get nervous. He didn't sweat. And no woman had ever intimidated him. Not until now.

Annabelle Vanderley intimidated the hell out of him.

"I can order room service for lunch, if you're hungry," she said as she laid her purse and key on the table just inside the entrance.

"Maybe later, unless you want something now."

She shook her head. "I just want to be with you."

Her soft voice wrapped the words around him like a silk blanket. Quinn closed his eyes and savored the moment. *God in heaven, don't let me hurt this woman.*

"Annabelle, I . . ."

She turned to him, there in the entranceway, her eyes glistening with unshed tears, her cheeks flushed and her sweet, pink lips parted on an expectant sigh.

He reached for her. As she came to him, he slipped one arm around her waist and brought her close, close enough to kiss. When she tilted her face up and gazed into his eyes, he desperately wanted to kiss her. Ravage her. Strip her naked and make love to her the whole afternoon. And then he wanted to start over again and pleasure her repeatedly, all night long.

"You don't know me, honey," he told her, his mouth almost touching hers.

"I know all I need to know." Breathless, she closed her eyes and brushed her lips over his.

Instant hard-on.

He pressed his cheek against her. "Do you know that I call all women honey?"

She wrapped her arms around him and laid her head on his shoulder. "Are you trying to warn me that I'm just like all the others?"

No! You're not like all the others and that's the problem. I never cared what the others thought of me, just as long as they considered me a great lover. But with you, Annabelle . . . ? With you I want—no, I need—your respect. "Would you believe me if I said no, that you're special? Very special."

Her breasts pressed against his chest; his erection pressed against her belly.

"Don't say it if you don't mean it," she told him, then dotted tiny kisses up the side of his neck.

He swallowed hard, ordering himself to go slow, to not lose control.

He grabbed her by the shoulders and shoved her backward, forcing her to open her eyes and look up at him.

"Quinn?"

"I want it to be different with you," he said. "I want it to be different for the two of us. I need more than just sex with you. I need to make love to you. I want us to make love to each other."

She sighed. "That's what I want, too."

"Then let's slow down, honey." He grimaced. "No, not honey. Darling. My darling Annabelle." He spoke the words slowly, in his sexy Texas drawl, then said in Spanish, *"Querida."*

Although his father had been Mexican and many of his friends had been Hispanic when Quinn was growing up,

English was his native language because he'd been raised by his Anglo mother. Sheila Quinn Cortez hadn't known more than a dozen words in Spanish. He'd picked up the language on the street, where he'd picked up most of what he'd learned as a kid. He spoke Spanish fairly fluently and was told with barely any accent.

Annabelle looked at him as if he were the dearest thing on earth to her. And that's when he knew he could have her. Right now. He could lift her into his arms, carry her into the bedroom and . . .

"Honey's an easy word. A meaningless endearment as far as I'm concerned," he told her. "And by calling all women honey, I never make the mistake of saying the wrong name at the wrong moment." He grasped Annabelle by the nape of her neck. "I've never called a woman *querida* before."

Quinn kissed her. Using every ounce of his willpower to not ravage her, he settled his lips on hers with tender force and savored the taste of her. She opened her mouth, inviting him inside, and he accepted her welcome. Deepening the kiss, his tongue dueled with hers. Savage, yet tender.

He ached. Ached with the need to be inside her.

When they were both breathless, he lifted his head and gazed into her eyes. He wondered if she saw in his eyes what he saw in hers. More than passion. Something far beyond mere desire. A wanting that went soul deep. A need as essential as air to breathe.

What was this thing between them—this powerful element that defied description?

"Annabelle . . . *querida* . . ." He cupped her face with his open palms. "Why did I meet you now when my life is falling apart?"

"I've asked myself that same question," she said. "And the only answer I can think of is that fate likes to play cruel jokes on us. Why else would I have fallen in love with a man I barely know, a man who is a suspect not only in my cousin's murder, but in the murders of four other women?"

A fiery strumming radiated throughout his body as if he

were burning from the inside out, the blaze ignited by Annabelle's confession of love.

"I—I don't know what to say. Annabelle, I—"

She placed her index finger over his lips to silence him. "I don't want you to tell me that you love me. Not now. Not ever—unless you mean it."

Quinn didn't know what love was—any kind of love. He understood friendship and loyalty and duty. He revered power and wealth. He played fair, but he played by his own rules.

"I swear to you that I'll never lie to you," he told her. "I care about you in a way I've never cared about anyone else. Is that enough for you?"

"For now."

Quinn lifted her up and into his arms. Squealing softly, she flung her arms around his neck and put her cheek to his. He carried her across the room, then sat on the sofa, cradling her on his lap. She snuggled against him.

"We might be more comfortable in the bedroom," she said.

"Later," he told her. "Right now, I think we should get to know each other. Talk, kiss, do a little light petting."

Annabelle smiled.

"Quinn Cortez, are you trying to be a gentleman?"

He traced the back of his hand down her cheek and held it against her chin. "*Si, querida*, I'm trying, but it's not easy for a bad boy like me."

Chapter 23

Annabelle reclined on the sofa, her back resting against Quinn's chest, her legs spread out across the seat and her ankles crossed. The back of her head lay against his shoulder, his chin pressed against her temple. They had spent the past couple of hours talking, mostly about the days and nights she had recently spent at home in Austinville . . . and about Lulu, both of them choosing to remember only the good things about her. Annabelle had ordered lunch, which they had eaten leisurely and had only a few minutes ago finished with dessert and coffee. The remains of their meal littered the small dining table across the room and their empty coffee cups and dessert plates cluttered the cocktail table. Except for when they'd eaten lunch, they had sat together, Annabelle curled in Quinn's arms, here on the sofa, soft kisses and lingering caresses interfused with their conversation.

A comfortable togetherness. Easy and relaxed. No pressure. No demands. Only a sweet, gentle prelude to lovemaking, tender expressions of two people who wanted to be with each other more than they wanted anything else on earth.

After lunch, while she had poured their coffee, Quinn had found a jazz station on the radio, one that played mostly cool jazz, then he'd brought their dessert plates over to the cocktail table. They had wound up eating first her dessert and then his, each feeding the other. Quinn had licked whipped cream from the side of her mouth and she had wiped chocolate from his lips with the tip of her finger, then licked her finger. The whole experience had been romantic and sensual. The moments they had shared seemed to be moments out of time, when nothing and no one else existed.

As he wrapped his arms around her waist and planted his big hands across her belly, Quinn kissed her temple. "What were you like as a little girl?"

"I was spoiled terribly by two parents who adored me. My father helped run Vanderley, Inc., but he never put work before his family." She sighed. "Something my Uncle Louis didn't do with Wythe, but he learned from his mistake and then devoted himself to Lulu." But he had failed his daughter, too. He had loved her dearly, but had failed to protect her from her own brother's sexual attacks.

Don't think about that now. It's too late to do anything to help Lulu. In truth, it had been too late to help Lulu even a few years ago when she'd finally told Annabelle the truth about her relationship with Wythe.

"What was your mother like—like you?" Quinn asked. "Beautiful and smart and sexy?"

"Sexy—me?" She pivoted her head so she could look him in the eyes.

He cupped the back of her head, kissed her tenderly and replied, "Yes, you. Don't tell me that you aren't aware of how sexy you are."

"If you say so." Annabelle smiled, then turned back around and laid her head against his shoulder. "My mother was beautiful and kind and loving. I have her build and smile, her mouth, but I really look more like my father. He was a blue-eyed blond. Very Vanderley looking." She laid her hands over Quinn's where they rested on her stomach. "What were you like as a boy? Precocious? Into everything?"

Quinn didn't reply immediately and she wondered why he was considering his answer so carefully. Weren't childhood memories easily recalled and happily recounted?

"My parents got married because my old man knocked her up. She did a lot of barhopping, liked to party, screwed around. Rico Cortez didn't think beyond getting laid one night and was none too happy when she told him she was pregnant with his baby," Quinn said, his choice of words crudely descriptive. "Their marriage lasted less than a year. The old man split when I was too little to even remember him."

"Oh, Quinn, how terrible for you and your mother, being deserted that way." She nestled against him. "So, did you grow up without a father? Or did your mother remarry?"

"She got herself engaged a couple of times, but the guys wised up before saying I do. As for my old man leaving— yeah, it was bad for me," Quinn said. "But lucky for him. He got away from her, and left me stuck with her for the next sixteen years."

"She wasn't a good mother?"

Quinn harrumphed. "Let's just say Sheila Quinn Cortez wouldn't have won any Mother of the Year awards. She'd leave me for days at a time with anybody who'd keep me. Then she'd come back and get me after she sobered up. My mother was a lush and the older she got the worse the drinking. We didn't have any money and there were times I stole things just so we wouldn't go hungry. If it hadn't been for her men friends . . ." Quinn grunted. "I had so many damn 'uncles' over the years that I lost count."

"Didn't your mother have any family? Didn't you have grandparents who would have—"

She felt the tension as it gripped his big body. "My mother's parents didn't want anything to do with her wetback baby. She went home once, when I was about five or six. They told her that she could stay, but that no son of some dirty, lazy, good-for-nothing Mexican would ever be welcome in their home."

"Quinn . . ." She turned in his arms and hugged him, burying her face against his chest. What must it have been like for a little boy to hear his own grandparents say such terrible things about him?

He wrapped his arms around her and stroked her, from neck to hips. "She might have been a sorry excuse for a mother, but I'll give the old lady credit—she told her parents they could kiss her happy white ass, grabbed my hand and dragged me back to her old ragged Pinto and then we hightailed it out of there."

"You loved your mother, despite everything, didn't you?"

Silence.

With her head resting on his chest, she listened to the rapid thumping of his heart. She sensed his pain, knew how badly his childhood must have affected the rest of his life.

"Quinn?"

"Yeah, I guess I loved her, at least as much as I hated her."

"Is your relationship with your mother the reason you—?"

His hand shot up and grabbed her chin, jerking her head up from his chest. With wide eyes, she stared at him, startled by his actions. But before she had a chance to react, he lowered his head and kissed her.

This kiss was different from the sweet, almost reverent kisses they had been sharing. His mouth took hers not only with hungry desire, but also with desperate need, as if seeking something from her that he hoped she could give him. Could it be love he wanted, needed, and didn't even realize it? Suddenly the kiss consumed her, took her over completely and ended rational thought. So swept up in the tide of Quinn's passion that she could barely breathe, Annabelle returned the kiss, participating fully and on an equal level. Eventually, Quinn moved his mouth from hers, over to her cheek, then down to her neck. He nuzzled her. Her neck drooped languidly to one side as she floated back to reality. When he lifted his head and looked at her with heavy-lidded eyes, she smiled.

"Let's leave discussions about my mother and my childhood for another time," he said. "Why ruin a perfectly beautiful afternoon?"

Annabelle wanted to ask him more about his mother and their relationship. Playing amateur psychiatrist, she could put together several scenarios to explain why apparently Quinn had never been in a long-lasting, committed relationship. He probably didn't trust women in general because he'd never been able to trust and rely on his own mother. And since his only example of male/female partnering had been his mother's promiscuous liaisons, becoming a ladies' man must have seemed the most natural thing in the world to him.

"All women aren't the same, you know," Annabelle said as she cuddled once again in his arms.

"A man knows some things, here." He tapped the side of his head. "And some things here." After tightening one hand into a fist, he pressed it against his belly.

Annabelle grasped his hand, unfurled his fingers and placed his open palm over her heart. "And some things in here." She kept her hand over his. "That's where I want you to know how you feel about me and how I feel about you."

"I'm not very experienced at using my heart," he admitted. "I use my brains, my gut instincts and on occasion, my animal needs. Feelings are something I don't think about much and I sure as hell don't talk about them." He flipped his hand over and grasped hers, then dragged it down her body until they reached the apex between her thighs. "I know more about what a woman feels down here than I do about what's going on in her heart." He pressed their joined hands against her mound.

At his touch, her body clenched and tingled, sending out sexual signals. "I want us to make love and if that's all you can give me, then I'll take it and be glad to be your lover," Annabelle told him. "But I'll warn you, Quinn Cortez, I want more. I'm one of those women who prefers that sex and love be combined in a relationship. And even if you think you aren't capable of loving someone the way I want to be loved, it doesn't change the fact that I've fallen in love with you."

He hugged her fiercely, yet tenderly. Leaning forward and burying his face against her neck, he whispered, "That fact should scare me. It should make me want to run. But it doesn't scare me and God knows I never want to run from you." He lifted his head and rubbed his cheek against hers. "But Annabelle, my darling Annabelle . . . you deserve so much better."

She turned in his arms again and wrapped herself around him. "What you're really thinking is that you don't deserve me."

"You're right—I don't deserve you. You're much too good for the likes of me."

"I don't see it that way," she told him as she caressed his cheek, the light beard stubble rough on her soft fingers. "I think you need me. I think I'm the woman you do deserve, a woman who can love you with all her heart. A woman who is capable of devotion and fidelity, a woman you can trust."

Quinn closed his eyes as if her touch and her words combined were more than he could bear. "You deserve a man capable of giving back those same things to you."

She cupped his face, then ran the tip of her thumb across his slightly parted lips. "I hear reformed bad boys make great husbands."

Quinn grinned. "You heard that, did you?"

"Mmm-hmm. It's like sinners who get religion and become religious fanatics. It's a scenario as old as time—bad boy meets good girl and changes his ways. The beast learns that being loved by the right woman can turn him into prince charming."

"Do you believe in fairy tales, *querida*?"

"Yes, I do."

He took her hand and brought it to his lips. "I should have known you were a romantic."

She sighed. "When I was twenty-two, I became engaged

to someone I thought was the love of my life. Christopher. He was everything I wanted in a man, in a husband, in a father for my children."

Quinn tensed. "Why are you telling me about this man?"

"Only a short time before our wedding, Chris nearly died in a horrific car crash. His injuries left him paralyzed. I wanted us to marry, but he wouldn't marry me because . . ." She swallowed. "Chris wasn't able to have sex."

Quinn said nothing.

"I loved Chris with all my heart and we remained engaged until the day he died, two years ago. During all those years, I remained faithful to Chris, except for . . . I had a one-night stand with an old friend over five years after Chris's wreck and later I had a brief affair with a man I admired and respected, but there was never anyone in my heart, except Chris." She shivered when Quinn kissed her fingers. "When I love, I love completely, with all that is in me. No half measures. If our relationship goes beyond a brief affair, I will be yours—heart, mind, body and soul."

Quinn kissed her fingers, her hand, rubbing his mouth over her flesh as he closed his eyes. "Somehow I knew—instinctively—the moment I first saw you that you were different, that you were special. The feeling hit me like a bolt out of the blue." He opened his eyes, held their hands between their bodies and gazed adoringly at her. "Getting involved with me is wrong for you. You should kick me out of here, tell me to go away, leave you alone and never bother you again. If you were smart you'd—"

"I'm in love with you. Maybe it's foolish. Maybe I'll live to regret it. But I can't change it. I don't think I'd change it if I could. Loving you feels so . . . so incredible."

He settled her back into his arms and held her. The quiet hush of the afternoon, alone together in Annabelle's suite, enveloped them. They lay there on the sofa, savoring the delicious contentment of being wrapped up in each other, physically and emotionally. There was no place on earth Annabelle would rather be, no other man she wanted. Now or ever.

* * *

Marcy looked at her watch again. Eight-fifteen. Where the hell was Quinn? Why hadn't he bothered to call her? Didn't he realize that she worried about him? She glanced at the wall phone there in the kitchen, wishing it would ring.

"Why don't you just call him?" Aaron said as he came into the room.

"What?" Marcy snapped around and glared at him.

"The boss man hasn't checked in all day and you're worried. Call him."

"I shouldn't bother him."

Aaron slipped his arms around her waist and dragged her back against him, then kissed her on the nape of her neck. "If you're worried about Quinn, you'll fuss and fume all evening instead of mellowing out with me and a good bottle of wine."

"What makes you think I'm going to mellow out with you?"

"Because you want more of what I've got to give. And don't deny it."

"I didn't intend to deny anything," she told him.

"So call Quinn, find out where he is and ask him if he's coming home tonight. If he is, you'll want to make sure he doesn't catch us. After all, you're still fantasizing that one of these days you'll be the love of Quinn's life."

"Shut up."

"Just call him, will you?" Aaron released her, went to the refrigerator and grabbed a canned cola.

"I do need to know whether or not he'll be home for supper."

"Good enough excuse."

Marcy's hand wavered over the wall phone. *Just dial his cell number. When he answers ask if he'll be home for supper. Like Aaron said, it's a good excuse to contact him.* She glanced over her shoulder at Aaron.

"I'm leaving," he said. "I know you want your privacy for when you talk to lover boy."

The minute Aaron walked out of the kitchen, she lifted the receiver and dialed Quinn's cell number. The phone rang and rang and rang. Finally, just when she thought voice mail would pick up, she heard Quinn's voice and she also heard music in the background. And something that sounded like the drone of voices.

"Quinn, it's Marcy."

"Yeah? What do you want? Has something happened?" Quinn asked.

"No, no. Everything is okay. I—I just wondered—"

"Talk louder, will you, honey?"

She hadn't realized that she'd been practically whispering. "Where are you?"

"At Chez Philippe, at the Peabody. Annabelle and I are having dinner."

"Oh." He was with her. Lulu's cousin. How could he wine and dine his former lover's cousin? What kind of woman was she to succumb so easily to Quinn's advances? "I guess that answers my question."

"What question?"

"I just wanted to know if you were coming home for supper."

"Oh, Marcy, I'm sorry. I should have called you. I wasn't thinking. Annabelle and I have spent the day together and I just forgot to phone."

He'd spent the day with her. Had they been making love? Had Annabelle Vanderley become Quinn's latest conquest? "Aaron told me that neither you nor he turned out to be the father of Lulu's baby. That's good. For both of you."

"Yes, it was. But unfortunately it doesn't let me off the hook," Quinn told her. "Look, I'll explain everything to y'all tomorrow. Okay?"

"Okay."

Marcy thought she heard a woman's voice. Soft, wispy. Annabelle?

Quinn laughed quietly, a sensual tone in the sound. "Marcy, I won't be home tonight."

That's what Annabelle had said to him, wasn't it? Those were the words Marcy had thought she'd heard the woman say. *Tell her you won't be home tonight.*

"Have a nice time," Marcy finally managed to say.

"See you tomorrow, honey." The line went dead. Marcy stood there in the kitchen, the phone clutched in her hand, and cried. *Idiot. You're so stupid, Marcy. You knew there would be another woman. There always is. And you figured it would be Annabelle Vanderley.*

Damn Annabelle. Damn her and all the other women Quinn had ever been with. She hated Annabelle. She hated them all. Every last one of them.

Chapter 24

Sanders served Griffin coffee while he checked his e-mail. "Would you care for anything else, sir?"

"No, nothing." Griffin opened the e-mail from Lieutenant Craig Stovall, Baytown PD. Stovall had been the lead detective on the Kelley Fleming murder case two years ago. Ben Sullivan would be in Baytown by morning, looking for a photo of Kelley and digging up all the information he could find.

Scanning the message quickly, Griffin hit PRINT, then turned to Sanders who was halfway across the room. "Wait up."

Sanders pivoted quickly. "Yes, sir?"

"See if you can track down Jim Norton," Griffin said. "If you can, ask him to drop by this evening if he will. I have several other phone calls to make."

Sanders nodded.

Griffin telephoned Ben Sullivan, issued him some last minute orders, then phoned Judd Walker's room.

"Walker here."

"Judd, it's Griffin. I just received an e-mail from Lieutenant Stovall from the Baytown PD. He'll fax me a crime scene photo of Kelley Fleming tomorrow morning, but he went ahead and gave me the basic info on her. The woman was forty, had lived in Baytown for only a couple of years. She worked as a waitress. Didn't have any close friends. Lived in a duplex apartment. Kept to herself. The neighbors said a teenage boy lived with her, but the police didn't have any luck tracking down the kid. He wasn't enrolled in school and nobody even knew his name."

"That's interesting," Judd said.

"Gets more interesting. Kelley Fleming was an alias. Her driver's license, social security card—everything—was bogus. They ran an article about her and the only photo they had of her in the newspaper, asking anyone who had information to come forward, but got no response."

"Do you think Quinn might have known this woman under a different name?"

"Possibly. We'll show him the crime scene photo and see if he recognizes her."

"Did the police think maybe the kid killed her?"

"That was one theory and a boyfriend was another, but they never found the kid or a boyfriend," Griffin said.

"Could be the teenage boy was her boyfriend."

"Could be. Another theory was that the murderer might have been a serial killer, but when they checked for similar murders, they came up with zero. But if she was the first . . . Quinn's involved in this somehow, someway. He didn't murder these five women, but someone is killing them because they were involved with Quinn."

"That means Kelley Fleming or whoever the hell she was must have been one of Quinn's girlfriends."

"Why would someone want to kill Quinn's girlfriends?"

"Jealousy," Judd said. "A woman who wants Quinn all to herself and is killing off the competition."

"Hmm . . . Or a man who hates Quinn and wants to pin these murders on him."

"Quinn has probably made a lot of enemies over the years, broken quite a few female hearts and pissed off more than his share of men."

"Looking for a possible murderer among Quinn's enemies will be like looking for a needle in a haystack."

Quinn held Annabelle in his arms as they danced slowly, languidly to the soft strains of a quiet-times, cool jazz number playing on the radio. The alto sax mourned low and sweet, while the bass strummed the lazy beat. With her head on his shoulder and her arms draped around his neck, Annabelle sighed. When, with very little interruption, one tune ended and another began, they barely noticed and stayed in each other's arms, their bodies continuing to sway. As the next tune began, a moody, melancholy rendition of "Body and Soul," Quinn brushed his lips across her temple and down her cheekbone.

Nothing had ever felt this right. Being with Annabelle, holding her, dancing with her, kissing her. Despite the horrors surrounding them—the unsolved murders in which he was a suspect—they had been able to separate themselves from the rest of the world this afternoon and evening. After tender, loving hours spent on the sofa in each other's arms, Quinn had called Chez Philippe for dinner reservations. They had dined on one of Chef Jose's specialties—filet de veau. After dinner, Quinn had ordered chilled champagne and an assortment of desserts to be delivered to their room.

For the past hour, they had been sipping champagne, nibbling on chocolates and dancing. Mostly dancing. Neither wanted to be out of touching distance. And the closer, the better.

Quinn had spent hours making love to a woman before and he'd also enjoyed his share of quickies. He had wined and dined plenty of lovely ladies. And on occasion he had forgone any preliminaries and just screwed a woman. But nothing in his past compared to what he was sharing with Annabelle.

They had been making love for endless hours, in the old-fashioned sense that equated to romantic foreplay. Lingering glances, gazing into each other's eyes. Touching tenderly, caressing, stroking. Kissing, tasting, licking. Every heartbeat connected, every breath simultaneous.

"I wish this night never had to end," Annabelle told him, her voice enticing, her words seductive.

Leaning his head over onto hers, he whispered, "I wish that, too."

She inched the fingers of one hand up and into his hair, while the other hand gripped his shoulder. "We can't pretend there aren't any problems to be overcome, but—"

"Leave those problems until tomorrow," he told her as he slid both hands down her back and cupped her buttocks, lifting her up and into his erection. "Tonight, there are no problems. There is no tomorrow."

As the dreamy music filled Annabelle's hotel suite, she stopped dancing, stood on tiptoe and kissed Quinn. "No problems. No tomorrow. Only now, tonight and the two of us."

They kissed again and again, all the while their hands roamed, exploring, discovering. When she was breathless and trembling, Quinn lifted her up and into his arms. She flung her arms around his neck as he carried her across the room to the sofa. He laid her on the soft cushions, then came down over her, balancing his body over hers with his knees and elbows on either side of her. She lifted herself up to meet his kiss. He undid the tiny pearl buttons on her silk blouse, kissing each new inch of flesh he exposed. She mimicked his moves and unbuttoned his shirt, then jerked it free from his pants. While she planted kisses over his smooth, muscular chest, he threaded his fingers through her hair and cradled her head with one hand. When she came up for air, he undid the front hook on her satin bra and spread it apart to reveal her high, round breasts. He couldn't resist touching them, cupping them in his hands. Each were more than a handful, neither small nor large. Just right. Perfect.

When he flicked her nipples with the pads of this thumbs, she keened softly and arched her back so that her mound aligned with his straining erection.

He was so ready. Wanted her so badly. Needed to be inside her now.

"Oh, Quinn, please . . ."

He lowered his head and kissed her directly below her breasts, then unzipped her black slacks and smiled when he saw the black satin bikini panties she wore. He shoved the slacks aside and the panties down far enough to expose a glimpse of dark blond hair covering her mound. He licked a path from between her breasts to the edge of that curly hair.

Tugging on her slacks, he managed to maneuver them down her legs and off, taking her panties, too. She lay before him wearing only her open shirt and bra, her body exposed.

"You're lovely," he said. "But I knew you would be."

When she tried to reach for his belt, he gently slapped her hands away. If she touched his penis, he might not be able to wait. And he wanted to wait. There were things he wanted to do before he took her completely.

"Quinn?"

"Later, *querida*. For now, leave everything to me."

He spread her legs apart and placed himself between them, then lifted her thighs up and over his shoulders, giving him easy access to his objective. He kissed her inner thighs, first one and then the other. She clutched his shoulders. He licked around her pubic lips, tasting the musky sweetness. She shuddered.

His lips encompassed the soft, pink tissue and sucked gently. Annabelle gasped, then panted when he tongued her clitoris.

"Oh, God, Quinn."

Her moisture gushed, dampening his mouth. He worked his tongue over her sensitive nub. Relentlessly. Passionately. When he realized she was on the verge of coming, he reached up and pinched her nipples, then rubbed them between his thumbs and index fingers. She cried out, then fell apart, her climax hitting her hard. But he didn't ease up, didn't slow down. With his fingers tormenting her breasts, his tongue took her over the edge and beyond, until she was totally spent and begging him to stop. Her body shook and shivered, almost convulsing in the intensity of her orgasms.

Jim and Griffin talked about old times for a good hour, drinking the Guinness beer that Griffin remembered Jim liking so much when they'd worked together a number of years ago on the art store robberies. He'd had Sanders go out and buy this particular brand, just for Jim. They had been college buddies, teammates, even double-dated several times back in the good old days. He knew Jim wanted to ask him about those mysterious ten years of his life when he had disappeared off the face of the earth, but he couldn't talk about those years, not even to an old friend, a guy he would trust with his life.

When there was a lull in the conversation, Jim asked, "What's up? It's not that I'm not enjoying your companionship and your beer, but you didn't ask Sanders to call me and invite me over just because you wanted to see my ugly face again so soon."

"Actually, I did have an ulterior motive."

Jim chuckled. "No kidding?"

"I've got a client I believe is innocent and the only way to prove he's innocent is by finding the guilty party," Griffin said. "Just like Quinn and Annabelle Vanderley, you and I want the same thing. Hell, all four of us want the same thing."

"Okay. We all want to find out who murdered Lulu and Kendall." Jim held up his hand to signal Griffin to let him finish before he spoke. "And yeah, you think the same guy killed both of them and those three other women—the two in Texas and the one in New Orleans."

"I think we should be working together. Unofficially, of course. We each have resources we can use. There are things you can do that I can't because I'm not law enforcement. And there are things that I can do that you can't because I'm a private investigator."

"If I agree, it would have to be unofficially. So, what comes first?"

"We decide on the most likely scenario," Griffin said.

"Which would be?"

"A serial killer with a direct tie to Quinn Cortez," Griffin said. "Either a woman who wants to eliminate the competition or a man seeking revenge. Somebody with a reason to want to hurt Quinn, either by making him feel guilty or by pinning these murders on him."

"It's a reasonable scenario." Jim took another swig from his second bottle of Guinness. "But it works only if Kelley Fleming was one of Cortez's women."

"I'm assuming you know what I know about Kelley." Griffin sipped on the Guinness, a strong, dark, Irish brew.

"And that would be?" Jim smiled.

"Okay, I'll give first—that her name was an alias, her ID all fake, that she either had a teenage kid or she had a boyfriend who was a teenager."

"Did you talk to Lieutenant Stovall?"

"I left him a message. He e-mailed me the info. Said he'd fax the crime scene photos in the morning."

"Then you don't have a photo of Kelley?"

Griffin shook his head.

Jim placed his beer on the cocktail table, then stuck his hand into his inside coat pocket and pulled out a folded piece of paper. "I talked to Stovall's partner, a guy named Estes. He faxed me the photos just a few minutes before Sanders called." Jim opened up the folded sheet and handed it to Griffin. "He sent several shots, but this is the only one that gives you a really good look at her face."

Griffin took the faxed photograph and studied it carefully. The woman appeared to be sleeping. "She was only forty, according to her phony ID. But she looked older."

"Maybe she was. Or maybe she'd just lived a rough life."

"Possibly both."

"She's not especially pretty, but not butt ugly either," Jim said. "Just haggard looking."

"I know what you're thinking."

"Do you?"

"You're thinking that she's not Quinn Cortez's type," Griffin said. "All four of the other women had something in common, besides being Quinn's lovers. They were all very attractive women."

"Kelley might have been attractive at one time."

"Years ago, maybe, but not two years ago when this photo was taken."

"Then it could be that there is no connection between her and Cortez. Your theory could be wrong."

"It could be," Griffin agreed. "But I don't think so. Maybe Kelley knew Griffin ten or fifteen years ago, back when she might have been attractive."

"That blows your theory, too. Why would the killer have waited all those years to murder her? And if he did wait ten or fifteen years to start killing Cortez's lovers, why start with her? Why leave all the women in between then and now alone?"

"Damn good question."

"Yeah, and if we can find out the answer, we might be able to figure out who our murderer is." Jim paused, looked right at Griffin and said, "Unless Cortez turns out to be our guy after all."

Chapter 25

Unbelievable. Deliciously, wickedly, astoundingly incredible. Annabelle lay there on the sofa, her senses sated, her bones soft, her body floating on a wave of pure satisfaction. Quinn lifted himself and moved up her body, trailing kisses from her mound to her breasts. When he flicked one nipple with his tongue, she gasped with an intense pleasure/pain that signaled to him the hypersensitive state her body was in right now. Chuckling quietly, he came up and over her, then lowered his head and kissed her mouth. She accepted him greedily, kissing him back, tasting herself on his lips.

"How do you feel?" he asked, a devilish twinkle in his black eyes.

"Wonderful. No, I feel more than wonderful." She lifted her hand and shoved back the lone curl that had fallen onto his forehead.

Quinn eased up and off her, then reached down and brought her to her feet. "We're just getting started, *querida*. We have all night."

Annabelle sighed heavily, contemplating more pleasure as the aftershocks of fulfillment still rippled along her nerve endings.

He scooped her up into his arms.

She had never loved life more. She loved this moment . . . and this man.

After carrying her into the bedroom, he laid her atop the covers, then eased her unbuttoned silk blouse and unhooked bra down her shoulders and her arms. While he flung her clothing aside, she kicked off her one-inch heels and peeled off her knee highs; then she scooted over into the middle of the bed and propped her back against the headboard. Sitting there gloriously naked, she became aroused anew simply by being near Quinn.

Taking his time, Quinn undressed. First came his unbuttoned shirt. He tossed it on top of her discarded bra and blouse, which he'd thrown onto a nearby chair; then he sat on the edge of the bed and took off his shoes and socks. When he stood again, she watched as he shed his dark slacks and added them to the pile of their clothing. He shoved his hand into his pants pocket and pulled out three small shiny packets, each containing a condom; then he laid them on the nightstand.

Annabelle surveyed him, from his curly black hair to his large, wide feet. His shoulders were massive, his back broad, his waist narrow. His butt round and tight. When he turned to face her, he grinned and butterflies danced wildly in her stomach. He was, without a doubt, the sexiest man alive.

He stood there by the bed, allowing her to look at him, to rake her gaze over all seventy-three inches of his magnificent body, from head to toe. When her vision focused on his crotch, his erection straining against his black briefs, he slipped his thumbs underneath the elastic band on either side and slid them down his hips.

Annabelle held her breath with anticipation. When his briefs hung on the large bulge in front, he hesitated. Teasing her.

"Take them off," she told him, practically licking her lips.

Quinn whipped off his briefs, stepped out of them and left them lying on the floor.

God, he was—impressive.

When he sat on the bed, she came up behind him and wrapped her arms around him, crushing her breasts against his back. Leaning her head to one side, she swooped down and nibbled on his ear, then licked a circle around the inner curve before whispering longingly.

"Make love to me," she said, "I want you inside me, loving me, showing me how good it can be."

He leaned over and took one of the condom packages from the nightstand, ripped it open and removed the rubber. Annabelle peeked over his shoulder to watch him apply the protection.

Naked, fully aroused and projecting a savage power, Quinn turned and looked at her, then he caressed her face. His touch was electric, sending shock waves through her body. She closed her eyes and savored the moment. He gripped the back of her head and brought her mouth to his, then kissed her. Hard. Demanding.

While still kissing her, his mouth devouring hers, he maneuvered her backward and down onto the bed. Using his knee, he parted her thighs and slipped between them, pressing his penis against her mound. Her hips bucked upward in invitation. His mouth left hers and journeyed down her neck to first one breast and then the other. When he suckled her breast, she shivered as pure sensation shot through her body. Longing. Desire. A primeval need to mate.

"Now, please, Quinn, please."

Running his hands beneath her, her cupped her buttocks and lifted her up so that he could easily take her completely with one fast, deep lunge. She gasped when he filled her, stretched her, giving her all of himself. Her body accepted him, expanding to accommodate his size.

The feel of him inside her was ecstasy. And when he began to move, to retreat and lunge, retreat and lunge, the pleasure intensified. Falling into the rhythm he set, her body undulated with each strong thrust. The tension inside her built again, faster and faster as he increased the tempo. Knowing she was close to climaxing, she encouraged him with hot, erotic words—alien words that she had seldom used. And he told her, in no uncertain terms, what he was going to do to her and how he was going to do it. His gutter vulgarity sent her over the edge, but she didn't go alone. Just as the first wave of her orgasm exploded inside her, he jack-hammered into her. When he came, he shivered and jerked and uttered a deep, guttural groan. Quinn surrendered to the animal in him, then dissolved on top of Annabelle.

Breathing heavily, wet with sexual perspiration, they clung to each other, sharing wild, damp kisses. He eased off her and onto his side, then drew her into his arms.

As she lay there, cocooned in his embrace, one coherent thought wafted through her foggy brain. *That was the best damn sex I've ever had in my entire life.*

The nightmare came again, as it so often did, seeming so real, as if it were happening at this very moment instead of in the past. Sometimes, like now, he knew he was dreaming, that he was asleep and would eventually awake, drenched in sweat, shivering and frightened. If only he could make himself wake now, before reliving those terrifying moments, but his subconscious mind would not allow him even that small mercy. This time, like the countless other times, he would be forced to recall the entire event, from beginning to end.

"How many girlfriends do you have?" she asked him, her voice deceptively sweet and calm.

"None, Mama. I swear I don't have any girlfriends."

"You're lying to me. You know it's not nice to lie, don't you?"

"I'm not lying. I swear I'm not."

"They're calling the house, asking for you. Two of them called just this afternoon, not thirty minutes after you got home from school. One's named Sherry and the other's name is Brittany."

"They're just girls I know from school."

She grabbed his arm and dragged him across the room.

He dropped his book bag on the floor and tried to jerk away from her. He was growing bigger every day, taller and stronger. One of these days she wouldn't be able to overpower him. He was nine years old now and although small for his age, he knew that it was only a matter of time before he would be bigger than she was. When that day came . . .

She grabbed his shoulders and shook him soundly. "What have I told you about fooling around with girls? You're too pretty, too charming. You'll break their hearts. It's not fair for one person to be able to do that to another person."

When she stopped shaking him, she kept a tight hold on his shoulders, her long, thin fingers biting into him painfully. A glazed expression darkened her eyes. He'd seen that look before and knew enough to be frightened. Her mind was wandering off somewhere, to another time and place. Whatever had happened to her there, it must have been terrible because it had filled her with hatred. And cruelty.

Taking advantage of the moment, he jerked away from her and backed several feet from her before she realized he had escaped. Her head snapped up and her gaze punctured him with a dare. He froze to the spot.

"I will not allow you to hurt anyone else," she told him and when he made no response, she asked, "Did you hear me?"

He shook his head.

"You gave those girls our telephone number, didn't you? You wanted them to call and make fools of themselves. They both think you like them. They both think they're your girlfriend. You lied to them, made each one of them think she was special."

"No, I didn't. I swear, I didn't."

"You're doing an awful lot of swearing today, aren't you? Bad, bad Quinn."

Don't pee in your pants. Whatever you do, don't wet yourself. If you do, it'll just make her madder and she'll hurt you worse.

"I'm not—" He caught himself before he corrected her.

She didn't like it when he told her she was wrong about anything. But he kept trying to tell her the truth. *Just agree with her,* he told himself. *If you do that, she'll go easier on you.*

"I'm sorry I gave Sherry and Brittany my phone number," he lied. He hadn't given either girl his number. "I promise that I'll never do it again. I'll never give another girl my phone number."

"Good. I'm glad you understand what a bad thing you did."

God, please, don't let whatever she does to me hurt too much.

She curled her index finger and motioned for him to come to her. It took a couple of minutes, but he finally managed to make his feet move in her direction. He had learned from past experience that disobeying her only made things worse.

When he stood in front of her, a couple of feet separating them, she reached out and patted his cheek. He gulped.

"You know you've been a bad boy."

"Yes, ma'am."

"And what happens to bad boys?"

"They have to be punished."

"That's right, darling. They have to be punished for their own good so that they will learn they can't use their handsome faces and charming personalities to take advantage of other people and hurt them."

He trembled inside, but managed not to shake outwardly.

"You know I love you. If I didn't love you, I wouldn't care. And I wouldn't work so hard to make you a better person."

He nodded. Sweat broke out on his upper lip. An involuntary quiver jiggled his hands, which he held down to either side of his thighs.

She grabbed him by the nape of his neck, then she drew back her other hand and slapped him hard across the face. He reeled from the impact, but didn't cry out even though his cheek and jaw hurt really bad. Using her hand on his neck to force his head to turn in the opposite direction, she hit him again. Harder. He moaned, unable to stop himself. She smiled. God, he hated it when she smiled that way.

She hit him again and again, until she had busted his lip, bruised one cheek and blackened an eye. Then she stopped, looked at him and frowned. "Why do you force me to do these things to you? Now you won't be able to go to school for a few days. Not looking like that."

"Please, don't keep me at home," he begged. "I'll tell the teacher I fell off my bicycle."

"She won't believe you, dear. You know how teachers are. They don't understand my type of punishment. If they knew it was the only way to control a person like you, they'd understand. But we don't want to have to move again, do we? If they send a social worker to the house, we'll have to leave here, maybe even move to another state."

He knew it wouldn't do any good to argue with her. The only time he felt secure and unafraid was when he was at school. She couldn't touch him there. But if he stayed at home the rest of the week, he'd do something to upset her every day. And she would punish him every day.

"Go to your room," she told him. "There won't be any supper for you tonight. No food for bad little boys."

Thankful to escape from her, he grabbed his book bag off the floor, then turned and ran down the hall and into his room. Just as he started to close the door, he heard her call, "Leave your door open. I don't want you doing something naughty in there. I'll come check on you in a little while, after I've had my dinner."

He left the door wide open—he had no choice.

Hoisting his book bag onto his bed, he sat down, opened the top flap and pulled out his math homework and a pencil. He read over the first problem, but he couldn't concentrate. All he could think about was how much his face hurt, how bad the blood in his mouth tasted and what his mother would do to him later when she came to his room to check on him.

I wish she was dead. I wish one day I'd wake up and she'd be gone to Jesus. If she could just go to heaven, she wouldn't suffer anymore and she could never hurt me again. He glanced up at the ceiling and prayed. *Wouldn't it be better for both of us if she died? Couldn't you just strike her dead? Please.*

But he knew God wouldn't kill her. God left things like that to people here on earth. He understood that God expected him to help his mother. And he would—someday, when he was older, when he had the power to ease all her suffering.

You will be the one to give her peace, he heard a voice inside his head saying. *It will be your duty someday to send your mother to heaven.*

Quinn tossed and tumbled. When he groaned, he rolled over and flung the sheet off, his big arm waving in the air before it came down across Annabelle. His restlessness the past few minutes had roused her, but not until he draped his heavy arm over her and moaned in her ear did she awake completely.

"Don't. Please, don't." He talked in his sleep.

Annabelle touched his forehead. He was warm and sweaty.

"Quinn?"

"Kill you . . . I'll kill you. Please, don't," he mumbled.

Every nerve in Annabelle's body went numb, her muscles stiffened. It was apparent that he was dreaming and had no idea what he was saying. But listening to his words unnerved her. Hearing him pleading with someone, telling someone— what? that he'd kill them? frightened her.

He's having a nightmare, she told herself. Who wouldn't have terrible dreams about death, about murder, if they'd been through what he had? Four of his former lovers had been killed and even though he wasn't the murderer, he still felt guilty. If someone had killed those women—including Lulu—because they'd been Quinn's lovers, it was only natural that he'd feel partly responsible.

"No!" Quinn cried out, then shot straight up in bed, his eyes wild, his breathing erratic.

Annabelle put her arms around him. "It's all right, darling. You were just having a terrible nightmare."

Blowing several times, then drawing in some deep breaths and releasing them, Quinn quieted. She felt the tension in his big body subside, but his muscles remained somewhat taut.

"I'm sorry." He turned to look at her. "I didn't mean to wake you."

"It's all right." She reached up and shoved his unruly, damp curls off his forehead. "Want to tell me about it?"

"About my nightmare?"

She nodded.

"It's an old nightmare, one I haven't had in years, but I suppose after all that's happened recently . . ."

He grabbed her hand, flipped it palm up and kissed the center, then lifted his gaze to hers. "I wanted to wake early and make love again." He nodded toward the nightstand. "We've still got one condom left."

"You changed the subject. I thought you were going to tell me about your nightmare."

"You don't want to hear about that."

"Yes, I do."

He looked at her, an inquiring squint to his gaze. "I said something, didn't I? I talked in my sleep. What did I say?"

"You said, 'please don't.' And then you said, 'I'll kill you.' You said it twice."

Quinn eased out of her arms and stood, fully naked there in the semidarkness of her bedroom, only the faint glow from the nightlight in the bathroom saving them from total darkness.

"If we're going to talk about old demons that still haunt me after all these years, I'm going to need a drink first."

Quinn got out of bed, rummaged through their pile of clothes on the chair and found his pants. After putting on his rumpled slacks, he headed toward the door.

"I can make coffee if you'd like," Annabelle called to him.

He paused before opening the door and glanced over his shoulder at the digital clock on the nightstand. "It is nearly five o'clock, isn't it? Why don't we fix the coffee together and then later order breakfast. And if you're very good to me, *querida,* I'll make love to you between the coffee and our bacon and eggs."

"I like the sound of all of that," she told him as she got out of bed. "The coffee, the bacon and eggs. But mostly the making love."

She fumbled through their clothing until she found Quinn's shirt, then she slipped it on and buttoned it up to the vee between her breasts. Barefooted and eager, she followed him out into the lounge. He flipped on one lamp, which partially illuminated the room, but left most of it in shadows. On his way to the coffeemaker, he paused and pulled the curtains open, revealing a dark, starless sky. A heavy patter of rain-drops hit the window. Off in the distance lightning flickered, then by the time Quinn removed the pot from the coffee-maker, a low, faraway rumble of thunder echoed.

Annabelle opened the coffee packet as Quinn poured the water into the reservoir. While the coffee brewed, he drew her over to the windows, draped his arms around her and held her back to his chest as they stared outside at the city lights below and the rain peppering down steadily.

"The dream was about my mother," Quinn told her, his voice just above a whisper. "I told you that I nearly beat a guy to death because of her."

"Is that what the dream was about—you defending your mother?"

"Yeah. I relive that night from time to time. I can see him hitting her, hurting her. And I tell him to stop, but he doesn't listen. Then I beg him to stop. But he just keeps hitting her. And then I tell him that if he doesn't leave her alone, I'll kill him."

Annabelle tensed despite her best efforts to control her immediate reaction to what he'd said.

"I know. I know. You'd rather think I'm not capable of killing someone." He turned her in his arms, forcing her to look him in the eyes. "But I am. Not in cold blood, but to protect someone I care for. I wanted to stop that man from hurting my mother and I would have killed him if that's what it took to make sure he never hit her again."

"I'm so sorry that you had to go through something like that." She hugged him, wanting to comfort him, longing to erase the unhappy memories that plagued him. She couldn't imagine what it must have been like for him as a boy seeing his mother brutalized.

"It's in the past." He stroked her back as he held her. "And it stays there, at least most of the time. He wasn't the first man who'd knocked my old lady around but until then, I hadn't been physically big enough to stop them. I'm telling you, Sheila could pick some real winners, including my father."

"Your parents must have possessed some good qualities," Annabelle said, lifting her face to his. "Otherwise they couldn't have produced such a remarkable son."

Quinn's lips twitched. "You think I'm remarkable?"

"Remarkable. Extraordinary. Incredible." Annabelle smiled. Quinn kissed her. Featherlight. Tender.

"Those are words I would use to describe you, not me."

"Then you must feel about me the way I feel about you," she told him, seeking the answer in his eyes.

"If you love being with me, love making love to me, want me more than anything on earth and never want me out of your sight, then yes, I'd say I feel the same way you feel."

Her heart laughed with joy. Whether Quinn realized it or not, he had just told her that he loved her. "Don't leave later this morning," she said. "Stay with me. Stay all day and again tonight."

He kissed both of her cheeks and then her forehead. "You just try getting rid of me."

Marcy got out of the rented SUV that she had parked down the street from the Peabody and walked in the rain, not caring that she was getting soaked to the skin. She had let Aaron screw her again last night. And yes, she had enjoyed it, but she didn't love Aaron. God, she wished she did. She'd give anything if she could love anybody other than Quinn. But what could a woman do when she was hog wild crazy about a guy and he kept her at arm's length because she was the best damn assistant he'd ever had?

As she trudged up the street, her feet splattering water right and left, she wondered if she should threaten to quit her job and see what Quinn would do.

He'd let you go, you ninny. He can hire another assistant. They'd be lined up six deep and two blocks long just for an interview, just for a chance to work for him. And even if by some miracle Quinn did become your lover, he'd leave you, just as he's left all the others. You'd be just one more in a never-ending stream of available women.

She was an idiot for coming here, but she hadn't been able to help herself. When she'd woke at four and couldn't go back to sleep, she'd crawled out of Aaron's bed and started to her room, but instead she'd opened the door to Quinn's room and looked at his empty bed.

He had spent the night with Annabelle Vanderley. He'd held her in his arms and made love to her.

Even with her eyes wide open, Marcy could see the two of them together. Naked. Fucking their brains out.

Marcy hated Annabelle. She despised her more than all the others, because she sensed that this woman meant something more to Quinn, that she was different.

Marcy had gone into Quinn's room and had lain on his bed, thinking about what it would be like to lie in his arms, to have him make love to her. She had opened his closet and ran her hands over his tailor-made suits, then she'd gone into the bathroom, opened the lid on his cologne and sniffed.

A couple of minutes later, she'd thrown on a pair of sweats and her sneakers and gone outside to the SUV. Like a real nutcase, she'd flown along the mostly deserted Memphis streets, running one stop sign and one red light in her eagerness.

Now she was here. At the Peabody. Standing outside in the pouring rain, looking up and wondering just where Quinn and Annabelle were and just what they were doing right now. Lying in bed together, listening to the rain? Making love at dawn?

You should be with me, Quinn, her heart cried. *No one will ever love you the way I do.*

Over the years, she had disliked all those other women, but she'd kept telling herself that one day Quinn would look at her and realize he loved her and only her. Then as time passed and Quinn never saw her as more than his faithful assistant, she had begun to hate his other women. But she had never despised any of them the way she did Annabelle.

What will you do if he loves her?

As she stood there on the cool, dark street, gazing up, her tears mingled with the rain. Inside, she was dying. Dying and no one gave a damn. Least of all Quinn.

Chapter 26

Quinn and Annabelle had enjoyed their early morning coffee as they'd sat together on the sofa and watched the dark, rainy sky lighten at dawn, presenting them with a gray, rainy day. They had talked some, but mostly cuddled, savoring the quiet moments alone. And when passion had renewed between them, they had gone back to bed and made slow, sweet love, then fallen asleep afterward and had been awakened less than an hour ago at ten o'clock by Griffin Powell's telephone call.

Breakfast had arrived only a few minutes ago and while Annabelle finished up in the bathroom, Quinn lifted the covers from their plates and poured coffee into their cups. Just as he removed the cellophane wrap from his freshly squeezed orange juice and took a sip, Annabelle emerged from the bedroom. He loved looking at her, every inch, from her long, silky blond hair to her slender feet, which he had discovered were extremely sensitive. Pausing in the doorway, she smiled at him and his gut tightened with awareness. He wasn't sure exactly what was going on with him, whether what he felt for her was love, but he knew that a brief affair wouldn't be enough. He wanted so much more from her, wanted to spend days—no weeks—just being with her, holding her, touching her, making love to her. Or simply looking at her.

"Think we'll have time to eat before Griffin arrives?" Annabelle came toward him, kissed him as if she hadn't seen him in days, then took the orange juice from his hand and drank from his glass.

"If not, he can have some coffee while we eat." Quinn seated Annabelle at the small dining table, but before he could join her, someone knocked on the door. "That'll be Griffin." Quinn checked his wristwatch. "Right on time. Precisely eleven."

"I'll pour him some coffee."

Quinn opened the door to Griffin Powell and found that he was not alone. Lieutenant Norton stood behind and to one side of his old UT teammate. Just the sight of the detective sent up a red warning signal in Quinn's brain. It wasn't that he had anything personal against Norton—not the way he did against Sergeant George—but irregardless, Norton was a Memphis cop and at present the Memphis PD was his enemy.

Ignoring Griffin entirely, Quinn pinned his gaze on Norton. "Should I call my lawyer?"

"I'm not staying," Norton said. "I'm just here to see if you recognize Kelley Fleming from the photo we have of her. No other questions and definitely no interrogation that will require your lawyer."

"That's good since Judd went back to Chattanooga," Quinn said. "I saw no reason for him to hang around here when he can fly back to Memphis in an hour's time if I need him."

"We can have Mr. Walker flown in on the Vanderley jet," Annabelle said as she came up beside Quinn and laced her arm through his.

At that moment, Quinn felt about ten feet tall. And all because of the woman at his side, the woman who believed in him. Trusted him. Loved him.

"May we come in?" Griffin asked, his tone marginally irritated.

"Of course." Annabelle tugged on Quinn's arm, prompting him to move backward so that Griffin and Lieutenant Norton could enter.

"I'll pour two more cups of coffee," Annabelle told Quinn. "Close the door and"—she lowered her voice to a whisper—"be nice to Lieutenant Norton."

Quinn grinned, then when she turned to go back into the lounge area, he closed the door, took a deep breath and joined the others. Both Powell and Norton remained standing.

"Coffee?" Annabelle offered a cup to Norton.

"No, thank you, ma'am."

"Griffin?"

"Yes, thanks." Griffin accepted the coffee, then glanced at Quinn. "Jim's got a photo from the crime scene when Kelley Fleming was killed. It's all we have right now, although I've sent one of my best men to Baytown, Texas, to track down all the information he can get on the lady. And by the way, Kelley Fleming was an alias."

Norton eased a manila envelope out from under his jacket and handed it to Quinn. "Take a look and tell us if you recognize her."

Quinn took the envelope, opened it and removed the photo. His muscles went taut as he looked at the picture, halfway hoping he would recognize the woman and halfway praying he wouldn't. Either way could work in his favor or against him. He studied the woman's face, then her features, one by one.

"I don't recognize her." Quinn slipped the photo back into the envelope.

"We didn't think you would." Jim held out his hand for the photo. "She's not exactly your type."

Quinn handed the envelope back to the lieutenant. "Meaning?"

"Kelley Fleming, or whoever she was, might have been attractive at some point in the past, but let's face it"—Norton waved the envelope back and forth—"this old gal looked like hell. And not just because this is a photo taken post-mortem."

"Does the fact I didn't know her help me or hurt me?" Quinn asked.

"Neither, actually," Norton replied. "At least not at this point."

"Jim needs to know where you were on the date that Kelley Fleming was murdered," Griffin said. "Since Baytown is within easy driving distance of Houston, let's hope you were out of town because that would prove you couldn't have killed Kelley."

"When did she die—two years ago?" Quinn frowned. "I'm not going to remember an exact date from that long ago, but records from my office might help us."

"All I need is your permission to access that information," Griffin said.

"When y'all can give us the answer, call me," Norton said. "In the meantime, I'm going to go out on a limb and assume we have ourselves a serial killer."

"Then that rules out Quinn as a suspect," Annabelle said.

"Not necessarily," Norton replied. "Mr. Cortez could be a serial killer, although I seriously doubt it." Norton looked right at Quinn. "Don't leave Memphis. If we call you in again, we'll be charging you with at least one of our two murders."

Quinn looked the detective squarely in the eye. "I appreciate the fact that you're not concentrating strictly on me as the only suspect."

"I don't have any real leads," Norton said. "But there are a few things I'm going to look into and if we're lucky, we'll find our killer."

Quinn and Norton shook hands, then Griffin walked Jim Norton to the door. Norton paused, glanced back at Quinn and said, "The coroner's office has released Kendall Wells's body. I understand her funeral will be Tuesday."

"Thank you for telling me," Quinn said.

Norton nodded, then left.

After closing the door, Griffin came back into the lounge,

picked up his cup and sat down on the sofa. "You two eat breakfast while I talk. I heard from Derek Lawrence this morning. He's the former FBI profiler we hired to give us some insight into our killer. Using the preliminary profile, Jim and I put our heads together and have come up with a couple of ideas on who the killer might be. Jim's input was unofficial, of course."

"How are we supposed to enjoy our breakfast while you talk about murder and mayhem?" Annabelle glared at Griffin as she speared her scrambled eggs with her fork.

"Sorry," Griffin said, "but if you two don't want me hanging around all day, let's get this over with this morning." Griffin cleared his throat. "And just as a word of caution—if I were y'all, I'd consider staying in and not going out, unless you want the fact that you two are a couple now broadcast all over the news. At least one TV station has a cameraman posted across the street and my guess is there's a reporter or two lurking about."

"Do they know I'm here at the Peabody?" Quinn asked.

"The manager informed me that an employee was let go this morning because he was overheard telephoning someone— probably a reporter—and telling them that Quinn Cortez spent the night in Annabelle Vanderley's suite."

"Goddamn son of a bitch!" Quinn pounded his fist on the table, clinking the silverware against the plates and sloshing his and Annabelle's coffee out of the cups and over into the saucers.

"Cool down," Griffin said. "Until you two are seen leaving the Peabody together, it's only supposition. So, Quinn, when you do get ready to leave, either we'll find a way to slip you out of here or you and I will go out together and Annabelle will stay safely behind."

"I don't care if the whole world knows that Quinn stayed here with me last night." Annabelle dropped her fork, then reached across the table and covered Quinn's fist with her hand.

Quinn stared at her, a sense of well-being flourishing inside him. He had never known anyone like Annabelle. No pretenses. No lies. No hidden agenda.

"If Annabelle doesn't care, then I sure as hell don't." Quinn opened his fist, grabbed her hand and squeezed.

Griffin cleared his throat again. "Business first."

Blushing, Annabelle slipped her hand out of Quinn's. "Of course."

"You said that you've already heard back from the profiler," Quinn said. "That was quick, wasn't it?"

"You get what you pay for and we paid dearly for him. Derek Lawrence is one of the best." Griffin slipped his hand inside his coat pocket and pulled out a small notebook. "This is only a preliminary profile, of course, but it certainly gives us something to go on."

"Where would you even begin to look for a serial killer?" Annabelle asked.

"We start with this profile," Griffin replied. "Lawrence says our guy is nomadic. The word is self-explanatory. He or she isn't stationary or territorial. He's killed in Texas, Louisiana and Tennessee. Thirty-four percent of serial killers are nomadic. And our guy—or gal—is probably a mission killer. This person believes it's his duty to eliminate a certain type of woman. In this case, a woman who sleeps with Quinn Cortez."

"What are you saying?" Annabelle's eyes widened. Surprise? Fear? "All the women Quinn slept with in the past have not been murdered. And he didn't even know Kelley Fleming or whatever the woman's real name was."

"Just because he didn't recognize Kelley Fleming doesn't mean he didn't know her," Griffin said.

"If I knew her, I would have recognized her." After speaking hurriedly, defending himself, Quinn considered the possibility that Griffin might be right. "But what if I knew her five or ten years ago and she'd changed so much that—"

"Save that supposition for when I present the scenarios that Jim and I came up with," Griffin continued. "If all of these women, including Kelley, were Quinn's lovers, then that's why they were killed. Either by someone on a mission to eliminate the competition or to punish these women, thus he or she is a mission killer."

"Why did the murders begin only in the past couple of years?" Annabelle asked. "Actually, except for Kelley, only in the past year?"

"Good question," Griffin said. "If the murders began with Kelley and if we can figure out why she was the first, we'll be one step closer to finding our killer."

"The person we're looking for is a nomadic, mission killer," Quinn said. "What else?"

"The murders seem to be victim and method specific," Griffin told them. "The victims were all Quinn's lovers and the way in which they were killed—smothered with a pillow—is the same, as is the postmortem removal of the right index finger."

"A nomadic, mission killer whose murders are both victim and method specific. What does this really tell us?" Annabelle shook her head as she spread her hands, palms up, in an exasperated manner.

"Lawrence said the person we're looking for was probably abused as a kid, suffered severe emotional trauma and maybe physical abuse. Removing the right index finger of each victim could be symbolic of a female authority figure who pointed her index finger at him while chastising him. A mother, a teacher, a foster parent, a nun . . ."

"People who had shit childhoods number in the millions," Quinn said. "And I'm one of those millions, as are some of my friends and employees. The Judge Harwood Brown Boys Ranch is filled with guys who came from very unstable home environments."

"Since you mentioned the ranch, I'll go ahead and toss out one of our scenarios," Griffin said. "You've helped a lot of kids over the years, mostly boys from the ranch, but several troubled girls, too. Three former delinquents make up your personal entourage. What if one of the kids you came into contact with through your work for the ranch fixated on you for some reason and transferred his hatred of this female authority figure in his life onto your lovers."

"You aren't suggesting that Aaron or Jace might—"

"I'm not suggesting either of them is guilty of anything. But I would like your permission to dig around in their pasts. And put out some feelers about other alumni of the ranch."

"Go ahead and dig," Quinn said. "You'll find that both of them—Jace and Aaron—were abused as kids. That doesn't make either of them a killer."

"No, it doesn't. But they do travel with you and would know your itinerary. And that includes Marcy Sims."

"Marcy? A female serial killer." Quinn laughed. "Good God, Marcy wouldn't hurt a fly."

"Never underestimate the rage of a jealous woman," Griffin said.

"I know what you're suggesting and you're way off base." Quinn's gaze connected with Annabelle's inquisitive glare. "Marcy's got a crush on me. She has for years, but there has never been anything romantic between us. For heaven's sake, when I first met her, she was barely sixteen."

"Once again, I'm not accusing anybody of anything, just presenting possibilities." Griffin stood. "Are you going to Kendall Wells's funeral?"

"Yes," Quinn replied.

"The press will be there. And her family may not want you to attend."

"Screw the press. As for Kendall's family—who are we talking about anyway? Her ex-husband, some cousins, an elderly aunt. Kendall was an only child and her parents are both dead."

"By not going to the funeral, you could avoid a possibly ugly scene," Griffin said.

"Kendall was my friend and my lawyer, not just an old lover. The least I can do is go to her funeral."

"If you'd like, I'll go with you," Annabelle said.

Griffin groaned. "The press will be there, lurking about, hoping for a scoop. You two are asking for trouble."

Annabelle smiled at Quinn, then looked right at Griffin. "Together, Quinn and I can face anything."

Griffin shrugged, then headed toward the door. He paused and glanced over his shoulder, spanning his gaze across the table from Quinn to Annabelle. "Love can't conquer all, you know. You two can shut the world out today, but when to-morrow comes . . . Annabelle, I don't think you should be alone. Our killer is apparently targeting Quinn's lovers and that now includes you. I suggest you let me assign a guard for you whenever you aren't with either Quinn or me."

"You believe I'm in danger?" Annabelle asked.

"Griffin's right," Quinn said. "From now until we find this guy, you can't be alone. When I can't be with you, Griffin will be or one of his agents."

"Yes, of course, if that's what you think is best."

"Good decision," Griffin told her. "I'll talk to y'all tomor-row or before then if I have any relevant news."

As soon as Griffin left, Quinn shoved his chair back from the table and got up, leaving behind his untouched breakfast.

"Quinn?"

With his back to her, he inhaled and exhaled, trying to calm his anger. Anger directed at himself. What had he been thinking becoming Annabelle's lover? Hell, he hadn't been thinking and that was the problem. He'd wanted her more than he'd ever wanted anyone. And what Quinn wants, Quinn gets.

"I've put you in danger by becoming your lover," he told her. "God, Annabelle, I'm sorry. So sorry."

With his own heartbeat pounding in his ears, he didn't hear her approach, didn't know she was behind him until she slipped her arms around him and laid her head on his back.

"Don't do this to yourself. You didn't become my lover without my full cooperation, you know."

"But what if he comes after you?" Quinn couldn't bear the thought of anything happening to Annabelle.

"If he does, you'll stop him. Or Griffin will. Or Lieutenant

Norton." Annabelle gasped. "Quinn, what if . . . if the police were to set a trap for him and use me as bait."

Quinn whirled around, grabbed her and hugged her fiercely. "Don't think such a thing. And never, under any circumstances, suggest such a thing to the police. Do you hear me?"

When she didn't respond, he grasped her shoulders and shook her. "Annabelle? Do you understand?"

She wrapped her arms around him and whispered, "Yes, I understand."

They hadn't gone out at all today, instead they'd stayed in Annabelle's suite and made love. After leaving their uneaten breakfasts on the table, they'd talked for a while, then Quinn had made a phone call. Half an hour later, a bellman had come to the door and delivered a small sack, which Annabelle soon discovered contained a box of condoms.

"What if he tells the reporter?" she had teased Quinn.

"You don't care any more than I do."

They had made love in a wild frenzy, then slept for a couple of hours and ordered a late lunch. After devouring every bite on their plates, including a sinfully rich dessert that they shared, they made love again.

What better way to spend a rainy Sunday afternoon? Annabelle stretched her arms above her head, then rolled over and snuggled up against Quinn, who suddenly seemed a million miles away as if he were thinking very hard about something. Was he still worrying about the fact that the killer would find out they were lovers and possibly come after her?

"Penny for your thoughts," she said.

He slipped his arm beneath her shoulders and kissed her forehead. "I don't want us to have any secrets. I've told you why you shouldn't be with me, why I'm such a poor risk for any woman."

She placed her index finger over his lips. "That's the past.

This is the present. You may not realize it yet, but you love me."

"Is that right?"

"That's right."

"Before we take things any further—make any kind of plans—there's something I have to tell you."

For about half a minute, Annabelle couldn't breathe. "What?" she asked in a whooshing gasp.

"About a year ago, I had an odd sleepy episode, sort of a blackout of some kind. And I've had three more since then."

"Have you seen a doctor?"

"No. I didn't think much about the first two, just chalked each one up to being overly tired. And even the third time, I wasn't sure. But the fourth time, I knew something was wrong."

"We'll make an appointment with the best doctor in Memphis and—"

"No, not yet. I can't. I . . ." He sat up in bed, pulling her with him, then turned her to face him. Looking at her, but not touching her, he said, "The first spell happened the morning Joy Ellis was murdered in New Orleans and the second happened the night Carla Millican was killed in Dallas."

Annabelle thought her heart stopped at that moment. For half a second at least. "And the other two times?"

"The night Lulu was killed and the night Kendall was killed."

Oh, God! What was he trying to tell her?

"Annabelle . . . *querida* . . . what if when I blacked out, I didn't know what I was doing and I actually killed—"

She grabbed him and wrapped her arms around him. "No!" She screamed the word. "You did not kill anyone and you know you didn't."

Silence.

"Quinn Cortez, I love you. And I trust you."

"You don't know what it means to me for you to say that

to me now. I don't think I'm capable of cold-blooded murder, but it can't be a coincidence that I've passed out each time one of my lovers was murdered."

"You're right, it can't be a coincidence, which means someone is drugging you. Someone wants you to think you might have killed those women. And they're making sure you don't have an alibi for the time the murders occur."

He enfolded her completely in his embrace and pressed his cheek to hers. "I won't let anything happen to you. I swear I'll protect you. If I lost you—"

"You aren't going to lose me. Not ever."

"Is that a promise?"

"That, my darling, is a solemn vow."

Chapter 27

Jim Norton didn't subscribe to the daily *Commercial Appeal* or any other paper or magazines. He usually glanced over the newspaper at work, but got the bulk of his news from TV, the way most people did. So, today when he'd been running late and hadn't even flipped on the nineteen-inch television in his small living room, he had missed the news that the entire Criminal Justice Center was abuzz with this Tuesday morning. He heard snippets of gossip in the elevator, just enough to pique his curiosity. Something concerning the big story in the *Commercial Appeal* about four of Cortez's lovers being victims of a serial killer. After getting off the elevator on the tenth floor, he went in search of a newspaper, which wound up being easy to find. Sandra Holmes handed him a copy when he stopped by her cubicle.

"Somebody's going to be in deep shit," she said. "Only a handful of people were in possession of this information, right?"

Jim scanned the headlines—DEADLY LADY-KILLER—and then the accompanying article that informed the readers about Quinn Cortez's connection to four murder victims, the two most recent here in Memphis.

"Goddamn," Jim cursed under his breath. "Where's Chad?"

"He's in Inspector Purser's office. And the director is in there with them. Why do you ask? You don't think Chad—"

"It's a sure bet that Cortez, his lawyer or Griffin Powell didn't leak this information to the press, so that leaves the Memphis PD. I know I didn't breathe a word of this to anyone, so by process of elimination . . ."

"Jim, don't go in there half-cocked and make accusations you can't prove," Sandra warned. "For all you know, Chad's in there right now covering his ass if he did do it."

"I wouldn't put it past the little prick to try to implicate me."

"I doubt he'd do anything that stupid. Purser has known you for a long time. He knows you're a man of integrity."

Jim halfway smiled. "Thanks for the vote of confidence."

Sandra looked at him with a soft glint in her eyes as if remembering their recent night together. That hungry look lasted all of thirty seconds, then she smiled back at him and glanced at the newspaper he held. "Why would Chad, or anyone else, leak that info?"

"To sway the court of public opinion. Chad wants Cortez to be guilty, but we don't have enough evidence against the man to arrest him. If the public demands an arrest, that will put pressure on Director Danley, which in turn puts pressure on Ted Purser to make an arrest."

"I don't like to think that one of our own would try to manipulate the situation. I know Chad's got his faults, but maybe you're wrong about him." Sandra reached up and grasped Jim's arm. "Don't do or say anything you might regret later."

Jim pulled loose of her hold and handed her the newspaper. "Anything I have to say, I'll say one-on-one to Chad. But you can be sure that Cortez's lawyer is going to be demanding some answers. I see an all-out inquiry into this matter. Somebody's going to get blamed for this and it sure as hell won't be me."

"Norton!"

Recognizing Ted Purser's gravelly voice, Jim groaned.

"Jim, please . . ." Sandra issued him a cautionary look.

He smiled at her, then turned and headed toward the inspector's office, where Ted stood in the doorway waiting on him.

"Yeah, what's up?" Jim took his time, sauntering leisurely toward his boss.

"We need to talk. Now," Purser said.

As soon as Jim entered the inspector's office and the door closed behind him, he glanced around at the small group assembled there. Ted Purser, of course. And Director Danley, Chad George and DA Campbell.

"You've seen this morning's *Commercial Appeal*," Purser said in a matter-of-fact manner.

Jim nodded.

"I've already had a call from Cortez's lawyer," Director Danley said. "He's demanding somebody's head on a silver platter and he wants it served to him ASAP."

"I was just explaining to the director that I do not believe anyone in my department leaked this information," Ted Purser said. "Chad's assured us that neither he nor you were in contact with any reporters."

"Jim and I aren't the only ones who possessed this information about Cortez's link to these four murder victims," Chad said. "There are others in homicide who could have leaked the info to the press. Sandra Holmes ran a check—"

Jim growled, the sound coming from deep in his chest. Before he hit Chad with a scurrilous glare, the sergeant stopped midsentence.

"I wasn't implying that Sandra is the one who did it," Chad said. "As a matter of fact, I don't think she did. She'd have no reason to have done it. Right, Jim?"

"That's right," Jim said. "But all we have to do is find someone who did have a reason to want the public up in arms about Cortez, someone who wants Cortez arrested, even without hard cold facts to back up that arrest. Now, who would that be?"

Chad flushed. Inspector Purser glanced back and forth

from Jim to Chad. Not picking up on Jim's subtle accusation, the director and the DA looked at him with puzzled expressions.

Ted Purser cleared his throat. "We'll be doing an internal
investigation into this matter. We wanted you two to be fore-
warned since you're the detectives in charge of the Vanderley
and Wells murder cases."

"Will that be all?" Jim asked.

"For now," Purser replied.

"Chad, you coming?" Jim asked.

"Sure thing."

Jim walked out of the office, then waited for Chad to
emerge, knowing his partner would have a few choice words
for him. Right on cue, the minute Chad came out, he nailed
Jim with a you-son-of-a-bitch glare, then motioned to Jim to
follow him. They wound up in the restroom.

Chad looked around, checking to see if they were alone,
then when he saw that it was just the two of them, he said,
"What kind of game are you playing, Norton?"

Jim grinned. "I think that should be my question, don't
you?"

"You practically accused me of being the one who leaked
the story to Bob Regan."

"Is that the name of the *Commercial Appeal* reporter who
wrote the article about Quinn Cortez?"

Chad clenched his teeth, then took a deep breath. "I could
have pointed the finger at you, but I didn't. You're my partner. It's my job to cover your back, right? I expected the
same from you."

"I can't prove you gave confidential information to the
press," Jim said. "I'm not even a hundred percent sure you
did it. But you're the only one I know who wants Cortez to
be guilty so badly that you'd resort to underhanded, unethical methods to get the man arrested."

"You're a good one to talk about underhanded, unethical
methods. At least I never went rogue and killed my partner's
murderer with my bare hands."

Jim saw red. Literally. Anger welled up inside him at an alarming rate. *Do not let him get to you. He knew the right button to push to shove you over the edge. Don't react. Don't give him that satisfaction.*

When Jim moved, Chad jumped, then eased back away from him. *The little shit's afraid of me. Good. He should be.*

Without saying a word, Jim shoved open the restroom door and walked out, leaving Chad to stew in his own juices.

Kendall Wells's funeral at Memorial Park Funeral Home chapel in East Memphis didn't involve the pomp and circumstance that Louisa Margaret Vanderley's funeral had, but it was a solemn, dignified affair, with a respectable number of mourners. Those in attendance included not only Quinn and Annabelle, but Quinn's entourage. Marcy Sims sat between Jace Morgan and Aaron Tully, on the same bench as Annabelle and Quinn. From time to time during the service, Annabelle felt someone staring at her and twice caught Marcy glaring her way. Apparently Marcy did have a major crush on Quinn and must be feeling quite jealous of Annabelle because, for the moment, she was the woman in Quinn's life.

One of Kendall's partners in the law firm, Calvin Jeffreys, gave a rather touching eulogy, recounting not only Kendall's professional accomplishments, but recalling several personal stories about his friend.

Two teenagers flanked Kendall's ex-husband, Dr. Jonathan Miles, who had glared daggers at Quinn as he made his rounds before the funeral, speaking to those in attendance in his role as grieving widower. Apparently, he'd seen the front-page article in this morning's *Commercial Appeal* and, like most of the people in Memphis, probably thought Quinn was a murderer. No, not just a murderer, but a serial killer.

Annabelle and Quinn had spent the past two days together in her hotel suite, making love, becoming better acquainted and trying to shut out the rest of the world. But this morning, just as he had Sunday morning, Griffin Powell brought the outside world to them. This time in the form of the Tuesday issue of the *Commercial Appeal*.

"I've already called Judd Walker for you," Griffin had said as he came barreling into Annabelle's suite at eight o'clock this morning, a ferocious look on his face as he brandished the newspaper at Quinn. "Someone in the Memphis PD is going to lose his job over this."

Having awakened only when Griffin called and said he was coming straight to Annabelle's suite, she'd still been in her gown and robe and Quinn had been wearing the rumpled slacks and shirt that he'd worn since Saturday.

Quinn had grabbed the newspaper, hurriedly read through the article and cursed under his breath. "Once again this bastard, Bob Regan, stopped just short of accusing me of murder, but by printing the facts the way he did, it makes me look like a monster."

"Judd's contacting Director Danley and demanding a thorough investigation," Griffin had said. "Judd thinks the article may be grounds to sue the newspaper as well as the Memphis PD. He said to tell you that he'll catch the first plane out of Chattanooga later today."

Annabelle had read every word of the article while Quinn and Griffin discussed strategy. If she didn't know Quinn, if she were just a Memphis citizen, she would assume the worst about lady-killer Cortez. Bob Regan had stated the facts—that four of Quinn's former lovers had been murdered and the police knew Quinn had no alibi for the time of the two Memphis murders. Other than the four of them—she, Quinn, Griffin and Judd—only the Memphis PD possessed those facts. Since she knew for certain that none of them had shared the information with Bob Regan, that left only one other source. Someone in the police department had deliberately given a reporter confidential information.

Her first thought had been Chad George. Was this all her fault? Had Chad's jealousy of Quinn pushed him into disregarding the very law he'd sworn to uphold?

Suddenly Quinn grasped Annabelle's hand and urged her

to stand, bringing her abruptly back to the present moment. Kendall's funeral. Only then did she realize the service had ended. Snapping her mind back to the here and now, she rose from the pew and, holding Quinn's hand, walked at his side down the aisle and out of the building. Kendall's interment would follow at the Memorial Park Cemetery, but she and Quinn had agreed earlier that they would not attend.

The very second they emerged from the South Chapel, a horde of reporters swarmed down on them like manic bees. TV cameras zoomed in on them, microphones were thrust in their faces and a dozen voices bombarded them with questions.

"Is it true, Mr. Cortez, that you murdered four of your former lovers?"

"How did you kill them, Quinn? Love 'em to death?"

"Ms. Vanderley, are you Cortez's latest ladylove?"

"Aren't you concerned you'll be his next victim, Ms. Vanderley?"

"How does it feel to sleep with a killer, the man who murdered your own cousin?"

"How many others have there been, Cortez? Just how many women have you killed?"

"Does it turn you on to kill? Is that the reason you do it?"

Quinn draped his arm around Annabelle's shoulders and did his best to push through the crowd, but the reporters en masse kept them trapped within a vicious circle.

"Leave him alone!" a female voice shouted.

All heads turned toward the sound of that voice and the reporter nearest the woman shoved his mike as close to her as he could get it. "Who are you? And why are you defending Quinn Cortez? Are you another of his lovers?"

"Who I am doesn't matter," Marcy Sims said, her voice loud enough to gain the attention of all the other reporters. "Quinn Cortez is a good man. He hasn't killed anyone. You have no right to accuse him of such horrible things."

"Oh, God," Quinn groaned. "It's Marcy. They'll eat her alive."

"What can we do?" Annabelle asked, whispering the question in Quinn's ear.

Quinn glanced nervously around as if searching for someone. She followed his line of vision and saw that he'd made eye contact with Aaron Tully, who had gotten separated from Jace and Marcy after leaving the chapel.

"Maybe Aaron can get to her," Quinn said. "He's closer to her than we are. Besides, we're trapped."

"She's Marcy Sims. She's the lone woman in Cortez's entourage. She's on his payroll," one of the reporters called, informing her fellow tormentors of Marcy's identity. "You can bet she's one of Cortez's lovers."

Suddenly, the focus left Quinn and Annabelle and became directed on Marcy.

"Are you in love with Cortez, Ms. Sims? Is that why you're defending him?"

"Tell us what you know about Cortez. If you two are lovers, why are you still alive?"

"Yes, I love Quinn!" Tears streamed down Marcy's flushed cheeks. "I love him because he's a good man. He's not capable of murder. Someone is trying to frame him. And y'all are making matters worse by tormenting him, by accusing him of things he didn't do."

Aaron knocked aside several reporters in his quest to reach Marcy, but before he could get to her, sirens shrilled and several police cars arrived on the scene. Within minutes, half a dozen uniformed officers cut a path through the unruly crowd, a path by which Jim Norton and Griffin Powell reached Quinn and Annabelle, just as Aaron got close enough to grab Marcy around the waist.

"The calvary to the rescue," Quinn said as Griffin approached.

"Come on, let me get you two out of here," Griffin said.

"I'm not leaving without Marcy and Aaron and Jace," Quinn said.

Jim looked at Griffin. "You get them to their car. I'll bring the other three along in a few minutes."

Before she realized what was happening, Annabelle found
herself not only protected by Quinn's strong arms, but by
Griffin and two other men in dark suits to whom Griffin had
issued orders. She recognized one of them as her part-time
bodyguard, Bruce Askew. Within minutes, the threesome
had taken them through the crush of reporters, several of
whom were being apprehended by the police.

When they reached Quinn's Porsche, he refused to leave
until he was certain his employees were safe. Annabelle
waited at his side and a few minutes later, Jim Norton and a
uniformed officer escorted Marcy, Jace and Aaron directly to
Quinn.

Quinn grabbed Marcy and hugged her. She wrapped her
arms around him and held on for dear life.

"What on earth were you thinking, Marcy?" Quinn
grasped her shoulders and pushed her back, then looked
right into her eyes.

Instead of making eye contact with Quinn, Marcy's gaze
pierced Annabelle. "This is all your fault. You should get out
of his life now and stop complicating things."

Marcy jerked free of Quinn's hold and moved toward
Annabelle, her finger pointing like a loaded weapon as she
raged. "You don't love him. You're just using him the way all
the rest of them did. He doesn't deserve to be treated like a
criminal." When Marcy lunged at Annabelle, both Quinn and
Aaron reached for her. Aaron grabbed her and yanked her
back, then whirled her around and shook her.

Suddenly, all the fire went out of Marcy and she crumpled
into Aaron's arms. "Jace and I will take her home," Aaron
told Quinn. "Maybe after you take Ms. Vanderley back to the
Peabody, you should come on home and—"

"Yeah, I'll be there soon. Just take care of Marcy, will
you?"

"Sure thing."

Quinn turned to Griffin. "Either you or one of your men
stay with Annabelle. I need to go home and talk to Marcy
and I can't be in two places at once."

"I'll drive Annabelle back to the hotel and make sure she isn't alone," Griffin said.

Quinn caressed Annabelle's cheek. "I hate to leave you, but I have to check on Marcy. I've never seen her lose control the way she did today. You have to understand that she didn't mean the things she said to you. She wasn't herself."

Annabelle grabbed Quinn's hand. "You go do what you need to do. I'll be fine. Griffin will take good care of me."

"Not too good a care," Quinn said, then kissed Annabelle hurriedly before getting into his Porsche. He zoomed out of the parking lot, forcing several people to jump out of his way.

Shaken by the combination of events, Annabelle trembled as Griffin helped her into the passenger seat of his rental car, a black Lincoln. She sat there quietly as he secured her seatbelt, then she rested her hands in her lap. Neither she nor Griffin said a word until they were a couple of miles from the funeral home.

"Could Marcy Sims be the one who killed Quinn's lovers?" Annabelle voiced the question, but she suspected Griffin had been wondering the same thing.

"It's a possibility. She's obviously in love with Quinn and apparently hates every other woman in his life. She's close enough to Quinn to know his every move, to be able to execute the murders when she'd know Quinn was in the area and wouldn't necessarily have an alibi."

And she's a trusted employee, someone close enough to have drugged Quinn so that he couldn't account for a couple of hours during the time each woman was killed.

If he was drugged . . .

"Could you find out where Marcy was when each of the murders occurred?" Annabelle asked.

"I've already got agents checking on Marcy's, Aaron's and Jace's backgrounds and their whereabouts when each woman was murdered. Of course Jace wasn't working for Quinn when Kelley Fleming was murdered. And Marcy's been in Quinn's life for ten years. Why would she just all of a sudden start killing his lovers?"

"Maybe she finally realized that Quinn was never going to be hers."

Griffin grunted. "If we could just tie someone else to all five dead women . . ." He paused, obviously thinking about something in particular. "Aaron Tully had a connection to Lulu. They'd been lovers, too. And he knew Kendall Wells."

"Do you think Aaron Tully is the murderer and not Marcy?"

"I'm not certain of anything. I have no way of knowing if Aaron or Marcy or Jace killed those women," Griffin told her. "But if we rule out Quinn, then—"

"What do you mean *if* we rule out Quinn?"

Griffin shot her a quick, speculative glance. "I know you're in love with the guy, but you can't tell me that the thought hasn't crossed your mind—"

"Don't say it. Don't even think it."

"But you've thought it, haven't you? Even though you love him and you want to believe him wholeheartedly, there's a tiny kernel of doubt deep down inside you, isn't there? Don't be ashamed to admit it. What you say to me will never be repeated."

"I know Quinn didn't kill those women. I believe in him. I trust him."

"But?"

"But God forgive me, the thought did cross my mind and that thought lingers."

"For what it's worth, I agree with you. I don't think Quinn killed those five women, but I can't say I'd stake my life on it."

Tears moistened Annabelle's eyes. She turned her head and stared out the window at the quickly passing scenery of downtown Memphis. The ache in her heart intensified. How could she doubt Quinn for even one second? How could she consider the possibility that he had killed five women? But what if he had committed the murders and had no memory of what he'd done? What if those blackout spells . . .

Quinn is innocent! Someone else killed Kelley, Joy, Carla, Lulu and Kendall. But who? Marcy? Aaron? Jace? Or some unknown serial killer who, for his own perverse reasons, had targeted Quinn's lovers?

"She's gone into her room and locked the door," Jace told Quinn when he arrived at their rental house. "Aaron's trying to talk to her, but I don't think he's having any luck."

Quinn nodded. "Whose idea was it for you three to show up at Kendall's funeral?"

"I don't remember." Jace scrunched his features into a pondering frown. "I think maybe Marcy mentioned at breakfast that we should all go, just to show the world that we support you."

Quinn sighed. "I know she meant well, but damn it if she didn't make matters worse. Did you or Aaron have any idea she was on the verge of losing it that way?"

Before Jace could respond, Aaron called out from the hallway, "No, we didn't know she was going to go berserk." Coming into the living room, rage in his dark eyes, Aaron walked right up to Quinn. Man-to-man. "But hell, it was only a matter of time. She's crazy about you and you treat her like a kid sister. She's been pining away for you as long as I've known her. Man, she'd lie down and die for you. You should have told her a long time ago that there was no way in hell you'd ever love her, not the way she wants you to love her."

"I knew she had a crush on me, but—"

"A crush?" Aaron raised his voice to a shout. "A crush! Man, that's rich, calling what she feels for you a crush."

"Don't talk to Quinn that way," Jace said. "None of this is his fault. He can't help it, can he, if women fall in love with him? You're just jealous of him because you've got a thing for Marcy and even after you two became lovers, she still wanted Quinn."

Silence. Utter, complete silence.

Jace gasped as if all at once realizing the impact of what he'd said.

Aaron paled, his anger seeming to drain away, leaving him mute.

Quinn focused on Aaron. "You and Marcy are lovers?"

Aaron nodded.

"Since when?"

"Since we came to Memphis."

"Do you love her or is she just another one of my women you wanted?" Quinn asked.

"She's never been one of your women," Aaron said.

"Not one of my lovers, no, but—"

"I care about Marcy," Aaron admitted. "Yeah, maybe I love her. And it has nothing to do with you. Or at least it wouldn't if Marcy wasn't in love with the great Quinn Cortez."

"Do you hate me?" Quinn had never even suspected that Aaron had any negative feelings toward him, that he resented him in any way.

"Hell no! I don't hate you. I just hate that Marcy's in love with you."

"I'll talk to her," Quinn said. "I'll make her see that you're better for her, that there can't ever be anything between us, nothing more than friendship."

"She won't believe you. She'll just go on deluding herself, telling herself that someday you're going to realize that she's the love of your life."

"I'll tell her she's wrong to think that."

"As long as you go through women like Kleenex, she'll keep hoping."

"What if I tell Marcy that I've found the love of my life? What if I make her understand that Annabelle Vanderley is more to me than just a brief affair?"

Chapter 28

Quinn left Aaron to think over what he'd told him. He hadn't planned what he'd said, hadn't actually been thinking about his feelings for Annabelle. But the words formed in his mind one second and came out his mouth the next. As he walked from the living into the hall, his mind a jumble of mixed thoughts and confused emotions, only one sentiment emerged from the chaos. What he'd said to Aaron was the truth, coming through loud and clear, drowning out all other thoughts.

I've found the love of my life.

There was no point in denying it to himself or to anyone else. How it had happened or why now, he had no idea. As if a light had been turned on in a dark room and illuminated the pitch-blackness, he knew that he loved Annabelle.

He certainly needed time to think about his feelings. Something he'd never really done. He had to consider how to handle things. Should he tell Annabelle now? Or should he wait?

But first things first. Marcy. He had to take care of her, make sure she would come out of this all right.

When Quinn reached the closed door to Marcy's room, he paused. Poor Marcy. He'd never meant to lead her on, to give her any false hopes where he was concerned. Aaron was right—he needed to make her understand that there could never be anything beyond friendship between them.

He lifted his hand to knock, then caught a glimpse of Jace and Aaron as they came up behind him. Looking over his shoulder, Quinn said, "Everything's going to be all right." He knocked.

No response.

"Marcy," Quinn called.

No answer.

"Marcy, honey, open the door and let me talk to you."

"Go away," she told him.

"I'm not going anywhere until we talk."

"We don't need to talk. I know I made a fool of myself and embarrassed you in public. I'm sorry. Really, I'm so sorry. You have every right to be angry with me, even fire me."

"It's all right, Marcy. I'm not angry and I'm not going to fire you. But we do need to discuss things and we need to do it now."

"If you're going to tell me you don't love me, save your breath. I already know."

"That's not exactly true. I do love you, but as a good friend, someone I can always count on."

He sensed the same trepidation tensing his nerves were wreaking havoc on Aaron and possibly Jace, too, as they waited anxiously for Marcy's reaction.

Finally, she unlocked the door and eased it open just a crack. When she peered out into the hall, she looked right at Quinn, ignoring Aaron and Jace. "You're not angry? You don't hate me? You—you aren't going to fire me?"

"No to all three questions."

She opened the door all the way, came outside and rushed into Quinn's embrace. When he closed his arms around her and held her as she cried, Aaron turned around and stomped back down the hall. Within minutes the sound of the front door slamming shut reverberated through the house.

"I'll be in my room if you need me," Jace said as he raced off up the hall.

Marcy lifted her head and looked at Quinn through tear-filled eyes. "I can't help being in love with you."

He released her, then lifted his hand and wiped her tears away with his fingertips. "You just think you're in love with me. You're grateful to me. You find me charming and irresistible. All women do." Quinn smiled, hoping she'd smile, too. She did. "We could have had a fling, had some meaningless sex and then when you realized I wasn't in love with you, you'd have quit your job and left me."

When she opened her mouth to respond, he tapped his index finger playfully on her nose. "I've always found you attractive, and it would have been the easiest thing in the world to have taken advantage of the crush you had on me, but I cared too much—loved you too much—to ever hurt you."

"You love me?" she asked hopefully.

"Like a kid sister. You're a good friend and a good assistant. I want you to be happy, but you can't find the happiness you deserve with me." He cupped her chin between his thumb and forefinger. "One of these days, you'll find the right person, the one meant for you, just as I have. Would you believe that after all these years, I've actually met the love of my life?"

"Annabelle Vanderley." Marcy spoke the name in a reverent whisper.

"Yes, Annabelle."

Fresh tears gushed from her eyes. "I figured as much."

"Ah, honey . . . Marcy . . ."

She swallowed. "I'm happy for you. Really, I am."

"You realize that Aaron's in love with you, don't you? Who knows, you could turn out to be the love of his life."

Laughing, Marcy swatted away the tears dampening her cheeks. "I doubt that. Besides, I've got to find a way to get over you before I can be of any good to somebody else."

"What can I do to help you?"

"I don't know if anyone can help me. It's just something I'll have to find a way to work through on my own."

Quinn nodded, wishing he could do something—anything—for Marcy. "Well, I can order supper for us. It's nearly five and we've got to eat."

"You aren't going back to the Peabody to have supper with Annabelle?"

"No, not tonight. I'm going to stick around here, eat supper with y'all. I'm sure Aaron will come back soon, after he's worked off some of his anger."

"Yeah, he'll come flying in before long and be starving to death," Marcy said. "Hey, why don't you call Annabelle and check on her. Tell her I'm sorry for the way I acted. And while you're doing that, I'll order supper."

Quinn ran the back of his hand along Marcy's cheek. She closed her eyes and sighed. He slipped his hand away and headed up the hall toward the kitchen. All of a sudden, he was thirsty. He'd pour himself a glass of iced tea and take it upstairs to his bedroom before he called Annabelle. He would miss her tonight. But he was needed here. Marcy needed him.

Annabelle would understand. She had a kind and generous spirit. A loving heart.

God help him. During the past couple of days, Annabelle had become as essential to him as the air he breathed.

How the mighty have fallen.

Quinn chuckled to himself as he opened the kitchen door.

But what a way to go.

Annabelle changed out of her black dress, hung it in the closet and put on her jeans and long-sleeved cotton sweater. Her suite seemed empty without Quinn. Quiet and lonely. Odd how essential he had become to her in such a brief period of time. She had fallen head over heels in love and there wasn't a darn thing she could do about it.

Even now, alone in her suite, the door locked and Bruce Askew posted outside, Annabelle felt uneasy, as if something terrible was about to happen. She had decided to forgo supper, knowing she was unlikely to eat a bite. Her nerves were frayed and her conscience was bothering her. How could she have confessed to Griffin that she harbored even the slightest doubt about Quinn's innocence?

Because you're human. Because despite the fact that you're madly in love with the man, you don't really know him.

Just as she picked up the dirty coffeepot, intending to wash it and put on fresh decaf coffee, a knock sounded at her door. She tensed. After sitting the pot down, she walked to the door and peered through the keyhole. Griffin stood there beside Bruce Askew.

"Annabelle, it's Griffin."

She opened the door.

He dismissed Mr. Askew, then came into her suite. "I've ordered dinner for us."

"That's nice of you, but I'm really not very hungry."

"I won't force you to eat, but you can keep me company while I enjoy my dinner, can't you?"

"Of course." She went back to the coffeemaker. "I was going to make some decaf coffee. Would you care for some?"

"Sure. Dinner won't be here for another forty-five minutes. Coffee sounds good."

After washing the pot and filling it with clean water, she returned to the lounge and found Griffin sitting on the sofa. He glanced up at her and smiled. "Judd Walker's staying in my suite tonight and I plan to bunk here on your sofa."

Annabelle's mouth gaped. "Is that necessary?"

"I promised Quinn you wouldn't be left alone."

"Quinn may be back tonight."

"If he comes back, I'll leave immediately."

"You are staying simply because Quinn asked, aren't you? Not for any other reason."

Griffin chuckled. "As attractive and desirable as I find

you, my dear Annabelle, I'm not a fool. I realize that there is only one man for you and I'm not that man."

Quinn set the glass of tea on his nightstand, then kicked off his shoes and sat on the edge of the bed. He picked up the phone and dialed the Peabody. As he waited for Annabelle to answer, he grasped the frosty glass and sipped the unsweetened tea.

She answered on the fourth ring. "Annabelle Vanderley's suite."

"Hello, Annabelle Vanderley."

"Quinn." He heard the rush of joy in her voice.

"Miss me?" he asked.

"Terribly. Are you coming back tonight?"

"Not tonight. Things are unsettled here. Marcy's going to be okay. She asked me to tell you she's sorry about the way she acted. She's ordering supper for us. Jace is holed up in his room, not wanting to be around in case of any emotional fallout. And Aaron's gone off in a huff because he happens to be in love with Marcy and he's pissed at her right now, and at me, too."

"That's quite a mess you have on your hands over there."

"Yes, it is. Marcy and Aaron and Jace are almost like my kids. I care about them and I feel like it's my duty to look after them."

"I understand. You stay there and take care of all your little chicks."

"I want to be with you. You know that, don't you?"

"Yes."

"Does Griffin have someone posted outside your door?"

"He did."

"What do you mean he did?"

"Griffin's here with me now," she said. "He ordered supper for us. He's in the lounge and plans to spend the night on the sofa."

368   *Beverly Barton*

"I'm not sure I like the idea of another man sleeping on your sofa."

"He will be on the sofa and I'll be alone in my bed. There's only one man I want in my bed now and for the rest of my life."

"I'm glad to hear you say it."

"Are you?" she asked.

"I feel the same way."

"Do you?"

"You want me to say it, *querida*? You want the words?"

"Yes, I'd like to hear you tell me how you feel."

"It seems that I discovered just this afternoon that you, Annabelle Vanderley, are the love of my life."

Silence.

"Annabelle?"

"I'm here." He heard the tears in her voice.

"I love you," he said.

"I love you, too."

"I'll see you in the morning. I'll be over to share breakfast with you and Griffin."

Annabelle laughed. God, how he loved the sound of her voice, the sound of her laughter.

"Night," she said.

"Good night, *querida*."

Quinn scooted back in the bed, bracing himself against the headboard, and drank the iced tea as he thought about a future with the woman he loved.

Marcy ordered supper from a nearby Chinese restaurant that delivered, then went back to her room to change out of the dress she'd worn to Kendall Wells's funeral. She couldn't believe that she'd made such an ass of herself, and in public! How could she have lost control that way, confessed to the world that she loved Quinn and almost attacked Annabelle Vanderley?

Quinn's forgiven you, so how about forgiving yourself?

Just as Marcy was peeling off her pantyhose, she thought she heard someone walking down the hall. Probably Jace. Or maybe it was Aaron. He could have cooled off already and come back home. Wearing only her panties and bra, she rushed across the room and eased the door open enough to peep into the hall. She looked right and left, up and down, and saw no one. Odd. She must have been hearing things.

Looking in her closet, she decided on jeans and a baggy sweatshirt. After supper, she'd clean up the kitchen and then talk to Aaron. If Quinn thought Aaron loved her, then it was possible he actually did. And if he did love her, what would she do about it? She enjoyed making love with Aaron. She liked knowing he cared about her. But even if she could eradicate Quinn from her heart, could she love Aaron? Could she love any other man?

The guy who'd taken her order at the Chinese restaurant had told her it would be at least an hour before delivery, so she had an hour to kill. She figured Quinn was on the phone with Annabelle and Jace was hiding in his room, keeping well out of the line of fire. She'd been wanting to paint her toenails with the new polish she'd bought the other day. Shocking Pink to match the new sweater she'd bought in one of the Opryland Mall boutiques while they'd been in Nashville. She'd bought it because she remembered that Quinn always complimented her when she wore pink.

Forget impressing Quinn. You'll have to let that fantasy die a natural death. He's in love with another woman.

After getting all the paraphernalia she'd need for the pedicure lined up in the bathroom, she rolled up her jeans and grabbed the polish remover. Just as she wet a cotton ball and started rubbing the chipped coral polish off her big toe, she heard a noise out in the hall again. Someone was out there. She tossed the cotton ball in the wastebasket and walked out of the bathroom, through her bedroom and to the door.

"Who's out there?" she asked.

Silence.

"Jace, is that you?"

No response.

"Aaron?"

Nothing.

An odd little niggling feeling fluttered in Marcy's stomach. Not fear. Just uneasiness. She opened the door and scanned the hallway. It was empty.

Either I'm going nuts or somebody's wandering around in the hall and not answering me.

"Quinn?" she called loudly. "Jace!"

Could an intruder have entered the house without any of them knowing it?

Without warning, the lights went out, turning everything pitch-black in the hallway. Panic gripped Marcy. She walked backward into her room where the remnants of twilight came through the lone window in her bedroom, casting spooky shadows on the walls and across the floor.

"Hey, guys, what happened?" she called loudly to anyone who might hear her.

"The electricity is off," a voice said. Quinn's voice?

"Is that you, Quinn?" She noticed a man's dark shadow in the doorway.

"Yes. Don't worry. I'm here."

An overwhelming sense of relief washed over her. Quinn was here. Everything would be fine.

"I don't know if there are any candles in this place, but I know there's a flashlight in the kitchen," Marcy told Quinn as she headed toward him.

"We don't need any light, do we?" he asked.

What was wrong with his voice? He didn't sound quite like himself.

"Are you all right?"

"Yes, I'm fine," he replied and came toward her.

Broad shouldered, six one, muscular yet trim. She loved Quinn's body.

When he came nearer, she could make out his dark curly hair and the thrust of his high cheekbones. "Poor Marcy.

You've suffered so, haven't you? You've loved a man who can never love you."

Why was he saying such things to her? Didn't he realize how much his words hurt her? "Quinn, please, don't—"

He reached out and circled the back of her neck with his hand. She gasped when he pulled her close, eye-to-eye. She gazed into his black eyes and saw no kindness, no gentleness. This was not the Quinn she knew and loved.

"You're a very foolish woman, Marcy. You know what I do to foolish women? I put them out of their misery." He tightened his hold on her neck. "I kill them softly."

Oh, God, no! It couldn't be. It wasn't possible.

"You killed all those other women, didn't you?" Marcy tried her best to escape from his tenacious hold.

"I put them out of their misery. I eased their pain. I ended their agony."

"And you're going to kill me, too? But why, I've never—"

He pressed his thumb against her windpipe so hard that she could barely breathe. While she struggled against his superior strength, he shoved her backward and onto her bed. Flaying her arms and doing her best to knee him in the groin, Marcy fought like a wildcat. But he managed to subdue her by crawling on top of her, pinning her to the bed and yanking her arms over her head and down against the pillows.

Marcy let out an earsplitting scream.

"No one can hear you."

She kept screaming.

"Poor, sweet, stupid Marcy."

He jerked one of the pillows off the bed and brought it down over her face, all the while she squirmed and cried, doing her best to stop him.

"It'll all be over soon, honey."

No, please, please, don't kill me.

He held the pillow securely over her face, cutting off her air completely.

Chapter 29

"Wake up, Quinn. Goddamn it, wake up!"

Quinn opened his bleary eyes. His head hurt like hell and he felt really groggy.

"Huh? What?"

"Wake up and get your act together," Jace Morgan told him. "The police are on their way here. You've got to be alert when they get here because they're going to ask you a lot of questions."

Quinn sat up in bed, scooted himself around and eased his legs off the side. The last thing he remembered was talking to Annabelle, then finishing off a glass of iced tea. He glanced at the nightstand. The glass wasn't there. Where was it? Had he taken it back down to the kitchen?

Shit! Did I have another blackout spell?

"Look, I know you didn't do it, okay," Jace said. "But the police are going to want to know how it happened. Did you hear anything? See anything?"

"What the hell are you talking about?" Quinn rubbed his aching head.

"You mean you don't know or do you just not remember?"

"Know what? Remember what?"

"Marcy's dead." Jace's voice trembled.

Quinn shot up off the bed, grabbed Jace's shoulders and speared him with a shocked glare. "Marcy's dead?"

"Yeah. Aaron found her. He's sitting down there now, holding her in his arms and crying. I—I called the police. They'll be here soon."

He must be having a nightmare. That was it. He was dreaming. This wasn't real. *Wake up,* he told himself. *Wake up now!*

He didn't wake up, couldn't wake up because he wasn't asleep. He hadn't been dreaming. This was really happening. Jace had told him Marcy was dead. But how was that possible? He'd been with her, talking to her, reassuring her, just a few minutes ago.

"What time is it?" Quinn asked.

"I'm not sure. About seven-thirty, I guess."

"Seven-thirty?" He had come up to his room to call Annabelle a little after five. If it was now seven-thirty, that meant he'd lost a good two hours. Again. And once again someone had died.

"What happened to Marcy?" But Quinn knew before Jace answered, knew that the killer had struck again, this time in Quinn's own household.

"I—I don't know for sure, but Aaron said she had a pillow over her face so I figure she was smothered." Jace looked at Quinn, his hazel eyes wide and round beneath his glasses. "God, Quinn, he—he cut off her finger. Just like he did with those other women."

Sour bile rose up into Quinn's throat, the bitter taste threatening his tongue. "You were here, too, Jace. Did you hear or see anything?"

Please, God, let him know something—anything—that will place suspicion on someone else. I couldn't have killed Marcy. I couldn't have. No more than I killed Kendall or Lulu. Or the others.

"I wasn't here," Jace said. "I took the SUV and went to the drugstore to get some Imodium. You know how my stomach gets when I'm upset. And today was pretty upsetting . . . even before Marcy was killed."

"Are you saying that as far as you know I was alone in the house with Marcy when she was killed?"

"You were out cold, sleeping like a baby," Jace said. "But you weren't the only one here. The killer was here, the guy who killed Marcy and all those other women."

Quinn walked out into the upstairs hall, Jace following right behind him. "Aaron found Marcy's body?"

"Yeah."

"He's got to be out of his mind, hurting really bad. He loved her. We all loved her." Quinn couldn't quite come to grips with the fact that Marcy was dead. Sweet little Marcy, with her blond curls and infectious smile. God, no, not Marcy.

"He is in a bad way. He was saying some crazy stuff about you. He—he thinks you killed her."

Before they reached the foot of the stairs, Quinn heard the shrill of sirens and then car doors slamming. Confused and still groggy, he barely knew what was happening and didn't know what to do first—mourn Marcy or think of a way to prove he didn't kill her.

"Police. Open up."

"Go let them in," Quinn said.

While Quinn entered the foyer, Jace rushed to the front door, then unlocked and opened it. Two uniformed officers entered.

"Are you the person who called?" one officer asked.

Jace nodded.

"Where's the body?" the other officer asked.

"Back there—in her bedroom." Jace said.

"Did you touch anything?"

"I—I haven't been in her room. I didn't find her body. Aaron did."

"Is that Aaron?" The first officer pointed to Quinn.

"I'm Quinn Cortez. This is my house."

"Holy shit," the other officer said. He touched his holster

nervously as if he thought he might have to draw his weapon at any moment. "You're the guy who—" He turned to his fellow officer and issued an order. "Get in touch with downtown and tell 'em if they've sent anybody besides Lieutenant Norton out, they'd better get in touch with Norton and tell him we've got Quinn Cortez at the scene of another murder. At Cortez's house."

"Quinn didn't kill Marcy," Jace cried out abruptly.

"How do you know he didn't?" Officer Number Two asked.

"I know. Quinn's no killer."

"You two go in there—" He motioned to the living room. "I'm staying right with both of you until the detectives get here. When Officer Griggs gets back from contacting downtown, he'll keep watch over y'all while I check out the scene."

"Aaron's in there with her," Jace said. "He may not let you get near her."

"Who's this Aaron you keep talking about?"

"He's her . . . er . . . her boyfriend."

"Did he kill her?"

"I don't know. I wasn't here. When I came back, I heard Aaron screaming and I ran down the hall and found him holding Marcy in his arms. He was crying like crazy. I stood there, outside the door for a couple of minutes, then Aaron told me to call the police."

The officer nodded toward Quinn. "And where was Mr. Cortez?"

"I was upstairs," Quinn said. "Asleep."

"Went to bed kind of early, didn't you?"

"Considering the situation, I think it best for me to not answer any more questions without my lawyer present."

Before the policeman could respond, the other officer came into the living room. "The ME just pulled up outside. And Lieutenant Norton is on his way."

En route to the crime scene, Jim Norton made two phone calls. First he called Griffin Powell. Then he got in touch with his partner, telling him where to meet him, but not giving him any names. All he knew was that Marcy Sims had been killed and her body was in her bedroom at Quinn Cortez's rental house. Once the press got wind of this, they'd have a field day.

If Marcy had been smothered and her finger severed, this would make murder number six. And she'd be the fifth woman out of six who had been personally involved with Cortez. In her case, Marcy had been a friend and employee instead of a lover, but she had, only today, confessed her love for Cortez.

When he parked his car behind Udell White's black Chevy Trailblazer, Jim noticed several neighbors standing on their porches and a few more in their driveways. But no one had ventured into the street. Not yet.

He knocked on the front door and was met by Officer Griggs. Jim flashed his badge. "Where's the ME?"

"Still back there with the body."

"Who called this in?"

"A guy named Jace Morgan. Just a kid really. He and Cortez and another guy named Aaron Tully are in the living room. Tully's pretty torn up. We had a problem getting him to let go of Ms. Sims's body." Griggs lowered his voice. "The guy was sitting on the bed holding her in his arms, crying his heart out. It took me and Bobby both to prize him away from her."

Jim groaned. The crime scene had been compromised even before the patrolmen arrived.

When Jim passed the living room, he saw the other officer standing guard. Glancing toward the sofa, he noticed that Quinn and Jace sat side by side, and Aaron Tully sat across from them, a dazed look in his eyes. Jim and Quinn made eye contact, but Jim glanced away hurriedly.

"Which way?" he asked.

"Down that hall. The door's open," Griggs replied.

By the time he got to Marcy Sims's bedroom, Udell was walking out into the hall. He paused and spoke to Jim.

"Another one. Smothered to death. Right index finger cut off."

"Damn!"

"The guy who was holding her in his arms when I got here—Aaron?—he was making some pointed accusations. He said Quinn Cortez killed her, that he was alone in the house with her, so it had to be him."

"I guess he didn't stop to think that he might be a suspect, too."

"Guess not."

"Can you give me an estimated time of death?" Jim asked.

"Recent. No more than an hour or two."

Jim nodded. His gut instincts told him that one of the three men sitting in the living room had killed Marcy Sims. One of them was possibly a serial killer. But which one? Chad was going to say it was Cortez. And he might be right. Unless Cortez had an alibi, this sixth murder might be the last nail in his coffin.

By the time Judd Walker and Griffin Powell arrived, Quinn's rental house was crawling with law enforcement. Quinn had cautioned Jace and Aaron not to answer any questions until Judd came. Jace complied. Aaron didn't. He talked and talked and talked. About Marcy and how much he'd loved her. About Jace and what a worthless piece of shit he was because he hadn't protected Marcy from Quinn.

"You crazy son-of-a-bitch, you killed her, didn't you?" Aaron had lurched at Quinn and it had taken both officers to pull him away.

Aaron was manic, wild with grief. Quinn was numb. Jace had been nervous at first, fidgeting, making trips to the bathroom every five minutes, but now he'd settled down and seemed relatively calm.

Judd informed Lieutenant Norton that he wanted to speak

privately with his client and Norton told them to go into the kitchen. When they entered the kitchen, they found police officers searching the room.

"I'm Mr. Cortez's lawyer and I'm taking him out back," Judd told the officers. "We won't be going any farther. Feel free to check with Lieutenant Norton."

Once they were just beyond the back door, standing on the stoop, Judd turned to Quinn and said, "Tell me what happened."

"I don't know what happened. I had another one of those damn blackout spells. I was asleep when Jace came upstairs and woke me."

Judd frowned. "Where were you when Marcy was killed?"

"Upstairs, in my bedroom. Asleep."

"What's the last thing you remember?"

"Calling Annabelle and then drinking a glass of iced tea."

"Where's the glass? Still in your bedroom?"

"That's the funny thing," Quinn said. "When Jace woke me up, I looked for the glass on the nightstand where I was sure I'd left it, and it was gone."

"I want to have you tested for drugs," Judd said. "Tonight."

"You think someone drugged me?"

"It's highly possible."

"But who—?"

"Jace or Aaron."

"No, they wouldn't. You can't think either of them killed Marcy. Aaron loved her. Besides, he's no killer. And Jace. The boy's shy. And scared of his own shadow."

"If one of them didn't kill her and there is no sign of a forced entry, that leaves only you. Did you kill her, Quinn?"

"No, I didn't kill her."

"At least you don't remember killing her."

"Fuck you, Walker."

"You're the one who's fucked," Judd told him. "Unless we can prove you were drugged, you could be looking at a murder charge, especially considering you're Suspect Numero Uno for the Lulu Vanderley and the Kendall Wells murders."

"I saw Griffin come in with you. He was with Annabelle tonight. Does she know what happened? Did he tell her?"

"No, he didn't tell her. He made some excuse about a business emergency that he had to handle, then he left one of his agents to guard her."

Quinn heaved a deep sigh. When Annabelle heard about Marcy's death would she think Quinn had killed his lovesick young assistant?

The back door opened and Jim Norton stuck his head out and looked at Quinn, then said, "You two had better come back inside. Now."

"I haven't finished talking to my client," Judd replied.

"You can talk to him downtown," Jim said.

"What's happened?" Quinn asked.

"Please, come back inside."

When Judd and Quinn entered the kitchen, Quinn spotted Sergeant George across the room, a self-satisfied smirk on his face. That was a bad sign, a really bad sign.

"Read him his rights," George said. "Or do you want me to do it?"

"What's going on?" Judd asked.

"While searching the house, we found evidence in Mr. Cortez's bedroom that not only links him to this crime, but to five other crimes," Lieutenant Norton said.

"What sort of evidence?" Judd glanced from Norton to Quinn.

"A small case was found in Mr. Cortez's closet, inside an empty shoe box," Jim said. "And inside that case were five small vials containing fingers preserved in what is probably formaldehyde."

"What?" Quinn cried. "But that's not possible. The case isn't mine. I—"

"Inside the shoe box was something else." Chad George smiled. "We found a bloody finger wrapped in a small hand towel. What do you want to bet it's Marcy Sims's finger?"

Chapter 30

Fending off the descending horde of reporters who'd been camped out for hours, some all night, waiting to attack Quinn the moment he was free on bail, Griffin Powell and Bruce Askew escorted Quinn and Judd to Griffin's rented Lincoln. While Griffin and Bruce kept the jackals at bay, Judd and Quinn hopped in the backseat, then Griffin joined them as Bruce slid into the front with the driver, whom Quinn recognized as Sanders, Griffin's assistant. Wasting no time in making a quick getaway once everyone was safely on board, Sanders practically peeled rubber. Overzealous reporters were forced to jump for their lives or be squashed under the sedan's large wheels.

"Who's with Annabelle?" Quinn asked, her safety his main concern above anything else, even his own horrific problems. "Tell me you didn't leave her alone." With sweet little Marcy dead, Quinn now understood that no woman in his life was safe from a crazed killer. If anything happened to Annabelle . . .

"Tobias took Bruce's place around six this morning," Griffin said.

Quinn breathed a sigh of relief. "How many agents have you brought to Memphis?"

"Three. Bruce and Tobias were already here. Bridges came in last night."

"Have you spoken to Annabelle personally today?"

"No, I thought it best to wait and let you explain the situation to her," Griffin said. "I told Tobias to make sure she doesn't receive a morning newspaper and I requested that all her calls be routed through me."

"You'll have to talk to her. Tell her what's happened and why I've made certain decisions," Quinn said. "I won't be seeing her today. Actually I won't be seeing her at all. Not until this mess is over, until we've proved I didn't kill Marcy or anyone else. I want you to take Annabelle back to Austinville and keep a bodyguard with her twenty-four/seven until we catch this maniac."

"You've got it all planned out, haven't you." Griffin snorted. "I thought you knew Annabelle, but apparently you don't. Do you honestly think she'll go back to Austinville when she finds out the trouble you're in? That woman is going to stick to your side like glue."

"It'll be your job to convince her—"

"There will be no convincing her," Griffin said. "There won't be anything I can say or do that will make her desert you."

"Then I'll call her and tell her whatever I have to in order to make her go home, where she'll be safe. At least safer than she would be anywhere near me."

"You'll call her, huh? Can't face her eye-to-eye, can you?"

The distinct ring of a cell phone interrupted the debate about Annabelle. Judd Walker removed his phone from his coat pocket and answered quietly. Quinn heard several uh-huhs, a yes and a thank you. Then Judd returned his phone to his pocket and glanced from Quinn to Griffin.

"That was the doctor who took a blood sample from Quinn last night at the jail," Judd said. "He had the lab do a rush job for us and the results just came in."

Everyone in the car, except Sanders who only glanced quickly in the interior rearview mirror, focused on Judd.

"Traces of some type of benzodiazepine showed up," Judd said. "The generic name is Lorazepam and it's sold as Alzapam, Ativan, Loraz and so on. It's an antianxiety and sedative/hypnotic. An overdose could knock a person out for an hour or two and then when they came to, they'd be disoriented. The pills could be easily dissolved in coffee, tea or cola."

"Son of a bitch," Griffin said. "You told us you drank a glass of iced tea right before you lost consciousness yesterday evening, right?"

Startled by the details of the doctor's findings, Quinn simply nodded. Why was it so hard to believe he'd been deliberately drugged? That someone had betrayed him?

"Someone drugged you," Judd said. "Who made the iced tea you drank?"

"Marcy," Quinn replied.

He wasn't sick, wasn't having a mental breakdown.

"I think we can rule her out." Griffin narrowed his gaze as if deep in thought. "The other times you blacked out, did you drink anything right before getting sleepy?"

Quinn tried to remember each incident, starting with Kendall and working his way back. "I'd drank iced tea at the house before I left to drive over to Kendall's the night she died. I got so sleepy, I had to stop and . . . Goddamn! The night I drove from Nashville to Memphis, the night Lulu was killed, I brought along a thermos of coffee and drank it during the drive."

"Who prepared the coffee for you?" Judd inquired.

"I'm not sure. I think Marcy fixed the coffee, but I believe Aaron brought the thermos to me after I'd gotten in my car and was ready to leave."

"One of your employees has been drugging you so that you'd lose consciousness and wind up with no alibi for the time of each murder," Griffin said.

"That means either Aaron Tully or Jace Morgan could very well be our killer."

Judd stated the obvious.

Quinn shook his head. "No, that's not possible. I refuse to believe either of them is capable of cold-blooded murder." It couldn't be Jace or Aaron. It just couldn't be!

"Well, you'd better believe it," Griffin told him. "Because if we can't prove someone else murdered those six women, you could wind up convicted of multiple murders. And Annabelle won't be safe until we catch this guy."

Knocking the waiter in the head and leaving him bleeding and unconscious, possibly dying, had been easy enough. He'd simply followed the man into the service elevator when he rolled in the breakfast cart. He had taken the waiter completely by surprise. Stupid bozo hadn't known what hit him. In fact, it had been the butt of his gun that had rendered the man helpless. Well, not technically his gun, but it was in his possession now, even though it was registered to Quinn Cortez. He'd dragged the guy off the elevator and dumped him into the stairwell, figuring it would be hours before anyone found him.

When the elevator opened on the correct floor, he shoved his duffle bag underneath the cart, and the white linen tablecloth hid the bag quite effectively. As he rolled the cart off the elevator and down the hall, he whistled a catchy little tune.

Sitting there outside her suite, just as he had expected, was a bodyguard. A big, burly black guy who looked as if he might have been a prizefighter or possibly a football player. Roughly six three and a good two forty.

"Morning," he said. "I have Ms. Vanderley's breakfast order."

"As far as I know, Ms. Vanderley didn't order breakfast." The black man studied him closely as if trying to decide whether he was on the up-and-up or not.

"She must have. They sent me up here with it. Eggs, bacon, toast. Hot tea."

He could tell the bodyguard was considering his options. "I'll call down and check to see if she placed an order."

"Yeah, sure. Or you could just ask her."

The big guy nodded. "Stay here."

"Yeah, sure." He backed the cart up a couple of feet, showing the guard that he was just a delivery man who was no threat to anyone.

The bodyguard knocked on the closed door to Annabelle Vanderley's suite. "Ms. Vanderley? It's Tobias."

She opened the door almost immediately, wide enough for him to get a really good look at her. She wasn't as gorgeous as Lulu, but this Ms. Vanderley was a real pretty lady. And from what he'd heard about her that's exactly what she was—a lady. But then, Carla Millican had been a lady. A nice lady. Kendall Wells had been a smart lawyer. Lulu had been a whore and so had Joy Ellis.

And what about Kelley? he asked himself.

Kelley hadn't been sweet or nice or a lady. But she also hadn't been a whore.

What Kelley had been was a mother. His mother.

"Ms. Vanderley, did you order breakfast?" the guard asked. "There's a waiter here with a tray—"

He eased the gun from where he'd tucked it beneath the white waiter's jacket, just under the waistband of the black slacks that were a tad too short for him. Moving lightning fast, he came up behind the big black man.

"Watch out, Mr. Tobias!" Annabelle screamed.

Too late. Just as Tobias turned, he shot the man right between the eyes. He dropped like a huge tree downed in the forest. Blood splattered everywhere. Annabelle screamed again and tried to close the door, but Tobias's body blocked the doorway. Realizing the danger and her inability to shut him out, she turned and fled. He jumped over the guard's body and raced after Annabelle, catching her just as she

went into the bedroom and was trying to close the door on
him. He yanked her toward him.

"If you scream again, I'll shoot you. Do you understand?"

Standing stiff as a poker, she nodded.

"We're leaving here, right now. We're going back down in
the service elevator and if you give me any trouble, I'll kill
you."

"It was you, wasn't it?" she asked. "All this time, it was
you."

"Shut up and get moving."

When they reached the outer door, she halted when she
saw Tobias's body.

"Just step over him."

She did. Reluctantly.

When they entered the hallway, several doors opened and
people peered outside. He brandished the gun around and
fired two shots into the ceiling. Every door closed instantly.
He reached underneath the serving cart and grabbed his duffle bag.

Within minutes, they had descended to the bottom level.
He had left the SUV parked up the street, but he didn't dare
use a vehicle that could be so easily identified. Before entering the hotel earlier, he had commandeered a delivery truck
after disposing of the driver. He really hated harming so
many innocent bystanders, but it couldn't be helped. If things
went as he'd planned, today would be the culmination of a
year's hard work. Today good Quinn and bad Quinn would
meet face-to-face. At long last.

He marched Annabelle to the delivery truck, opened the
back doors and forced her inside the dark interior. He crawled
in with her, picked up the rope he'd placed there, then tied
her hands and feet.

"Where are you taking me?"

"Someplace private, where you can spend some time with
the bad Quinn."

"What?"

He yanked a handkerchief out of his pocket and stuffed it in her mouth, then used one of the rags he'd brought with him to gag her.

There, that would do. She was as snug as a bug in a rug. She might roll around a bit in the back of the truck, possibly even tumble into the driver's lifeless body, but it wouldn't matter. She couldn't scream.

Sanders pulled the Lincoln up in front of the Peabody and three men emerged. Bruce Askew stayed in the car with Sanders.

"You two go on up to my suite." Griffin tossed Judd the key. "I'll stop by and speak to Annabelle, tell her that you want her to go home to Austinville, but if I can't persuade her, you'll have to see her."

Quinn nodded as they entered the hotel. But they didn't get very far before they realized something was going on, something out of the ordinary. Hotel security had the elevators blocked.

"Wonder what this is all about?" Judd paused and studied the situation.

"You two wait here and I'll find out." Griffin walked over and spoke to one of the hotel guards, then turned and rushed back to Judd and Quinn. "Don't jump to any conclusions." He looked right at Quinn. "But there's been a shooting upstairs, on the floor where Annabelle's suite is. One man is dead, possibly Tobias. And they found an unconscious and nearly dead waiter in the stairwell."

"He's got Annabelle." Quinn's heart stopped. Whoever this guy was, the one who had already killed six women, had somehow overpowered Griffin's agent, had either killed Annabelle or would soon kill her.

"I have to get upstairs," Quinn said, but when he started for the stairwell, Griffin grabbed him and none too gently shoved him up against the wall.

"You and Judd go out in the lobby and sit down. I'll find

out what happened and if Annabelle was involved. If she was—and I'm saying if—then we'll precede from there."

No! Quinn's mind bellowed. *I can't just wait here. I have to find out if Annabelle is safe. I have to do something.*

As if reading Quinn's mind, Griffin said, "You do anything stupid and you'll wind up back in jail, then you'll be of no use to Annabelle. Is that what you want?"

Judd grasped Quinn's arm and led him toward the lobby. But he couldn't sit down. Instead he paced the floor. Finally, after what seemed like hours, but had actually been only a few minutes, Griffin reappeared. He could tell from the look on Griffin's face that the news was bad.

"Tobias is dead," Griffin said. "Shot at close range, right between the eyes."

Quinn felt as if all the air had been knocked out of him.

"Annabelle?"

"She's gone. Some of the people in the other rooms got a glimpse of a young guy dragging a woman down the hall. Their descriptions of the guy all vary too much to do us any good. Young. Tall. Brown hair. Wearing a white jacket and dark slacks."

"Young, tall and brown-haired could be either of your employees," Judd said.

"Yeah, it could be either Aaron or Jace," Quinn agreed, despite his need to believe neither was involved. Two young men he had saved from lives of crime. He had befriended them, given them jobs, trusted them, thought of them as surrogate sons.

"The police are on their way," Griffin said. "I think we should call Lieutenant Norton. Annabelle's been kidnapped and is in the hands of a serial killer. We're going to need all the help we can get."

Annabelle didn't know how long she had been in the back of the truck. All she knew was that she'd rolled into a dead body and screamed inside her mind for a long, long time.

Whether an hour or two or more had passed, she wasn't sure. Time had ceased to be of any importance to her. Not when she was at the mercy of a madman.

Sunlight hurt her eyes when the door opened and a big hand reached inside and yanked her forward. She hadn't realized she'd been lying so close to the door. He grabbed her legs and hurriedly undid the rope binding her ankles together. He pulled her out of the truck and onto the ground. Wobbly on her feet, she fell into her captor, who all but dragged her along with him as he sneaked around the side of a building she recognized as a motel. Surely someone would notice them and realize she'd been kidnapped by this man.

Your feet are free, even if your hands are tied and you're still gagged. Don't just go passively with him. Do something. Anything. Kick him and run.

Annabelle did just that. Her kick missed its mark, striking him in the thigh, but it stunned him just enough for her to get away from him. She made it a good ten feet before he tackled her, shoving her down onto the concrete walkway in front of the motel. She lay beneath him, the breath knocked out of her and her body screaming in pain.

He jerked his gun from the back of his pants and pressed the muzzle against her temple. "Try something like that again and I'll have to shoot you. I don't want to shoot you, Annabelle. I'm not a cruel, unkind person. Not to the women we love. I kill them softly, tenderly and put them out of their misery. I'll do the same for you."

What was he talking about? What misery? What did he mean by *we*? And he couldn't possibly love her. He didn't know her, had only seen her—what—once?

When he hauled her onto her feet and marched her toward Room Ten, she looked right and left, hoping and praying she would see someone—that someone would see her. Not a soul in sight. That's when she noticed there were no vehicles in the parking slots and the one-story motel looked shabby and rundown. The place was abandoned, probably on the brink of being demolished.

He shoved open the unlocked door to Room Ten and pushed her inside. The stale air reeked with various unpleasant odors. The interior lay in semidarkness.

He forced her toward the bed. "Sit down."

She sat.

"I'm going to take the gag out of your mouth," he told her. "Scream if you want to waste your breath. Nobody will hear you."

When he untied the rag and pulled the handkerchief out of her mouth, she gasped, then sucked in a deep breath.

"I'm going to tie your hands to the headboard, just so you won't try to run."

When he loosened the rope, she head-butted him. Damn, but that hurt. Hurt her as much as it did him. But she took advantage of his surprise, leaped to her feet and ran to the door. He caught her just as her hand touched the doorknob.

Something hard hit her in the back of the head.

Quinn's cell phone rang. He started not to answer it, considering he, Judd and Griffin were in the middle of a discussion with Jim Norton.

"You'd better get that," Griffin said.

Quinn moved away from the others to take the call. "Cortez here."

"Hi, Quinn."

He recognized the voice instantly. Fear clutched his gut. "Where are you?"

"In a little out-of-the-way motel."

"Are you alone?"

"Of course not, silly. Annabelle is with me."

"Don't hurt her." The roar of his heartbeat thundered in his ears. "Whatever you want, you've got it. Just don't hurt her."

"Quinn Cortez begging. Hmm . . . I like that. Have you ever begged before, Quinn? I have. She used to make me beg and plead. She'd point that damn finger at me and laugh when I cried in pain."

"Who did that to you?"

"Who do you think? Kelley. My mother. The woman you used and forgot about, the woman you destroyed."

"Kelley Fleming?"

"Fleming wasn't her real name. She used lots of different last names. She changed our name every time we moved. I think her real last name was Ford. After you dumped her, she finally married some loser named Tony Ford, but he didn't hang around for long." He chuckled. "But at least he married her, that was more than you did. You don't remember her, do you, Quinn? That tall, skinny girl who tutored you in English your first semester in college. You screwed her a couple of times and she thought you loved her."

"Kelley . . ." Oh, my God!

He did vaguely remember an odd young woman who had tutored him that first difficult semester. But he'd forgotten her name was Kelley. Back then, he'd hump just about any willing female and Kelley had been no exception. When he'd broken things off with her, she'd stalked him for months, then she disappeared and he never saw her again. And to be honest, not once in all these years had he given her a second thought.

"Did you kill her, your mother?"

"Yes, I did. And I killed the others, too, just like I'm going to kill Annabelle. I'm going to put her out of her misery. She's in love with you, just the way the others were and you'll only break her heart and she'll never be able to get over you and she'll make others suffer because—"

"Annabelle isn't like any of the others. I love her. Do you hear me—I love Annabelle and I want to marry her. I'll never break her heart. I promise you."

"I don't believe you."

"It's true. I swear it's true. I can prove it to you if you'll let me. Just tell me how I can prove that I love Annabelle."

Silence.

"Answer me, damn you!" Quinn said.

"All right. If—if you love her then you can save her. But you'll have to die in her place. Are you willing to do that? Are you willing to sacrifice your life, to pay for all your sins, in order to save Annabelle?"

"Yes. Just tell me where you are and I'll come to you. You let Annabelle go and you can kill me in her place. Do we have a deal?"

"We have a deal." Pause. "But you come alone and un-armed. If anyone comes with you, I'll kill her. Or if I find out you have a weapon. Do you understand?"

"Yes, I understand."

Chapter 31

Annabelle came to groggily, her head pounding. For a couple of minutes she felt completely disoriented, wasn't sure where she was or what was going on. Then she began to remember the details of her morning, starting with when Mr. Tobias opened the door and a waiter had shot him right between the eyes. No, not a waiter . . .

"I'm glad you're finally awake," a voice said. An oddly familiar voice.

"Quinn?"

"Yes, honey, it's me. Bad boy Quinn."

She tried to sit up, but when her head started swimming, she lay back, resting her head against the dingy pillow. Then she turned to search for the voice and saw a shadowy figure on the far side of the semidark room, his shape outlined by a glimmer of sunlight peeking through the window where the curtains didn't quite meet.

He was the same height and had a similar build as Quinn. And his voice sounded a great deal like Quinn's. But Quinn didn't call her honey and only the two of them knew that to him she was his darling, his *querida*.

"I can't see you," she said as she once again tried to sit up. Still she couldn't manage to lift herself, but this time she realized why. Not because of her headache and slight nausea, but because both of her wrists were bound to the rickety headboard.

The shadow moved toward her. The closer he came, the faster her heart beat. He paused about three feet from the bed. She shut her eyes for a few seconds, then reopened them, hoping what she thought she'd seen would disappear. But no, he was still standing there. Curly black hair. Cocky smile. Quinn, and yet not Quinn.

What's wrong with this picture? she asked herself. *How can he look so much like Quinn and yet not be Quinn?*

"Please, come closer," she said. "I can barely see you."

He moved to the side of the bed, then leaned over and looked right at her. His black eyes were identical to Quinn's, too. The similarity between the two men was amazing.

"You look a great deal like him," she said.

He laughed. "I had you fooled there for a few minutes, didn't I? You actually thought I was Quinn Cortez."

"At a distance, the resemblance is remarkable."

"Yeah, I know, especially with the black wig and the dark brown contacts." When he spoke, his voice was his own again and not an excellent imitation of Quinn's.

"Why?" she asked.

"Why what? Why do I choose to look like Quinn when I perform my acts of kindness for his victims?"

Was that how he saw the women who loved Quinn—as victims?

"You killed those six women, didn't you?"

"It was the right thing to do, the only humane thing."

"I don't understand," she told him. "What do you mean it was the only humane thing to do?"

"They were suffering. I put them out of their misery. And I'll do the same for you."

Annabelle felt a rush of pure panic flood her senses. There had to be a way to stop him. She had too much to live for to give up without a fight. She tugged on her bound wrists.

He laughed again, then grinned at her, and she thought how eerily unbelievable it was that with only a few minor changes in his appearance, this man could easily pass for Quinn's brother. His younger brother.

"You're curious as to why I look so much like Quinn, aren't you?" he asked.

"Yes, of course. The resemblance isn't obvious at all when you aren't wearing the wig and contacts," Annabelle said. "And you're not wearing your glasses, so that changes your appearance, too."

"I have my mother's hair and eye color," Jace Morgan said. "But my features are a great deal like his. I'm the same height and the same size he was when he was a teenager. That's what my mother told me a couple of years ago."

"Who is your mother?"

"You mean you haven't figured that out? My mother was Kelley Fleming, one of Quinn's first victims. Kelley, the poor besotted fool who fell in love with Quinn when he was nineteen, the same age I am now. He got her pregnant, left her and never looked back. She loved him and hated him, all at the same time. And she never let me forget that I was his son, that I looked like him, that I had his cursed good looks and charm. When she punished me, she called me Bad Quinn."

"Quinn is your father?" *Oh, my God!*

"Yeah. Ain't that a kick in the head. The great Quinn Cortez is my old man. Only I didn't know his full name until two years ago. Whenever she got angry with me, which was almost every day, she'd call me bad Quinn. So I figured Quinn was his name. But not until I got old enough and big enough to stop her from terrorizing me did she tell me who my father really was. She told me his name was Quinn Cortez and he was a rich, hotshot lawyer in Houston. I knew then I had to make him pay for what he'd done to her—to us. He needed to suffer the way she'd suffered . . . the way I had."

"Quinn didn't even know you existed," Annabelle said.

"He knew. She told me he knew and that he didn't give a damn. And she told me she still loved him and she'd kept me only because she hoped that someday he'd come back to her. That's when I undertsood what I had to do. I had to put her out of her misery. It was the only way to give either of us any peace. Don't you see—she had suffered all those years and she'd made me suffer."

"So you killed her." His own mother! *And he's going to kill me, unless I can find a way to stop him.*

"While she was sleeping, I put a pillow over her head and held it there until she stopped breathing. I didn't hurt her. Not the way she'd hurt me so many times. I killed her humanely."

"Why did you cut off her finger?" *Keep him talking. Buy yourself some time.*

"So she could never point it at me again when she punished me for being bad. Bad Quinn. That's what she called me. But I told you that already, didn't I?"

"Oh, Jace, I'm so sorry. And if Quinn knew you were his son—"

"He'll know soon enough. He's coming here. He thinks he's coming to rescue you. I was going to let him hang for those murders, but this way is even better. He's exchanging his life for yours. But without him, you'd rather be dead, wouldn't you?"

Quinn knew where she was? He was coming to rescue her? *No, please, God, no. He'll be walking into a trap. Jace plans to kill us both.*

"He tried to make me believe he actually loved you, so I told him that the only way to save you was to swap his life for yours. Do you think he loves you enough to sacrifice himself for you?"

Yes, yes he does. There was no doubt in her mind that Quinn would lay down his life and die for her.

* * *

Quinn parked his silver Porsche in the back of the motel, directly behind the delivery truck, exactly where Jace had instructed him to park. On the drive here, to this ratty motel on the outskirts of Memphis, he had thought of nothing but saving Annabelle. She was his first priority. His only priority. He had no intention of dying today, but if that's what it took to save Annabelle, then so be it. It was his fault that she was in this deadly situation. When he'd been a teenager, he had messed around with an odd girl named Kelley Morgan and probably broken her heart and that woman's son had come into his life to destroy him. But why? Why would an old girlfriend's son hate him so much? Enough to have wormed his way into Quinn's life, pretending to be a troubled teen who needed rescuing.

Quinn felt inside the pocket of his leather jacket, reassuring himself that the Glock 30 Griffin had provided for him was still there, ready to draw and use at a moment's notice. If he could get one clear shot . . . just one. That's all he'd need.

Griffin had promised him five minutes to go in alone to rescue Annabelle. "If you can't take charge of the situation in five minutes, you can't do it in five hours," Griffin had said. "I'll make sure Jim keeps his partner out of the loop, so he won't be there to act like some cocky cowboy and get you and Annabelle and God knows who else killed."

"Just make sure Norton understands that if Jace even suspects that I'm not alone, he'll kill Annabelle before I can get in there to her."

As Quinn walked around the corner of the motel, his accelerated heartbeat hummed inside his head and a rush of adrenaline pumped through his body. He had never been so damn scared in his whole life. Nothing had ever been more important than the task ahead of him—saving the woman he loved.

A loud, repetitive knocking at the door brought all of Annabelle's senses to full alert. Jace jumped as if he'd been

shot, then raced over to her and sat down on the bed beside
her.

"Yeah?" he called.

"Jace, it's Quinn. I'm here. Ready to exchange myself for
Annabelle."

"You're really going to do it?" Jace asked.

"Yes, I'm here, aren't I?"

Jace pointed the gun directly at Annabelle's head. "If you
try to trick me, I'll kill her. And it won't be a kind, gentle
death. I'll blow her brains out."

"I understand," Quinn replied. "No tricks."

"Okay. Come on in, but keep your hands where I can see
them."

"No, Quinn, don't!" Annabelle yelled. "He'll kill you."

"She's right," Jace said. "I am going to kill you."

"But not before you let Annabelle go."

The door burst open. Jace jumped, the action shaking his
gun hand. Annabelle swallowed hard. Quinn stood in the
open doorway, the sunlight behind him outlining his powerful body. The light partially blinded her, so she knew it must
be having the same effect on Jace. She wriggled, longing to
be free so she could attack Jace, to stop him from harming
Quinn. But all her squirming accomplished was to agitate a
nervous Jace. He pressed the gun against her temple.

"I'm not coming inside until you take your gun away
from Annabelle's head and untie her," Quinn said.

"Hold your hands over your head," Jace told him.

"Take the gun away from her head and move away from
her, then I'll do as you asked."

Jace lowered his weapon. "Now, come on in."

The events of the next ninety seconds occurred so rapidly
that it was as if the world had gone into supersonic speed.
Quinn stepped through the doorway, drew his gun as agilely
as an Old West gunslinger and aimed at Jace. Annabelle
screamed, "No, don't! He's your son." Quinn hesitated for a
split second, long enough for Jace to fire his weapon. The
bullet hit Quinn in the shoulder. Screeching, Annabelle

fought the bonds that held her. Another shot rang out. Jace, who'd had his gun pointed at Annabelle, dropped to the floor before he'd been able to fire his weapon again. A single shot from directly behind Quinn had put an end to Jace's killing spree. The bullet had gone in one side of his head and out the other. Blood and brain matter spattered across the floor, the bed and the wall.

Lieutenant Norton and Griffin Powell came in behind Quinn. Griffin removed the unused gun from Quinn's trembling hand.

"How bad are you hit?" Griffin asked.

"Hurts like hell," Quinn said as he clutched his shoulder, blood dripping between his fingers. "But I'll live." He glanced at Jace, whose crumpled body lay on the floor.

Lieutenant Norton inspected Jace's body. "Would you look at that? He's your spitting image, Cortez, with that black wig on."

As Annabelle struggled unsuccessfully to free herself so she could go to Quinn, he came toward her. He walked around Jace's lifeless body, giving him only a quick glance, before hurrying to the bed.

"Quinn, you're hurt." Tears blurred Annabelle's vision.

He reached up, untied her hands and took her into his arms, then winced when she pressed against his injured shoulder.

She jerked away from him. "I'm sorry."

He circled the back of her neck with his big hand. "I'm the one who's sorry. Because of me, you nearly died."

"And because of you, I'm still alive."

He pulled her to his uninjured side. She wrapped her arms around him gently and laid her head on his good shoulder.

"He—he told me he was your son," Annabelle said. "His mother was Kelley Fleming. He had to be telling the truth. With that black wig and brown contacts, he looks so much like you." She lifted her head and her gaze locked with Quinn's. His eyes were filled with tears. "Oh, Quinn, I'm so very sorry. I couldn't let you kill your own son, not even to save me."

"I never knew. I swear to God, I had no idea I'd ever fathered a child."

She caressed his face. "Don't you think I know that? Despite all your faults, my darling, you would never have deserted a child the way your father deserted you."

Lieutenant Norton cleared his throat. "Let's get you two out of here. The local ME is on his way and the crime scene team will want everything as untouched as possible."

"And we need to get Quinn to the hospital ASAP," Griffin reminded them. "I'll drive y'all there. It'll be quicker than waiting on the ambulance."

Griffin had stayed at the hospital with Annabelle during Quinn's surgery and when she refused to leave, he stayed on with her throughout the night. He had left her only a few minutes ago, shortly after Quinn awoke. But before he left, he gave Quinn the report that had come in through his agents in Texas. A report on Kelley Morgan Fleming and her son, Jace.

Sitting on the edge of Quinn's bed, feeding him his breakfast, Annabelle had never felt so thankful. She had come very close to losing Quinn and if she had lost him, she wasn't sure she could have gone on living.

After eating half his meal and downing a full cup of coffee, Quinn told her, "That's enough." Then when she pushed aside the serving table, he reached out and grabbed her hand. "Since you're still here, does that mean you aren't going to run from me while you still can?"

"Silly, silly man." Lifting her hand to his forehead, she brushed back several stray curls. "Don't you know that you're stuck with me for the rest of our lives?"

"Annabelle . . ." He gazed at her pleadingly. "My stupid, careless actions when I was a teenager helped create that poor boy. I got a girl pregnant and never knew it. And my child—my son—grew up with a crazy woman who punished him because he reminded her so much of me."

"I didn't want Griffin to give you that report on Kelley Fleming and her son. I told him to wait until you'd recovered."

"Griffin knew I needed all the facts he could unearth and I needed them right away. I have a great deal to work through and I can't do that without the facts, without the truth."

"The truth is that you've made some mistakes in your life. Who hasn't? You can't change the past, can't go back and save Jace. But you can continue helping other kids in trouble, the way you've done for years. And I'll help you do it. We'll build a girls' ranch adjacent to the Judge Harwood Brown Boys' Ranch. We'll—"

With his good arm, Quinn reached out and pulled Annabelle to him, then lifted his head and kissed her. When the kiss ended, he smiled at her. "Don't ever leave me, *querida*. You're my only hope for salvation. You know that, don't you?"

"I know that I love you and you love me. And against all the odds, we found each other, fell in love and now have a chance for real happiness. I'd say that means you're as much my salvation as I am yours."

"Marry me, Annabelle. Marry me and help me become a better man than I've been in the past."

"You don't think being married, being tied down to one woman, will bore you in a few months?"

"Not if that one woman is you."

Her face lit up with a deliriously happy smile. "Then the answer is yes. Yes, Quinn Cortez, I'll marry you."

Epilogue

One year later . . .

Annabelle and Quinn lay in front of the roaring blaze burning brightly inside the rock fireplace in their rustic home on Quinn's ranch, deep in the Hill Country of East Texas. They had married two and a half months ago, in a small white church not far from here, with Aunt Perdita as her Matron of Honor and Quinn's long-time friend, Johnny Mack Cahill, as his best man. Griffin Powell, Aaron Tully and Johnny Mack's family were their only guests. Since first meeting the Cahills, Annabelle and Johnny Mack's wife, Lane, had become fast friends, and she adored the Cahill's children.

During their two-month honeymoon, which wasn't over yet, she and Quinn had barricaded themselves from the outside world, from the past and all its heartaches and regrets. It had taken them ten months to put their lives in order, ten months to endure three funerals, to bury family members and move beyond each tragedy.

Quinn had buried his son, a child he'd never known as his own. And although he had at first resisted the idea of therapy, he had finally seen a highly respected Houston counselor. After months of counseling, Quinn had accepted the reality of what had happened and the fact that all the self-hatred in the world wouldn't change anything, that it served no worthwhile purpose.

Only a few months after Jace Morgan's funeral, Annabelle's Uncle Louis had passed away quietly in his sleep. They had buried him near his beloved Lulu, in the family cemetery near Vanderley Hall, on a hot, humid day in late June. Uncle Louis had made Annabelle the executor of his will, thus putting her in charge of his vast fortune. Then, when his father hadn't been gone less than two months, Wythe had been arrested for raping a sixteen-year-old girl. Annabelle had used the Vanderley money to hire him a good lawyer, but she had refused to pull any strings to get him out of trouble. The family had saved him too many times in the past. But Wythe had never gone to trial. The father of the girl he had raped took matters into his own hands and shot Wythe with a long-range rifle, while Wythe was standing on the front veranda of Vanderley Hall one evening in early October.

Annabelle rolled over on the cushy rug in front of the fireplace and faced her husband, an adoring smile on her face. "So, tell me something, Mr. Cortez, are you bored with married life?"

He yanked her into his arms and kissed her passionately, then when she was breathless, he said, "Does that answer your question?"

Propping herself up on her elbow, she sighed contentedly. "We can't stay here forever, you know. I have an empire to run and you have a law practice that can't function much longer without you. Besides, all those delicious meals you've prepared for us while we've been here has put five pounds on me."

"Yes, I know." He stroked her hip. "On you those five pounds look great."

"Are you saying you'd love me if I got big and fat?"

"Yeah, I'd love you if you got big and fat and wore a tow sack."

"Ah, Quinn . . ."

He caressed her cheek tenderly. "I realize we have to return to the real world soon. Are you sure you don't want me to move my practice to Mississippi? I know it will be difficult for you to oversee Vanderley, Inc. from Houston."

"I can perform my duties as chairman of the board without living in Mississippi," she told him. "I plan to gradually, over the next seven or eight months, put trusted employees in key positions so that I won't need to personally oversee everything on a day-to-day basis."

He stared at her, a puzzled expression on his face. "Why would you do that?"

"Because I want to free up most of my time for the next few years so I can be a really good full-time mother to our child."

She waited and watched for his reaction when realization dawned.

"Annabelle? *Querida?* You're pregnant?"

Smiling, she nodded.

"How? When? Are you certain?"

"How? I'm pretty sure our making love had something to do with it. As for when it happened—probably on our wedding night. Am I certain? Yes, I am. I took a home pregnancy test that is supposed to be very reliable. And I have now missed two periods. And that bout with nausea this morning was the beginning of morning sickness."

Tears filled Quinn's black eyes as he laid his hand over Annabelle's still flat belly. "I swear to you that I will be the best father I can possibly be. I'll never let you or our child down. I'll—"

She kissed him. Then with tears of joy in her eyes, she said, "You'll love us. That's what you'll do. And we'll love you . . . your daughter and I."

"Daughter, huh?"

"Or son."

"Doesn't matter, does it?"

"No. All that matters is that she—or he—is part of you and part of me. Conceived in love."

"And brought up surrounded by love."

Quinn wrapped her in his arms and brushed her temple with a wispy soft kiss.

Annabelle closed her eyes and sighed contentedly. *Thank you, Lord. Thank you.*

Please turn the page for an exciting sneak peek of
Beverly Barton's new novel

THE DYING GAME

coming in 2008

The intensely bright lights blinded her. She couldn't see anything except the white illumination that obscured everything in her line of vision. She wished he would turn off the car's headlights.

Judd didn't like for her to show houses to clients in the evenings and generally she did what Judd wanted her to do. But her career as a realtor was just getting off the ground, and if she could sell this half-million-dollar house to Mr. and Mrs. Farris, her percentage would be enough to furnish the nursery. Not that she was pregnant. Not yet. And not that her husband couldn't well afford to furnish a nursery with the best of everything. It was just that Jennifer wanted the baby to be her gift to her wonderful husband and the nursery to be a gift from her to their child.

Holding her hand up to shield her eyes from the headlights, she walked down the sidewalk to meet John and Katherine Farris, an up-and-coming entrepreneurial couple planning to start a new business in Chattanooga. She had spoken only to John Farris. From their telephone conversations, she had surmised that John, like her own husband, was the type who liked to think he wore the pants in the family. Odd how considering the fact that she believed herself to be a thoroughly modern women, Jennifer loved Judd's old-fashioned sense of protectiveness and possessiveness.

When John Farris parked his black Mercedes and opened the driver's door, Jennifer met him, her hand outstretched in greeting. He accepted her hand immediately and smiled warmly.

"Good evening, Mr. Farris." Jennifer glanced around, searching for Mrs. Farris.

"I'm sorry, something came up at the last minute that delayed Katherine. She'll be joining us soon."

When John Farris raked his silvery blue eyes over her, Jennifer shuddered inwardly, an odd sense of uneasiness settling in the pit of her stomach. *You're being silly,* she told herself. Men found her attractive. It wasn't her fault. She didn't do anything to lead them on, nothing except simply being beautiful, which she owed to the fact she'd inherited great genes from her attractive parents.

Jennifer sighed. Sometimes being a former beauty queen was a curse.

"If you'd like to wait for your wife before you look at the house, I can go ahead and answer any questions you might have. I've got all the information in my briefcase in my car."

He shook his head. "No need to wait. I'd like to take a look around now. If I don't like the place, Katherine won't be interested."

"Oh, I see."

He chuckled. "It's not that she gives in to me on everything. We each try to please the other. Isn't that the way to have a successful marriage?"

"Yes, I think so. It's certainly what Judd and I have been trying to do. We're a couple of newlyweds just trying to make our way through that first year of marriage." Jennifer nodded toward the front entrance to the sprawling glass and log house. "If you'll follow me."

She whimpered. *Oh, Judd, why didn't I listen to you? Why did I come here alone tonight?*

"Are you afraid?" John Farris asked.

"Yes."

"You should be," he told her.

"You're going to kill me, aren't you?"

He laughed again. Softly.

"Please . . . please . . ." She cried. Tears filled her eyes and trickled down her cheeks.

He came closer. And closer. He raised the meat cleaver high over her head, then swung it across her right wrist.

Blood splattered on the cabinet, over her head, and across her upper body as her severed right hand tumbled downward and hit the floor.

Pain! Excruciating pain.

And then he lifted the cleaver and swung down and across again, cutting off her left hand with one swift, accurate blow.

Jennifer passed out.